If only

He'd not *meant* to put his hands on her, but Meade's men were too numerous to fight. Against the rock, they'd needed to hide. In the road, he'd needed the element of surprise. On the trail, the rain was too heavy to drag her. He'd had no choice but to scoop her up. Her position over his shoulder had been a practical matter, logistical; but then her hip had settled against his cheek and her thighs rested against his chest and his body had awakened at each point of contact. Muscles twitched, groin tightened, hairs stood on end. Gabriel's skin was like a thick, leathery husk, long detached from the sensations of softness. He rarely encountered female parts, or fragrant cloaks or wet curls, or lips against his throat. The husk had dissolved when he held her, every nerve ending tingled and throbbed and *sought*.

Physically, his body had climbed up that hill; mentally, he'd cataloged the contour of her breasts against his back; her hip against his cheek. It had taken all of his control to carry her away instead of dropping to the ground and touching and touching and touching every part of her until there was no earlobe or shoulder blade or the inside of a knee unknown to his hands. He'd wanted to gobble her up.

He hadn't gobbled her, he'd removed her from the road—and then he'd held her against his chest and slowly expired while she nestled into him.

And now he'd touched her again. In his own kitchen. And declared that she should stay the night.

Also by Charis Michaels

THE PRINCE'S Bride

A HIDDEN ROYALS NOVEL

CHARIS MICHAELS

AVON

An Imprint of HarperCollinsPublishers

THE PRINCE'S BRIDE. Copyright © 2024 by Charis Michaels. All rights reserved. Printed in the United States of America. No part of this book may be used or reproduced in any manner whatsoever without written permission except in the case of brief quotations embodied in critical articles and reviews. For information, address HarperCollins Publishers, 195 Broadway, New York, NY 10007.

First Avon Books mass market printing: May 2024

Print Edition ISBN: 978-0-06-328010-6
Digital Edition ISBN: 978-0-06-328011-3

Cover design by Amy Halperin
Cover illustration by Chris Cocozza

Avon, Avon & logo, and Avon Books & logo are registered trademarks of HarperCollins Publishers in the United States of America and other countries.

HarperCollins is a registered trademark of HarperCollins Publishers in the United States of America and other countries.

FIRST EDITION

24 25 26 27 28 BVGM 10 9 8 7 6 5 4 3 2 1

For "Michelle Next Door." This is how you're saved in my phone. The idea for this series came from you, but your proximity as my neighbor came from much higher up. I'm so grateful for both.

THE
PRINCE'S
Bride

CHAPTER ONE

Savernake Forest
Wiltshire, England
August 1811

*T*HE NIGHT WAS pierced by a woman's scream.

The sound, brief and raw, shot above the canopy and scraped down the hillside to bounce against the rock.

Deep in the forest, a man slipped from his saddle and fell into the shadow of a limestone crag and listened.

Gabriel Rein knew the sounds of the forest after dark. He knew nocturnal animals, he knew cave-dwelling smugglers, he knew drunken villagers who'd lost their way home. But a woman? A screaming woman?

Gabriel's life was so deeply embedded in the trees and rocks of Savernake, he rarely, if ever, encountered others. He employed three men to help him with the horses and an old woman to keep camp; beyond these, Gabriel had very little contact with the outside world. A screaming woman was not only unexpected, it was a moral dilemma.

After ten beats, she screamed again; a shrill rip of sound that grabbed him by the throat and shoved him back.

Gabriel swore and looked at the sky. He'd waited weeks for the threat of a storm without actual rain. His new commission was a young stallion terrified of storms and he meant to expose him bit by bit. No surprise, the horse was also unnerved by *screaming*. He stamped and huffed behind Gabriel, yanking the lead. They'd been picking their way along a rocky path, acclimating to the smell of rain and the flashes of lightning. They'd not gone far, and the horse had seemed willing to press on—until the screaming. Now the stallion's ears flicked back and his nostrils flared and he dug in, refusing to proceed.

Gabriel stepped to the horse and stroked his neck, assuring him with low words and the gentle clicking noise he used to calm frightened animals.

"No?" screamed the woman in the distance. A word this time. Her inflection spoke less of a retreat and more of a request? The screaming woman was negotiating.

Gabriel's grooms had told him that the highwayman Channing Meade was raiding again. Meade made camp on the edge of Savernake Forest in August because the weather was mild and the deer were fat and the constable was lazy. Perhaps the screaming woman had been swiped from the village for Meade's pleasure. Perhaps she'd come willingly, only to discover that Meade was a brute and his camp was a pit. Maybe the highwayman had set upon a carriage, and the woman inside objected to being robbed at knifepoint. Long Harry Road was little more than two ruts disappearing into a tunnel of murky green, and travelers should know better.

I don't care, Gabriel thought, stroking the horse.

The forest had been a sanctuary to Gabriel since boyhood. He'd grown up in a constant state of evasion, tracked by spies and bounty hunters and mercenaries. He knew stillness and quiet like other children knew lessons and sport. He was a champion at holding his breath.

Now he was a man, and Gabriel wasn't sure if the sanctuary was a necessity or simply a preference. He'd been here for so long, it was all he knew. The forest allowed him to owe nothing and rely on no one. His loyalties extended to his staff and his horses and no further. The work he did for clients was negotiated by an emissary; the same man provisioned his camp with supplies. The extreme seclusion had kept him alive for more than a decade. It kept everyone else alive. It was survival.

As to the survival of the screaming woman? He couldn't say. Except for rare encounters with women—professionals who kept things quick and anonymous—he knew very little of female companionship. And he didn't care about this screaming stranger.

I don't want to care, he thought.

The horse snorted and tossed his mane. Gabriel made the clicking noise and pulled on his lead, reining him around. They would return to camp. The rain wouldn't hold off forever. The horse shouldn't be subjected to rain *and* screaming.

"Please!" came another cry from the woman. "Help!"

Gabriel paused. There was a note of demand in her voice. An earnestness, a reasoning. This wasn't uncontrolled wailing, she was expectant. She *summoned*. The sound slid under his skin and burned.

Behind him, the stallion threw his head, yanking the lead. The horse was now properly agitated, dancing backward, snorting and hoofing the ground.

"*Help!*" the woman cried again.

Gabriel swore under his breath, keeping his hand steady on the horse's neck.

I don't care, he repeated in his head.

The stallion pulled backward, seventy stone of frightened animal straining against the lead. Swearing again, Gabriel allowed the horse to reverse from the path.

I don't care.

There was a circle of grass where the terrain leveled off, and Gabriel ripped up a handful of the fragrant sweet reed and held it out, inviting the animal to graze.

I don't care.

He looked around. A giant oak loomed nearby, and Gabriel tethered the horse to a low limb, his flank shielded from the wind by the trunk.

I don't care.

He'd fitted the stallion's bridle with blinders, and now he pressed the leather patches against Zeus's eyes, obscuring his sight. Each precaution was made with ease and gentleness, his movements rote. Soothing a frightened horse came as naturally to Gabriel as breathing, but he knew almost nothing about frightened women. And yet, his ears were acutely tuned to the sound of—

"Please help me!" came another terrified cry.

Gabriel—who really, truly *did not care*—pulled the ax from his belt and slipped into the trees.

CHAPTER TWO

ᴸADY MARIANNE "RYAN" Daventry was not, by nature, a screamer.

Ryan was a suggester. A stater of simple truths. A calm voice of reason when emotions were high and tempers lost. Her middle sister Diana had the flash temper and a very hearty scream. Their youngest sister, Charlotte, with her girlish fear of mice and bugs and branches scraping windowpanes, was also a known screamer. But not Ryan. Ryan, in fact, could only remember ever having screamed once or twice in her entire life.

But she screamed now. She was well and truly terrified, and she screamed the raw and desperate scream of a survivor.

At least she'd come into the forest alone. Her one consolation. Ryan was defenseless, yes, but her maid, Agnes, was safe back at the inn. Agnes had wanted to accompany her and Ryan had refused. Even without the threat of ambush, Agnes was unsuited for forest trespass. The maid was afraid of nice men in polite settings; she would never survive a snarling man with no life behind his eyes.

"Cry all you like," hissed the man with his hand

clamped to Ryan's jaw. "There's no one within fifty miles to hear you scream." With his other hand, he pinned her against his chest, her body dangling half a foot from the road.

Ryan couldn't really say how she'd gone from mounted on horseback to the painful grasp of this fetid, sneering man. She'd been plodding carefully through the forest, nudging the frightened mare onward, when she came upon a row of men on horseback just over the crest of a hill. They sat so heavily, their ranks so impenetrable, she'd mistaken them for a line of statues blocking the road. But they weren't statues: they were highwaymen and the brute who now held her was their leader. He'd emerged from the blockade like a cannon ball rolling into the chamber of a cannon.

Despite her fear, she'd kept control of her mount and reined around. But he'd been deceptively fast for his size and managed to swipe the reins before she could bolt. Then his hands were on her and he dragged her from the saddle like a basket of wash.

"Believe me when I say I've got nothing," she now whimpered to the man. "No money. No jewelry. Not even food. I rode from the inn in Pewsey to have a look at the forest's edge and lost my way."

"Of course that's your claim," the man said, releasing her chin with a teeth-rattling shove. Ryan tried to scuttle away, but his hand returned, this time with a dagger. He pressed the flat side of the dull blade against her cheek. "You've a horse, haven't you?"

"On loan from the inn," she insisted. "Please do not harm the mare. She is not valuable. They loaned her to me for no fee, but they'll want her back. They'll come looking for her."

He pulled the knife from her cheek and dug his hand into her hair, yanking her head back with a snap. The pain and helplessness of being steered by her hair took Ryan's breath away.

"Answer me with sass, will you?" the man mocked. "See how far that gets you."

"I'm telling you *plainly*," she insisted, "if it's valuables you seek, you'll be disappointed. I'm sorry, I simply don't—"

"Your body then," the man announced, wrenching her head back. "Easier to divvy up. A turn for every man. We'll make a game of it. Find anything you may have hidden in the process."

Without hesitation, Ryan screamed again.

CHAPTER THREE

WHILE HE RAN, Gabriel told himself all the things he would do when he reached the source of the screams.

He would *not* insert himself into the conflict, whatever it was.

He *would* observe it from a concealed location. Downwind. With a clear path to retreat.

He would ascertain *who* and *how* and *why*—all for his own information. It was pertinent to the peace and quiet of the forest and his solitude. This was reconnaissance, not a rescue; prevention, not preservation.

For a long, hopeful moment, the screams had paused, but now they rang on. Sometimes words, sometimes only sound. Always resonant fear. As long as she cried out, he knew she lived. The more she cried, the easier she was to locate. The sounds came from Pike Hill on Long Harry Road. He'd suspected this. The rise would conceal an ambush; the ledge would restrict escape. Gabriel kicked into a sprint.

The undergrowth was thickest between the trail and the road; serpent vines and spiked saplings, thorns thick and waist high. It was a nuisance in the dark, but Gabriel knew the land. He slipped easily through unseen gaps in brush, sidestepping bogholes and leaping over logs. He pushed deftly over, around, through, a silent piece of the night.

When he reached the last stand of trees before the roadside, he paused, allowing his breathing to slow, searching the undergrowth for stragglers or a watch. He saw no one. Channing Meade was sloppy. Not that it mattered. Gabriel had only come to look. He crept forward. Before he could see the road, he heard them.

"Cry all you like; there's no one within fifty miles to hear you scream," growled the man's voice. So it was Channing Meade. Gabriel had never met the man, but he'd observed him from various lookouts.

Gabriel shuttled from one tree to the next, moving silently closer. He heard horses—four, possibly five—their hooves stamping, the creaks of their tack. He squinted, trying to distinguish shadow from figure. There was a line of mounted riders, their backs to him. The men sat alert in their saddles, intently focused on the business in the road. The animals appeared sleepy, bored.

Gabriel inched closer, spinning the handle of the ax in his hand. He wouldn't need the weapon, he reminded himself. He meant only to be ready. It was easier to throw if it was in his hand.

A fallen tree stretched parallel to the road and Gabriel slunk to it, flattening himself against the damp, spongy floor of the forest. From here, he could see beyond the mounted riders to Channing Meade, unmistakable for his size, pacing before the men on horseback. Against his swollen belly swung the helpless figure of a woman in a cloak. Meade would dwarf most women, and this one was no exception. He clutched her back to his front and pressed a dagger to her cheek.

Gabriel closed his eyes. He exhaled. And now he'd seen her. A woman restrained. A knife. Five men looking on.

What did I expect? he asked himself. *You followed the sound of distress. She was literally crying out for help. You* knew. He swore in his head. His gut constricted like a taut rope, the fibers snapping under the weight of indecision. His own safety versus hers. Weakness versus might. The unprotected at the hands of the merciless. Lust and greed unchecked, and no one else for miles. His sanctuary disrupted.

When he opened his eyes, Meade was pacing back and forth, parading the terrified woman before his men. Gabriel squinted, trying to see. Her profile was partly obscured by hood, then her hair, Meade's round shoulder. Finally, the highwayman turned in the same moment clouds slid from the moon. He saw her. She had pale skin and big eyes; her expression was taut with fear. She was young but not a child. She was afraid but not hysterical. Meade wrenched her face upward and her delicate profile looked as out of place in the forest as a teacup.

Gabriel swallowed back something bitter and hot. He felt suddenly winded, his body coiled, eager to pounce. He forced himself to exhale and look away. He studied the five men on horseback, inventorying their weapons. He examined the mounts, trying to assess their age and fitness. He looked down the road to the east and up to the west and checked the position of the moon. He looked at everything and saw nothing so clearly than a woman in need of help.

"Please, sir," she said, her voice terrified but steady. "Believe me when I say I've got nothing. No money. No jewelry. Not even food. I rode from the inn in Pewsey to have a look at the forest's edge and lost my way."

"Of course that's your claim," Channing Meade snarled. "You've a horse, haven't you?"

"Please do not harm the mare," she begged. "She is not valuable. They loaned her to me for no fee, but they'll want her back. They'll come looking for her."

Meade shut her up by grabbing her hair and snapping her head back. Gabriel flinched. A hatch in his chest swung open. Cold, fresh air stung whatever was inside.

"Answer me with sass, will you?" Meade growled. "See how far that gets you."

"Please," the woman cried, "I'm telling you *plainly*. If it's valuables you seek, you'll be disappointed. I'm sorry, I simply don't—"

"Your body then," Channing Meade said, yanking back her head with a snap. "Easier to divvy up. A turn for every man. We'll make a game of it. Find anything you may have hidden in the process."

Gabriel was off the ground before Meade finished the threat. He pressed his hat low on his head, gripped the ax, and darted to the road.

CHAPTER FOUR

How, RYAN WONDERED, had she managed to be attacked by two different men in one night? It was a record, surely—especially when she factored in the third man—the one who'd attacked her in Guernsey. *That* man had been the reason she'd traveled to Savernake Forest in the first place. All told, she'd suffered three attacks in the span of a month. She was at capacity for marauding men.

She was not, however, afraid—no, that was inaccurate. She was afraid, but she wasn't *terrified*, not anymore. The current attacker had thrown her over his shoulder and run. He conveyed her, bodily, *away* from the ambush and the scrambling, shouting men. Her scalp burned from the highwayman's meaty fist, and the wound on her leg pained her, but no one in this moment was actively threatening her.

"Please, sir," Ryan asked, hoping to discover her agency in this particular abduction. Her voice came out like a wheeze. With every footfall, the man's shoulder nudged into her gut. Her hip was pressed into his ear and held in place by a tight arm around the back of her thighs. Ryan's face bounced, upside down, against the hard plates of his back. She held on by squeezing handfuls of his coat. The wound on her leg had begun to throb.

"If you please," Ryan tried again, speaking to her abductor's back. She turned her head to the side, sucking in a breath. "I should like to appeal to your sense of—"

"Quiet," the man huffed. "Do not speak. Meade will not stay down for long. Even now, his men will give chase."

"Yes, alright," she whispered, "but please may I be allowed to walk?" Surely this should be suggested by one of them. The puncture wound in her leg was four weeks old, and she no longer walked with a limp.

"No," he rasped.

"Perhaps you could turn me upright and swing my legs around so I could—?"

"No."

He was hiking them steadily upward, pushing around trees, climbing over fallen logs, trudging through sunken spots packed with forest decay. With every step, he dislodged a spray of rocks. Ryan watched the debris bump down the hillside in a waterfall of gravel. How they remained upright, she had no idea.

After five minutes of steady climbing, they reached a crest of exposed rock, and the man fell against it, breathing hard.

She cleared her throat and he brought a finger to his lips. *Shhh.*

Ryan switched to a whisper. "I beg your pardon? But if you would simply release me to—"

Shouts from men cut her off—voices from below that echoed up the hill. Amid the shouts, she heard thrashing and snapping, the sound of the forest disrupted.

The man who held her swore in another language (French, unless she was mistaken) and shoved from the rock. Tipping forward, he rolled her unceremoniously from his shoulder and flipped her. She was suddenly face up, lying across his arms like a woman in a swoon. The forest canopy swung into focus above her head, a cathedral of foliage with the night sky behind. Before she could react, he tipped her again and folded her roughly against his chest. She tumbled against him like a string of buoys. Gathering her up, he slowly, carefully, eased around the stone. He crouched down, matching the shape of their bodies to the shape of the rock and wedged his weight into the boulder. Then he exhaled and became perfectly, breathlessly still.

Ryan was given no choice but to fold into a ball in his lap. Her ear was pressed against his clavicle and her hands were bent at odd angles against his chest. Her knees pushed into his ribs. She heard his heart, and felt his beard, and smelled wind and horses and man. She was powerless to do anything but close her eyes and exist in his arms.

A minute passed . . . two . . . She'd been chilled on his shoulder but she was rapidly growing overwarm. Her stomach growled. The wound on her leg throbbed. She tried to shift, but he squeezed her tighter. She winced and tipped up her chin to draw breath. Her mouth brushed the whisker-rough skin at his throat. The contact was as unexpected as it was intimate— prickly and warm and tangy; she felt his pulse against her lips. For a long, fuzzy moment, Ryan's mind skipped away from the woods, and the chase, and the throb in her leg. She held her lips to his throat, sharing the air beneath the brim of his hat.

Downhill, the highwayman and his lackeys could be heard lumbering through the underbrush. After a time, silence prevailed; then more thrashing; and finally she heard complaining, curses, and the diminishing sounds of their retreat.

An eternity later, he released her. He simply dropped her and scooted away.

Ryan hit the damp, mossy ground in a tangle, sucking in air and scrambling to get her hands beneath her. The contrast between the tight, warm circle of his arms and the wet leaves of the forest felt like a throw from a horse. While she untangled herself, he slid backward, keeping his weight on one knee.

"Have they gone?" she whispered.

"Yes. They are lazy and underpaid."

"Th-thank you," she said. "I think. That is, if this is a rescue, I'm in your debt. If this is not a rescue, well—almost anyone would be better than the highwayman. I hesitate to ask, but I was riding a young mare when they attacked me. Do you—"

"The horse now belongs to Channing Meade," he said. He stood and made no offer to help her up. Ryan braced against the rock to keep from rolling down the hill.

"You are acquainted with the highwayman?" she asked.

"No, but highwaymen steal horses and yours was delivered to him on a platter."

He removed his hat, ran a hand through his hair, and pressed it back on his head. The clouds shifted and Ryan was able to see his face. His features matched his body; strong, angular, rough. Even so, she could tell that he was young; not much more than her own twenty-four years; certainly not thirty.

Also, he was rather handsome. He was bearded, and streaked with dirt, and scowling, but she understood handsomeness as a practical matter; the natural architecture of a face. Fine clothes and pomade only went so far. This man would be handsome in a bog.

Ryan herself was neither pretty nor plain. She was not known for her appearance, a circumstance she'd accepted years ago. Ryan's calling cards were reason and practicality and getting the job done. Her sister Diana was very striking and her sister Charlotte was very fragile—pretty, each of them, in their own way—and their beauty predicated everything they did. It was like a suffix. Lady Charlotte, the delicate one; Lady Diana, the radiant one. Lady Ryan was the one who held everything together. She was predicated by reliance.

Likely, this man's handsomeness was also deeply embedded in his personality. She'd only now seen his face, but she'd recognized the beauty of his physical form the moment he'd hefted her onto his shoulder. He had long legs and a broad chest, a rakish hat and dashing leather coat. All of it worked together to make him appear savior-y, rather than menacing. She reminded herself that even though handsome might *feel* safe, it was no guarantee.

"I'm going," he said suddenly, shoving to his feet.

Going? she thought, and she realized he meant to leave her. He had rescued her perhaps, but to what end? To desert her in the dark forest?

"Oh," she said, looking around. "Alright. Yes of course."

"It will soon rain. I've left a nervous horse tied to a tree."

"Right. Sorry, but can I impose on you to . . . to . . ."

She studied the trees around her. The landscape appeared the same in every direction: dark, steep, uncompromising. Her heartbeat ticked up. Perhaps this man wasn't a threat to her, but the forest certainly was.

"I'll have to bring you to my camp," he said. "We've no other choice. Can you walk?"

"Your camp," she repeated, dragging herself up. "How very . . ." she searched for the word ". . . kind."

She was relieved, certainly, but now the veneer of safety wrought by his handsomeness began to tarnish. *His camp.* She felt the prickle of unease. She didn't even know this person's name.

"Forgive me," she began, "but might I inquire . . . that is, can you tell me—? Do you have—? Will your family be there? At this camp? Will we be—"

"I live alone except for my horses."

Ryan blinked at him. He turned away and began walking along a rocky ledge.

He lives alone except for his horses.

But would he simply leave—?

Yes. Yes he would. He was walking away.

Ryan tested the ground in front of the rock—one foot, then the next foot, then the next. The forest floor was slick and uneven, but she been raised on the windswept cliffs of Guernsey. The island was steep and rocky, constantly doused by ocean squalls. She knew challenging trails. She knew storms. She knew survival.

"Right . . ." she began, speaking to herself, picking her way behind him. She stepped on a fallen branch and it snapped in two with a *pop*. Ryan jumped, fell sideways, righted herself on a tree.

The man glanced back but said nothing. He turned and walked on. Ryan narrowed her eyes. What choice did she have but to follow? Gathering her skirts, she trudged after him.

After a long moment, he asked, "Why are you alone in the forest after dark?"

"Foolish mistake, I'm afraid," she called. "I was out riding and lost my way. My maid and I have taken a room at the inn in Pewsey, and I borrowed a horse to have a closer look at the forest. I became disoriented in a clearing and couldn't find the path. Eventually I came upon the road, but the sun set before I'd reached the end of it. I was navigating by moonlight."

"With a storm coming."

"Yes. The storm, the nightfall, the forest—which has been described to me as *haunted* by more than one person. It was all very reckless." She glanced at the sky. "But I've actually traveled from London to Savernake Forest on urgent business. I cannot be deterred by weather or ghosts."

If she thought he would ask her the nature of this business, she was mistaken. If she thought he would congratulate her courage, he did not. He walked on in silence.

Naturally, the silence compelled her to explain. "London is actually only half the distance I've traveled. If I'm being honest. I hail from the Channel Islands. I set out from Guernsey nearly a fortnight ago."

Finally, he asked, "What's your business in Saver-nake Forest?"

"I'm in search of a man." Why not tell him the truth? Her intention was to leave no stone unturned.

He made no response and she pressed on, "I've been told he makes his home in the wood. Honestly, I'm desperate enough to ask *you* about him. You are local to the area, I presume, considering your . . . er, camp. Perhaps you know him. He's called Gabriel d'Orleans? He's a Frenchman—that is, he left France when he was a boy, and he's come of age in Britain. His last known location was . . ." and now she looked out at the misty, moon-bathed forest, crinkling her nose ". . . here. In this forest. Generally speaking. Regretfully, I've no specific direction."

The man stopped walking. His stillness was so sudden and so unexpected, Ryan almost collided with his back. She made a little yelp and jumped out of the way. Had he seen a snake, she wondered. Or a bog-hole? The highwaymen?

"Sir?" she asked carefully.

He stood motionless before her, shoulders raised, gloved hands balled into fists at his sides. When, finally, he began to walk again, he did not look back.

"I was mistaken to think my camp would be suitable for a woman," he said over his shoulder. "I'll take you to the corner of the village instead. You can make your way to the inn from there."

"Oh," said Ryan, surprised by this sudden accommodation. "Very well. If that is what you prefer. I'm in your debt—truly."

He made no reply. Ryan trudged silently behind

him, watching him open and close his hands. Lightning pulsed in the sky but he didn't look up; his gaze was fixed on the horizon. His stride lengthened. Ryan scrambled to follow, swatting at limbs and yanking at her cloak. If she didn't keep up, he would leave her—of this, she had no doubt. He'd hardly been pleasant, but now he appeared agitated, almost angry. Unless she was mistaken, he was running away from her.

Ryan cleared her throat. "Forgive me, but I would be remiss if I didn't ask again. This man, Gabriel d'Orleans, but do *you* know him? If not, have you heard tell of him? And if you have heard of him, do you know where he can be found?"

"No," he said.

"No you don't know him, or no you don't know where he is?"

"Gabriel d'Orleans," the man said, "is dead."

CHAPTER FIVE

THE WORDS WERE out of Gabriel's mouth before he could stop them, stones he couldn't unthrow.

"*Dead?*" repeated the woman behind him. "But are you certain? You *knew him? You knew* Gabriel d'Orleans?"

They were coming to the ridge above the River Kennet. Gabriel considered lowering himself over the edge—simply swinging down and climbing to the water. The fog would swallow him up, and he would swim to his camp. This woman and her questions and her screams would live on without him. She would be frightened and confused, but eventually someone would find her. He'd saved her from Meade, it was enough.

"But *when* did he die?" she asked, her tone suddenly razor-sharp.

He ignored this question and weighed the odds. Was it possible she wasn't the only person looking for Gabriel d'Orleans? She could be one woman alone, or there could be a bloody manhunt. For years, Gabriel had evaded government trackers and palace spies and even his own sister. He'd not hidden for years to be discovered now.

"How did he die? And when?" she pressed.

"I don't know," he said. "It was years ago."

"*No . . .*" she said on a breath.

"Yes."

Lies about d'Orleans had always rolled effortlessly off of Gabriel's tongue, as easy as locking a door. But this lie felt flimsy and unrehearsed. Yes, he'd locked the door, but what if this woman managed to crawl through a window?

"If Gabriel d'Orleans is dead," she was saying, "well . . . then . . . I've come for nothing. How can I return and tell them I came *for nothing*? This was our best, most feasible solution. Oh my God—what will become of us?"

Gabriel stopped walking and turned back. This felt like a trick question. Who were the "them" in this pronouncement? Return *where*?

It doesn't matter. He forced his mind to become a blank slate of all the obligations he did *not* have—not to this woman, not to anyone.

"What is your business with Gabriel d'Orleans?" he asked. If he had any obligation, it was to the name.

"Your French pronunciation is so natural," she observed. "But do you speak French, sir?"

Gabriel swore in his head. He'd said the name with perfect inflection; the pronunciation of a native, of a man saying his own name.

She caught up and rounded on him, stopping him on the path. Her eyes were the most defining feature on her face. Large and expressive; a dusky, foggy blue. He tried not to look at them. He tried not to look at any part of her.

When he didn't answer—when he averted his gaze—she murmured, "A question for another time, perhaps."

She'd lost her hat in the road, and her hair hung in limp, damp waves down the sides of her face. It looked dark in the moonlight, a striking contrast to her pale skin.

After a moment, she said, "Sorry—you asked about my business, didn't you? I might as well tell you." She took a deep breath. "Gabriel d'Orleans was my fiancé. Actually. If you can believe it. It was an arranged marriage. The betrothal was set in place by our fathers when we were toddlers."

"Fiancé?" he rasped. Gabriel experienced the bottomless sensation of stepping from solid ground into a deep well.

The woman nodded. "I've come in search of him. Because I need his help."

And now Gabriel was so deep inside the well, he could barely hear her.

"Sir?" she prompted.

He blinked at her. He gave a definitive shake of his head—*No*. And then he turned on his heel and trudged away. Actually, he ran.

"Wait—sir?" He heard footsteps behind him but he didn't stop.

Was he *running* from her? Yes—yes he was.

Did he *remember* her? Yes—yes, God help him, he did. He was awash in memories: an earl's daughter, the betrothal, the letters, his dead father, his former life.

He saw a brown-haired child in yellow ribbons, studying him with large eyes.

He saw his father, toasting an old friend.

He saw his father again, summoning him to the cavernous study inside the Palace Royale.

He heard the words *duty* and *tradition* and *covenant*; *a bond between two families.*

But how had she—?

"Please stop, Mr.—?" she called from behind him. "Sorry, I don't know your name!"

Oh the irony, Gabriel thought. He kept moving.

He'd hidden from his own sister Elise. *For years*, he'd hidden. He'd secluded himself so effectively, even *she* hadn't found him. Oh, she'd come close; her investigators had cornered Gabriel's emissary at a horse sale in Haymarket. They presented so much evidence and had so many good intentions, it had been impossible to evade them. When it was clear she intended to seek him out—to simply thrash through the forest and find him—he wrote to her and asked her to respect his privacy and the life he'd made and to *keep away*. It had been a harsh request, and he'd tried to soften it with the suggestion that they correspond. Elise had not understood but she'd conceded. She and her husband had also bought an estate not far from Savernake Forest. They were building a life in Wiltshire on the hope that he would, eventually, consent to see her.

But he would not consent. The melding of his old life and his new life was a collision he wouldn't survive. He didn't want his sister to see what he'd become—he didn't want to be seen by anyone. It was simpler and less painful and safer for all of them if he was left entirely alone.

I want to be alone, he thought.

Behind him, the woman called out, "I cannot keep up with you, sir."

Good, he thought.

"I'm usually not so feeble." Her voice was winded. "My legs are not as long as yours. And I've not slept. Nor eaten. And I've been lost in a wood. Also—*attacked*. You, yourself, have both *abducted* me and now, ironically, are *fleeing* from me."

"I'm taking you to the village," he called, not looking back.

It was another lie. He had no idea where he was taking her. They might've been walking in circles. Or off the ridge into the river. Or into a bog. Gabriel was lost, and found, and falling, and drowning, and losing his bloody mind.

He stopped rushing away and turned. She trudged to him with determined strides, her cloak fanning out behind her.

"Why," he demanded, "would the fiancée of Gabriel d'Orleans travel from . . . from . . ." He stopped, trying to remember the details of the betrothal.

"*Guernsey*," she provided, coming up to him. "I've traveled from Guernsey. My name is Lady Marianne Daventry. I'm called 'Ryan' by those who know me."

Her shoulders rose and fell with the force of her breathing. She staggered sideways and, on reflex, he reached out a hand.

Instead of clasping it, she took it up and shook it. "It's a pleasure to make your acquaintance, Mr.—?"

Gabriel frowned. "Why did you travel from Guernsey to meet a dead man?"

"Oh, right. *That*." She retracted her hand. "Well, I came because I didn't know he was dead, obviously;

and it was my very great hope that he would address the very troubling—to put it mildly—matter of *his cousin*."

"His cousin?"

"That's right."

"What problem is caused by his cousin?"

She sighed. "Well, the cousin of the prince—"

She stopped. She swallowed. "I might as well tell you, this man I seek, Gabriel d'Orleans, is French royalty. Or he was when France was ruled by a royal family. He is, in fact, an actual prince. His title is—*was* . . ."

And now she paused and looked upward, affecting the expression of someone reciting from memory. "I believe the full title is 'His Serene Highness, Gabriel d'Orleans, Prince of the Blood.' He was nephew to King Louis XVI. He went missing in the wake of France's Revolution, and no one has seen him for more than fifteen years."

She raised her eyebrows as if to say, *Can you believe it?*

Gabriel said nothing. In fact, he *couldn't* believe it—couldn't believe *her*. And yet—

"Prince Gabriel's father was executed in the Revolution," she explained. "His mother fled the country. And he and his sisters were separated and exiled to England for their safety. He was a boy at the time. I was a year younger—nine years old, perhaps?—and I grew up knowing that the missing French prince to whom I was betrothed, had, for all practical purposes, *vanished*."

"Did you mourn him?" Gabriel asked from the bottom of the well.

"Mourn the prince?" She frowned. "Well, I did, actually. If I'm being honest. I'd only met him twice, and he was a boy and I was little girl but he . . ." and here she took a deep breath ". . . he'd written me letters in the years before he vanished. Not a lot, but enough for me to develop a fondness for him. I replied to his letters and—" She paused again, as if to collect herself. "Well, even as children, we acknowledged the strangeness of an arranged marriage. But he hadn't seemed to hate the notion and neither did I. He seemed very wrapped up in the duty of the thing. There was an earnestness to him that I admired; I've never been much for cynics. And I lived on a remote island but had been engaged to an adorable prince—what's to hate in that? Very little if you were nine-year-old me. I would be lying if I said I did not worry for him when he fled France; nor that I didn't feel very great sadness when his letters ceased. It was a girlish affection, perhaps. But it felt very tragic at the time. It *was* tragic, honestly."

Gabriel breathed in and out, searching her words for judgment or callousness. Searching for truth.

She tugged off her glove and smoothed back her hair with a small pale hand. "These days, I've no remaining energy to mourn the past—not when the present is so very distressing. Any sadness spared for the missing prince is inconsequential compared to the *imposter* prince."

"What imposter prince?" asked Gabriel, annoyed at the man, whomever he was. He'd wanted to hear more about her girlish affection for the adorable prince.

"*His cousin,*" she reminded, sounding annoyed.

"Why do you call him an imposter?" asked Gabriel.

"Prince Gabriel's cousin turned up at my front door claiming that, in the absence of the long-lost Gabriel,

he had inherited the title, and that *he* was the new
Prince d'Orleans. As such, he was now in possession
of the d'Orleans coffers and d'Orleans property—and
also he intended to take possession of *me*."

"Possession of you?"

"Yes. To take as his wife. Because of my long-
standing betrothal to the missing prince. This imposter prince and I are to be united instead of the actual
prince and I. Regardless of the transfer of the title. Or
how I feel about the matter, which is horrified." She
took a deep breath.

Gabriel stared down. Extreme shock felt like a blow
to the head. Tiny lights flickered at the edge of his vision. He swayed on his feet. He hadn't drawn breath
since she'd said the word *fiancé*.

"Shall I carry on?" she prompted.

He blinked at her.

"I'll take your undivided attention to mean *yes*." A
smile. "So now this imposter prince is endeavoring
to . . . to . . . collect. *Me*. And assume possession of my
family's estate, which is an old manor house and lands
called Winscombe. My father is very ill and we've
fallen on lean times. Still, there is the house and acre-
age and sheep. I am the least of what he wants, honestly,
but also the means by which he acquires the lot."

She sighed and continued. "As I said, it's a tragic
tale with which I wouldn't ordinarily burden a stranger.
But you did ask. And I'm rather desperate to find any
trace of the *actual* Prince Gabriel d'Orleans. So . . ."

"What do you expect Prince Gabriel to do?" His
voice was a rasp.

"Well, I expected him to show himself. To reveal to
this imposter that he is, in fact, *not dead*. There can

be only *one* Prince d'Orleans, after all. Surely. Even in France."

"Which cousin is claiming to be the new Prince d'Orleans?"

"What?" Her features twisted in confusion. "Do you mean what is the imposter's name?"

Gabriel waited, his heart a hot ember in his throat.

"He's called Maurice Emile . . . Something-or-other." Her expression went sour. "And he's frightening. Truly. I wouldn't have left Guernsey, sailed to the mainland, and plunged into a dark wood, searching for an exiled prince, if the alternative was not *truly frightening*."

Gabriel took two steps backward. *Maurice.* Snide and petty and selfish Maurice; disagreeable, even when they were boys.

"But how did you know to come here?" he demanded, trying to keep his voice calm. "To Savernake Forest? How did you find"—he paused—"your way?"

"I've a letter," she said, and she began searching her skirts, digging deep into a pocket and coming up with a small leather satchel. She flopped it open and plucked out a piece of parchment, folded again and again.

"Remember I said Prince Gabriel and I used to correspond? My only clue was the last letter he wrote to me." She unfolded the parchment, careful to protect the limp paper in the rising wind. "His letters before the Revolution discussed his life in the Parisian palace with his family. He spoke of the French Court, his lessons—typical ten-year-old things. And then the people of France revolted and the letters stopped. Until this one."

Gabriel stared at the pale letter in her hand. The parchment was tattered, its age obvious even in the dark.

It was *his* letter.

She held *his letter*, written more than a decade ago. It had been the desperate effort of a terrified, lonely, uncertain boy, far from home. His childish attempt to behave with honor to the very end; to set things to rights.

Gabriel was gripped by an old heartbreak, stomach-churning and fearful. He took a step back. He scrubbed a hand over his face, trying to wipe away all the things he saw in memory and the vision of the woman standing two feet away. He contemplated turning on his heel and leaving her. He could dive into the forest, the only respite he'd known for years.

" 'Furthermore it would be imprudent to reveal my exact location,'" she was reciting, reading from his letter, "'but I will say that I'm in the county of Wiltshire in the south of England, in an ancient forest called Savernake.'"

She lowered the parchment. "That is what he wrote to me in . . ." she referenced the letter again ". . . 1799. So . . . close to twelve years ago? His last letter, as I've said. But it's the only clue I have. I used it to map out my search for him. As impossible as it may seem."

Gabriel was about to tell her that it *did* seem impossible; that she was asking the wrong man; that he didn't understand any of it. The words were on the tip of his tongue. He need only articulate the lie.

She cocked her head and studied him. "But you claim that I've come all this way for a dead man?"

He blinked down at her, grateful for a question he

could answer with a *yes* or a *no*. It was easier to lie
in fewer words. And yet, he couldn't speak. He was
too busy swatting memories. Faces, smells, snatches
of conversation—*letters*, swarming him like insects.
How long had it been since he'd thought of the girl
she'd been or the woman she might become? How long
since he'd thought of her *letters*? Images and emotions
flew at him from every direction. He *was* the prince,
of course. He *had* been affianced as a child. He *had*
written her, foolish boy that he'd been. He *did* have a
terrible cousin called Maurice.

He was just about to agree with her—to tell her,
Yes, for God's sake, the prince is dead—when lightning popped, and thunder cracked, and the sky opened
up. The forest was doused with sheets of cold rain.
She made a squeaking noise and quickly folded the
letter into the leather pouch. She ducked her head and
fumbled with the hood of her cloak.

All at once, Gabriel remembered the spooked stallion he'd tied to the tree.

"*Zeus*," he hissed, looking around, judging how
fast he could get to the animal.

"What?" she asked, shouting over the sound of
the rain.

"One of my horses! He's frightened by the rain! I
have to recover him! Can you—"

He looked at the sky. There was no help for it. He
could hardly leave her in the middle of the storm. He'd
have to take her to his camp and then recover Zeus.

"Can you run?" he shouted.

"What? Run? I suppose I can—yes."

He took up her hand and set out at a sprint.

CHAPTER SIX

$\mathcal{R}$YAN TRIED TO keep up—truly. She'd engaged all remaining strength, ignoring the pain in her leg, her fatigue, her unsteadiness on dark, slick, unfamiliar ground. But his strides were longer, and he knew the way. He'd pulled her behind him for only a few yards before he turned back, swept her off her feet, and tossed her over his shoulder again.

Ryan made a yelping noise but honestly, she was relieved. Given the choice between being dragged through the mud or carried, she preferred to be carried. Little known fact: it wasn't terrible to be foisted up by a tall, broad-shouldered man and carried about. After the night she'd had. And in the rain. And by *this* tall, broad-shouldered man.

For the second time that night, she found her head dangling down his back and her legs pinned to his chest. Her bottom stuck up to the sky, and he held her securely in place with an arm to the back of her knees. The contact just missed the wound in her leg. She was getting better at holding on. She clasped both hands around his middle and pressed her cheek into his spine.

Her eyes were closed, but she felt the rise and fall

of the terrain, heard the *thud* of his boots, smelled wet leaves. He splashed through a puddle and cold water splattered her face. She'd gathered up her hair with a hand, trying to keep it from trailing through the mud.

He said something over his shoulder—some growled request that she couldn't understand.

"What?" she asked.

"Close your eyes," he repeated.

"They're closed!" she called back.

But now she blinked them open and added, "Why?"

"My camp is ahead," he said, "and it's . . . it's very private. I prefer it to stay hidden."

Hidden? she repeated in her head. As if she would *return* to this terrifying forest on purpose and *intentionally* seek out this man's camp.

"They are closed," she assured him—although now she felt compelled to open her right eye, just a crack. Not that it mattered; the world was a blur of wet vegetation and the flapping corner of the man's coat.

Five minutes later, he grunted "here" and fell sideways against something hard and unmoving.

The relentless peck of raindrops had stopped, and she heard them tapping against an overhang above. A barrier protected them on one side from the wind. Ryan opened both eyes and looked around. He was leaning against a wall made of rough-hewn timbers, the gaps between the wood sealed with plaster.

"Can you stand?" he asked, sliding her toward the ground.

"Probably," she managed. She left his body in a controlled fall. Her feet were numb and the wound on her leg ached. She staggered when she landed. Large hands caught her around the waist, shoring her up. Ryan's sodden hair clumped in her face, and she smoothed it back, trying to see.

"Put a hand to the wall," he said.

"Thank you." She reached out, trying to look around without *seeming* to look around.

"You can look," he said. "It's a camp—nothing more. There's no time for a tour and honestly, nothing to—"

He exhaled deeply but didn't finish.

"Go," she said. "Your horse—please go. I'm perfectly happy to wait"—she looked around trying to identify where he'd propped her—"here."

With no warning, two large dogs emerged from the mist, plodding to them. Ryan reacted without thinking, gasping and shrinking against the wall.

"Careful," he said, frowning at her wariness. He made a clicking noise and held out his hand. In unison, the dogs stopped walking and sat, tails wagging. "Have you a fear of dogs?"

"No," Ryan managed, turning her face to the wall. "That is, I haven't been until recently. Sorry. I'm not—" She took a deep breath, trying to control her racing heart. "They are not aggressive—your dogs?"

"No. They help with the horses and are companions to me."

Ryan nodded to the wall, trying to regain composure. She loved dogs. Winscombe had been home to many dogs over the years, and several of them had slept nudged against her in her bed. One incident should not destroy a lifelong affection.

"Hugo," the man said gruffly, "Tatin—bed."

The dogs made a whining noise but retreated, padding into the night.

Ryan let out a slow exhale. "Thank you."

"I'll set you up inside," he said. "The dogs will be too curious not to return. And I assume you want in out of the rain."

"Well, only if it can be quickly managed. I would not detain you . . ." She glanced around but saw only a wash of dark greens and blues and grays. Somewhere nearby, horses whinnied and stamped. She smelled wet hay and manure.

"I would ask you not to . . ." he exhaled ". . . *touch* anything."

Ryan laughed in spite of herself. "Understood. But I've not come here to rob you, please be assured. Or if I have, I've been very inefficient about it, have I?"

"Don't touch anything," he repeated. He stomped away; she heard a door open and close. When he returned, he held a glowing torch. She peeked around the corner and watched him light lanterns on posts, illuminating the rainy night at intervals.

"Does this mean that I'll be left alone here? You live alone, sir?" She wanted to confirm this.

"It is only the animals and me." When four lanterns were aglow, he mounted the torch on a stake.

"No staff?" she pressed, just to be certain.

"No."

"No one at all to help you mind your horses?"

"I've two grooms, but they've gone for the night."

"Of course." Ryan looked at the sky. The rain was slowing and silver clouds parted to reveal a bright moon. "Honestly, it's not necessary for me to wait in your . . . dwelling if you prefer me outside. You've been so very kind and . . ."

Now Ryan stopped. In fact, she wanted very much

to wait in his dwelling. She was soaked to the bone and shivering, and, oh—to *sit down* for ten minutes. If there was water and a crust of bread, all the better.

"It's through here," he said, summoning her with a jerk of his head. She followed him around the corner of the structure. Was it a house? If so, the roof was very low, almost sunken, and—

—*underground?*

Ryan blinked at the domicile illuminated by flickering lantern light. It was less of a house and more of a . . . bunker? It protruded from beneath the gentle rise of a small, grassy hill. A wide, low doorway had been cut into the hillside like a human-sized mousehole. On either side of the door, the earth was held back by stone ledges.

It was half house, half hill; part bunker, part cottage. It was sunken and settled and clearly very old. A stout chimney poked from the side of the hill like a cork; a small window beside the door was one open eye. It was the type of abode that children in a storybook might stumble upon in the forest; a magical dwelling for fairies or wood nymphs or a witch. It looked far too small to accommodate the man who'd abducted/rescued her. It hardly looked large enough for Ryan.

"Shall I—?" she began, trying not to stare. She glanced behind her. She heard the horses milling in the darkness.

"I'll not be gone long," the man said.

He stepped to the door and Ryan had the errant worry that she was about to be led inside, knocked in the head, and baked into a pie. She never learned the *name* of this man.

"I beg your pardon?" She cleared her throat. "I've been remiss in not learning your name, sir. I should hate to impose on your hospitality without knowing to whom I'm indebted."

He wrenched open the heavy door with a creak and disappeared inside. She held back, hovering between the stone ledges.

"Sir?" she tried again, her mind conjuring terrible names, the names of madmen and murderers.

He didn't answer. She heard the scrape of iron on stone and saw orange flames flicker in a corner grate. Light tumbled from the fireplace, and she could see his silhouette amid the outlines of crude furniture. A chair. A table. A shelf.

"Come in out of the rain," he said.

Ryan swallowed. "Forgive me. I'm . . . I find myself grasping for the social constructs that usually govern these sorts of situations."

"You're grasping for what?" He was annoyed.

"Introductions, servants, an umbrella . . ."

"Sorry," he said, "you're out of luck."

"The great irony is that I typically care very little about these sorts of things. Social constructs saw me betrothed as an infant and would now see me married to a petty tyrant. Forgive me, I'm rambling, the point is, I really must insist upon learning your name, sir. Please."

"It's Rein," he said, emerging from the dwelling.

"I beg your pardon?"

"I'm called 'Rein.'"

"Rain?" She looked up at the weeping sky.

"Not 'rain,' as in a deluge, I mean 'Rein' like for a horse."

"Oh, '*Rein*,'" she repeated agreeably, as if this made all the sense in the world rather than lacking in subtlety for a man who described himself as "alone except for my horses."

"Thank you very much, Mr., er, Rein. Do go and see to your stallion. I'll make myself at home. Whilst touching nothing—just to be clear."

"I'll be back in half an hour," he said, cramming his hat on his head. "Close the door and turn the lock."

And then he was gone, striding into the wet mist, his coat whirling behind him.

Ryan turned to the open door and braced herself. Swallowing hard, she stepped gingerly over the threshold.

Slowly, her eyes adjusted to the dim light of the fire. She looked around. The house had a wet, earthy smell but was neat and tidy. She was gratified to see the floor was made of wooden beams rather than dirt; and the ceiling was—she looked up, squinted, and then stood on her toes to stretch an arm above her head and touch—*rock*. The ceiling was rock. Oh. She touched the ceiling again. And now she understood. Mr. Rein lived in a *cave*. Well, one side was a cave; the other side was built out like a house, with proper walls connected at proper angles. The seam where the rock met the timber was a ribbon-like crevice, packed with a quarry of stones. The cave part of the house and the . . . well, the *house* part of the house came together into a whole that was very cottage-like, with a door and a window, furniture and rugs; a hearth and—she looked around—a small kitchen. Unless she was mistaken, other rooms lay beyond the circle of light provided by the fire.

But how *incredible*, she thought, slowly spinning. There were candles, an old leather chair by the fire, a stack of books—actually there was an entire shelf of books—a desk and another chair.

Working quickly, Ryan disentangled herself from the dripping cloak and hung it on a peg by the fire. She laid her sodden gloves on the mantle and removed her wet shoes and stockings. She checked the wound on her leg—no worse for the wear, two arcs of teeth marks, nearly healed.

In the kitchen, she located a cloth and used it to dry her hair and pat down her dress. There was a barrel of fresh water and she scooped ladle after ladle, gulping it down.

For ten minutes, she stood before the fire, allowing the heat to lick the wetness from her skirts, warming herself. Only when sweat formed on the back of her neck did she light a candle and return to the kitchen. She poked around, looking for a stray apple or walnut or turnip—anything she might eat. She found a kettle and coffee and made the calculated gamble that Mr. Rein would value hot coffee more than his desire to have untouched possessions. She set about making a pot. While the water boiled, she perused the books on his shelf.

True to form, there were many titles about animal husbandry, horses, racing, and breeding. But there were also books about history and philosophy; mathematics and natural science; and novels—both classics and the popular literature of the day. Mr. Rein, it seemed, was an avid reader with diverse tastes and access to a bookseller.

She moved to the next shelf, running her finger

along the spines of religious texts, books about geography and economics and—

When she stooped to the third shelf, her finger stopped. She held the candle closer. The titles on the spines of these books were written in French. Ryan was fluent in French—her home was only sixty nautical miles from mainland France—so it took no effort to read titles on French history, French geography, French philosophers. There was a book of French artists and an illustrated guide to Paris. And Bordeaux. This collection went on and on—books about cities and provinces throughout France.

When Ryan had read every title twice, she stepped away and considered the shelves. In total, there were more French books than English. But how had a cave-dwelling horseman who called himself *Mr. Rein* manage to collect a small library in two languages?

Without thinking, she crossed to the small desk in the corner. The surface was bare, but the desktop concealed a drawer. Ryan bit her lip. Something, some unnamed curiosity, nudged her to test the handle. Glancing at the door and then back, she carefully slid open the drawer. It contained . . . nothing in particular. Parchment. Quills. Loose candles. Tucked deep in one corner, she saw a bundle of folded parchment tied with a string, the paper thin and flaking, bleached by age. She was just about to move on—she was not, by nature, a snooper, and she'd promised not to touch anything—when she noticed a trio of tiny shapes on the corner of the parchment. Ryan blinked, pushed the candle closer, and leaned down to examine the small scribbles.

The shapes had been formed by hand, not printed,

and crudely so. They'd been drawn in the shape of a
triangle, a pair of them above with one centered below.

Ryan straightened. She stared at the wall above
the desk. She took a deep breath and looked again.
She *knew* this upside-down triangle formed by
three little symbols. It was familiar to her. In fact,
she knew the three little symbols.

Glancing at the doorway and then back at the
drawer, Ryan carefully, gingerly nudged the bundle of
parchment, sliding it into plain view. It was a stack of
envelopes. They'd been placed in the drawer, inscrip-
tion down—so she couldn't see the address. A greasy
stain marked the old seal, the wax long since flaked
away. The crudely drawn trio of symbols was in the
corner of the topmost envelope.

It can't be, Ryan marveled, her heart beginning to
pound.

Checking the door once more, biting her lip, she
used the tip of one finger to touch the trio of doodles on
the envelope. They looked like fat, squat daggers with
a short blade pointed upward and a scabbard crossing horizontally just above the hilt. While the shapes
were dagger-like, the lines were curved like petals. A
fleur-de-lis; or rather, *three fleurs-de-lis*. The symbols
worked together to form a reverse triangle.

Ryan knew this, because it represented the crest of
the Family d'Orleans—and because she had drawn
the crest on every single letter she'd ever written to
her former fiancé, Prince Gabriel d'Orleans.

These were *her* drawings, on *her* letters, bundled
and stored in the drawer of a reclusive man living in
the last known location of the Prince d'Orleans.

Fumbling for the candle, nearly dropping it, burning

herself with wax, Ryan snatched up the bundle of letters and studied them at close range.

The name inscribed on the front, written in her precise, childlike hand, was His Serene Highness, Gabriel Phillipe d'Orleans. The address was the Palais Royale in Paris, France.

"These are my letters to him," whispered Ryan. "*Mine*. I wrote these. When we were children, I wrote these letters to him."

Ryan looked up and around, gaping at the small cottage-cave-dwelling-wherever-she-was. She heard a low *whoosh*, the rising tide of shock and hope. Her mouth literally fell open.

"Oh my God," she whispered. "It's him. I've found him. I've actually found him."

Just then the door pushed open, letting in a burst of cool air, rainwater, and scowling man in a dripping overcoat.

Ryan closed the drawer with her hip and slid the bundle of letters into the pocket of her skirts. Her hands felt bloodless, her heart felt like a bucket of coins being shaken in her chest. She spun to face the door.

Mr. Rein looked around, taking in the brewing coffee, the discarded stockings, her position by his books. His eyes narrowed on her face.

"What's happened?" he rasped.

"I've found you," Ryan said, the words spilling out in a breathless gush. "That's what's happened. It's you, I know it, it's you."

Almost too late, she remembered to bow. She dipped into a wobbly curtsy. She wasn't required to bow—he was *French* royalty, and she was English—

but on the two occasions she'd met him in childhood, her father had bade her to curtsy. It felt foolish and unfitting for two people in sodden clothes, standing in a cave, but she'd told herself that if she found him, she would do it.

She looked up. He gaped at her like a man with a rifle pointed at his face.

Ryan pressed on. "I've come to seek your help," she whispered. "Prince Gabriel. Please. I need your help."

CHAPTER SEVEN

"*G*ET UP," GABRIEL rasped.

"Will you—"

"I said, get up."

He didn't wait for her to comply. He turned away and trudged to the door. His hand was on the knob when he stopped. He asked himself where he intended to go. His lack of choices was devastating.

He could run away—like a coward, he could run—but to where?

He could evict her—simply, toss her out into the storm—but she *knew*. This woman *knew*, and it was too dangerous to trust what she might reveal to others.

He could hide somewhere nearby—close enough to observe her, to wait and see—but he'd *been* hiding for half his life. *For years*, he'd hid. And for what? So she could locate him on an otherwise unremarkable Tuesday night . . . no warning . . . on her very first foray into the forest?

He could simply admit the truth: he could tell her he'd been "Prince Gabriel" once upon on a time, but not anymore—not for years. But this admission would mean so much talking, explaining, *hours* of discussing it. He wouldn't survive it. Discussing his identity with someone who wanted something from his old life would feel more revelatory than walking up the high street in Marlborough and shouting his name.

But what if he simply told her that he had no idea what she was talking about? What if he carried on with the lie he'd been telling everyone, including himself, for all these years. He could tell her she was mistaken.

"I'm not mistaken," she said from behind him.

He craned around. She stood in the center of the room.

"I understand if you're not prepared to admit it," she said calmly. "Your life has been a trial, clearly but—I've found a stack of letters I wrote to you when I was a girl, Highness."

She reached into her pocket and extracted the bundle of letters that he'd carried with him from his chamber at the Palais Royale, to his jail cells—first in Temple Prison, and then in the Conciergerie—and finally, on his flight from France. She held them up like a stolen candlestick.

"Say what you will," she continued, "but I know who you are. I was led to this forest by your own letter—I've already said this—and now here are mine. I heard you pronounce your name as if it was the most familiar thing you'd ever said. You've a library of French literature. If that's not proof enough, well—I don't mind telling you that you resemble your late father. May God rest him. I've met him, remember? I met all of you. When we were children. Your family traveled to Guernsey twice and you were our guests at Winscombe. It was on the last visit that I recall the imposing sight of your father. He was tall and broad, with hazel eyes. Just like you. I'm sorry, Highness, but *I remember.* I've found you. I've actually managed to find you."

Gabriel did not feel found—he felt trapped. The storm was behind him. She stood before him, waving his private, personal keepsakes and calling them her own. Perhaps she had written them, but they'd belonged to him. They'd been one of the few things he'd managed to secret out of the palace during the arrest. Why he'd taken them, he couldn't say. Why he'd kept them, he also could not say.

I took them because I wanted them, he thought, staring at the small, crumbling stack of parchment. *I liked to read them. I respected my father's wish for my future with the daughter of his old friend.*

To Gabriel's young, terrified mind, clinging to the betrothal had seemed like the noble thing to do. He'd been forced to leave behind so much from his old life, but he'd wanted to keep her.

No, not her, he reminded himself, *her letters.*

And now those letters were being used to unmask him. *She* was unmasking him. Lady Marianne Daventry had found him, and trapped him, and threatened everything he held dear. She'd made him feel homesickness—something he'd not felt for years. It was a roiling, bubbling stew of emotion—too much for a man who subsisted on a diet of very bland, very simple feelings.

"Look," she continued, "we needn't commit to anything this precise moment. Not when you've just blown in from the storm, wet, stomping mud on the rugs. You're soaked through. But can you . . . ?"

She set the letters aside and extended her hand to

him. "Give me your coat. I've hung my cloak by the fire but there is another peg. I'll hang it while you see to your boots. I've made coffee—I hope you don't mind. Will you take a cup?"

"Don't placate me," he warned, not moving. He thought of how she'd rifled through his things. It was a profound intrusion, and how much easier to dwell on this than on her accusation.

"Forgive me," she said, retracting her hand. "It's not my goal to manage you. I've only one goal, which I stated even before I knew that you were, well, *you*. I—" She took a deep breath. "I can acknowledge that everything about me comes as a very great shock. I am not, by nature, a shocking person, nor a bold one. Seeing to wet coats and offering refreshment come much more naturally to me than asking a strange man for help. I am loathe to be a bother to anyone—the man who rescued me from certain doom, least of all—but my family have found ourselves in dire straits. The old betrothal has forced me to hunt you down, but I won't try to disguise it as anything less than an imposition. To you—that is. A very great imposition."

"More than an imposition, I'd say, to nose about in the personal possessions of a stranger, to ransack his property." He eyed the letters on his table. Where had she found them? The desk? The bedside? God, had she been in his bedroom?

"I asked you not to touch anything," he said, flinging his hat back and forth, shaking off water.

"Yes, you did," she allowed carefully. "The coffee was a practical matter, just to be clear, and I don't make a habit of nosing about the homes of strangers. I cannot say why I did it, except that . . . I *knew*? I'd sensed it. Deep down. And this *knowing* propelled me to explore. It's no excuse, but . . ."

She trailed off with a shrug and stared into his face. Her expression was forthright, and wary, and (if he was being honest) *contrite*. Her eyes were a smoky gray-blue; the color of a ribbon of mineral that bisected a chipped rock. It was subtle and cloudy and almost no color at all. And it cut him in two.

"Give me your coat?" she tried again, speaking gently.

He stared at her. He could feel himself wanting to comply. She had this quality—a calmness, an observational air. She seemed disinclined to argue with him. He shouldn't forget that she'd calmly, observantly pawed through his house until she'd lit upon his identity. Why argue when she simply did whatever the hell she pleased? But even so. She was the opposite of the flash and rattle he associated with most females. Not the radiant sunrise, the cool shade at noon; not the butterfly, the moth. She had been this way, even as a child. And perhaps that's why he'd kept her letters. Her even, neat handwriting . . . her earnest, everyday musings . . . made him feel steady and calm when his world spun into chaos.

She nodded to the coat and he held it out to her.

"This is a fine coat," she said, plucking it from his arm. "What is the material?"

"Oilskin."

"Oh, lovely. Is there a craftsman in Pewsey?"

"No."

"Marlborough, then?"

"No."

"But did you have it made in London? I ask, only

because my sister Diana—you may recall there were three of us girls. I'm the oldest, then there's my middle sister Diana? She manages the sheep and lands at Winscombe, and she is outside in every kind of weather. She could benefit from a coat like this."

"Your sister manages your sheep and lands?"

"She has a foreman who answers to her—they manage it together. Our father fell ill five years ago, and he was never much for estate management even before his heart gave out. Diana is keenly interested in it, and we're so very lucky for it. The grounds and livestock are her purview. I manage the house. Our youngest sister, Charlotte, is in the schoolroom at the moment, but our hope is that she'll escape the demands of Winscombe and marry. I should say, this is *her* hope, but we want what she wants. She is very much taken with the idea of a London debut and Season. We've an elderly aunt who can sponsor her, but one thing at a time. Forgive me, I'm prattling on. If you'll hand over your socks and gloves, I'll set them by the fire to dry."

His socks were sweaty and gnarled with patches and there was no world in which he would pile them in her small pink hands. But he extended his gloves and she plucked them away. He watched her arrange his disembodied gloves above the fire. It felt like she was stealing sections of his body, one at the time, and priming them to burn. And all the while, he simply stood there and . . . allowed it.

She turned back to him. "Forgive me, Highness—"

"Please refer to me as Rein."

"Right." She sighed. "Forgive me, *Mr. Rein*, but will you tell me about this house? I'm ever so intrigued. Is it—?" She ran a careful hand along the crevice of gravel where the timber wall met the exposed rock of the cave. Watching her, he felt the phantom caress of that same hand touching a crevice inside his chest. Her expression looked mystified, and something about that look caused a little inward tickle, like the swish of a feather over his heart.

"It is a *cave*, is it not?" she asked. "Unless I'm mistaken, we are *underground*?"

She looked so very delighted by the notion, he heard himself say, "Yes, it is a cottage built out from a cave."

"Astonishing," she breathed. "And yet you cook and raise heat by a hearth. There are proper floorboards and a window. You come and go through a door that locks. But is it damp? There are caves on Guernsey but the sea is a constant source of wet."

"It is not wet," he answered, looking to her. She had effectively trapped him in his own doorway. Did she mean for him to pad, shoeless, across the floor, to stand—where would he stand? The cottage was barely large enough for him, and now he was to navigate a woman?

"Will you stand before the fire?" she suggested. "I went to the grate immediately when I came in."

"When you came in," he corrected, "you ransacked drawers and cabinets."

"And, I made coffee. Will you take some?"

He watched her maneuver around him, taking up the kettle with a cloth to the handle. Her feet, he now saw, were bare. Oval toes poked beneath the muddy hem of her dress. He glanced around until he located her shoes; they were lined neatly beside the fire with her stockings draped across them. He looked away.

"Can you direct me to the cups and saucers, Mr. Rein?" she said from the kitchen. "Sorry to say that I failed to locate your dishes whilst engaged in my diligent ransacking."

"Above the basin," he said, his eyes returning to the stockings. They were ivory wool, splattered with mud, spread limply over muddy shoes. Even so, the sight of them felt like walking by the open door of a church and catching a glimpse of the beauty inside. Was it a sin, he wondered, to compare women's stockings to church? Certainly the sight of them felt a little spiritual. He was reminded of the feel of her legs beneath his arm when he carried her. He thought of her small bare feet.

Gabriel's adult life had afforded him with fewer women's undergarments than it had churches, and he'd not been to church in years. Any public gathering felt like a luxury; his true identity always put others at risk.

Women, on the other hand, could be arranged. When he absolutely could not take the solitude another night; when he was out of his mind with need; when he had the money. Endurance work with horses sometimes took him to the low hills on the opposite edge of the forest, near the town of Marlborough. It was his practice to never leave the wilderness in the light of day, but could slip into Marlborough's southern-most quarter after sunset and pay for an hour in the company of a woman. Stockings were never part of these encounters; they were dark, and silent, and anonymous.

Gabriel squeezed his eyes shut, blocking out memories of Marlborough. The women were perfectly cordial and seemed pleased that he was generous

with his tips, but the interludes were unsatisfying
and transactional. And that was the sum total of his
experience with females: nameless brothel workers
and . . . *this* person. She stood in his kitchen, pouring
coffee, and strewing wet garments about the hearth.
She challenged his identity and claimed to be the
grown-up version of his childhood fiancée. And he
couldn't stop looking at her.

He watched her crane up to the cabinet on her tip-
toes, reaching for a stack of cups.

"Oh, but look at your sturdy stoneware," she was
saying.

You mean primitive and crude, he thought. He was
just about to turn away when she tumbled backward.
She'd reached too high and the cups were too heavy. He
lunged just as the pottery fell. She windmilled backward, trying to both avoid the cups and catch them.

He grabbed her from behind, snatching her back to
his front and banding an arm around her waist. She
made a small gasping noise and grabbed his outer
thighs in each hand. Four cups hit the wooden floor
with a thud, but the fifth landed directly on her foot
and she yelped. Wincing, she curled her body into the
shape of a nine, bowing against him.

"Careful," he rasped, holding her tightly.

"Ouch, ouch, ouch," she whispered in short, pained
breaths. With each word, she burrowed more deeply
against him. Gabriel molded around her, tucking her
head beneath his chin. As he bent, he felt the tickle of
her hair on his throat; her ear against his chest; her hip
to his groin; the arch of her feet against his shins. He
memorized all of it, the woman-shaped imprint burning into him.

"I'm alright," she breathed. "I'm alright. That hurt like the very devil but, remarkably none of your cups are damaged. Look."

"You needn't make a fuss with coffee."

"I'm not usually so clumsy." She chuckled and relaxed the hand on his left thigh, laying it on top of his arm. Her other hand remained on his right thigh and he would feel her handprint forever.

"I'm really rather handy," she went on softly. "Everyone says it."

"I'm sorry," Gabriel breathed.

A chuckle. "For what are *you* sorry?" She lifted her chin, trying to see him.

I'm sorry, he thought, *that I'm inarticulate and mannerless. Sorry that you've been forced to make coffee like a servant. Sorry I snatched you up like you were trying to hurl yourself off a cliff. Sorry you found the letters.*

He didn't say this—he didn't know if it was true. She began to jostle against him, her hands sliding from his arm and his thigh. He loosened his grasp, a concession that felt akin to breaking off his hand, but she didn't pull away.

She pivoted, spinning in his arms until they were pressed together in a sort of face-to-face embrace. Her chest pressed against his ribs, the most urgently needy part of him pressed into her belly.

"Will you give me a tour of your house?" she asked quietly.

He ignored the question and looked down at her. Was this really Lady Marianne Daventry? Here? In his house—in his arms?

Her hair was darker, she'd grown obviously, but her

large bluish eyes were unchanged. She'd had a general air of quietness, and this was also the same. Her request to see the house came out like a gentle suggestion. Her voice was soft and her mannerisms were calm. He couldn't have borne brashness, he thought. He was accustomed to the quiet rustles and snaps of the forest. She fit nicely inside the small cave. She fit even more nicely in his arms.

"I've not prowled about, no matter what you think," she was saying. "I would hate to leave a proper cave without a tour. Do you mean to restore me to Pewsey tonight?"

"My intention was to take you to the edge of the village in the morning."

"Tomorrow, then. Thank you for harboring me. And rescuing me. Thank you for everything."

"I regret it," he said, the words out before he'd realized it.

"You regret rescuing me?" she asked on a chuckle. "That is a terrible thing to say."

"I am terrible."

"Your value, sir, is still in question. At least where I am concerned. It depends on what you're willing to do for me."

"I'm not willing to do anything for you." He forced himself to release her. He took a step back. "We'll ride to Pewsey and part ways."

"I don't believe you," she declared softly. "You rescued me from the highwayman. You've taken me in. You saved my letters these great many years. You've been very gracious about—" A pause. "About the collision of our lives. All things considered."

Gabriel stooped to collect the fallen cups and

clunked them, one by one, on the tabletop. Should he contradict her? Tell her she'd been *extracted*, not rescued? That he'd not taken her in, but stashed her out of the rain? That he was a rustic, primitive beast of a man who gaped at her like he'd never seen a woman? That he'd hauled her through the forest on his shoulder because that was what primitive, beastly men did?

What of the rest of it? Should he tell her that the freedom of his forest life was something he would never give up?

Being a prince was not an honor, it was a type of servitude. Princes existed at the pleasure of their families, and loyalists, and history, and money. Every aspect of royal life was controlled. And Gabriel would rather be primitive and free than to ever go back.

He was a man forgotten by civilization—or who'd forgotten how to be civilized. He'd allowed it all to slip away in order to survive. But there wasn't space in his life to also manage the survival of Lady Marianne Daventry. Regrettably. Selfishly.

And it made no difference that she seemed unfazed and accommodating, and that she hadn't challenged him about keeping her letters. And it made no difference that he'd managed to touch her ten different ways since he'd scooped her from the road and she hadn't seemed to mind.

If only he'd not *touched* her, he thought. If he'd not touched her, he probably *would* be stomping through the rain, hauling her to Pewsey tonight.

He'd not meant to put his hands on her, but Meade's men were too numerous. Against the rock, they'd needed to hide. In the road, he'd needed the element of surprise. On the trail, the rain was too heavy to drag her. He'd had no choice but to scoop her up. Her position over his shoulder had been a practical matter, logistical; but then her hip had settled against his cheek and her thighs rested against his chest and his body had awakened at each point of contact. Muscles twitched, groin tightened, hairs stood on end. Gabriel's skin was like a thick, leathery husk; long detached from the sensations of softness. He rarely encountered female parts, or fragrant cloaks or wet curls, or lips against his throat. The husk had dissolved when he held her; every nerve ending tingled and throbbed and *sought*.

Physically, his body had climbed up that hill; mentally, he'd cataloged the contour of her breasts against his back; her hip against his cheek. It had taken all of his control to carry her away instead of dropping to the ground and touching and touching and touching every part of her until there was no earlobe or shoulder blade or the inside of a knee unknown to his hands. He'd wanted to gobble her up.

He hadn't gobbled her, he'd removed her from the road—and then he'd held her against his chest and slowly expired while she nestled into him.

And now he'd touched her again. In his own kitchen. And declared that she should stay the night.

"Mr. Rein?" she was saying, trying to get his attention.

"Tell me your name again?"

"You know my name."

"Tell me."

"Alright. I'm called Ryan. Lady Ryan Daventry. When we were children, you knew me as Lady Marianne."

"I do not know you, Lady Marianne *Ryan* Daventry." He would say it, and say it, and say it.

"You do."

"I do not."

She exhaled, closed her eyes, opened them again. "You wish to speak in circles? Fine. Let us circle back to this: Will you show me your home?"

"Why?"

"Because I want to see it."

"I'll show you to where you will sleep."

"Oh, you've a guest room? Lovely."

"No. I do not have a guest room." *It's a cave*, he added in his head.

"Right. Of course. Lead the way."

CHAPTER EIGHT

*R*YAN WAS LYING when she said she wasn't trying to manage him.

Manage him was exactly what she was trying to do. He was caustic and evasive and *lying to her*— which, he lived in a cave (a very tidy cave, but still a cave); of course he would pretend not to know her. She could allow for some dancing about the truth from a man who'd been born in a castle and now lived in . . . *this*. But the situation wanted some productive way to *evolve*. There wasn't time to evade and lie forever. And his one-sentence utterances must stop. There was so much to be said—years of history and explanations and *strategizing* from both of them. He would simply have to find a way to be more forthcoming.

Ryan was adept at managing many things— household staff, the weekly budget for the market, her father, her sisters, sick tenants, gossiping villagers, just to name a few—but she had less of an idea how to manage a man. That is, she knew absolutely nothing about seduction.

No—that wasn't true. She knew enough about se- duction to identify this man's keen interest in human contact. That is, human contact *with her*.

Gabriel's regard for her and the regard of other men was the difference between memorizing a book and glancing at the title. And wasn't this an interesting development? It hadn't happened in the forest—in the forest, she was a parcel to be borne about. But in the hour since he'd returned to the cottage, he'd stared at her like she was a cool stream and he'd not had water for a week.

And perhaps it was a bold leap—to go from *his* stare to *her* seduction—but she was not a child. She was inexperienced and had no idea what she was doing, but when he'd caught her up by the cupboard and held her against him, she realized the advantage.

In the end, seduction—even an amateur one—was an easy risk for Ryan to take, because Prince Gabriel was so very much more . . . spectacular (was there any other word?) than what she'd imagined. It would not be a difficult chore to seduce him—or to *endeavor* to seduce him.

She'd prepared herself to find a frail man; a degenerate man; a man who lived beneath a bridge and subsisted on grubs and raw fish. Despite these predictions, she'd come for him because almost anything was preferrable to the imposter prince.

But the real Prince Gabriel was the opposite of frail, and if he was degenerate, he was very slow to reveal it. He was virile, and robust—a horseman who could carry her over muddy hillsides. He was a man who hadn't welcomed her snooping but also hadn't thrown her out. At least not yet.

And he'd clutched her against him like he was fighting an invisible force that was trying to peel her away.

And her letters. He'd kept the letters she'd written to him.

And now who was being seduced?

Ryan licked her lips, watching him. He said nothing, and she raised her eyebrows, inviting him to begin the tour he so clearly did not want.

"Kitchen," he said, gesturing to the tiny room.

"I do believe I've seen the kitchen."

"Fire," he said, pointing to the chair beside the fire.

A passage extended into darkness between the kitchen and the fireplace, and he took up a candle and stalked through the murk. Ryan followed, marveling at the uneven rock that formed the walls of this corridor. She skimmed a hand down the cold, hard surface, her fingertips snagging here and there on rough spots. It really was a cave. Gabriel d'Orleans, Prince of the Blood, resided in a cave. She thought back to his visits to Winscombe. How incredibly showy and over-provisioned they'd been. His family had arrived with a line of gleaming carriages they'd ferried from France. They'd worn what had seemed (even to her young eyes) unnecessary layers of formal clothes in metallic fabrics that reflected the sun. His parents brought so many servants Winscombe's basement couldn't house them all, and they'd been posted at the inn in the village.

And now he lived alone in a cave and referred to himself as Mr. Rein.

Ahead of them, Ryan heard the distinctive sound of falling water splashing against a hard surface. Was there a crag somewhere that allowed rainwater in? An underground river? They'd not walked three yards when the narrow blackness opened up into broader, higher blackness. She followed the light of the candle drawing a yellow line across the void. One by one, he lit sconces and a chamber came into view.

"Bedroom," he said.

Ryan blinked into the newly illuminated space. It *was* a room, of sorts. There was a low ceiling formed of solid rock. It just missed the top of Gabriel's head. There were walls, but they weren't straight or flat. These were also rock, cut away by whatever natural force formed caves. There was no timber embedded here; they were in the belly of the hill.

In the lowest, tightest corner, he'd situated a bed, the mattress neatly covered with a quilt and fluffy pillows. There was a chair, a wardrobe, another desk, a basin. A mirror hung from a stake driven into the rock. The floor was wooden and a rug stretched beside the bed.

Ryan considered all of it, keeping her face pleasant. The room was modest but not uncomfortable—a little cold, but not suffocating. She stepped to the bed and fingered the coverlet and dug a bare toe into the rug.

"Have you seen it?" he asked, stepping behind her.

"I can honestly say I've never seen anything like it, if that's what you mean."

The sound of splashing water was louder now, but the air was not damp. Behind him, she could just make out a gap in the rock, another passageway perhaps, but it was too dark to see where it led.

"What is that notch in the wall?" she asked.

"Nothing of consequence. This is the bedroom and there's not much more to see. It is a modest dwelling, obviously."

"Yes, alright," she said. "And for tonight, I will sleep by the fire."

"No, *I* will sleep by the fire. You may have the bed."

"Oh I couldn't possibly put you out of your bed, Mr. Rein. I'll not impose."

"It's no imposition. When Samuel was alive, he slept every night by the fire. It's perfectly comfortable."

"Who is Samuel?"

"My . . ." and here he paused. He looked pained. She worried she'd overstepped, but then he exhaled and said, "My guardian."

"Oh."

"I was his ward, I should say. He took me in when I was eleven years old. He was a surrogate parent to me, and I became a son to him and an older brother to his two young boys. This was his home and the horses were his trade. He welcomed me in and he taught me to heal animals."

"But where is he now?" she asked.

"Dead. Six years now."

"I'm so sorry."

"Thank you. I owe him my life."

"And many nights' good sleep," she said, trying to make a joke.

"I beg your pardon?"

"I simply mean that he was very generous if he gave his only bedroom to his ward."

"He made three small beds for this chamber. One for me and two others for his boys. He was a widower but a good father. He wanted us to be warm and safe. After Samuel died and his boys left the forest for school, I removed the small beds and built this larger one."

"Oh," she said, thinking of Prince Gabriel felling trees to hew his own furniture—and also rearranging beds in this cave as if it was a proper house. When his family visited Winscombe, her parents had vacated their bedchamber so that Gabriel's royal parents might enjoy the largest bed in the house.

"You should sleep now," he said. "Dawn is hours away. There's nothing more to do or say tonight."

Oh, no, not yet, Ryan thought. *Please keep talking.* She didn't look at him.

"Lady Marianne?" he prompted.

"Will you call me 'Ryan'? Or 'Lady Ryan' if you must. I cannot promise I will answer to 'Lady Marianne.'"

"How did you come by the name Ryan?" he asked.

How did you come by the name Gabriel Rein? Ryan thought. She liked this line of questioning. They were making slow progress. She smiled at him.

"When my sister Charlotte was learning to speak," she explained, "she could only say the middle piece of my name—the *riann* bit of Marianne. Even that came out distorted—it came out 'Ryan.' The name sort of attached itself to me. Honestly, it suits me more than the other."

"Why?"

"Oh, well, Marianne is a bit fussy, isn't it? It's not really two syllables, but also not really three. There are a great many vowels and *n*'s and the silent *e* on the end. It's a frilly name whereas I—as a person—am decidedly unembellished. I am not given to unnecessary letters."

She glanced at him. He was frowning. She took a breath and went on. "Also, I'm in rather high demand—around Winscombe, that is. It's no exaggeration to say that someone is always in search of me. Many days, I'm sought from the moment I awaken until I close the door to my bedchamber at night. Someone is forever calling, summoning, demanding, asking for my opinion. 'Ryan' is simply more to the point than 'Marianne,' I suppose?"

"Why is your attention so prized?"

Ryan shrugged. She'd not meant to complain about it. She loved her family and her home; their constant need for her was both rewarding and motivating. She was good at solving problems and giving assurances. It was why she'd dragged herself to mainland England and dived into a forest.

But she needn't explain that. She needn't tell him half of this—honestly, he probably remembered that her family called her Ryan. But he'd not yet admitted that he was Gabriel d'Orleans or that he *knew* her, so she would play along.

"My father is the Earl of Amhurst and the title is old and respected. The locals look to our family for leadership. Winscombe is large but was built several centuries ago. It's maintained by a staff that is more loyal than robust. And my father is in poor health. My sisters and I get along as best we can, but I'd be lying if I said there are not constant challenges. It's my nature to be less reactionary and more practical, I suppose? This makes me popular in a crisis."

He stared at her, saying nothing.

"Why are you called Rein, *Mr. Rein*?" she asked. He'd handed her this opportunity like a gift.

"My guardian was called Rein," he said simply.

"Oh?"

"Samuel Rein. I honor his generosity by taking his name."

"That *is* an honor," she said. "And what is your

given name, Mr. Rein? Do you call yourself 'Samuel,' as well?"

He didn't answer. He stared down at her.

"Not Samuel?" she confirmed. "What is it then?"

"Gabriel." A whisper.

An anvil dropped squarely on Ryan's chest—she could hardly squeeze in a breath. Even so, her mouth didn't fall open, she didn't exclaim *aha!* She blinked once, twice.

After a long moment, she asked, "Gabriel? Will you hear the story of this imposter prince called Maurice? The man who's pursuing us—pursuing me and all of Winscombe?"

He said nothing.

"Mr. Rein," she said gently. "Will you hear it? May I tell you what's happened?"

"No," he said.

"Will you hear the terms of the betrothal, then? I haven't a copy of this alleged *binding* document, but I've notes about what it says. Perhaps you can help me understand how to challenge it?"

"No."

"Is there no help you can give me?" she pressed. "No help at all?"

"No."

And now Ryan's composure slipped. She wanted to slap her palm against the wall of this cave. She wanted to make the unpleasant half-shrieking noise that Diana made when she was frustrated. She wanted to take Prince Gabriel by the lapels and say, *You cannot be this unfeeling!*

Instead she said, "Will you show me your horses, Mr. Rein? I find myself in need of fresh air."

"It's raining," he said.

"I don't care."

"It's night."

"By torchlight then."

"It's—"

She didn't wait for another refusal. She stalked to the fire, shoved her bare feet into wet shoes, and trudged to the mouse-hole door. Taking a deep breath, she pushed it open and stepped into the mist.

CHAPTER NINE

If SHE MUST see the horses, Gabriel thought, she would stand in the rain. If she must leave the glow of the lantern, she would squint into the shadows. What choice did he have? He'd refused her enough. And anyway, she was halfway to the fence, following the sounds of horses. Given the choice, he'd rather negotiate a muddy stable yard than tell her lies inside the house.

Half a dozen mares clustered at the far corner of the paddock, taking shelter beneath the leaning canopy of an oak. She went to them and they whinnied and blew, sniffing to discern the new and unfamiliar human standing in the darkness, peering over the fence.

Clicking softly, Gabriel held out a hand. The mares ambled to him, nodding into his palm with velvet noses, nuzzling his pockets, searching for feed.

"How many?" she asked. Her voice was flat. He'd made her angry.

"Fifteen of my own," he said. He didn't mind telling her. He might be a forgotten man who lived in a cave, but he did have responsibilities and motivations. He did have a contribution beyond the forest. "Plus three horses that belong to—"

He stopped. Telling her he had purpose was one thing, but details were reckless. He could talk about the horses as a way to *not* talk about his identity, but he would only reveal so much.

"Everything you see and hear in my camp is confidential, Lady Marianne," he added. It couldn't *not* be said.

"Confidential," she repeated. "I understand."

She was quick to promise—and also quick to do whatever she liked. It bore remembering. He'd picked up the letters and tucked them into his belt. They burned a hole in his side.

"I've no wish to interrupt your livelihood, Mr. Rein," she said, staring at the horses. "Truly. I'm single-minded in what I want, and it has nothing to do with horses."

"Then why ask about them?"

She turned to him. "Because I want to know. I am *curious.* Are you not curious about the lives of other people, Mr. Rein? Not me, obviously, but anyone else?"

"The lives of others are risky, foreign notions to me. It feels like you're asking if I'm curious about tying a millstone to my neck and stepping into the river."

"In what way?"

"Well, rivers can be cool and refreshing—and there is always the *possibility* that I would survive."

"I don't understand."

He sighed. "My isolation is also my safeguard, and isolation does not lend itself to curiosity about outsiders. However, to answer your question, I've fifteen horses of my own and three horses that belong to clients—two are here for training and one is healing from a fall."

"Oh, you've *clients*," she realized. "But how do you manage them—these clients? Are they blindfolded and led to your hidden camp?"

"I've an emissary—one of the sons of Samuel Rein—who meets with clients on my behalf. He also transports the horses to the camp."

"A partner. How enterprising."

"He is a university student. He manages the clients as a favor to me and out of obligation to his late father. This was his family business, but he and his brother chose scholarship, not horses. In the training, I work alone. There are two old grooms who've been with the Reins since before I came to live here. They help with the stables."

"But what is the nature of the training?" she asked. "Are these racehorses?"

"No, not racing—racing wants a different type of facility. But I train for most other purposes. Anything from making a difficult horse more docile to teaching a particular skill. I also breed, raise, and break horses for sale to private owners."

"What do you mean by teaching a particular skill?" she asked.

Gabriel exhaled and looked around. The rain, he realized, had mostly stopped. But the leaves hung heavy after the storm, and water fell in uneven drops. A silvery fog had rolled into the stable yard, thickening the space between them. He saw her only in outline. The mist served as a barrier, making her questions easier to answer.

"I've Scottish lairds, for example," he said, "who hunt on horseback in the Highlands. This requires more from the animal than fox hunting on level ground. Scottish clans write to me when their mares foal so their young stallions can have a place on my training schedule."

"Scottish lairds," she repeated. He could feel her studying him.

He kept his gaze on the horses. Had this impressed her? When had this become a goal? He meant to bore her, distract her, implore her to leave him alone. It made no difference if she was impressed.

"My services are not . . ." he exhaled. And now he was simply boasting, "Cheap."

"You are in high demand?"

"I've a list of clients awaiting a place on my roster."

"How fascinating," she enthused. "But do you enjoy the work?"

"Yes. I've a particular interest in injury recovery. And I do find it gratifying—yes."

"Healing lame horses?"

He nodded. The fog was dissolving and a shiny, post-rain moon poured silver light on the paddock. He could see her more clearly; large eyes rapt on his face. He looked away.

"Muscle injuries," he said, "but I've also worked on broken spirits—anxiety after an accident or abuse. These are animals who'd been in the prime of their lives but have become impossible to manage, or withdrawn, or easily spooked by everyday things."

"I've heard of this," she said. "In fact, some horses brought to Guernsey are spooked by the Channel crossing. Some never recover from being confined to the pitching hull of a ship."

"I've been a sort of last resort for animals who have failed with other trainers. Damaged horses are typically put out to pasture or destroyed if they cannot be healed. In the case of my clients, they may be sent to me."

"But this is *fascinating*," she said. She dropped an elbow on the fence railing and leaned a hand against her cheek. "But *how* do you heal them?"

"Samuel had an arsenal of unorthodox techniques. He took pride in them and taught me. He was an advocate of . . . *listening* to the wounded animal? Trying to understand what is going on inside his head, to understand his fear. After we understand, we gently coax the horse to conquer that fear."

"You *do* love this work," she whispered.

"Yes." The truth. A greater truth was that Gabriel himself had been healed by horses. His guardian, Samuel Rein, had saved him, but he'd used the animals to do it. Gabriel would heal horses for no fee at all, but Samuel believed that gentlemen valued the work more if it came at a high price. And his sons needed the money for their expensive schools. The result had been a waiting list of esteemed clients clamoring for his care and healing. It was a service available nowhere else in England; honestly, nowhere in all of Europe. His clients came from around the world.

"My sister would say this about the sheep," mused Lady Marianne. "She loves our animals; there is no better day in her view than tending the flock."

Gabriel made no reply. He would not be drawn into a conversation about her sister or their sheep.

"But are you happiest with the horses?"

"I've not considered when I am happiest."

"Come now, Mr. Rein, you cannot say that chopping wood makes you as contented as training horses?"

"I'm happiest when I am alone."

"Solitude is not an activity, it's a circumstance," she said.

He didn't answer.

"But are you never lonely?"

"I am safe."

"Safe from what?"

Not from you, he thought.

The mares had grown restless, hooking their heads over the fence, sniffing and nibbling at the pocket of his shirt. He reached for a bucket of carrots beneath the tree.

"Here," he said. "If you want to see happiness, offer a carrot to a horse."

"Treats?" she chuckled, taking a handful. "In the middle of the night? But what lucky horses."

"People assume that training amounts to restrictions and punishment and putting an animal through his paces. That is not the work I do. The horses I train have survived some traumatic event—a stable fire or a carriage accident or cruelty from a groom. I heal warhorses who've seen great carnage in battle. Wellness for these animals doesn't come from scarcity, but from abundance. Patience. Security. My first order of business is to earn their trust. I make them feel as if they're in a safe place; that I am a safe man. I show them that the work we're doing will benefit us both."

"But how do you show this?"

"A variety of ways. But an underlying principle is . . ." he extended his hand to a mare, "*liberty with carrots*."

For a long moment, she watched him. Eventually she reached for the bucket and picked out a dusty carrot. His dogs had crept from the stable and sniffed stealthily about the bucket. When Lady Marianne saw them, she let out a little yelp and leaped onto the bottom slat of the fence.

"Careful," he said, eyeing her.

"Your dogs." Her voice was a breathless squeak. "Sorry, I didn't see them."

Gabriel glanced at Hugo and Tatin, cautiously sniffing Lady Marianne, their tails wagging. They were well-behaved, but the fascination of a new person in camp was too much not to investigate. Also, they'd discerned *food* was on offer. They weren't much for carrots, but no food in camp escaped their interest.

"Hugo, Tatin, stand down," he said to the dogs. He looked back to her. She clung to the fence, regarding his perfectly docile dogs as if they might tear her limb from limb.

"I'll send them away," he offered.

Before she could reply, Hugo shoved his nose into her skirts, sniffing deeply. Lady Marianne startled. The sudden movement intrigued the dog; he raised his paws to her hip.

"Hugo, *down*," Gabriel said, but not before Lady Marianne cried out and scrambled higher. She hiked a leg over the top railing and balanced there, clinging to the wood with both hands. The mares in the paddock skittered backward, whinnying and snorting. Hugo didn't understand the game and he barked.

"Sorry, sorry, sorry," whispered Lady Marianne, squeezing her eyes shut. She dropped the carrot into the paddock and the horses clomped to gobble it up. The crowd of mares confused the dog, and Hugo barked again. Lady Marianne gasped and hiked her knee against the boards. This movement knocked back her wet skirts, and her leg was exposed.

Gabriel had been signaling to the dogs, trying to banish them to the stable, but the paleness of Marianne's bare leg caught the moonlight, and he turned to stare. The cream of her skin was streaked with mud, but beneath the dirt he saw—

"What's happened to your leg?" he demanded.

She didn't answer. She clung tightly to the fence, eyes squeezed. Gabriel stepped closer, leaning toward her leg. The skin of her calf was marred by an angry red wound. It wasn't new, and it appeared to be healing nicely, but clearly it had been a deep and painful spate of punctures and lacerations. There were two bloody arcs of red set end to end, the incisions in the shape of the letter *U*. An *open mouth*. She'd been bitten by an animal.

"Hugo, Tatin, I said go," Gabriel growled over his shoulder. The animals fell back.

He stared up at her. "What happened?"

"Hmm?" She'd opened her eyes and was now staring wildly after the retreating dogs.

"They've gone, you needn't worry. I'm asking about your leg. Did you suffer an attack?"

"Oh." She looked down, saw her bare leg, and yanked her skirts, dropping wet cotton over the wound. "Sorry I didn't realize my leg was . . . not covered. I'm not usually so panicked around dogs. I . . . Well, I suppose you can guess why."

"You were attacked. What happened?"

She looked at him, her expression desperate. She pinched her lips together and shook her head.

"Lady Marianne?" he repeated.

Another headshake.

"Was it a dog, then?"

"I—" she began. "Yes. Several weeks ago. It's nearly healed. It's why I give dogs a very wide berth. This new fear is almost as bad as the attack, actually. Previously, I was very fond of dogs. I love them still, it's just . . ."

"On what occasion were you *attacked by a dog*?" he asked—but suddenly he knew.

Instead of answering, she raised her eyebrows. She sat up straight on the fence.

"Maurice," he guessed. And now Gabriel felt as if *he* was in the grip of powerful teeth, like a beast was trying to dig out his very heart.

"It was Maurice's dog—yes."

"No."

She chuckled bitterly. "Yes."

Gabriel was accustomed to seeing abuse. The horses he treated had been beaten or neglected. He was never unaffected by the cruelty, although he forced himself to look ahead, to focus on the treatment and recovery. He only survived the reality of the suffering by embarking on the healing. But how could he facilitate this? Maurice, and Lady Marianne, and Winscombe were realities he couldn't heal.

"I challenged something he said," Lady Marianne was telling him. "I challenged everything he said, actually—and in this instance, his dogs felt threatened somehow. One of them lunged and . . . and he did not call her off."

"Come down from there," Gabriel said, her words ringing in his ears. "The mud is not good for a healing wound. It must be cleaned."

He forced himself to think only of this moment, of what he could control immediately. She wasn't asking him to leave the forest *now*. Not *tonight*. He needn't reckon with Maurice this moment. He needn't reckon with Maurice at all. Now, he need only lift her from the fence, get her out of the rain, tend to her wound.

"I am certainly filthy," she agreed, bracing her hands on his shoulders. "But have you a tub? Or I suppose any basin would—"

"I have a waterfall."

"I beg your pardon?"

"There's a third room inside the cave. A hot spring that falls from a crevice overhead. It's an underground waterfall. You can wash there." He'd purposefully concealed the waterfall before, but it would be useful now.

"Oh," she said.

Yes, he thought. *Oh.*

The reason he'd not shown the waterfall was because his brain did not need the vision of her wet, or bathing, or without her clothes. He'd been unsettled and aroused since the moment he'd carried her through the woods. To introduce warm water? Splashing? He knew his limits. She'd come to him for help. He meant to send her away. There was no place for—

"I'm struggling to picture what you mean," she was telling him. "*A waterfall*. It does sound rather enticing. After the day I've had. But the horses . . ." She was looking over her shoulder into the misty paddock.

"Forget the horses. You can wash now and we'll try to sleep. There are only a few hours until sunrise."

He would not sleep. He would not think of dog bites or waterfalls or the sunrise. He would exist in a state of agony and guilt and longing, and morning would come, and he'd deliver her to Pewsey. She would leave the forest but he would remain.

CHAPTER TEN

$\mathcal{J}$T WOULD NEVER occur to Ryan to simply *show the man* evidence of his cousin's abuse. Perhaps this had been her error all along. What finally got his attention had not been the damning proof of her letters or even her awkward thoughts of seduction, but evidence of what Maurice had done. Who could have guessed? Not Ryan. She was not a natural victim. She thought to appeal to Gabriel's sense of decency and duty; in a pinch, his loneliness. But his sympathies lay with wounded horses, so of course she should cast her lot with the bitten and beaten. God knew she had the wounds for it.

After he'd plucked her from the fence, she'd spent a long, mortifying moment fearing he meant to *carry her* inside. It was one thing to be borne through the forest for the sake of expediency; quite another to be conveyed about like an invalid. Which she was *not* (an invalid). The dog attack had been terrifying and hurt like the devil, but apparently she'd "been very lucky." The muscle had not been severed from bone; the bleeding had been stopped before too much blood had been lost. The doctor said she would recover, save an annoying new panic around dogs.

In the end, Prince Gabriel hadn't carried her. He'd walked silently behind her, reaching around to open the door, jerking his head in the direction of the bedroom. She kept ahead of him, plodding into the darkness.

"Is your, er, waterfall . . . secluded?" she ventured. She should maintain some sense of decorum, she told herself, even alone in the forest. Even in this cave.

"It's here," he said, stepping around her. They'd entered the bedchamber and Ryan was relieved to see the candles were still bright from the earlier tour. He strode to the notch in the wall she'd asked about earlier, holding a candle aloft.

"Careful," he called from behind the rock. "It can be slick."

Tentatively, Ryan followed. She was aware of the sound of splashing water, the smell of moisture, and a heaviness to the air. A soft, misty spray tickled her face. The walls of the cave were slicker here, shiny with moisture. It was—she squinted in the candlelight, peeking through the vapor—a little room.

"Keeping a flame can be a challenge here," he was saying, holding the candle to a lantern hanging from the stone. "It's the wetness."

When the wick caught, the light doubled. He stepped away to reveal a small underground waterfall splashing onto a slab of rock. The shower of water fell from a high crevice in a downward stream. The slab behind the waterfall was wet where water poured from above.

Mesmerized, Ryan looked to the floor. Floorboards had been laid like a small dock, extending from the shoulder of rock to the spot where the waterfall splattered into an iron grate. Large craggy stones lay beneath the grate and the falling water ran through the iron bars and drained away.

"Is it a natural spring?" she asked.

"Yes." He wiped water droplets from his face with his sleeve.

"And the water is warm?"

"Oh yes," he said. "It's very warm. This was Samuel's reason for building out the cave. Warm, running water is a rare luxury, indeed."

"Quite so," Ryan said. Her skin tingled, thinking of the heated water, and the cool air, and the thrill of bathing in an actual waterfall. She wanted to try it—in fact, she couldn't remember wanting the simple pleasures of warmth and cleanliness more—but she felt suddenly shy and uncertain. How did one transition from uninvited guest to . . . to *bather*? Undressed and splashing about in an underground waterfall? In the home of one's estranged fiancé? It was so unimaginable; it was like guessing the procedure for spinning straw into gold.

"Could I trouble you for a . . . a towel that I might use for . . ." Ryan scrambled for the correct word ". . . for after?"

He stalked to a cupboard in the bedroom and returned with a white towel. It appeared well worn but clean. He held it out to her. Ryan accepted it. He did not leave. Together, they stared at the waterfall. A tendril of steam unfurled between them.

"And sorry," she ventured again, "is there . . . soap?"

"There's a ledge beside the spray of water. Do you see it? There is soap on that ledge."

"Oh, lovely. All of this is very welcome, indeed.

My wound is almost healed, I assure you; but I'd be lying if I said a warm waterfall didn't sound very therapeutic."

More staring.

"After I've stepped into it," she went on, "can I trouble you to, er, collect my dress and hang it by the fire? Even five minutes of heat would do it well, I think. I'll just leave it—"

She glanced around.

"On the floor? Shall I?" she suggested. "It will soil your bedding if I lay it out."

"I've a woman who comes several times a month to tend to the laundry and the floors. Please do not worry about the house."

Ryan stared in the direction of the bed. Would it be too much to ask, she wondered, to request a change of clothes? She glanced back to him, clutching the towel.

"But can I impose on you for an old nightshirt or dressing gown that I might wear for sleeping . . ." She let the sentence trail off.

He made a second silent trip to the cupboard and returned with a folded garment in white linen. A man's night shirt. She stacked it on top of the towel.

Ryan waited a beat, hoping he would say or do something to facilitate how she might go from standing there, clutching linens, to splashing about in his waterfall. It was a vain hope. He was silent. He was nothing if not consistent.

"Are you afraid?" he asked finally.

"Oh no—not afraid, more like uncertain. We bathe in a large copper tub at Winscombe. And when we swim, it's in the Atlantic Ocean."

He shook his head. "This is like standing in a warm

summer rain, only better. Here—sit on this ledge." He pointed to a shallow ridge of rock beside the waterfall.

"Now?" she heard herself ask.

"I'll show you," he said.

Still clutching the towel and nightshirt, Ryan settled on the ledge. The mist was thicker here, more like fog. Warm droplets dampened her face. She could feel her hair growing heavier, absorbing the moisture. A fine sheen of condensation settled on her dress and her hem soaked up water at her feet. She snatched up her skirts, exposing her ankles.

"Wait," he said, frowning, "but have you worn your shoes?"

"Oh, well I'd not yet— You marched me here from the paddock."

"First rule of the waterfall," he said, taking a knee in front of her. "No shoes."

While Ryan watched, he took up her heel and tugged off her left shoe. She'd not bothered with stockings, and her bare foot slid free. She settled it on the damp stone floor and he reached for the other foot, tugging at her shoe.

"The floor is so warm," she said.

"The hot spring heats the rock." He set her shoes away from the water. "Now put it in," he said.

"In?"

"Put your foot beneath the spray."

Ryan cinched her skirts higher and tentatively extended one foot to the stream of water.

"Ouch!" she gasped, snatching back her foot. "It's boiling hot."

He shook his head and reached for her foot. His fingers grazed her arch on the underside and the ball of her ankle above her foot. Ryan felt the contact up and down her leg.

"One stream of the water is very hot—yes," he told her. He propped her foot on his bent knee. "The hot band of water comes from the thermal spring. But there's another stream that falls beside it, and it's very cold—the temperature of any stream you might encounter. When you bathe, you mix the two together. May I?"

Mesmerized, Ryan nodded. Carefully, he lifted her foot from his knee, extending her leg. With his other hand, he cupped the cascading water and ladled it over the proffered foot. Ryan jumped, afraid of being scalded, but the water from his palm was warm.

"Do you see?" he asked, his voice had gone hoarse. She looked to his face, studying his profile. He was intently focused on cradling her foot in his hand and diverting the falling water.

"Oh yes," she said softly, "that's very nice, actually." She wiggled her toes and leaned back, giving him more leg. He slid his hand from her heel to her ankle, splashing the water higher. Ryan's breath caught. The warm water on her cold foot sent tingles up her leg; his large hand on her ankle set off a fizzier, bolder wave of sensation.

"Give me your other foot," he said, settling her first foot on the grate. He took up her other foot and squeezed, enclosing it in his large hand.

"You're freezing," he mumbled, massaging her foot. "It was careless to go back out."

Ryan had some vague notion of carelessness and outside, but it was hardly her focus. Every pulse of attention was on his hands. She struggled to stay upright on the ledge. She had no words. She could only stare, vision blurred, at the top of his head as he bent over her foot. He knelt so close to the waterfall, moisture saturated his shirt. The fabric had gone translucent in the candlelight, and it clung to his muscled arms and shoulders. She'd known he was powerful—he'd carried her up a mountain—but seeing the size and shape of him kneeling at her feet? She couldn't look away. Mindlessly, she settled a hand on her skirts and ever so carefully tugged, inching up the fabric to bare more ankle to him . . . then shin . . . then calf.

"Dip it in." He extended her foot to the waterfall. His voice was now winded and rough. His chest rose and fell. He was . . . he was—

He feels it, too, she thought.

Ryan knew too little of men to assign a name to the "it" in question, but she could identify a shared experienced. She was also short of breath. Her hands shook. Did his heart pound? Her heart beat so furiously, it could fracture the walls of this cave.

"How does it feel now?" he rasped.

"What?" A whisper.

"The water? How does it feel?"

Glorious, she thought, but she said, "Hot and cold. Both at once. I feel heat around the edges and little stabs of cold in the middle. But also somehow warmth throughout?"

He glanced up at her. His eyes were half lidded. She wanted to touch his face.

"Yes," he said, "it's a mix; but you should feel warmth most of all."

"I feel very warm, indeed," she whispered. She

used both hands to cinch up the hem of her dress, raising it to her knees.

"Allow me to . . ." he said, but he didn't finish. He settled her foot on the grate—both feet now stretched into the cascade—and began to gently massage the warm water into her legs.

"Does the puncture wound pain you now?" he asked roughly.

She shook her head. She felt the opposite of pain. She felt only tingly, prickled pleasure and an urgent sort of building, a sense of anticipation, of breathless longing. His hands massaged higher on her leg with every swipe, and Ryan had never known such humming pleasure. She leaned against the damp rock and closed her eyes.

"Shall I help you unfasten your dress?" he rasped.

Her eyes sprang open. "Um . . .".

"It's a waste to wash only your . . ." he turned back to her legs, bare now to the thighs ". . . feet," he said.

"Well, I suppose if you don't mind about the dress."

He shoved up. "Turn round."

Ryan blinked at the sudden command in his voice. Her heart twisted toward him, like he'd called it by name. Pulse racing, skin tingling, she retracted her legs and dropped her skirts. She stood on shaky legs and slowly revolved, presenting him with her back. He stepped to her.

For a long moment, he did nothing. She felt his looming presence like the hot vapor from the waterfall.

"Your hair is in the way," he said.

Move it, she thought, but she couldn't bring herself to invite this.

"Lady Marianne?" he prompted gruffly.

"Sorry." She scooped her hair and swept it over her shoulder.

"There are no buttons," he said.

"Oh—right. Well, they are hooks, I believe? You'll take up the fabric on both sides of the seam and work it together until each hook releases. There are a great many of them unfortunately. The neck on this dress is rather high. But you need only do the top half. This will loosen the bodice, and I can spin the dress and manage the rest."

These instructions were a miracle of composure. Her ability to concentrate had drained like the water in the grate—and good riddance. She didn't want to think, she wanted only to feel.

He puffed out a breath like a man bracing to leap over a ravine. He brought his hands to the back of her neck, just below her hair. Ryan's heart stopped. She grabbed handfuls of her wet skirts in both hands. Her whole life, she'd been dressed and undressed by other people; fussy maids, impatient sisters, her brisk, efficient mother. The feel of his large hands was as different from these as climbing a ladder was from falling to the ground. Now Ryan fell. Every nudge and jab reminded her that he was a man and his work was with saddles and rope, not ladies' dresses. He fumbled with the first hook, but the second and third came easily. He jostled her as he worked, listing her this way and that, holding her steady with his own body, pressing his leg against her for leverage. Ryan could feel his breath on the back of her neck. By degrees, she felt the loosening bodice droop—

"What's this?" he said suddenly, his hands going still.

"I beg your pardon?"

His voice was alarmed, sharp. The gruffness was gone. He sounded . . . angry.

"You've an abrasion on your neck," he said. He retracted his hands and her bodice sagged. He stepped away. A chill rose up her spine.

"The skin is broken on your neck," he said. "It looks as if you've been—but has someone *garroted you*, Lady Marianne?"

Ryan pressed the loosened bodice to her chest, holding it in place. "An abrasion?" she repeated, trying to comprehend. Her brain was swimming through the mist and the tingles and the closeness. She put a hand to her neck and—

—and remembered. How could she have forgotten?

"Oh," she said. She turned to him, her cheeks burning. "Forgive me. It . . . it must look very gruesome indeed."

"What's *happened* to your neck?"

She raised her eyes to his. His expression was volatile.

Ryan felt the sting of sudden tears. *He* was angry? *Him?* He'd brought her here, he'd lied about his identity, he'd bathed her—*touched her*—and now he was angry with her?

She should feel the volatility. She'd not planned to tell him about the marks on her neck—or the dog bite, for that matter. She'd planned to request his help plainly, calmly, with due gratitude and self-respect. It was how she preferred to be asked for help.

"*Lady Marianne*," he repeated, "what's been done to your neck?"

"I . . . lost a gold chain."

"Lost it *how*?"

"It was a simple gold chain with a locket given to me by my late mother. It was . . . torn from me."

"Torn?"

"Well, snapped off, I should say. It was a fine piece, in the end, because it refused to give without considerable effort. It took five or six firm yanks. The chain cut my skin." She exhaled. "It's healing. Like the wound on my leg, it's healing—*I* will *heal*."

"Maurice?" Prince Gabriel hissed.

She nodded, not taking her eyes from his.

"Why? Why would he tear jewelry from the body of . . . of his betrothed?"

"*Do not say* I am his betrothed," she corrected, blinking back tears. "If I must be betrothed, it is *to you*."

Gabriel squeezed his eyes shut and shook his head, a convict refusing his sentence. He took two steps back.

"Oh yes—deny it," she said. "That is your luxury. Meanwhile, I've tried to deny the betrothal of the imposter, and he set his dogs on me and torn away my gold chain."

"He's a thief on top of everything else?" he gritted out.

"He didn't steal the locket. He tossed it into the pond. My mother's necklace. To *make a point*."

"What point?"

"That he mustn't be told no."

"Told no for what?" he asked.

"For any reason," she said, tears now spilling down her cheeks. "*No* I will not marry him. *No* he may not assume control of Winscombe. *No* he may not release our staff and install his own. *No* a manager from

France may not replace my sister in tending the sheep. *No* I will not relocate to Paris to live in his castle. *No* he may not leer at my younger sister, nor corner her in passageways, nor grope her, nor intimidate *any of us*. It's a rather long list, all the things I denied him; and he was spitting mad in the end.

"*Even so*," she finished, swiping away tears, "no one was more shocked than me when he allowed his dog to attack me and then he garroted me—excellent description, by the way—with my own necklace."

"Are there more?" he rasped.

"More *what*?"

"Do you harbor more wounds by his hand?"

"No," she exclaimed, so very annoyed that it had come to this. "Surely one dog bite and the abrasion to my neck is enough."

"Enough for what?"

"Enough to justify me leaving my home and asking this very great favor of you." Her neck burned and her leg ached and Ryan was suddenly cold all over.

He eyed her warily.

"Forgive this outburst Prince Gabriel," she said—but then she remembered this wasn't his preferred name. "Sorry, *Mr. Rein*. I find myself reeling from the carousel of emotions brought on by our introduction. My only goal in meeting you was to ask for a very little bit of help. Not a lot. I simply wanted you to publicly say your name and discredit your cousin. It was meant to be an inconsequential, totally reasonable request. Instead, I'm digging through your drawers and baring my cuts and bruises. I've somehow become the busybody; even worse, I'm *the victim*—which I hate. Not my planned method of persuasion, I assure you."

"Saying a name publicly may seem reasonable," he said, "but it can have far-reaching consequences, Lady Ryan. It's no small thing to bring someone back to life after they've been given up for dead, least of all a prince. Even so, please do not misunderstand. I am very concerned. From the beginning, you've had my concern."

"Let me be more clear," she said tiredly. "I need *less* than a solution but *more* than concern. I need *help*. Not a lot, as I've said—just a little. At the moment, I'll settle for this: Admit it. Admit that you are Prince Gabriel. The real, living Prince Gabriel d'Orleans."

He stared at her, breathing in and out, in and out. Finally, he said, "I will hear it. I'll hear what's happened with Maurice. You can say it and I will listen."

"Truly?" A rasp. She barely understood how they'd gone from feet washing to quarreling—and now he was inviting her to discuss Maurice? She'd begun to shiver; small, jarring shudders vibrated through her body. She was cold and hopeful and frustrated all at the same time.

"Now?" she said through teeth rattling.

"Have your bath," he said. "Get warm. I will set out something to eat. We will . . . talk." He began to back away.

She looked over her shoulder at the waterfall.

"Can you manage?" he called.

"Yes," she said, "I can manage."

In her head she thought, *I can manage, I can manage, I can manage.*

If only he understood how very proficient she was at managing . . . everything.

"I don't mean to be a burden," she said quietly, mostly to herself. She sighed quietly. She stepped toward the little ridge. "I simply need a favor."

CHAPTER ELEVEN

$\mathscr{G}$ABRIEL GATHERED A loaf of bread, a bowl of raspberries, and a triangle of cheese, and set them on his small, rough-hewn table. He hung the kettle over the fire to reheat. He kept only one set of utensils, and he clonked these down next to the food. There was a cloth for a napkin and butter and salt and jam. He stepped back, staring at the spread but seeing nothing. In his mind's eye, he saw only a man hurting Lady Ryan. Not just "a man." His own cousin, marauding about with Gabriel's title. How deep a cowardice, he thought, to brutalize defenseless young women. Maurice had clearly survived the French Revolution hale and hearty. With so many dead or lost, he was climbing the ranks of their shattered family. And his response was cruelty to Lady Ryan and her family?

Gabriel coped with cruelty by healing it away— he'd said this when he'd explained his work, and it was true. But he couldn't heal Lady Ryan, he couldn't even help her.

Lady Ryan. He repeated her name in his head and thought of the moments before he'd seen the abrasion on her neck. She'd welcomed his request to undress her. Before that, he'd knelt before her and she'd bared

her legs to him. He'd picked up her tiny foot and held
it in his hand. Their time beside the waterfall had
evoked a surge of desire so potent, he'd thought he
would expire from it. The memory of it—of kneeling,
and touching, and unhooking—was too new to regret
and he repeated it, over and over, in his mind.

The kettle whistled, and Gabriel jumped. He
stepped to the fire to move it to a higher hook. She
might not want coffee, so he poured cider into a clay
goblet. Was this enough? Gabriel knew virtually nothing of entertaining guests.

"Oh, how lovely."

Gabriel looked up. Lady Marianne, skin glowing,
head tipped sideways, padded into his small kitchen,
drying her hair with the towel. The borrowed nightshirt swallowed her shoulders and fell loosely to the
middle of her legs. Her feet were bare.

"I'm famished, actually," she said, sliding into a
seat. "Do you mind?"

How natural she seemed. Unaffected. He'd known
so few women in his adult life, he couldn't say if this
was remarkable, or fleeting, or feigned. The memories of his own mother were not steeped in calmness.
She'd been beautiful and demanding, and life inside a
cave would have sent her into hysterics.

Gabriel didn't know Lady Ryan, not really, but he
remembered a sort of serenity—a steadiness—from
the letters she'd written as a girl. She was curious
rather than judgmental; hopeful rather than preoccupied with dread. Their betrothal hadn't seemed to
distress her. In their two, brief meetings, he remembered her as pleasant and matter-of-fact. She wasn't
so very different now. Channing Meade had evoked

her screams—and rightly so. But she wasn't scream-ing now; she hadn't screamed since he'd collected her. How, he wondered, had he almost not gone for her?

"Will you be offended if I eat while we talk?" she asked, studying a raspberry before popping it into her mouth.

He shook his head, watching her chew. But he *had* gone for her. He'd brought her inside his home. He'd invited her to tell him everything. The screaming was over; now the recruitment would begin. And he would be forced to refuse her.

Gabriel wanted nothing to do with life outside the forest. He could exist perhaps; eat food, brush past strangers on the street, find some work. But he could not bungle through inane conversations, he could not relax in crowds, he couldn't breathe in layers of stiff clothing. He couldn't spend hours a day *inside* of doors. He couldn't stomach the way horses were handled by untrained grooms or work in a stable that was not his own. He couldn't trust anyone. He would never sleep.

And these were only his preferences. What he could never, not ever, survive was the mantle of being a prince. Royalty meant ceding a colossal measure of control that he'd vowed never again to release.

"Mr. Rein?" she was prompting. "Shall I begin? Will you hear it?"

"Yes." He exhaled. "I will hear it."

She froze for a moment, perhaps not expecting him to agree. His stomach gave a flip. She was so very pretty. Her hair had begun to dry. Loose brown waves swung about her face. She shoved up the sleeves of the nightshirt and took up a slice of bread.

"Right. Thank you. Let's see, where shall I begin?" she wondered.

"Why don't you start by telling me how your sisters are safe alone in Guernsey? Where is this imposter prince now?"

"Excellent question," she conceded. "We've no guarantee of their safety, actually. The imposter prince departed Guernsey more than a fortnight ago—in late July—claiming some pressing business in Paris. He's vowed to return on the fifteenth of October. He is a very precise person. Particular and fussy. He gave us no reason to believe we would see him before that date. We were meant to use the intervening time to . . . 'come to terms with our future.'"

"Your future?"

"The future with him in charge. *He* manages things. And he marries me." She took up another slice of bread and nibbled the crust. She did not gobble or smack. She was hungry, clearly, but her manners prevailed—small bites, slow chewing, shallow sips of cider. She was a lady. This made Gabriel think of his father, a gentleman—a *prince*—and the boy Gabriel once had been. Even as a child, he'd spent hours with his nanny and tutors to refine his manners and comportment. All of it was a faint memory now, like watching a familiar dance but having no notion of the steps.

"Naturally, we've come to terms with nothing," she was saying. "Instead, we've made a careful study of our options. My sister Diana wants to fight, and Charlotte wants to beg—but I know better. Fighting him would invite harsher punishments and begging would only play into his inflated sense of entitlement. Our only choice is to outsmart him. October fifteenth is like the swinging door of a jail. Until it clangs shut, we'll slip in and out, trying to find a way to subvert him."

"And your way has been to wander about an unfamiliar forest in mainland England until you stumble upon Gabriel d'Orleans?"

She stopped chewing and stared at him. Too late, he realized he'd again pronounced his name like a native.

"Yes," she said, taking a drink. "Well no, not entirely. We also contacted solicitors to challenge the betrothal. We looked into hiring a man who might serve as a sort of bodyguard and advocate, speaking in lieu of our sick father. We even thought of marrying me off to someone—*anyone*—else. But when I showed my sisters the last letter from yo—er, my last old letter from the *true* Prince d'Orleans, we agreed it was worth the effort to try and find you—er, *him*. The most efficient and least expensive way to extricate ourselves from the imposter prince was to present the real prince."

Gabriel lowered himself into the opposite chair, trying not to think of himself being *presented* to someone. Even worse, to claim he was "the real prince." It would be like digging up a dead man and wheeling him about, telling the world he's not dead, only a little dirty and asleep.

"Just to be perfectly clear, I'm not on a mission to *marry* the real Prince d'Orleans," she rushed to add. "He need not follow the terms of this old betrothal, simply . . . make himself known so that the imposter prince steps down. His mere presence will end the fight, in our view. There would be no dickering with solicitors or documents. We've no desire to engage in a lengthy negotiation with this man. He is unreasonable, to say the very least." She touched a stray hand to the scab on her neck.

"I don't understand why marriage to you would give Maurice so much power over your father's estate?" Gabriel said. "I understand you have no wish to marry an abusive man, and I don't blame you, but why is Maurice's stake in the betrothal so far-reaching?"

She shrugged. "The terms of the union state that all of Winscombe goes to *my* husband, the Prince d'Orleans, on the occasion of my marriage."

"Like a dowry," he said. He'd not understood the terms as a boy, but he had some notion of the way marriage merged fortunes.

"Yes, exactly like a dowry, I suppose."

"Why would you be dowered with your family's *entire estate*? What if your father had had a son?"

"Well, my father did not have a son, but I suppose if he had done, that boy would have inherited the title only. Not the lands or the house. They are tied to *my* marriage."

"But why?" Gabriel hadn't questioned the betrothal as a boy, but in hindsight it was a very odd arrangement, indeed.

"Money," she said. "Your late father gave my Papa a loan at the time of the betrothal. Sorry, it's a challenge for me to continue speaking as if you're a stranger in all this."

"I might as well be a stranger," he tried.

"I'll bear that in mind," she said tiredly. "To answer your question: Papa has become too ill to explain his motivations, but I believe at the time, he desperately needed money. He's a good man—well-liked and respected—but he is prone to bad investments. Your father was an old friend and he gave Papa the desperately needed loan. The terms of that exchange saw *you* betrothed to *me*, despite the fact that we were toddlers. And my dowery would be Winscombe. It was all my father had at the time."

"Your future marriage was the collateral on the loan?"

"Not just collateral," she said, "it was the repayment."

"But why did they—"

"The benefit to your father was . . . you would eventually own Winscombe, which is an ancient English estate so very close to the coast of France. The benefit to my father was money in the short term and a prince for his daughter in the long term. It was a bit of a shortsighted arrangement, honestly—rash and unorthodox. But there is a friendly history between our two families; generations of intermarriage and alliance. And our fathers were great friends, weren't they? There was an understanding that you would grow up to be a generous steward of Winscombe. This was all before French princes began losing their heads to the guillotine of course."

"Yes. A lifetime ago," he said.

"Sorry. That was insensitive. What I mean is, I'm no student of French foreign affairs, but the French Revolution happened and we never heard from any of the d'Orleans family again. Until now. I can only guess things are looking up for royal sons of France, because this person, this imposter prince *Maurice*, is not shy about flaunting the title and staking claim to everything to which he feels entitled."

"If Maurice is flaunting the title," said Gabriel, "why pursue your obscure estate in the English channel? The portfolio of d'Orleans properties is extensive— everything from seaside villas to castles."

"Money. Again, money—it's the answer to so many questions, isn't it? Maurice intends to sell Winscombe. French aristocrats have been left with very little. The rioters gutted Crown property during the Terror and now Napoleon is leading the country into its eighth year of an expensive war. Money and lands are scarce for the average French princeling, I believe."

Gabriel thought of this. He read the papers, but it was difficult for him to guess at his family's solvency. His father was dead, of course, but he'd lost touch with everyone else, even his mother. He tried to remember this man—his second cousin Maurice. He was older than Gabriel; a lanky youth who ran with other cousins in their teens. Gabriel outranked him, of course, but he remembered that Maurice went out of his way to treat Gabriel like a child. And he was so very preoccupied with the family's royal blood, despite the fact that everyone in their circle was related to the king in one way or the other.

Gabriel also remembered Maurice's zeal for almost (but not quite) taking cruel advantage of servants for sport. If a footman brought tea, he would badger the man to fetch small additions to the spread, one item at a time, for the novelty of seeing him scramble. Back and forth to the kitchens he'd send the man for a salt cellar, a larger spoon, a smaller spoon, a dish of olives, a husk of vanilla seeds, a fresh napkin, milk for the cat, open the drapes, draw the drapes—on and on it went. All of this, just for a snicker from other cousins, but Maurice thrived on the attention. Even as a boy, Gabriel had been bothered by this unnecessary abuse of rank.

"Honestly," Lady Ryan was saying, "I would have married the imposter prince if he'd been decent and fair-minded—a man who I could remotely tolerate." She stared into her cup. "I'm twenty-four and unmarried, with no proposals to speak of. I had no debut in London, but I've been out in Guernsey society—such that it is—for years. My childhood betrothal was not common knowledge. As far as anyone knows, I'm fully available. Even so, there has been no interest, so—"

She glanced at him and then away. "Why shouldn't I consent to an arranged marriage? When the proverbial wolf has been at our door for so many years? Winscombe can be profitable, I believe, as soon as we dig out of our father's mismanagement. He is dear to us, obviously; but his health and our financial problems are dueling burdens that encroach on two sides. As soon as we curtail one of them, the other flares. My sisters and I live with the pervasive feeling of almost-but-not-quite *drowning*, as if we're just about to reach the surface and take a breath, but then—no. We gulp down only the smallest little watery gasp, and under we go again."

She made a sad little chuckle. "If some man turned up, claiming to be my betrothed, and he consented to join our good fight toward solvency and gave me the chance to have a family of my own, I would've gone along. *If* he wasn't terrible. But the imposter prince is *so* very terrible. And he has no interest in our father or increasing the productivity of Winscombe. He means to sell it off in parts and relocate me and my younger sister to France. He would leave Diana and our father behind to rot. He wants no family with me, although he does seem keenly interested in making my younger sister something like his concubine. I know it all sounds unbelievable—and trust me, it is *beyond all belief*—but it's happened. And we are scrambling to subvert it. Scrambling tooth and nail."

Gabriel put aside her comments about her willingness to marry "just about anyone" and tried to learn more about his cousin Maurice. There must be some way to turn him out without Gabriel, himself, leaving Savernake Forest.

"This imposter prince, as you call him," he asked, "did he simply turn up with his dogs and begin ripping jewelry from your neck? Did he size up everything at once and claim it?"

She shook her head. "No, not at first. He arrived unannounced on an ordinary summer day. He was accompanied by two carriages, a retinue of servants, and a great many trunks and dogs and horses. I was actually in the kitchen garden with our cook when they arrived. We were sorting out what vegetables we may put up for winter to clear room for autumn planting. When I saw his procession, I thought, *What's this? A traveling band of actors?* I'd never seen so many flags and banners and liveried horses and trunks lashed to carriage rooftops.

"I met his herald—the man travels with his own *herald*—on the front stoop and, after five minutes of convincing the man that I was *not* a servant and, in fact, Lady Marianne Daventry, the man bade me to make myself 'presentable for His Serene Highness, the Prince d'Orleans.'

"I was so confused by all of it—the carriages, and the bandying about of this royal title, and this man tsking over my perfectly presentable day dress—that I mistakenly believed the herald *was* the prince himself—a grave insult, apparently. Also, proof of my poor breeding. It was the last straw, and the herald actually returned to the vehicles in a huff and closed himself up inside. I was standing on the stoop, trying to decide what to do, when Charlotte opened the front door."

"Your sister?"

She nodded. "The youngest. And . . ." an exhale ". . . a singular beauty, if I do say so. Everyone else does. When she was in view, four men spilled from the carriage, and the herald announced Maurice, Prince d'Orleans, without further delay, and on and on it went. We were given no choice but to invite them inside. I rang for refreshments and Charlotte and I received them in the drawing room. The man came to ruin our lives and I served him tea. Kind of like what's happened here between me and you," she said taking a bite of cheese.

Gabriel ignored this. "And then they broached the topic of the betrothal?"

"No, first the lot of them—the imposter prince, his herald, various courtiers, and a steward—made certain we were all properly introduced and they understood who was who. *I* was the eldest. My sister Charlotte was the youngest, barely fifteen. Our middle sister, Diana, was in the stables that morning. My father, the earl, was indisposed. When this was sorted, they asked when they might speak to Papa."

"Who is ill," provided Gabriel.

"It's his heart, we believe," she said. "He drifts in and out of consciousness, and even when he is alert, it is only enough to eat and be washed. That day, he'd been particularly lethargic. I offered my apologies and told them the earl was not well. If I'd known their true purposes, I would've lied and said he was in London, or Scotland, or on the moon. But I did not know, and the imposter prince launched into a thinly veiled interrogation about Papa's fitness, including questions about what male guardian looked after us. By the time I comprehended the very great risk of revealing too much, Charlotte had rattled off thorough answers to all of his questions. Within ten minutes, the imposter understood that we were three women living alone on a vast estate with an invalid father and no other protection. It's obvious that Winscombe is weather-beaten and in need of repairs. He could also see that I'd remained unmarried all these years and was perfectly situated to honor the original betrothal. Finally, he saw that I had at least one beautiful sister who might be swept up to sweeten the deal."

"So when did he raise the topic of the betrothal?" he asked.

A shrug. "Not for several wretched days."

"What excuse did he give for calling to Guernsey if he waited days to mention the betrothal?"

"He reminded me of the great friendship between our two families," she said. "He said he wouldn't hear of departing until he'd gained an introduction to my father. He gave us a little explanation of his inheritance of the d'Orleans title—how his cousin Gabriel had been missing these great many years and was presumed dead."

"He used these words?" confirmed Gabriel. "Missing and presumed dead?"

"That is what he said," she answered carefully, watching him. "And then on the third day, he approached me alone in the drawing room. He told me that, as the new prince, he was also the proud owner of everything in the d'Orleans estate—*including* the decades-old betrothal that bound the firstborn daughter of the Earl of Amhurst to the current prince. He said it was a union that had happened time and again down through the centuries—a tradition of the two families—and now it was our turn, that *we* would marry."

"He demanded it," guessed Gabriel. "And you fought?"

"Well, the first time he raised it, we were both perfectly . . . civil, I suppose you'd say. He believed me to be under his charming spell and dazzled by his title. He also mistook me for someone who is easy to command. I stammered out something about having no wish to marry. He replied that I had no choice in the matter, that I should prepare myself—that we should all *prepare ourselves* for sweeping changes at Winscombe.

"After he'd said it, I remember I sat alone in the drawing room and sort of . . . absorbed my own shock. You've heard of someone screaming into their pillow? This moment was like screaming into a pillow. It was far worse than the dog attack that happened later, worse than the temper fit when he ripped away the necklace. We'd foolishly allowed ourselves to be vulnerable. We have a beautiful estate but little money. Our father is too ill to advocate for us. But we got on

so happily in Guernsey. Our family is well-liked and
our neighbors are decent and respectful. No one took
advantage. Until your cousin."

"But the violence," Gabriel pressed, "when did he
drop the pretense and begin to bully you?"

"Ah yes, the dogs," she said. "Please believe me
when I say I had no intention of trotting out my battle
scars."

"I've known great violence in my life, unfortunately. My own father was executed. Before that, our
family was terrorized."

"Yes," she said, watching him. He'd just revealed
himself. She knew it, and he knew it. His identity was
proven. She said nothing. She waited.

Gabriel forged on, trying to remember his point.
"My early exposure to mindless violence has made
me a student of that moment."

"Moment?"

"The tipping point where civil debate turns to ag-
gression."

"Oh right," she said. "I don't suppose I've thought
of it in those terms. Every minute of his visit was so
very wretched. Never did Maurice engage in 'civil
debate.' He's very underhanded about doling out punishments. For example, he didn't set his dog on me
outright; the dog attacked, and he refused to call it
off. He didn't strangle me, he fingered my necklace
and then pulled so hard, it snapped. Both incidents
could be explained away as accidents unless a witness
happened to be there to see it."

"I'm sorry for what you've suffered, Lady Ryan,"
he told her—the truth. He *was* sorry. He lived a solitary life, but he understood injustice and vulnerability

and abuse. Injustice and vulnerability and abuse were the reasons for his isolation.

Not for the first time, he thought of asking her to stay here, in the forest, with him—to stay hidden and safe from the threat of Maurice, or the burden of managing an old estate and an infirm parent. But of course her troubles were shared among sisters, and love for her home was obvious. She didn't want to hide away in the forest with him. She didn't even know him. And forest life was not easy. Even Samuel's sons—twin boys who'd been raised to love the forest and horses—had, in the end, chosen a different life. Hiding was not the answer for everyone.

"And *I'm* sorry I've thrust our crisis on you," she said. "I'm sorry to have opened your desk and found out your real name and forced you to admit it. Your privacy and solitude are priorities, clearly. What I've done to you resembles Maurice's crimes against me—we both turned up, claimed to be *owed* something, and waved proof in everyone's faces. I see the unfairness of it. I am loathe to draw anyone else into our nightmare, but if I could just compel you to *challenge* this person."

"I . . . *can't*," Gabriel told her.

She stared at him, her face creased with concern. "But, *why not*? If I must beg you, I will."

"Please don't," he whispered harshly. "Look, I will try to help you in some way. I cannot go myself, but I have money. You may use it to hire lawyers."

"I don't want to *fight* the imposter; I want him gone. Why would I travel all the way here, risk all the dangers of the forest, only to *find you* and then hire a lawyer?" Her voice was filled with tears.

"You're not hearing, me, Lady Marianne. I cannot—"

"Please do *not* refer to me as 'Lady Marianne.' That is what *he* calls me. I am *Ryan*. Lady Ryan if you must, but 'Lady Marianne' is the helpless woman betrothed to a terrible stranger and that is *not me*."

He swallowed. "Lady Ryan, will you listen?"

She closed her eyes, took a deep breath, and brushed away tears.

"You're exhausted," he told her. "You've been through a storm, and an ambush, and were lost in the wood. I have misrepresented myself to you, and I can imagine the frustration of it."

"I'm not one of your horses," she said. "I needn't be soothed into docility. I'm perfectly docile. I *can* accept that you won't do it—I can—but I should like to know why. My sisters will want to know. *I want to know*."

"Will you sleep now and let us talk again in the morning?"

"You're joking? You would send me to bed with a vague promise of revisiting this topic 'in the morning'? No sir, I will not. I would know it *now*."

"You want to know, and I want to be left alone," he growled, pushing back from the table. "We can't always have what we want, can we?"

She laughed a little at this, thank God. The irony was, he did not want her to go away. Even though she asked the impossible, everything about this conversation had thrilled him. Having a real conversation with a real woman—not just any woman, but the girl from the letters, all grown up—was invigorating. He never wanted to stop talking to her or looking at her. He could watch her eat raspberries every day for the rest of his life.

Well.

And wasn't this a truth he didn't want to acknowledge?

He could hardly tell her that.

"Look, Lady Ryan. You are articulate and determined, and good for you. I go days without speaking to anyone at all—and now you would have me reveal deep convictions that were borne of the darkest moments of my life?" He began walking the perimeter of the room. She kept silent, watching him.

Finally, he said, "The forest is safe and private. It requires nothing from me but survival. If I leave it, I would have to relearn how to carry on. And I don't want to relearn. My old life betrayed me in terrible ways." He paused beside the wall and leaned back, staring at her. He crossed his arms over his chest. "That is one reason."

"Alright," she said carefully. Her expression had softened.

"I don't know anything but horses and living off the land. And these have been enough—for years, this was enough."

She nodded.

He pushed off the wall and started again to prowl the room. "People will expect me to behave like a prince. Not only have I forgotten how to be a prince, I don't want to know how. The world assumes that a prince manages things, rules over a kingdom. Perhaps he does and perhaps he doesn't, but the result is—as I've experienced it—a prince is actually ruled by his subjects. Sometimes, they love him and he is obligated to retain their love. Other times they hate him, and he is compelled to win back their regard.

Sometimes they hate him so much, they cannot be won over, and they kill him. Regardless, his life is not his own—not his work, not his study, not whether he marries or who. His enemies are chosen for him, as are his allies. He's given almost no choice in how he spends his time. All of these very basic things are controlled by his duty and his country. Various members of my family have been in exile for years, and I can only guess that they have suffered—but not me. I am finally in control. No longer at the mercy of nameless, faceless subjects; of governments; of my family's bloody place in bloody world history."

"Gabriel—"

"Lastly," he said, cutting her off, "there was a culminating event—a disaster—that caused me to take shelter in the forest. That disaster convinced me without a shadow of a doubt that I am not safe outside the forest, nor is anyone with whom I share my life. I can't elaborate further, so please do not ask, but I have freedom from fear in the forest; outside of it, I do not."

"Gabriel, enough," she said softly and he looked up. He'd not realized his voice had risen. He'd almost forgotten she was there.

"Enough," she repeated. "You're safe here in a way you're not safe elsewhere; and I'm sorry. It has been selfish of me to not accept no for an answer. I couldn't see around my own crisis. I was entitled and short-sighted."

"You deserve an explanation."

"And you've explained—and I believe you. I've been—" And now she sighed. "Thank you."

This was unexpected. She watched him now with eyes bright; her pretty face gentle, her body relaxed.

She looked like she could listen to him prattle on about the safety of the forest all night.

Gabriel frowned. "You're exhausted. You should sleep while it's still night."

She considered him a moment longer. She glanced to the direction of his bedchamber and back to him. Finally she said, "Alright. Will you walk with me? I'm not sure I can navigate the room when the candles are snuffed."

His eyes flicked to hers. She stared back. Gabriel felt a blast of something hot and potent. It was hazy and breathless and smelled like a thermal spring. He'd taken her to the waterfall to help her, not—

He breathed out. *Touching her* had simply happened. His current impulse was not to help, it was to indulge. Arousal crawled through him like a wolf. The rawness of their conversation was rapidly fading away and a deeper connection, a greater intimacy, smoldered between them.

"Gabriel?" she prompted.

Of course he couldn't refuse her; not after everything else. He was not a miser. He was simply not a prince.

"Yes," he said. "I'll get the lamp."

She waited for him to collect the light and then preceded him down the dim corridor.

CHAPTER TWELVE

$\mathscr{G}$ABRIEL'S EXCUSE WAS insufficient, but Ryan had always been a little helpless around people who told the truth. Vulnerable friends, neighbors who shared worries, tenants who bared their souls. Her sister Diana said Ryan's heart was too soft and her patience too loose; that Ryan invited these confessions. Ryan preferred to think of it as prioritizing the authentic.

If Maurice the Imposter Prince had been authentic—if he'd come to Ryan and said that he was short on funds, had no remaining relatives, and was adrift in a country that hated royal cousins, it was possible she would've determined some way to help him.

Meanwhile, Gabriel Rein, also known as His Serene Highness, Gabriel d'Orleans, the man now stalking silently behind her, had genuinely confided in her. He'd shared an elusive, fleeting blink of honesty. And it had been enough.

He described his love for the forest, and a need for safety, and the obstacle of losing control over his own life. It wasn't an *I won't*—it was an *I cannot*. And hearing this was enough to soften her heart, just a little.

Meanwhile, her body cared nothing for soft hearts or obstacles. Her body wanted more of the waterfall.

His hands. His attention. His coiled strength kneeling before her. What had begun as a hodgepodge of attractive qualities had piled up for Ryan like logs on a fire; now she felt ablaze. His eyes, for one thing. He gazed at her with an intensity that made her stomach flip. And the *power* of him—the height and muscles and broad shoulders. He'd *carried her* through the forest and into his waterfall and she did not hate it.

Also, his home was tidy and warm, with thoughtful touches like rugs and a little curtain on the window.

And his nose was so very proudly French.

And the bread he'd served her with soft butter and a small dish of salt was delicious.

And the way he'd touched her—

"Will you be comfortable in the nightshirt?" he asked from behind her.

And that was another thing, she thought. The intimacy of wearing his loaned nightshirt made Ryan so very aware of her half-dressed body. The shirt was enormous but smelled clean. The fabric was rough, and it brushed against her nipples in a way that made her tingle. And it belonged to him.

"Oh yes, thank you very much," she said. "If I'd worn the soggy dress, I wouldn't have slept, not really, and it would've ruined your sheets."

"I hope the nightshirt will keep you warm," he said. "There is no fire in the bedchamber."

"No I don't suppose there is. I hadn't realized about the fire."

"No way to remove the smoke," he said. "The chamber is too deep in the hillside for a stovepipe or chimney. A window would be impossible. It can be chilly without a fire. I'll fetch another blanket."

"Thank you. But how do you know when it's morning if there is no window?"

"Rooster," he said.

"Of course. Rooster."

The bedchamber was dimly lit by the sconces, half of them now burned out. Around the corner, the waterfall splattered. Ryan eyed the bed. Should she simply draw back the covers and crawl in?

"Did you find the waterfall suitable?" he asked.

"Oh yes. I should love to have such a thing at Winscombe. The maids resent lugging buckets of heated water upstairs, and I don't blame them. I've converted a little side parlor on the ground floor into a bathing room. And we use a trolly for the buckets."

"How many floors have you at Winscombe?"

"Five. If you count the cellar and the attic. It's the largest home on the island, actually. Plenty of space for ancestors to tack on leaky additions and impossible-to-heat solariums."

She'd reached the edge of the bed and stopped. She could feel him standing behind her, as tall and thick as a stone wall. She need only drift backward to ever so idly lean against him.

In the kitchen, they'd sat across from each other, talking across his table. Her gaze had been drawn to his big hands on the small cup. She'd thought of him holding her foot, massaging her ankle; she'd fought the urge to reach out, to feel the roughness, to see her own hand disappear inside of it. Her parents had held hands, she'd remembered. When her mother had been alive and her father had been well, they'd walked hand in hand to the village, they'd danced together at assemblies, and her father had put his arm around her at church. Ryan remembered her naive childhood assumption that *she* would grow up and one day marry the Prince d'Orleans, and they would hold hands, and dance, and snuggle together on shared pews.

But her mother had died, and the prince had gone missing, and her father had fallen ill. For whatever reason, suitors had not come—not the missing prince chosen by her father, and not the sons of the small circle of local gentry. Ryan had realized that there were no guarantees. She was not the sort of woman that men viewed as . . . well.

She was not the sort of woman whom men looked upon with interest. To presume some man might court her? Marry her? These were fairy dreams.

By the time she and Diana discovered that Winscombe was in debt, Ryan had forgotten all about the Prince d'Orleans and any other man. Her life was full of sisters, and her ailing father, and the grief of a mother who had fallen very ill, very quickly, and then died the next week. She took on the responsibilities of managing a household when she was barely out of the schoolroom. Her life had not been without trials, but it was very full; and she truly believed it was a privilege to be so very needed and to have the cleverness and energy to provide for everyone in it. Ryan had been given many gifts, she knew this.

But *oh*.

Oh, how this deep forest, and this dark cave, how this *giant man* plucked and pulled at some long-overlooked yearning inside of her. It was like the errant string on the sleeve of this nightshirt; her fingers returned to it again and again, fingering, twirling, tugging gently until it snapped. She wanted to be touched and twirled; she wanted to have her strength tested. She wanted to snap.

In this moment, it didn't matter so much that he'd refused to oust his cousin. In this moment, she was crawling into a bed located beneath a *hillside*. Surely she could indulge in the fantasy of snapping. Just for one night. If only in her mind.

"Shall I . . ." she began, unable to endure their silent observation of his bed. "Shall I sleep on top of the coverlet? It's not necessary to disturb the—"

"Get in. You'll be chilled on top."

"Thank you." She gathered her courage and dragged the covers back. She took up a pillow and fluffed it.

"Use the light of the candles to get settled and I'll snuff them," he told her. "This will mean total darkness. When the last one goes out."

"Total darkness?"

"Because the passageway has a bend," he said. "Any light from the fireplace is cut off. It becomes as dark as . . . well, as dark as the inside of a hill."

"I'm not afraid," she said, although she had no idea if this was true. Her bedroom at Winscombe was never without the bright coals smoldering in the grate. If the fire burned out, there was always moonlight from the window.

Without looking at him, Ryan climbed gainfully into the bed, sweeping her legs quickly beneath the covers. The spring in the mattress surprised her, not to mention the cool, crisp sheets. He really was very comfortable inside this hill. She wanted to tell him that he'd be comfortable at Winscombe, too, whether he stayed one night or forever. Of course he'd not refused her for lack of comfort. Ryan, meanwhile, was rather a purveyor of comfort. She loved fresh flowers in vases, and soft cushions in chairs, and raging fires on snowy days, with hot chocolate and currant buns.

When she was settled, Ryan watched him stalk about, snuffing the wall sconces. The room grew darker by degrees. With every new pool of shadow, Ryan's heart beat faster. She pulled the covers to her chin.

"Would it be unsafe to leave a single candle lit?" she asked.

"I don't know, I've never done it." He snuffed the candle in the last sconce. Darkness dropped over the room like a black cloth. The only light was the candle inside the lamp in his hand. His face and chest were illuminated by a flickering glow. Her eyes followed it as he made his way around the bed.

"You're exhausted," he said. "It invites sleep, actually—the complete darkness."

"Will you . . ." she began—but then she stopped. Her heart beat wildly. She squeezed the coverlet.

She tried again, "Before you go, may I see what it will be like? Will you stay a moment after you snuff the lamp? Could you find your way out with no flame?"

After a long beat, he said, "If you prefer."

She glanced up, watching him in the tiny oval of light. He tipped his head down.

"Will you come closer?" Ryan whispered.

"Alright." He walked four steps and loomed beside her. Could he see her nestled in his bed? How far did the halo of his candle extend? She didn't know, but she could see him, and his gaze was half lidded. Heavy. He blinked slowly.

"Thank you," she whispered. "I'm being ridiculous. I've never been afraid of the dark."

"Shall I extinguish it?" he asked.

"You'll not leave the chamber until I'm ready?" she asked. In her head, she thought, *Please stay.*

"I'll not leave until you're ready."

"Right," she said, releasing her grip on the covers. "Thank you. Alright, then. On with it."

He lowered his mouth to the glass globe that protected the candle and blew. The bedchamber, which previously seemed very dark indeed, was plunged into total blackness.

"You're alright," Gabriel whispered.

"Yes?" she said, her voice like a squeak.

"Lady Ryan?"

"You did not misrepresent—it's very dark indeed."

"If you give yourself time, your eyes will adjust."

"I can feel myself searching for some source of light—a tiny glimmer somewhere in the distance—but there is nothing."

"In two minutes, it will not seem quite so disorienting. You will grow accustomed. You will sleep."

The darkness was like being dropped into a void, cold and thick and disorienting. Spreading her fingers wide, she slid her hand in the direction of his voice. She felt cool sheet and the boxy edge of the mattress. She reached farther. Her fingertips brushed the back of his hand. He jumped at the contact but did not move away. Ryan went still, one trembling finger pressed to his knuckle.

When, finally, he moved, it was all at once. He snatched her hand from the mattress and interlocked their fingers. Ryan squeezed and closed her eyes. For a long moment, she lay with fingers clinging, heart running away, breath held.

"You're alright," he said lowly, his voice a rumble.

She didn't answer. Ever so slightly, she gave a slow, slight *tug* to his hand. *Stay*, she thought.

"Lady Ryan?" he whispered, a plea.

She said nothing. She blinked her eyes open. There was no difference between the inside of her eyelids and the black chamber. It emboldened her, this blindness. She increased the strength of her grip on his hand and pulled.

Stay.

"*Ryan*," he warned.

Heart pounding, eyes open or closed—she didn't know—she increased the slow, steady pull of his hand. She didn't yank. It was more like she was trying to prevent him from drifting away.

Gradually, he allowed her to draw him down. He nudged closer, then closer, then finally, all at once, he sat heavily on the bed beside her. The weight of his body caused a slant in the mattress, and Ryan tipped in his direction. She let out a small, desperate sound. Triumph.

Without pausing to think, she released his hand and began to feel her way up his arm, sliding, tracing, using the tips of her fingers to see.

"Ryan," he rasped. His breath was faster.

She didn't answer. She swam through the dark and found his thigh—hard muscle encased in buckskin—and then felt her way to his waist. Above his waist, she found his elbow, his bicep.

Her hands moved at a moderate pace, not frantic but swift. She touched him like she was carefully searching for the handhold on a rock face. In truth, she searched for the trigger that would release him, that would ignite him, that would lure him from hiding place and . . . and—

She could not say what she hoped his trigger would do. Could he touch her like he had in the waterfall; hold her like when she'd fallen from his cupboard? Could he *not go*?

He remained, but he didn't touch her or hold her. Her hands roved over him, and he sat, bolt upright, frozen, breathing hard.

"Gabriel?" she whispered.

"Please," he said.

"Gabriel?" she called again. Her hands had reached his neck. She lifted from the bed, feeling his beard, cupping his face.

It was enough.

On a growl, he reached for her, scooping her to him, dropping her against the pillows, and coming down on top of her.

She whimpered—part thrill, part relief—and slid her arms around his neck. Her head sank into the pillow and he buried his face in the crook of her shoulder, his mouth against her throat. He didn't kiss, he didn't nuzzle, he simply held her tightly and *breathed*. Ryan struggled to catch her own breath, and they lay there in the blackness, holding each other, sucking air in and out. He smelled like rain, and horses, and *him*. His hair tickled her face. His hand cradled the back of her head. His body was so very heavy against her, deliciously heavy—heavy like an anchor, like a hillside.

"What do you want?" he whispered into her skin.

"I . . . I don't know," she breathed. "I want you to stay."

"If this is a game, it's a dangerous one, Lady Marianne."

"Please don't call me that."

"Please don't . . ." and here he paused, as if he couldn't say what he didn't want. Finally he said, "Please don't make this more of a challenge than it already is."

"This?" she whispered. "What do you mean—this? We are two lonely people who . . . who need not be lonely tonight. For once. Here and now."

"What is meant by 'not be lonely'?" he rasped.

"I don't know," she breathed. The truth. She knew only that she didn't want him to go.

"What do you *want*?" he demanded softly.

"I don't know how to say it. In the waterfall you . . . you—" She could not finish.

"If you mean to tease me or trap me, have mercy. Please. You feel—so—good." Each guttural, raspy word washed over her like a warm, gentle wave. "How can you feel so good?"

Yes, she marveled, *how can I?* Her body hummed.

"Am I hurting the abrasion on your neck?" he asked.

She thought of this. She felt only tingles and warmth and pleasure on her neck. She felt tingles and pleasure everywhere. She shook her head.

"May I touch you?" he rasped.

"*Please* touch me."

"May I touch all of you?"

This, she had not considered. Ryan Daventry had never been kissed, and the thought of a handsome prince/horseman/fiancé touching *all of her* hadn't been something she'd expected to consider. She allowed her body to decide. "Yes," she said.

Gabriel let out a feral-sounding moan and rolled off of her. For a second, she thought she'd said the wrong thing. He'd been pressing against her, and now he was gone, and it was too dark to see. But she heard the sound of two heavy boots hitting the floor, felt the mattress depress near her knees and felt the coverlet being peeled back. Cool air moved in, and she let out a little gasp. Beside her, the mattress shifted.

"Oh," she whispered, her heart pounding like it would knock down the walls of this cave. A shimmer of anticipation tingled up her body. She gasped for breath.

Lowly, he whispered something in French, the words too fast for her to interpret. And then his hands were on her thighs, grasping her through the nightshirt. He skimmed downward, massaging as he went, until the fabric ended and he touched bare leg. He rubbed lower, taking care around the wound; and lower still to clasp her ankles. He squeezed her heel and massaged her feet, tracing the arches, circling each toe and then sliding back to her leg. It was like in the water but firmer, more lingering. The water had made his fingers slide, but here there was a friction that allowed him to dig in. After a fortnight of travel from Guernsey, a day on horseback, and their flight through the rain, his hands felt heavenly.

"Vous êtes belle," he said in French. This translation she knew. *You're beautiful.* She wanted to laugh, she wanted to tell him that she'd prefer he not speak if he must tell her lies, but it felt too good to protest. He was bathing her without water; fizzy, tingling sensation dripped from his fingers and radiated across her skin. She descended into warm, shimmering pleasure.

Her consciousness narrowed to his hands, strong and thorough and sure, working their way up her legs in deep, probing strokes. She said nothing, and thought nothing, and very occasionally moaned a vague, "*Oh.*" She lay before him, half languid, half coiled in anticipation, and simply *felt*.

When his fingers nudged the hem of the nightshirt, he stopped, his breath coming in heavy pants. Ryan let out a whimper, frustrated with the pause.

"There you are," he rasped. "Like the waterfall."

"More?" she whispered, emboldened by the darkness—emboldened by the threat of him moving away.

He let out a growl and continued his assent, his hands now above the nightshirt. She missed the warmth of his fingertips but reveled in the new sensation of rough fabric scraping her skin. He dug in more deeply, massaging the muscle, exploring the shape. Vaguely, Ryan became aware of his progress so very far up her leg; he'd reached the apex of her thighs. If he continued on his current path, he would surely brush up against—

"*Oh,*" she gasped, a wave of pleasure rolling from her core.

He'd flattened out his hand across her belly and slid it downward, scooping her sex with his open palm. Pressing in with the heel of his hand, he cupped her, setting off a delicious burn that made her mind go blank.

"*Oh!*" she called again. The shape of his large hand through the cotton of the nightshirt, the pressure— these became the titillating answer to a question she hadn't known her body was asking. It was an upward journey to the very heart of pleasure. They'd not reached the destination—she knew this somehow—but the journey had begun, and she wanted to *fly*.

He pressed more firmly now, cupped her tighter, stoking that mind-erasing burn. Every twitch of his hand set off a jolt of pleasure that took her breath away. Ryan shoved to her elbows and blinked, trying to see him, but the blackness endured. She saw only sparks and twinkles of sensation glowing behind her eyes.

"Gabriel," she panted, "it feels . . . it feels—"

He muttered a French curse, cutting her off, and lowered himself—actually, it was more like he *fell*—on top of her. One moment he'd been kneeling, then she heard the curse, then the hard, heavy weight of him was stretched out on top of her.

She dropped back on the pillow, reveling in the pressure, the closeness, the smell of him. His hand slid from between their bodies, replaced by a thick, hard ridge that nestled exactly, perfectly in the hottest part of the burn between her legs. Ryan whimpered and pushed up, seeking the hardness.

"What are you doing?" Gabriel whispered into her hair.

"I don't know," she whispered back. "I'm doing nothing. For the first time in perhaps a very long time, I'm doing nothing at all." It was true. The darkness had collided with days of fatigue and weeks of worry, and that collision was reason enough to give in. To simply *feel*. To indulge in the incredible thrill of him wanting her, of him indulging her; worshiping her body and giving her pleasure. Making her forget. And no other indulgence would be quite as thoroughly effective as this, part forbidden, part mindless, part transporting, all pleasure.

"I could stop," he breathed, although the words sounded like he could not, in fact, stop.

"*No,*" she gasped, it was the last thing she wanted.

He swore again and scraped his beard from her neck, across her ear, until his lips found her mouth. Ever so gently, he lashed the very tip of his tongue against the corner of her lips. A lick. A taste.

"Please, Gabriel . . ." Sucking in a shaky breath, she turned her head, seeking the tip of his tongue.

Gabriel moaned and shifted, squaring his mouth to hers. The kiss was hungry and demanding and all-consuming. It felt pure and uncomplicated, like the first voracious bite of an apple. He was in charge and she was grateful. She need only drag her hands into his hair and hold on.

When, finally, he drew back and sucked in air, Ryan whimpered, not wanting to stop. She made a keening noise and tried to pull him back down.

"You're killing me," he rumbled.

"Again?" she pleaded.

He complied, dipping to find her mouth. This time, he nipped. He licked. He pecked with tiny, teasing kisses. Eventually, when she was raising her head off the pillow to seek him, he went deeper; he lingered, he feasted.

This was a complicated kiss, with tasting and savoring, and Ryan became a student of rhythm and angle and depth. She was a quick study, aided by the darkness. Her only desire at that moment was this— kissing him, touching him, feeling him.

If she worried he was not equally affected, if she

worried he was merely going along, she need only listen to his groans of pleasure, feel his labored breath on her cheek, revel in the urgency of his body pressing against her. He devoured her like a maelstrom devours ships at sea and she welcomed it, she let herself be sucked down.

And yet . . .

The drowning seemed to want something else to be fully consumed. Through it all, she experienced a leading, pleading, burning need for . . . *more.* For . . . something. For—

For what? As if *this* was not enough? As if she would not relive the glow of this night in her memory until the day she died. Even so, her greedy body insisted it wasn't enough. Despite the abundance, she should have more. She needed, she needed . . .

She couldn't say what she needed. She knew only that she would absolutely require more, and he should absolutely give it to her, and he should do it very soon, and it made no difference that he was currently doing every perfect thing that had ever been done to a woman by a man.

"Gabriel?" she panted.

"Like this?" he whispered. And then he pumped his hips—once, twice—rocking the hard ridge of his body against the demanding burn between her legs.

"Oh!" She sighed.

"Ryan?"

"Yes," she breathed. "Like that."

The pumps melted into a steady rhythm of rocking thrusts that stoked the burn in her center, setting off wild sparks of pleasure.

"I don't—" she panted. "I can't. You must—"

"Wait," he urged, his voice strained.

"Wait for . . . ?" Surely he would tell her. Surely one of them would find words for what needed to happen next—not her, of course. She was rapidly drowning and sinking and thrashing against rocks and surging and dying and should not be expected to predict the future. Nor to wait, for that matter. She *could not wait*.

"Gabriel!" she cried out.

He answered with a guttural noise that was primal and wrenching but also somehow fitting for this moment. He increased the thrusting motion with his hips, grinding, a heavy, muscled, panting man. He'd removed his boots but nothing else, and the texture of his buckskins imprinted through the roughness of the nightshirt. Behind that, she felt the hardness of his arousal. Layers of texture rubbing against her and—

Oh.

She rose up to meet all of it—the weight and the roughness and most of all the hardness. When she pressed, every other thought vanished. She lived only to relieve the yearning fire that throbbed from her center. She pressed, and pressed, and pressed, and then—

A gasp.

A plunge into the dark and the light. She was launched into a swirling spray of pleasure, and colors, and tingling, delicious shimmers. Breath froze in her throat, her body clenched, she clung to his shoulders. She hovered in the dark cave, an ethereal mist shaped like a woman, while a million little particles of pleasure kissed her inside and out.

When she came back to herself, she was being kissed by an actual man, by Gabriel; his mouth swallowing her gasps of pleasure, drinking it in.

"You're killing me," he growled between kisses.

"I don't care," she said, trying to keep up with his mouth.

"I can tell."

He kissed her hard and deep, an assault to her mouth that felt just as shocking and intimate as every other shocking and intimate thing he'd done, and then pulled back. She felt his breath on her face.

"Have you kissed a man before, Lady Ryan?" he rasped.

She shook her head but then realized he could not see her. "No," she whispered.

He swore in French and lowered his face again, kissing her more softly. Little pecks. Longer pecks. The swipe of his tongue.

Ryan kissed him back. Now she understood, and it was nice—less mindless, which she appreciated. She valued reasoned thought and now she could almost, almost manage it.

"Gabriel?" she whispered between kisses.

"Yes?"

"Can I have a baby from this?" She was reluctant to ask this, but it was among the first reasoned thoughts when her brain returned. No responsible woman could allow this to remain unknown. She didn't *think* she could have a baby from what he'd done—but it was so explosive and life-altering and incredible, she had to be certain. She'd taught herself many things since her mother had died, but she had not learned this. Not specifically.

"No," he said. "Can you feel my clothes? I'm fully dressed, Lady Ryan."

What Ryan felt was the large, thick hardness, still

nudging between her legs, but he seemed to be making a point.

"Yes," she said. "I can feel you—er, your clothes."

"You cannot get pregnant without . . . without me."

"Thank you," she said, squirreling away this information for later examination. *Without him.* She wanted to ask more but the simple *thank you* seemed like the most concise, most polite thing to say, considering how wonderful it was and how wanton she'd been.

"Can you sleep now?" he asked.

"Will you stay?"

He made a groaning noise but said, "Yes. Alright. I will stay."

He rolled from her body and Ryan made a small noise of protest, her fingers scrambling to retain some part of him. He settled beside her and she sighed in relief.

He moaned softly and reached for the coverlet, pulling it over them.

"Close your eyes," he said, gathering her body up and tucking it against him.

And now Ryan felt an entirely different pleasure: strong arms pulling her against warm man; one hand slid round her waist, another beneath her and between her breasts. She felt safe and satiated and exhausted; she felt she'd been given permission to tumble into sleep. She saw new colors in the darkness, more muted, but no less incredible. Her breathing was slow and steady. It was so very dark, she didn't know if her eyes were opened or closed, but she knew he was beside her. Knowing this, she fell asleep.

CHAPTER THIRTEEN

GABRIEL HAD NOT intended to fall asleep. He'd not intended to hold her. His vague plan had been to leave her as soon as—

Well, none of it had been planned. Obviously.

He stomped through the stable in the misty light of dawn, feeding the animals. His actions were rote, mechanical, he moved blindly. His brain was consumed with memories of last night and all the things he'd done to Ryan Daventry. Making almost-love to her had been . . .

He couldn't say what it had been. He knew only that he'd wanted it at the time, which also seemed to be the same moment *she'd* wanted it. The darkness had been so complete, and the day had been the most agonizing in recent memory, and *damn it all to hell*.

He grabbed the slats of a stall with both hands and dropped his head between his shoulders, breathing in and out.

Making almost-love to Ryan Daventry was not a change of heart. It was not a compromise. It was base, and primal, and he hadn't realized it ran so very deep until he'd touched her. The moment he'd plucked her from the road and held her against him had been like popping the cork on a vessel that was bone-dry inside. Now all he wanted to do was fill it, and fill it, and fill it. And so what had he done? He'd brought her here, to his camp, so she could immerse it with her scent and her wet undergarments and *her*; so she could be everywhere at once. In his waterfall, in his kitchen, in his head, in his bed.

The bedroom and the darkness had awakened something inside of him so ferocious but also so very latent. It was a version of himself he'd never met. She made him feel entitled to abundance; like mere safety and isolation were not enough. She made him feel like a man who said bollocks to loneliness, even if being alone served a purpose.

With Lady Ryan, he was allowed to be a flesh and blood man instead of a stone-cold survivor.

And where did that leave him? If she was going— and she *was* going—and he carried on surviving by himself? When you'd tasted warm bread with butter, it would be very hard to eat raw turnips and call them delicious.

But this wasn't about only him. He remembered enough about society to know you did not hurl yourself onto a young woman, hours after meeting her, and ravage her. Or nearly ravage her. She'd asked him to touch her, but she'd not been thinking clearly. She'd been terrorized by the highwayman. She was exhausted. She'd been overwhelmed with the responsibility of saving her family. He'd not taken advantage so much as sat down to an abundant feast when he should have eaten the rations he'd packed from home.

The honorable thing to do would be to apologize, and make some excuse, and remind her that nothing had changed. And after he'd suffered through those great many words, she would go, and he'd be left in a wretched state of yearning for the rest of his life. Because—*bloody hell*—it hadn't been enough. Not the sleepy hours holding her nor the mind-blowing minutes touching her. They'd been a fraction of what he wanted and an infinitesimal drop of what he would need again. *If* he ever had the opportunity to lie again with Ryan Daventry. Which he would not. She would go—she *had* to go—and he would remain and never again their paths would meet.

The realization of this made him so very angry. He shoved from the stall and knocked about the stables with terse, agitated movements. His jerks and grunts disturbed the horses, which only irritated him more.

"You said the rooster would awaken me."

At the sound of her voice, Gabriel went still. He dropped a scoop of barley into a trough and slowly turned around. She was standing in a hazy pool of sunlight, hair pulled back, a cautious look on her face, hands folded. She was dressed in her muddy gown, her cloak hanging down her back. She gave him a shy smile.

A *whoosh* of sensation swept from his throat to the bottom of his feet. And just like that, he felt like a man entitled to abundance.

He turned away. "It's early yet. I'm glad you slept."

"When did you leave me?"

Why did she want to know this? Of all the things to ponder about last night, what difference did it make when he'd left her? Had he stayed too long? Should he have waited for her to wake up? He'd never lain with a woman more than ten minutes after—

He trudged to the next stall. "I've been awake for an hour."

"Thank you," she said, "for staying with me. In the dark."

"You are not . . ." he began, but he could not finish. He scooped another cup of barley and moved to the next trough.

"You're not troubled by last night?" he said finally, speaking to the bowed head of the gelding dipping his nose into the feed.

"No," she said. "Not troubled."

His shoulders had been tense, full of knots, and now the tightness eased. The tight pinch when he breathed was gone. He examined her tone for sincerity. He glanced back, checking her expression. She raised her eyebrows and he felt the *whoosh* again. He turned away.

"Are you?" she asked. "Troubled?"

Yes, he wanted to say. *Of course. Entirely.* But that would be a lie.

They'd come to the stall of the stallion called Xavier, and Gabriel made his clicking noise, summoning him to the trough.

"He's afraid," Ryan observed. "Should I go?"

"It's not you," he said. "He's a deep fear of me, and you, and any human, actually. He's slowly warming to one of my grooms, thankfully. He was stolen from his owner and treated horribly by the thieves, only to be recovered and returned home. The abuse he suffered was severe, and he'll no longer acknowledge his owner."

"How terrible," she whispered. "But is the horse so essential that the owner cannot simply put him to pasture? After all he's endured?"

Gabriel shrugged. "He belongs to the son of a wealthy lord. The horse had been a gift of his late father; his first horse when he was a boy. He is attached to the stallion's larger meaning within the family. Xavier, the horse's called. He'll not approach the food until we're gone from the stable. Although, every day, I try." Gabriel reached into his pocket and pulled out a carrot, extending it to the horse. He made the clicking noise again. The horse eyed him from the shadows at the end of the stall but did not move.

"When we've gone," Gabriel said, "he'll eat."

"When we ride to the edge of the forest, so I may return to the inn," she added.

He felt this statement like a pin to his shoulder. He moved down the stalls, measuring feed. After a moment, he said, "I've a new proposition."

"Oh?"

He came to the last horse and emptied the remaining feed into a barrel. Stalking across the stable, he took up his saddle and carried it to his own horse, Anton.

"Something to consider," he said. "The least I can do."

"Alright."

He took a deep breath. It was not physically painful to say words. He wasn't accustomed to talking, but he could do it. He need only open his mouth and speak. Still, making this offer to her felt a little like pulling himself free from a trap. He'd been ensnared by her arrival here, and he was freeing himself, but the means of freedom would tear away skin and bone.

"Gabriel?" she prompted.

"I've a sister," he forced himself to say. "Elise, she's called. You may remember her. She was older by seven years than I."

"Princess Elise," said Ryan. "Yes. I believe I do remember."

"We are no longer acquainted, unfortunately, but she and her husband have purchased an estate on the southern edge of Savernake Forest, not far from the village of Pewsey. I cannot say for sure, but I think if you were to go to her—to call upon Elise and her husband and appeal to them—they may be able to help you. With Maurice. Particularly with the legal aspects of this twenty-year-old betrothal. Her husband was formerly employed by St. James's Palace and worked directly for the king. He sorted out complicated problems in unconventional ways, I believe. He is creative and connected and Elise herself is very clever. Together, the two of them may be able to help you."

"What do you mean, you're no longer acquainted?" Ryan asked.

Gabriel rolled his neck. Of course she would ask this. *This* was why he'd not wanted to make the offer. In the end, his desire to help had been greater than not wanting to discuss it. And now she would pick over the skin and bone of his decision.

"I *mean*," he said, tightening the saddle, "I've not seen my sister since we were separated as children in France. Before we were exiled. Not for fifteen years."

"*Fifteen years?*" repeated Lady Ryan.

"Yes."

Silence settled around the admission and Gabriel went about the business of securing Anton's saddle. She watched him, he could feel it, and he was bothered by it. He knew silence very well but he wasn't accustomed to being watched. Did she judge him?

Probably. Yet another reason he lived apart from all society. Freedom from judgment.

"We have written to each other, Elise and I," he finally said, speaking to the horse.

"You've *written*," Lady Ryan repeated.

"Yes. Back and forth. Not a lot. Enough. We are friendly."

"Friendly?"

With every repeated improbability, the pinch in his shoulder squeezed tighter.

"She approached one of Samuel Rein's sons in Newmarket," he said. "Roderick—his name is Roderick—was negotiating client business on my behalf, and she approached him, and Roderick brought her inquiry back to me. I agreed to correspond with her."

"But are you . . . *angry* with Princess Elise?"

"No. Not angry."

"But you don't see her? Not in person? No proper meeting, no reunion? Not even once?"

"No," he said, stretching the reins over Anton's mane.

And then, to his extreme irritation, she fell silent again. No further questioning. No suggestions. No admonishment. She simply watched him ready the horse.

Say it, he thought tersely. Call him a coward, or unfeeling, or a maddened recluse. Better to challenge him than to force him to define it. He knew his choices were indefensible.

When he could take the silence no more, he said, "I've not met with her for the same reasons I cannot travel to Guernsey with you. I never leave the forest, Lady Ryan. Not ever. I came here to protect myself and to protect others. My sister's safety—the safety of her young family—is my priority above all things. Leaving the sanctuary of the forest is not worth the danger."

He kept a spare sidesaddle to train mares for female riders. He took it and the saddle pad to the horse called Fleur. Lady Ryan made no reply. He wondered if they were having a conversation or if he was simply dribbling out his terrible life story for her shock and bafflement.

"But have you," she finally ventured, "considered inviting your sister here, to your home, in the safety of Savernake Forest, to reunite?"

"No. Actually. I've not," he gritted out. "And I didn't mention my sister so that I could defend my choices to you. I meant only to offer an alternative way to help."

A pause. Damn her pauses. They compelled him to say too much. Then they compelled him to stew in his own admissions.

After a long, painful moment, she said, "Forgive me. My own sisters are very dear to me and it's difficult to imagine a life where we might correspond rather than—well, rather than anything else. Your reasons are for you, alone, to know. I am grateful for any help you can give me, including an introduction to Princess Elise. I'm grateful for everything you've done, truly."

I've done nothing for you, he thought, but he said, "I regret that you came all this way. I know you do, as well."

And now his pounding heart stopped and he held his breath. He was waiting for her to say, *I don't regret it.*

She did not say it. And he would not *un*say it. And

so it was a reality. Silence stretched over the stable again.

"Is there anything I can do to help get underway?" she asked.

"No."

"I saw the breakfast you laid and helped myself," she offered. "I hope you don't mind."

"That is why it was there." He led the mare to the hitching post.

"That's a fine-looking horse." She followed him into the sunlit paddock.

"Fleur, she's called. You were riding through the forest when Meade set upon you, so I assume you're proficient on horseback."

"Oh I'm proficient," she said on an exhale. She tightened her gloves. "I've a multitude of problems, but riding a horse is not one of them."

If NOTHING ELSE, Ryan was behaving more like herself today. She was listening, she was waiting. No implorations to remain; no begging for passion. Also, a man was sending her packing. How familiar it was to be overlooked, or passed by, or whatever was happening here with the saddled horses and the handing off to a sister.

At least she had last night.

It was not Ryan's nature to feel sorry for herself and she tried very hard to shake the feeling that she was being *un*chosen. She would focus on her next plan of action instead. And on empathizing with Gabriel's struggles, which were clearly significant to him—they would be significant to anyone. He was sending her away, but he was not a happy man with an easy life.

Meanwhile, her life before Maurice had been rather charmed, the loss of her mother notwithstanding. Gabriel was clearly a stalwart, deep-feeling man, and one did not live in the forest unless the outside world was untenable. She should see his challenges and encourage him to endure. Seeing and encouraging were restorative gestures. The more she felt for others, the less sorry she felt for herself.

Gabriel stalked to the stables to bring out his own mounted stallion. Compared to his house, the interconnected maze of paddocks and pens was new and modern. The fence gleamed with a fresh coat of paint. The shingles were straight and flat. The sod was trimmed. There was a kitchen garden and rose bushes in large pots. The contrast surprised her; she'd seen the outside last night, but only by torchlight.

In the stalls and the paddock, horses grazed or stared languidly out, watching Gabriel. The dogs—the pair of them—had clearly been warned to keep their distance, because they sat in the open doorway of the stable, alertly observing her. There was a coop for chickens and pens that housed swine and goats. It was a bustling enterprise, as tidy and well maintained as the house. And to think, all of it buried so very deep in the forest.

"The facilities for your livestock are beautiful," Ryan called to him.

"Samuel Rein's family sustained themselves on a perfectly workable layout here for fifty years," he said. "Samuel trained me in this paddock—or rather, a cruder version of it. I've made improvements over time. Space is limited in a small valley at the base of a large hill, but I've managed to make the most of it."

"And you find that no one disturbs you here? No other forest dwellers, no travelers who have lost their way? Huntsmen? No one? You're completely alone?"

"It is very remote."

"Your preference," she observed.

"My necessity." He rounded the stallion at the hitching post, reached for his saddle horn, and put a boot into the stirrup.

"But we're going *now*?" she asked.

"My grooms will arrive soon to start their day. I'd rather we be gone by then."

"Oh, right. Of course." Ryan took a step toward the saddled mare.

"Forgive me," she said, "but can I trouble you for a hand up?"

Gabriel paused, halfway in his saddle.

"Or," she tried, "I can lead the horse to a mounting block?"

Gabriel dropped his foot to the ground.

"I *can* mount up without help," she volunteered, "but it's an ungraceful enterprise. And it will upset the balance of the saddle." She shaded her eyes and looked at him.

"Sorry," he said, speaking to the horse.

"My sister Diana can leap into a saddle without assistance, but she rides astride." A nervous chuckle.

"There is no mounting block," he said. "Can you use the slat of the fence?"

"I suppose I could do; but it will be difficult in a dress. The fabric snags. It becomes a bit of a fight between the post and gravity."

But had she offended him by asking for help? Ryan looked to him and realized he was blushing.

He studied her position beside the mare but would not meet her eye. He took off his hat and swiped his brow. Had she upset him with the suggestion of closeness? Was the prospect of touching her again so terrible?

Slowly, almost tiredly, he released his horse and came to her. Ryan smiled cautiously. There was no ulterior motive here. He needed her to ride, and she needed a hand into the saddle to do it. She thought about apologizing again, but he was upon her—coming closer and closer and so close, he stood six inches away. The smell and heat of him came over her in a rush, and Ryan felt a *zing* of sensation shimmer down her body. She took a step back. He'd need room to kneel and she'd need space to hitch her foot into his hands. The grooms at Winscombe took up position about two feet away.

She took another step back. Gabriel closed the distance, following her.

Ryan bit her lip. She glanced at the mare. If there was any hope for reaching the saddle horn and the reins, he must—

With no warning, he fastened his large hands around her waist and lifted. Ryan let out a little yelp and her hands flew first to his wrists, then to his shoulders. He lifted her up, *up*, past his face, past his hat. He lifted her so high, she looked down into his face.

"Wait, wait, wait," she said in a small, breathless voice. "Gabriel, let us—can we begin again?"

He frowned and lowered her. Now they stood chest to chest. The fabric of her skirts enveloped his legs; the bodice of her dress brushed the lapels of his coat.

The zing in her chest was now a cascade, raining down on her pounding heart.

"Sorry," she said on a breath, "I wasn't expecting you to—" She laughed. "That is, the grooms at Winscombe stoop like this . . ." she demonstrated going down on one knee ". . . and make a cradle with two hands by interlocking their fingers, and I step into their hands. I wasn't expecting you to lift me from— well, I wasn't expecting to be lifted."

He took a step back.

"Although," she said quickly, following him, "your way is perfectly alright; I simply—"

"I've never seated a woman on a horse before," he cut in.

In the same moment that he said it, she blurted out, "I've never had a man *lift me* onto a horse before."

She laughed and raised her hands to his shoulders. His blush persisted, brighter now, and he was still frowning. She was just about to suggest that he lift her again, that she was *prepared* this time, when he dropped to his knee and interlocked his fingers. Because of their closeness and the position of her hands, she tipped forward when he went down. He was given no choice but to grab her around the legs to steady her. She fell, leaning into him, pressing her thighs into his shoulder and her belly into his cheek.

"*Oh*," Ryan exclaimed, her hands sliding from his shoulders to the back of his head. His hat dropped to the ground. For a long moment, they hovered there: Gabriel on one knee, his face pressed into her middle, Ryan clutching his head. The memory of last night swept over her, the closeness, the safety, the intimacy. She squeezed her fingers into his hair and closed her

eyes, basking in the feeling of being held by him
again, of his shoulder against her legs, of his hands
tangled in her skirts.

He would pull away, she knew—any moment he
would go—but until he did, she held him. But then he
didn't move, and so she didn't move, and she nudged
closer. He hesitated a moment and then encircled her
legs in his arms, crushing her against him, burying his
face against her breasts.

Ryan stifled a whimpering noise and closed her
eyes. She folded over him and dropped her mouth
to the top of his head. Oh, the *rightness* of it, she
thought. How could he feel so familiar after only one
night? She moved her fingers through his hair, inhal-
ing the scent of him. The embrace was sweet, and unexpected, and restorative. After everything he'd not
said, and she'd not said.

It wasn't a moment for chatter, but her mind cast
around for something to say. *I'm sorry.* Or, *It feels
very good when you hold me.* Or, *Please don't send
me away.* These were wrong, of course. She wasn't
sorry. And his arms felt far better than "good." And
the problem wasn't that he sent her away, the problem
was that he refused to go away *with* her. He would
remain, and she would not challenge him.

After a second, a minute—she didn't know—he
drew back his head, let his hands fall away, and
shoved up from the ground. He turned briskly away.
Ryan staggered a little—he'd released her as swiftly
as he'd snatched her—and she reached out a hand to
the mare. The moment dissolved.

Breathing hard, she watched him walk to the paddock fence, grip it, and turn back. His face was tight and unreadable. Was he angry? Pained? Sad?

"But are you angry, Gabriel?" she asked.

It was one thing to say too much, but quite another to say nothing and simply *guess*. Ryan preferred to understand.

"Or hurt?" she offered. "Sad? Forgive me, I don't understand what's happened between us."

"Nothing's happened," he said. "I've never seated a woman on a horse before. I've never had a woman hover at such close proximity. I've never—" He stopped himself.

"I apologize," he said, clearing his throat. "Shall we mount the mare your way or shall I lift you?"

She blinked at him. "Your choice."

"Fine. Up you go." In one swift movement, he picked her up around the waist, lifted her, and plopped her on the saddle. Her skirts and cloak got in the way and she scrambled to hook her knee around the pommel and arrange the fabric.

"Thank you."

He nodded and climbed into his own saddle.

And that was that.

One minute she'd been holding him, and now he'd tossed her onto the horse. When she gathered the reins, her hands shook.

"There is a path to a thicket," he said.

"A path?"

"Aye. Your mare will follow Anton. When we enter the thicket, however, the path disappears. I take a different route every time to hide the direction to my camp. This involves doubling back and winding around trees. It's slow but not difficult. You can mirror me to the right or left. Fleur should comply with no effort. Just watch for holes in the sod. The thicket is home to every manner of creature."

"Alright," she said, shading her eyes. She'd lost her hat in the ambush the day before. "And you're taking me to . . . ?"

"We'll ride to the edge of the forest, just outside Pewsey. You'll have to walk from the outskirts of town to the inn—it's not far—because I cannot be without this mare. I'm sorry. I've money for you to give to the innkeeper to cover the price of the horse stolen by Channing Meade. There is also money to hire a carriage to convey you to the home of my sister Elise. It's also not far. Her estate is called Mayapple. Any local driver will know the way."

"The money, Gabriel," she said, "it's not necessary, really I—"

"Please do not argue. Please take what very little I can give."

These words seemed to pain him, so Ryan simply nodded. "Alright. Thank you."

He exhaled then—it was clear he expected to fight her on every point—and then kneed his horse into motion. Ryan followed suit, reining the mare behind his stallion.

"Shall I close my eyes," she volunteered, "so as not to see the way back?"

"No," he said. "Please do not close your eyes."

It was the last thing he said for half of an hour, and Ryan did not disturb the quiet. What more was there to say? He couldn't help her; he couldn't tell her exactly *why* he couldn't help her; and he would not discuss what had happened last night. They had exhausted all relevant topics. Everything else would be chatter.

She studied the shape of his shoulders and back, marveling at the power of him. Had he felled the trees to construct his stable yard? Did he hunt and skin his own game? Ryan was hardly a city dweller, but Winscombe was staffed by loyal servants and she and her housekeeper shopped in the village every week. She knew every comfort.

They cleared the thicket using his zigzag route and then turned to follow the ruts of what appeared to be a sparsely used road. There was room for Ryan to ride beside him, and she kneed her horse forward.

"Gabriel?"

"Yes?"

"Would you have me say anything in particular to your sister? When I call on her? Shall I simply knock on her door?"

"I've written a letter that you may give her. This will help explain. It's inside a packet with the money."

"Thank you. This is all very helpful. But do you expect your sister to welcome me? Just like that? I'll not have to convince her to indulge my tale of woe?"

"I believe she will be very open to receiving you. She is—" An exhale. "She is eager for any connection to me. It will interest her very much that you have seen me. Please . . . can you assure her that I am well."

"Yes, yes—alright. But Gabriel? Is there no explanation for why you'll not see her yourself? What if she asks me why I've seen you and she has not?"

Gabriel said nothing.

"You've said there was no falling out," she continued. "I only raise it because disagreements have a way of healing themselves over time. Or perhaps you dislike her husband? Have you—"

"There was no row," he said, cutting her off. "And I've never met her husband. She speaks very fondly of him in her letters. If she is happy, I am grateful to him."

"Alright. Fine. I'll simply tell her what I know of you—which is almost nothing—and also that—"

"I cannot meet her outside the forest because it's not safe," Gabriel stated, his voice pained. "And I'll not meet her inside the forest, because I'm not prepared for her to see what I've become."

What he'd become? Ryan scrunched up her face, trying to understand.

"When last she knew me, I was a prince," he said. "Now—now I don't even know how to help a woman onto a horse."

"Oh, yes, well . . ." Ryan was beginning to understand. "Please be advised, I've never been helped onto a horse by a gentleman before. I'm accustomed to grooms."

He didn't answer, and they fell quiet. Only the plod of hooves and birdcall filled the void. All around them, the forest was a lush tunnel of green. It dripped with vines and swayed with feathery groundcover that bent easily under the horses. Ryan saw the wildness, she registered the beauty, but she didn't care. She repeated his words in her head. *I'm not prepared for her to see what I've become.*

In her view, Gabriel had not transformed in such a way that his own sister would not welcome him. He was hardly a London dandy or a country squire, but she'd found no objection with him. Obviously. Quite the contrary; if pressed, she would say he was magnificent. Was Princess Elise, whomever she was, so judgmental that she'd rather *not* see her brother than see his evolution?

They came to a brook and Gabriel allowed his stallion to drink. Ryan's mare dipped her head but clomped into the water to take the clearest depths.

After a moment, Gabriel said, "I was not meant to exile with Samuel Rein."

"No?"

"No. When I fled France, the arrangement was to exile in Marlborough. I'll—" A deep breath. "I'll tell you what happened. *Then* you may form your opinion. About me."

"I'm no judge of circumstances, Gabriel," she said. "What I value is honesty. When someone reveals his true self, I'm rather at their mercy."

"Do not place yourself at my mercy, Lady Ryan."

Too late for that, Ryan thought miserably. *Too late.*

Chapter Fourteen

He WOULD SAY it very quickly. An overview. The bits that provided an overview.

They were ten minutes from the edge of the wood. He could devote five to his history and use the remaining five to tell her again about the money and his letter for Elise. Five minutes to say it would be sufficient. He owed her nothing more than general motivations for his life's choices. After that, they'd part ways. She could form her opinion and remember him accordingly. She could report to his sister that he was a man living life on his own terms. Or not. Whatever she wanted. It wouldn't matter. She would be gone.

She glanced to him, eyebrows raised, waiting. He'd seen that expression before. Expectant; almost hopeful. A stab of something sharp and uncomfortable pierced his heart. He fixed his eyes on the trail ahead. He lifted his hat and then reseated it. He gripped the reins.

"My life and the challenges I face are . . ." he began ". . . they're no greater than what you face."

"Well, let us not make it a contest."

He closed his eyes and snorted. She was clever. She was clever and generous and she had a serene, steady quality. She was like cool shade on a hot day. He wanted to nudge his horse closer and bask in it. He wanted to unseat her and settle her in his lap. He wanted to turn their horses around and take her back to his camp and keep her.

And now he was thinking like the reclusive, forest dweller. Which he was, honestly, so what did it matter? He cleared his throat.

"I was ten years old when my sisters and I were taken into hiding in England," he said. "Elise was taken by a nun. I was taken by a soldier. I cannot say what happened to our baby sister, Danielle. According to Elise's letters, no one will tell her where Dani was taken or by whom. This is another example of the control exerted over anyone with royal blood. The location of an exiled baby has been concealed. And for what? Sometimes, we're controlled by what is said; other times, we're controlled by what is not said."

"Control exerted by whom?" she asked gently.

"Family. Loyalists. Advisors. Counselors. Tradition. History. Allies. Enemies. Anyone with a stake in power."

"Your bitterness and frustration are justified," she said, "but your change of heart is fascinating to me. When we were children, you seemed so very proud of your title. You seemed in awe of your father."

"Forest life afforded me ample time to read, and I became a student of history and government and philosophy. And I witnessed the brutal execution of that father. Even at my young age, I knew his only crime was being a prince. Our family was torn apart—never to be restored. Danielle was not three years old when she entered exile. She's been lost to us since then."

"Your sister was very young, indeed," said Ryan, "but you were hardly grown. To be taken from your family at the age of ten? You were a child."

He shrugged his shoulders. Must he say what happened, and how it shaped his views, and also how it made him feel?

"This had to be the same year your family visited us at Winscombe," she said. "You were ten and I was nine when we—when I last saw you. My memory of it is patchy, but I remember."

"Aye," he said. "We visited Guernsey in the summer. The Revolution would not rage out of control until late autumn."

"I know you were old enough to remember meeting me and to write letters. We'd already begun to correspond, hadn't we? You were old enough to forge our friendship, to know royal protocol, but not old enough to survive in the larger world alone."

"Well, here I am," he said. "Some version of me has survived."

"How?" she said softly. "How did you survive?"

Another exhale. "I was ferried to England, obviously. The soldier who volunteered to steal me out of France delivered me to a small regional boys' school in Marlborough, not far from here, actually. The school's headmaster harbored me as an asylum seeker—he and his wife took me in."

"Oh no, Gabriel—not a school for boys. The stories I've heard about boys' schools—the abuse and neglect and bullying? I can't imagine going from a *palace* to a boys' school in rural England."

"It was the best circumstance for exile, honestly. You're correct, it could've been wretched, but the headmaster was a kind man, and his wife—who was French, and responsible for taking me in—was lovely. They had four children who were happy to share their parents. I was a student at the school; given a new name and said to be an immigrant from Flanders. At holidays and breaks, the headmaster's family included me in their celebrations. The setting of the school allowed me to continue my studies, and the headmaster's family meant I was not quite so alone. The other boys were curious but friendly. It was different than the Palais Royale, obviously; but there were no angry mobs and no executions. My final days in France . . . the imprisonment, the execution of my father? These put me off of palaces for good."

"I don't blame you."

"We're almost to Pewsey," he said, changing the subject. "Are you fit to walk after an hour in the saddle?"

"Oh yes, I am well. But will you say the rest of your history? Before I go?"

"About France?"

"Well, no. Although, I'm happy to discuss your life in France. I was wondering about the school for boys. If you were fond of it, how did you wind up in the forest?"

He thought of the school, thought of his friends. For a moment, he could not speak.

She must have seen his struggle because she added, "Or can you tell me what became of your sister Elise? Did she pass exile in England in a girls' school?"

He took a deep breath. This, he could answer. "Elise was not so fortunate in exile. She was neglected, or shall I say, she was 'endured' by her hosts. In a way, she was a prisoner."

"Held prisoner, oh dear," said Lady Ryan. "But where?"

"St. James's Palace."

"*St. James's?* But do you mean with King George and Queen Charlotte?"

"Yes." He sighed, thinking of what his sister had described in her letters.

Ryan made a whistling noise. "Who could guess that a rural school for boys would be better than the home of the king? But who designed your exile?"

He shook his head. "We know very little about who arranged it or why. Before he was executed, my father told us that royalist sympathizers were plotting to rescue and steal us away. He said we would enter exile in another country and be safe. He told us to be ready, that they could come at any moment. He did not tell us where, or how, or how long. It's been nearly twenty years, and Elise has received very little explanation. I've vanished so they can hardly inform me. And we've no notion of what became of our sister, Danielle. I would not have made the connection with Elise, except she searched tirelessly for me. She searches for Dani still."

"She searched *tirelessly* for you?" whispered Ryan.

"She looked for me, and she found me—or rather, she found the general location where I reside—and now we correspond. I've not been prepared to meet her, but we do write."

Ryan said nothing, and he braced for her to press him. He knew his estrangement from Elise was odd and unjustified, but theirs was not a conventional family.

"So what happened?" she finally said. "How did you go from the boy's school to the forest?"

He took a deep breath. "The short answer? A fire. The school was burned to the ground. The dormitory, the cottage that housed the headmaster and his family, the lecture halls, the stables. All of it."

"*No*," breathed Ryan. "Was anyone harmed?"

"No one died," he said, determined to rush through this bit. "That is, so far as I know, no one died. After the fire, I left my host family for the woods and we have lost touch. They moved to Yorkshire and I fled to Savernake Forest. I've been here ever since."

"The fire was so very devastating," she guessed. "It was the last straw. After the trauma of the Revolution?"

"The trauma of being hunted and hounded was the last straw," he corrected.

"What?"

"The fire that burned the school was set *because* of me. *I* was the reason for it. Seventy-five boys, countless teachers, the headmaster and his young family, staff, the livestock. All of us could have burned alive. All because the school harbored an exiled French prince. And that says nothing of the danger to the other families on the street if the fire had not been contained."

"But what do you mean it was because of you?"

"I mean that—although I'd managed some semblance of a normal life at school—I was never fully at peace. Instead, I was constantly, maliciously, *hunted*. Sought by spies, and revolutionaries, and soldiers, and mercenaries. From the day I fled France, some party or faction have *wanted me*—a male grandson of the former king; nephew to the most recent king— captured, extradited, or dead; all three if it could be managed. They've wanted me so urgently, they dispatched agents to track me. I can only assume they would've tracked me to the ends of the earth. The headmaster and his wife were shocked that these spies and mercenaries found me so very deep within the English countryside—but they did. And eventually they *burned a school* to flush me out."

"But are you certain?" she asked, sounding appalled. "This is terrible, Gabriel. I'm horrified for you—for all of you."

"Yes," he said. "I'm certain. My life reads like a very bad, very improbable novel, but I assure you, it's all happened. Before the fire, there were repeated harassments from men hired to hunt me down and capture me. There'd been failed break-ins to the school. Mercenaries turned up in our high street and waded into groups of classmates, scattering boys as they searched for a missing prince. They threatened local shopkeepers for information about a French orphan. The headmaster's wife was frequently followed to the market. The carriage of my best friend was attacked after his parents collected him for holiday. The school and the boys were constantly surveilled, frequently harassed. The headmaster and his wife were, God love them, determined that I should have a normal life. They brought in dogs; they begged shopkeepers not to answer questions from strangers; they even hired a boxing instructor and taught all of us boys to fight.

"I survived only out of luck," he said. "And also because the spies never knew exactly where to look or which boy I might be. And my classmates were very loyal. For more than a year, I hid in plain sight. And then, they set fire to the school."

He hadn't meant to say more than that. The edge

of the forest was around the next bend. Still, once the story began to pour from him, he couldn't seem to stop.

"They blocked the dormitory entrances after bedtime," he told her. "Can you believe it?"

"No," she said quietly. "I cannot believe it."

"They blocked the entrances and set the building on fire. Only one door remained unlocked, and their plan had been to force us out that door so they might search the face of every boy. It was a shite plan—all of the mercenaries who came for me were sloppy—but this represented a new level of danger. But I knew, even as a boy, that I could ignore it no longer. The fire itself was fast-moving and voracious. Within minutes, it had become an inferno; a petrifying, hot, blinding monster. If you've never seen a building catch fire, it truly looks like hell come to earth. The outline of the structure is visible, but its shape is made of fire. Flames shoot upward to the sky. Meanwhile, the inside of the building becomes translucent, so you can see through the walls. It's this skeletal framework that rapidly dissolves into a living furnace. All the while, chaos reigns. People were frantic, trying to save the surrounding buildings; trying to account for the missing; trying to reckon with the loss of their every possession.

"I remember looking around at my classmates, standing barefoot in the snow. I heard the cries of the livestock, stampeding in terror. For a terrible quarter hour, the schoolmaster's baby daughter was lost in the confusion, and his wife was inconsolable, sobbing in the middle of the street. The child was later found, but she could have easily been killed."

He took a deep breath. "And you'll have to remember, this was not my first trip around the sun. I knew the escalating nature of bloodlust. The week leading up to my father's beheading was . . ." He shook his head. *This* he would not discuss.

He finished, "I knew that the only safe thing was to remove myself from the school, from Marlborough, from society. And so I did. The forest was not far from the school—close enough that my classmates and I had trooped through the trails and swum in the streams. The great expanse of it was not known to me, but I was familiar with the first mile or so."

"And so they simply let you go? The headmaster? Your teachers? A boy of eleven was allowed to make his life in the forest?"

"I ran away," he said. "That same night, I ran. The schoolmaster was busy looking after his family and finding temporary lodging for the boys. I scribbled out a note and shoved it at a teacher. Then I walked to the forest, sought out the darkest, windiest, most formidable path, and threw myself down it, running as fast as I could. I had no destination in mind, no plan for survival; I wanted only to remove myself from the men who hunted me so that my classmates and host family would be left in peace."

"But how did you survive?" she asked.

"Samuel Rein," he said. This part of the story was easier to tell. His chest loosened. He could breathe again. "Samuel Rein discovered me—or actually, it was his dogs. I'd passed out beneath the upturned roots of a felled tree. I was hungry and cold and rather belligerent, but he coaxed me to his camp; he clothed me, fed me, gave me time and solitude. And then, he suggested I stay on, just for a while. He was a widower with twin sons. The boys had only rudimentary schooling, and he wanted them to learn to read and write. I told him that I was a danger to him and his children, that I was hunted, that no one was safe in my company—he laughed. He actually laughed. I was offended, of course, but then he showed me how very hidden they were—how far from Pewsey; farther still to Marlborough. No roads, not even a trail. Also he was a giant bear of a man. Formidable looking. It would take a very large ransom for any mercenary to take on a man like Samuel Rein."

"And you considered it. You said yes," she guessed.

"Do you know what convinced me? At least in those early days? The animals. I'd always had a deep love of horses, and I could not resist the promise of riding every day, of learning how he healed wounded animals. He saw my indecision and offered a trade. If I would teach his boys to read and write, he would teach me to break horses. It was meant to be temporary; but a fortnight turned into a month, a month turned into the spring. And then I found myself living among them in the camp like a member of his family. It was . . ." he breathed in and out ". . . a saving grace for me. I would be dead if not for him, I'm certain of it."

"And your fear about bringing danger to his doorstep? You were able to release this?"

"Well, I do feel safe in the forest, obviously. I also felt safe with Samuel, as I've said. His boys were vulnerable but he was teaching them to be woodsmen and horsemen and fighters—he was teaching all of us to be resourceful. And there were no women in camp. The image of the schoolmaster's wife, sobbing in the road during the fire? The thought of her baby burned alive? I was so very haunted by these. With just the four of us living rudimentary lives, our existence felt inconsequential. No, that's not true. It felt profound and of no consequence at the same time. But what mattered was, I felt far less afraid."

"And that is when you wrote me for the last time. The letter that led me to you here."

"Yes." He sighed. "My final princely act. I hadn't written from the school because it did not feel safe. The forest felt more secure, I suppose. I wanted you to know that I was 'out there' somewhere. I wanted to tell you goodbye. It was foolish, I—"

"It was a very great relief to me," she cut in. "That letter. I read it a hundred times. I prayed for you. When Maurice came, it was my first thought. I hope you don't regret sending it to me."

Gabriel thought of this. "No," he finally said. "I don't regret it."

After a silence, Ryan said, "You mentioned that Samuel Rein was a widower?"

"Yes. His wife died of a fever," he said. "Sadly. It was why he moved to the forest. Grief. Also too much interference from relatives about how to raise his boys. Samuel had grown up in Savernake Forest. When he lost his wife, he returned to it."

"Did he ever leave the shelter of the wood, or did he seclude himself like you?"

"It was his strong preference to never leave, but he was compelled to attend market days in surrounding towns to meet with clients. Once or twice a year, he traveled to Newmarket. But these were very quick, very detached forays into society. He made camp in whatever wood was nearby—he never lodged in an inn. Outside craftsmen were hired only as necessary for essentials that couldn't be made by his own hand."

"So resourceful," she marveled.

"Yes. He would consider my current lists of store-bought 'necessities' to be very extravagant, indeed. 'Indulgences,' he would call them."

She chuckled. "Like what?"

He glanced at her. When she smiled, her face was so very pretty, it made his chest ache. He looked away. "Sweets, for one. Newspapers from London and Paris. Proper linens and down pillows. Clothing I don't have to sew by hand. New hats and gloves when the leather wears thin."

"Oh yes, indulgences, indeed," she laughed. "But Gabriel, is there truly a lingering threat? Even now? The Revolution in France has been over for more than ten years. As I mentioned, Maurice believes the monarchy may be restored in France. We think this is one of the reasons he's so covetous of Winscombe. He needs money if he is to reclaim his position in court."

"The Prince d'Orleans," Gabriel said, "whomever he is—be it me, my cousin Maurice, whomever—is a potential challenger for the French throne. My guess is, he doesn't want a *position* in court, he wants to *be king*—head of the court himself, head of everything. He always harbored delusions of grandeur."

"But is that possible?" she gasped. "Could the Prince d'Orleans ascend to the throne if France restores a monarchy?"

"If the monarchy returns to France, my uncle Louis-Stanislas should be king—in theory. However, the Orleans branch of the family *could* challenge him for it. I know this because my sister has been harassed by the courtiers of our uncle in recent years. The school that burned? That was most likely done by revolutionaries. Ten years on, there are fewer of those zealots running about, but loyalists have taken over where they left off. Someone is always hunting an exiled prince."

"What do you mean, they harassed your sister?" she asked.

"They've hounded Elise for my location; but her husband is rather forceful and he's put a stop to it. Luckily she doesn't know exactly where I am. She couldn't tell them, even if they reached her."

"But if your uncle's men found you," she asked, "could you simply tell them—now as a grown man— that you have no aspirations to the French throne, that you simply wish to be left alone? Are you still so vulnerable?"

And this, Gabriel knew, was the crux of the matter. The line between life-and-death solitude and preferred solitude was as thin as the leaf of a fern. Did he simply want to be left alone? *He* wasn't afraid of the outside world, but he would always be afraid for the safety of Elise and her family—even for Lady Ryan, if she left here bandying about his name and title. Furthermore, the customs and crowds and chaos of society repulsed him. He knew himself to be wholly unprepared to return, and he had no notion of how to condition for that sort of thing. The mere thought of it made his shoulders ache, and his chest tight, and his palms sweat.

Lady Ryan was gracious about his life in the wood, but to most people, he would be a spectacle. He wanted no part of their judgment. And that said nothing of the filth and soot, the noise, the buildings that blotted the sun, the rivers that teemed with offal and the runoff of latrines, the clocks that counted off hours of the day so no moment was wasted?

Worst of all would be the loss of his freedom. From anonymous woodsman to obligated prince. He could not.

"I don't want to defend my solitude, Lady Ryan," he said. "It's best for everyone that I'm believed dead. I'm loyal only to myself. It's safer that way. For everyone. I'm—" He glanced at her and then away.

"I'm sorry I cannot help you," he finished. "I'm sorry I'm passing you off to Elise and Killian Crewes, her husband; but I pray they can help you. And I pray you can forgive me."

"There is nothing to forgive," she said. She flashed him a genuine smile. "I understand everything you've said and I don't fault you. How could I? You've endured so very much, and you've carved out a life that is safe and fulfilled. You deserve this peace, Gabriel. I want nothing less for you."

Her words were sweet and sincere but instead of absolving him, his stomach twisted into a knot. He was angry at himself, angry at his cousin, angry at the plague of being born a prince.

"Stop—please," he breathed.

"Stop . . . riding?" she asked.

"Stop *talking*."

"Alright. I wasn't actually speaking at the moment but alright."

"Enough has been said."

"I understand, Gabriel."

"The trail to the village of Pewsey is just there." He pointed through a screen of saplings at a clearing, splashed yellow with sun. "You'll turn right beyond the tree line and see a small brook with a little bridge. Cross the bridge and follow the path to the stone fence. There's a gate to the left. Through it, you'll find the main road into town. It becomes the high street within a quarter mile. Do you understand?"

"Yes. Yes, I understand."

"I'm sorry I cannot go closer. I'm sorry I—"

He stopped and closed his eyes again. He sighed. "You should be perfectly safe. It won't take ten minutes to reach the inn from here. You're sure you understand?"

"Oh yes. It's perfectly clear."

He nodded and forced himself to think of everything she needed to know about the money and the letter. If he focused on these logistics, he would not think of letting her go. He reached into his coat for the packet. She shifted in the saddle beside him, preparing to dismount.

"Wait," he said. "Let me help you."

He swung from his horse and tethered him to a tree. Striding to her, he reached up. His hands closed around her waist and he had the errant thought: *I'll not touch her again. I'll not lie with her again. I'll not hear the sound of her voice, ever again.*

She laughed a little when he lifted her. It was a delighted, heartbreaking little trill, and he marveled that she could find joy despite everything she faced. Shouldn't she be jerking from him and stomping through the trees, shouting *thank you for absolutely no help at all*?

When she had her footing, he tipped his head

down, unable to resist a final look at her pretty face. His hands gripped her waist. He could smell her. The wind tussled her hair. Her smile went a little off. Her lips were turned up, but her eyes grew very bright. She blinked. She crinkled her nose.

"Sorry," she whispered, lowering her eyes. When she looked up again, her eyelashes were wet. She was crying.

Gabriel frowned and tugged off his gloves. "What's happened? Why are you crying?"

"May I ask you a different sort of question? Before I go?"

"Alright." His heart was pounding.

"My letters," she said. "Why did you keep them? All this time, from France to the school, from the fire to your camp?"

"Oh," he said. It was the last thing he'd expected. He wasn't sure how to answer. "Will you stop crying if I tell you?"

"I'm not crying."

He smiled. He took a deep breath. "I cannot say why I kept them except . . . I wanted them? For one thing, I suppose I felt duty bound. Believe it or not, but I was quite invested in being a prince, once upon a time. And my father had compelled me to carry on like a member of the royal family, even in exile. I was too young to know how to embody that, except to remember my commitments. And the most outstanding commitment in my life was my betrothal to you.

"Secondly, I was fond of you, Lady Ryan." He smiled, thinking of the boy he'd been. "We'd met twice, and on both occasions, I'd been impressed at how *not-awful* you were. Even though you were a girl.

And English. Our correspondence began, and your letters . . . in a way . . . delighted me." He gave a shrug. "When the time came for me to escape the mobs, I simply grabbed them up. And I haven't been able to let them go."

Now she let out a little whimper and dropped her face into her hands.

"You're still crying," he observed.

"Because I will miss you," she said simply, looking up. "And because our history has broken my heart. Ignore me. Please."

"Don't, Ryan. Please."

"Will you kiss me once more, Gabriel?" she whispered.

"What?"

"I would not ask except . . . what could it possibly matter now, if we mean to say goodbye?"

"You're killing me."

"If we part ways, I needn't worry about how I may seem, or how out-of-character I may behave, how bold or how brazen. It won't matter, will it, after you've gone?"

"You cannot want this," he whispered, his heart racing. He'd felt heavy and tired, revealing these truths to her. Now his body lurched to life.

She bit her lip. "Oh yes. Yes, I do want it."

He should've challenged this; he should've asked her again if she was certain. He should've bowed over her hand, kissed her knuckles, and stalked to his horse.

Instead, he locked his mouth over hers with a force so strong, she tipped backward. He caught her with a hand between her shoulders and another behind her neck and leaned over her, holding her at a slant. True to her request, she didn't pull away, she clung to his biceps, pinning herself to him and kissing him as if she would perish if she did not.

Gabriel showed no restraint. He kissed her until he had no breath. When, finally, he raised his head to gasp for air, Ryan scrambled forward, burying her face in his neck, nuzzling his beard, breathing him in.

Gabriel returned for more, pulling her upright and walking her backward. He hustled them beyond Fleur, beyond Anton, and backed her into a fat sycamore. He pressed her against the peeling bark and aligned his body against her, using the leverage of the tree to press against her, kissing her all the while. With one hand, he felt his way down her side and cupped her bottom, tilting her hips into his need. With the other, he gripped the back of her neck, raising her face up to him.

"*Ryan*," he breathed, coming up again for air.

"I am here," she whispered, gathering the lapel of his coat in greedy hands.

He glanced down. Her eyes were closed, her mouth parted, her face flushed. He'd never seen anything as beautiful. He had no idea how he'd managed the restraint not to make love to her last night. He wanted to hear her laugh, he wanted to bask in her attention, he wanted to earn her forgiveness, he wanted *her*.

"I'm sorry," he said simply. She'd come here offering many of these things, possibly all of them, and he'd refused them.

She didn't answer. She kissed him again. She kissed deeply and frantically, and he wondered if she felt the same urgency he felt; the desperation and hunger? He was out of words for his desire. She was like a missing piece of himself he'd not known he'd been searching for his whole life.

And then, without warning, she turned her head to the side, she gasped in and out, and she allowed her hands to fall from his coat.

Gabriel pulled back, studying her, memorizing her. Her tears had stopped. She was neither laughing nor frowning. She was simply looking through the trees in the direction of the clearing.

Releasing her felt like hollowing out a piece of his chest with a knife. He reminded himself that she was only doing what he'd asked. It was what he wanted and what he didn't, in the same terrible moment.

"Do you have the letter?" she asked, still breathing hard.

"What?"

"The letter, Gabriel. For your sister Princess Elise."

With a final squeeze of her hips, he let her go. He took a step back. His hat had fallen and he stooped to get it. He wiped his mouth. "Yes. I have it. And the money. Pay for the horse stolen by Meade. Hire a carriage to take you to Mayapple. Do you remember the way to the high street? Shall I tell you again?"

She shook her head and rolled off the tree. She staggered a little, smoothing her cloak over her shoulders.

"Can you manage?"

"Yes. I can manage."

"Here," he said, handing her the packet of money and the letter.

She nodded and extended a trembling hand.

"Goodbye, Gabriel," she said, taking two steps back.
Wait, he thought. *Not* yet. *Not* this *second*. *Not*—
But she took another step. And another step. And
then was walking away, winding through the trees.
She slid a hand along the neck of the mare when she
passed. She did not look back.

CHAPTER FIFTEEN

IN FLASHES, RYAN became aware of Gabriel following her. It took no effort to see him through the trees, keeping pace as she walked to Pewsey. She looked three times—one long, hard, disbelieving look, and then two more quick assurances—and then forced herself to face forward. Well. If this constituted "keeping hidden," he was failing at it. She hoped he knew. She also hoped he would walk into a tree. Or fall into a bog. Or leave the cover of the trees and return to her.

Good lord, she was wretched. Tears dropped down her cheeks; her throat was tied into a tight knot, and she struggled to breathe without hitching her breath. She swiped at the tears in frustration. What a sight she was for village gossips; a stranger, trudging up the high street with no hat and a filthy dress, silently weeping.

And why? It wasn't because he wouldn't help her—oh no. Ryan barely thought of her family crisis in the least. (And wasn't that selfish and shortsighted?) She cried because the jagged edges of her fractured heart hurt so much.

She'd wanted him. Of all the things she'd not expected when she'd ventured into the forest to seek him

out, who could've guessed that she might actually enjoy his company? Or be fascinated by him, and his
horses, and his camp, and all he'd overcome? Who
could have guessed she'd be attracted to him?

She sniffed and swiped away more tears and
glanced to the trees. There he was, thirty yards away,
riding the stallion and pulling the mare on a lead,
watching her. She hadn't lied to him; she understood
why he could not help her. He was correct not to leave
the forest if it wasn't safe.

So why then is he following me?

The great irony was, he hadn't seemed to *reject* her.
If the kiss against the tree was a rejection, then she
knew far less about men than she'd thought. In fact,
he'd seemed to *want* her. Against the tree. And at the
hitching post. And in his bed last night.

And wasn't this a small personal triumph—a man
wanting her? Naturally when a man finally wanted
her, he would be a prince. And also naturally, he
would refuse to show his face in public or claim his
title—or claim her.

So, there you have it, she thought bitterly. What
more could she do but indulge in a watery cry on her
long walk back to the inn? While he stalked her but
would not *have* her?

Ten minutes later, eyes puffy, throat still tight, she
was forced to placate her maid Agnes. Ryan's long absence had traumatized the girl, and it took two minutes of imploring to convince her to open the door to
their room at the inn.

"*My lady!*" the maid exclaimed, horrified at the
sight of her.

"It's me, Agnes." Ryan sighed, repeating what she'd

said fifty times in the hallway. "Will you let me inside, please?"

"Oh, Lady Ryan, I was sick with worry," Agnes exclaimed. She'd opened the door only enough to grab Ryan by the wrist. Agnes pulled her through and slammed it behind her, bolting it and spinning round.

"My lady, what's happened?" said the maid on a tearful breath. "You didn't return, and then it was midnight, and then it was morning—and I didn't know what to do. I was certain you'd been devoured by wolves. But were you attacked and ravaged and left for dead?"

Ryan bit her lip, thinking how—for once—Agnes's wild imagination had lit upon two out of three.

"I was not left for dead," Ryan told her, "but I did have a rough go of it in the . . . er, forest. Also, I've located the prince, if you can believe it. However, he is unable to help us. Sadly."

"Located the prince?!" whispered Agnes, her hands up, fingers spread, as if Ryan might pull a prince from her cloak and toss him on the rug.

"Yes. But, he cannot leave the forest for reasons of personal safety. However, his sister Princess Elise d'Orleans—now a *Mrs. Crewes*—lives in a manor house nearby, and he has bid us to call on her to ask for advice and help."

"*A princess* . . ." marveled Agnes. The maid was too young to have met the original Orleans clan, and she only recently learned that her mistress had been promised to a prince. Every mention of French royalty sent Agnes into the throes of disbelief and anxiety and wonder.

"Yes, a princess; but Agnes, we must move quickly.

I am loathe to remain in Wiltshire longer than necessary. Can you help me get out of these clothes and redress my hair? If Princess Elise cannot help us, we must return to London and seek out the counsel of lawyers to make sense of the old betrothal. First thing's first. We'll leave the inn and travel by carriage to the estate of Gabriel's sister—"

The maid's hands went still as she peeled back the damp cloak. "*Gabriel?*" the girl repeated.

Too late, Ryan realized her error. "Gabriel," Ryan clarified, "the Prince d'Orleans. He . . . he prefers informal address now that—well, he prefers informal address. He does not carry on as a prince in his work with horses. In the forest. Obviously."

AN HOUR LATER, washed and wearing a clean dress, Ryan sat across from Agnes in the hired carriage.

"This estate is called Mayapple," Ryan told the maid. "Prince Gabriel said the driver would know it, and so he does. I've asked the man to wait after I've knocked, because I'm not certain Princess Elise will have time to receive me. We're dropping in with no invitation. You'll have to wait in the carriage, I'm afraid. Do you mind? You must make certain the driver doesn't pull away before I've managed to dash off a note, at the very least."

"Oh yes, my lady, I prefer it," assured Agnes. Ryan had given her a very cursory overview, complete with half-truths and flat-out lies, about meeting Gabriel in the forest. The maid was respectful enough to withhold judgment, but it was clear she was highly suspicious of all this business with a French fiancé; and a deep, dark wood; and horse training; and calling on princesses with no invitation. It took no cajoling to convince Agnes to watch from the safe distance of the carriage.

Ryan turned to stare out the window, idly patting Gabriel's letter in her pocket. He'd not bothered to seal it, and she was tempted to take a peek—if for nothing else, to read how he'd described Ryan's situation. But of course Ryan could not read his private correspondence; she'd already rifled through his drawers and found her letters.

Fingering the parchment again, she forced herself to strategize the best way to describe Maurice. In hindsight, she'd blurted out too much, too quickly when she'd explained him to Gabriel. No matter how gracious or compassionate Princess Elise revealed herself to be, given the choice, she'd probably rather *not* have Ryan's problems introduced into her life.

Outside the window, the deep greens of late summer cast the cloudy morning in a dark, almost pickled light. Mainland England was so very green compared to the brown, earthy crags and cliffs of Guernsey. Plant life was plentiful in the Channel Islands of course; but not like the mainland, with its grassy meadows, dense trees, and the mosses and ferns that furred over rocks and stone walls. She hadn't realized there were quite so many shades of—

Ryan stopped, midthought, and squinted at a decidedly un-green movement in the trees. But was it—?

She leaned closer to the window, using her glove to clear away a smudge.

Oh my God.

There was a rider keeping pace with the carriage. She fell back against the seat. She blinked, trying to interpret what she saw. But it made no sense. She raised up to look again.

Yes, yes, there he was *again.*

Someone was *riding his stallion* in the forest that bordered the road. Flanking the carriage at a distance of about thirty yards, deep in the trees.

Gabriel.

The sight of him—and there was no doubt it was him, his size and posture on horseback were unmistakable—crashed into Ryan like a wave. She grabbed hold of the seat, blinking into the dimness of the carriage.

But what did he mean? They'd said goodbye. Ryan was no expert, but surely their *particular* goodbye— with the tree and the heavy breathing—promised the finality of battlefields and deathbeds and walking the plank.

And yet, here he was.

Ryan sat very straight against the seat, her body pinned back by the shock of seeing him.

"Are you quite well, my lady?" asked Agnes, eyeing the window cautiously.

"Yes," said Ryan carefully. "Perfectly well. I merely—I saw something that reminded me of home."

"Of Winscombe?" asked the maid. Agnes had been very vocal about the flatness and muddiness of mainland England, about the endless buildings and crowded streets and the sooty, airless smell. So far, she had not been impressed.

"It was nothing," said Ryan, "I was taken by surprise, that's all."

Ryan fought the urge to look again; Agnes existed in a constant state of alarm. Ryan need not heap on more erratic behavior. And what was solved by watching him keep pace with the carriage? What if she looked again and he was gone?

It means nothing, it means nothing, it means nothing, she chanted in her head, even as she pretended to stretch forward and *lean*. Just as she broached the window, the carriage turned from the main road onto a long drive.

"Oh, perhaps we've arrived," Ryan said, and pressed her face to the window again. The small road led away from the forest, positioning the tree line behind them.

"But are you certain you're alright, my lady?" Agnes asked.

"Yes," she said. "Fit as a fiddle. Forgive me, Agnes, I'm simply . . ." she turned away from the window ". . . I suppose I'm just nervous to drop in on a royal princess unannounced. How do I look?"

"You look . . ." Agnes studied her with a wary expression ". . . well, you're rather flushed, to be honest, my lady. But are you overwarm?"

Ryan shook her head, raising her hands to her cheeks. She felt nothing through her gloves—in fact, all feeling seemed to have left her body. Or was it that she felt everything? She was hot, and cold, and dizzy, and sitting perfectly still in the center of this road while the world spun around her.

Why had he come?

"Did the luncheon disagree with you?" Agnes wondered, and Ryan was forced to pay attention. My God, how ill did she look?

"Luncheon was perfectly suitable. It's merely nerves, as I said. Oh look, here we are."

The carriage slowed, and Ryan used this as an excuse to dive to the window. Gabriel was nowhere to be seen. They'd reached the main house and the tree line was some hundred yards away, at the edge of manicured parkland. He was gone. Naturally. Or perhaps she'd imagined the whole thing. Ryan took a deep breath and forced her brain to the matter at hand.

The centerpiece of Mayapple was a charming manor house in the Palladian style. The smooth stone shone gold and gray in the midday sun. There was a small rise of steps and a little stoop and a giant front door. Ryan swallowed. She must pull together some little speech that would introduce herself and her problem without sounding deranged. She must mount the steps and knock on the door. She must save her family and not think about Gabriel Rein/Gabriel d'Orleans, riding with breathtaking balance and grace through the wood beside her carriage.

"Right," she said again to Agnes. "Here we are. If the family are at home and have time for us, I'll send for you. If not, I'll turn round and we'll negotiate with the driver about travel to London. You're sure you don't mind the carriage? Are you comfortable, Agnes?"

"Oh yes, I'm very comfortable, my lady. But are you certain you're—"

"Fine, fine, everything is completely . . ." a deep breath ". . . fine." She gathered her skirts and reached through the open door for the driver's outstretched hand.

"If you are unwell, we can always depart for London now and *write* to these princesses or whomever they are?" Agnes called after her.

Ryan gave her a reassuring wave and spoke briefly

to the driver about waiting. After that, she raised her chin, took up her skirts, and strode across the gravel drive to the steps. At first glance, the house appeared smaller than Winscombe, but the closer she got, the grander it seemed. Winscombe was large but crooked and slumped and bleached ashy by sea winds and rain. This house was pristine and immaculate—a small palace, if Ryan was being honest.

And good for you, Princess Elise, Ryan thought. To have a lovely home after all she'd been through.

Ryan reached into her pocket and felt for Gabriel's letter. She patted the bun at the back of her head. She adjusted her hat. She'd worn her pale green dress—not her favorite, but it was a nice dress, just the same, not to mention her only remaining garment after ruining the blue traveling suit. The green dress had been her mother's, remade in a more modern style. Say what you would about Agnes, but she was an excellent seamstress and took loving care of Ryan's wardrobe.

Do not look, Ryan thought, trying to slice through the nonsense in her brain. *Don't look for him; don't expect him; do not think of him.* The trees were a green wall in the hazy distance. If he was there (a very significant "if"), he would not leave that wall. It was pointless to look.

And then Ryan was at the front door, and she felt so charged with jittery energy that she did not hesitate, she rapped on the door three times, very quickly.

After the knock, silence. No footsteps from within. No movement at the nearby window.

Tightening her gloves, Ryan reached up to knock a second time. Before her knuckle made contact with the wood, the door was wrenched open.

"Hello," said a woman in a pretty lavender dress with dark hair and hazel eyes. In her arms, she held a baby—a girl—gnawing toothlessly a crust of bread, crumbs dribbling down the front of her dress.

The woman looked informal—no hat, no gloves, hair loose—and a little harried, but very beautiful. And not unkind. She smiled expectantly at Ryan.

"Can I help you?" She hitched the baby higher on her hip.

"Sorry, Mrs. Crewes!" came a man's voice behind. "You are too quick for me. Again."

"Noelle was making a run for the door, Wallace," the woman said over her shoulder. "It's no problem. I can manage."

A resentful-looking butler appeared behind her. Now all three of them—the pretty woman, the butler, and the baby—stared at Ryan. After a beat, the baby held the bread out. "Bah!" she said, a wordless offering.

"Hello," Ryan began.

The trio in the doorway considered her.

"Forgive my calling unannounced," she continued. "My name is Lady Marianne Daventry, and I am from the island of Guernsey." Another swallow. "In the English Channel."

Ryan blinked. Of course they would know Guernsey. Everyone knew Guernsey, didn't they? She was not accustomed to formal introductions—she rarely met someone she'd not known her entire life. In hindsight, perhaps it'd been best that she'd met Gabriel in the midst of a highway ambush.

She took a breath and smiled. The baby made the offering noise again and thrust out the bread.

"No, no darling, the bread is for you to eat," said the woman. "Our visitor does not want it." She looked again to Ryan.

"I—" began Ryan. She stopped and reconsidered. "That is . . . *my family*." Another pause. "*I've* come in search of Mrs. Killian Crewes, the former Princess Elise d'Orleans? Of France?"

"I am Mrs. Killian Crewes," said the woman, her voice a degree more cautious.

"Shall I fetch Mr. Crewes, Mrs. Crewes?" asked the butler.

Mrs. Crewes made a dismissive gesture, not taking her eyes from Ryan.

"How do you do," said Ryan, bowing slightly. "Again, I'm so sorry to drop in on you with no warning, but I've come to mainland England on business pertaining to my family—and yours, that is, your childhood family—and I first sought out your brother, Prince Gabriel d'Orleans . . ."

Mrs. Crewes's expression turned from cautious to wide-eyed. Her pallor went white. Slowly, she began to slide the baby down her hip. The child resisted, grabbing her mother's sleeve and holding on. While Ryan watched, the child clung to her mother's side, chewing, as Mrs. Crewes reached for the door facing. Ryan was just about to reach for the baby when Mrs. Crewes hoisted her up again. With her free hand, she braced against the door.

"I beg your pardon?" rasped Mrs. Crewes.

"I'll just go fetch Mr. Crewes, shall I?" the butler said. He looked to the baby, made an expression of distaste, and then hurried away.

"Forgive me," Ryan said, "I've no wish to alarm or

distress you—and in fact nothing is amiss . . . well, nothing is immediately amiss . . . it's just that I've come seeking . . . well, seeking advice. By a wild turn of luck, I was able to locate—"

Before Ryan could finish, a pack of dogs—one, two, three, four . . . well, there must have been *six* of them—pushed past Mrs. Crewes and the baby and bounded onto the stoop, tails wagging, noses probing, tongues hanging.

Fear coursed through Ryan and she sucked in a breath. She clutched her chest and skittered back, falling against the house.

Her distress and retreat only intrigued the animals and they followed her, forming a panting half circle at her skirts. Immediately, the wound on her leg began to throb. She looked from one animal to the next, trying to remind herself that she needn't be afraid of every dog. But one of these dogs, she noticed, looked exactly like the breed favored by Maurice. She locked eyes with it and began to breathe quickly in and out, in and out. She looked right and left, wondering how she might evade them. Could she outrun them? *All* of them? She let out a whimpering noise.

"Oh, sorry, sorry, sorry," Mrs. Crewes said, pushing off the door and wading into the dogs, reaching for collars. She swung the baby from her hip and settled her on the stoop. The animals seemed delighted by this game—the terrified caller, the frantic host, the laughing baby on the floor who waved delicious bread. The pack of them shifted and spun, jumping and sniffing. They were like eels in a tidepool, everywhere at once, impossible to catch.

"Marie? Sofie?" Mrs. Crewes called, shouting back through the door. *"Bartholomew!*

"They won't harm you," Mrs. Crewes assured Ryan. "These are my nephew's dogs. He's on break from school and insists on transporting them from his own house to mine so he might not miss a moment in their company. And yet—where is he? Nowhere to be seen, while the dogs are omnipresent. My husband will speak to him. We forget how terribly behaved they are because our small daughters maintain their own version of unrelenting chaos."

With no warning, one of the dogs, the biggest one—the one who looked like Maurice's dog—began to bark loudly.

"Oh God, that one's called—? Oh I can't remember," muttered Mrs. Crewes, reaching for the dog. "Quiet, you worthless hound."

Ryan was just about to throw herself from the stoop. It was lofty—twenty steps high, at least—but she could jump off the side and crash into the flowerbed. She'd break a shrub or two, but at least she'd escape the dogs. She *needed* to escape the dogs.

"Stand. Down."

A firm voice rang out, freezing the dogs where they stood. Ryan froze, too, her foot dangling over the edge of the stoop.

Mrs. Crewes clutched the scruff of two different dogs but her head snapped up. Even the baby went still.

Gabriel.

He appeared from nowhere, clipping up the steps and positioning himself between Ryan and the dogs. When he blocked her, he reached behind and grabbed her waist, nudging her from the edge of the stoop.

"Careful," he said to the animals, "careful." Mesmerized, the dogs went immediately quiet and still.

"She has a fear of dogs," he said to Mrs. Crewes.

There was a long, heavy pause. Ryan craned to see around Gabriel's shoulder.

Mrs. Crewes was staring at her brother with an expression of such shock and disbelief and joy, Ryan's throat cinched.

"Gabriel?" whispered Mrs. Crewes.

"Bah!" said the baby on the stoop, holding out her bread to Gabriel.

One of the smaller dogs padded over and began to eat from the child's hand.

But now another man was there. He popped through the doorway, the butler on his heels, his face creased with concern.

"What happened?" He glared at Gabriel. "Who the devil are you?"

He glanced at the baby on the floor; she'd tipped to her side and begun crawling in his direction. "Noelle—?"

"Forgive me," interjected Ryan, "but I do believe Mrs. Crewes is about to—"

And then Mrs. Crewes made a small noise and collapsed into a faint.

"Bloody—" The man in the doorway lunged forward just in time and scooped her up. Six dogs crowded around him, pressing noses into her limp form.

"Bartholomew!" the man bellowed before he bent down to press a kiss to the top of her head.

CHAPTER SIXTEEN

GABRIEL STOOD IN the midst of utter chaos, keeping the dogs off of Ryan. His sister had fainted at the sight of him. One man caught her up; another recoiled against the wall. Two small girls dressed in dueling shades of pink spilled from the house, jabbering and spinning, reigniting the dogs.

Gabriel stared down at the two children, the baby, his sister (unconscious), the man holding her (suspicious), at Lady Ryan, and the second man on the wall, and all six of the dogs. It was more people than Gabriel had encountered altogether in five years.

His sister's eyes fluttered open and she began squirming in the man's arms. "I'm alright," she proclaimed. "I'm alright, I'm alright. Killian, *I'm all right*. But can you put me down?"

The children were momentarily silenced by her protestations—but only just. Now they bobbed up and down, shouting, *"Maman!"* and reaching small hands to her skirts. "Put her down, Papa!" the girls ordered, "Put her down!"

Slowly, carefully, the man—she'd called him Killian, so he must be her husband—settled Elise on her feet. She held to him and searched every face until she locked eyes with Gabriel. In a breathless, tear-choked voice, she whispered his name.

Gabriel did not answer; it hadn't seemed like a question. Also, he had no words. The mere sight of her knocked him backward as squarely as a punch. He landed dizzyingly in the past. Her eyes were so familiar; her expressions exactly as he remembered. Her posture was the same, and the set of her chin. She was the most important face of his boyhood—but now a grown woman. She looked so very much like their mother. She was somehow . . . *shorter*? That couldn't be right, she wouldn't have shrunk. No, of course not, he'd grown.

Elise—living, breathing, *tearful* Elise. Adult Elise—with three children who referred to her as *Maman*. The sight of her flipped him forward and backward in time, like thumbing through the pages of a book. Only, the middle had been torn away. How could he make sense of their story if the intervening years were lost?

Also how must *he* appear to *her*? He was a man now, obviously; with a face and bearing probably very much like their father's—if their father had been bearded and disheveled and dressed like a common woodsman.

"I'm sorry for the shock," he finally said. The words came out in French.

"No apologies," Elise whispered also in French. She wiped away a tear.

Behind him, Lady Ryan pressed a gentle hand to his back. He leaned into the pressure. The warm imprint staked him to earth as memories streaked through his mind. He saw the swing in the garden at the Palace Royale, Elise pushing him too high while their nursemaid begged them to stop. He saw the two of them diving into the water at their seaside villa in Nice, coming up with handfuls of perfectly round stones, swimming to the beach and making a nest of their pretend eggs. He saw the darkness and fear of the prison and bright sun through the bars of the executioner's wagon. He wasn't sure he could've borne the memories if Ryan hadn't been there with a firm hand to his back: It was imprudent to rely on her, he knew. He took a step to the side. He wasn't a child or an invalid, and she need not protect him. But he didn't feel protected, he felt calmed. He pulled off his hat, remembered his crude haircut, and crammed it back on his head.

"Killian," Elise was telling her husband, "*this* is my brother. But can you believe it? My brother. *Here*. He's come. After all of this time." She laughed, an elated, tear-choked sound.

One of her daughters clung to her skirts and the other pressed against her, hands raised. Behind them, the baby on the stoop began to cry.

Elise seemed not to notice any of it; her gaze was locked on Gabriel. She took a step forward and he braced, unprepared to be touched. Sweat cooled the back of his neck; his throat was dry. She touched the sleeve of his coat and Gabriel looked down, staring at her small, clean hand on the stiff mud-streaked fabric. He thought of the clothes beneath the coat; simple, rustic, mended. He thought of his filthy boots. He tried to conjure up something to say.

The baby's cries grew louder and Killian Crewes scooped her from the floor. "Everyone on this stoop . . ." Killian Crewes announced, "who is the height of my elbow or *shorter*, will now *retreat* to the nursery, select any book, and read it for the length of one hour."

"But *Papa*, we cannot yet read!" reminded one of the girls, jumping up and down.

"How will we know when an hour has gone?" said the other girl. "We cannot tell time!"

"Where is Nanny?" He hitched the baby on his hip.

"Nanny requires ten minutes of total silence and total stillness to lie down in a dark, cool place," recited the first girl.

Killian Crewes made a growling noise and narrowed his eyes on the bouncing girls. "Marie—take Noelle, will you? You're big enough to hold her, surely."

"Oh yes, Papa!" said the girl called Marie, reaching skinny arms and tiny hands for the baby.

"Brilliant." Killian deposited the baby with her sister. The child was too heavy—more than half the weight of the girl herself—and Marie staggered under the burden. The baby sensed the instability and let out a protesting screech.

"Quiet, Noelle," lectured Marie. "We must choose a book and learn to read for one hour."

These are my nieces, Gabriel thought. *I am in possession of nieces.*

He'd known he was an uncle from Elise's letters; but seeing the girls in life affected him in a different way than reading about them. They were beautiful. Their names were French. They were not afraid of him or of dogs or of their tall, imposing father. They appeared fearless. Beautiful and tireless and fearless.

Elise paid them no mind; she'd not taken her eyes

from his face. Tears rolled down her cheeks. Gabriel tried to hold her gaze, but he found himself unable. The force of her attention seemed to rip open something inside him, something bound, and creased, and sealed with wax. He didn't like it—not the openness, nor the bareness of it. He felt unprotected, exposed, vulnerable.

"Hallo!"

And now a shout rose above the chatter of the children. Gabriel tensed. He wasn't accustomed to shouted greetings. He wasn't accustomed to newcomers spilling from doors or around corners.

The shout came from a youth—aged anywhere from sixteen to twenty. The boy came around the side of the house with a fishing pole and pail. The dogs sprang from the stoop and raced to him, leaping and barking. He was a tall boy, broad shouldered, with black hair and a broad grin.

"Bartholomew, thank God," snapped Killian. "Call off your mongrels, we've guests and they've been terrorized by your unruly wolfpack."

"Sorry, Killian!" called the boy. He whistled to the dogs and made a gesture with his hands. The animals bolted around the side of the house. He dropped his pole and pail.

"What's happened?" the boy asked, bounding up the steps. "Why is everyone on the stoop?"

"Can you take Noelle?" asked Killian.

"*Hello, you . . .*" the boy sang to the baby, taking her from Marie and swinging her into his arms. He turned to Gabriel and Lady Ryan. "Are you the terrorized guests? My apologies about the dogs. Truly. I snuck away to . . ." and now he pantomimed casting a line with his free hand. "The dogs love the water but frighten the fish. I've better luck if I leave them."

Gabriel stared at him, trying to place a young man among the cast of family members in his sister's letters. The boy had positioned the baby facedown over an arm, like a footman might drape a napkin. She gnawed blithely on his wrist. The two girls leaned against him and strained arms upward, as if he might carry all three of them. They spoke over each other, imploring him to take them fishing.

"The dogs must be restricted to the stables, honestly," Killian was telling him. "We've enough chaos. For now, take the girls inside, will you? Seek out Nanny and tell her to contain them in the nursery until I come for them. Tell her also that I wish to speak to her at her earliest convenience."

"No, Killian, you mustn't threaten Nanny," Elise said distractedly, casting a glance over her shoulder.

"Sorry again about the dogs," the boy volunteered. "I'm Bartholomew by the way. If you're thinking of how long to stay, please do not consider the threat of my dogs. Truly—banish all thoughts of them from your mind. You'll not see them again."

Gabriel stared at him. He'd not thought of how long he might stay; he'd no intention of staying any time at all. He'd only come to protect Lady Ryan. This wasn't a visit, it was a . . . a chance meeting.

"Pleasure to make your acquaintance," Lady Ryan called from behind him. "The dogs were no bother. Please don't think of it again."

"Come on then, girls," Bartholomew said, "you're to be 'contained,' did you hear your Papa?" He limped inside, holding the baby on his arm, dangling Marie from the opposite wrist, and dragging the third girl on his boot. When he passed the frowning butler cowering against the wall, he called, "Hello, Wallace!"

"My nephew is to blame for the dogs," Killian Crewes said with a sigh, "but the children are not so easily explained. Elise, we must find a replacement nanny. Also, we cannot remain on the stoop all day. What is your vision for entertaining the guests?"

"I've no vision for it," said Elise, not taking her eyes from Gabriel's. She was shaking her head back and forth.

RYAN FELT GABRIEL's body go rigid. He did not, she was certain, wish to *go inside*. He would not chatter away with the sister he'd not seen in fifteen years—not with her dazed and fainting and weeping over him.

"Would it be possible," Ryan cut in, "for us to become more acquainted in your garden?"

Mr. and Mrs. Crewes turned to consider her.

"Anywhere outside would be lovely, actually. If it wouldn't be too much bother."

Their stare endured. Finally, Mr. Crewes said, "Forgive me, but you are—?"

"Oh sorry," Ryan said. "I am Lady Marianne Daventry. Of Winscombe. In Guernsey."

"How do you do?" he said cautiously. "And you're acquainted to Elise's brother . . . how?"

"Right. That. How can I explain it? Well, I was once *betrothed* to, er, Prince Gabriel? That is, I still am, or so I'm told. We were betrothed as children. By our fathers. So I'm hesitant to say I *know* him, more like I know *of* him? Or rather, I *knew* of him?"

"Oh, *now* I remember," exclaimed Mrs. Crewes. "Yes,

yes, *yes*. You're the Earl of Amhurst's eldest daughter. From *Guernsey. Lady Marianne*—I completely remember." She clapped her hands to her cheeks, smiling back and forth between the two of them.

"I am, in fact," said Ryan. "All grown up, I suppose. And I'm called Lady Ryan—or simply Ryan, as is my preference. We do not stand on ceremony at Winscombe."

"But we visited Winscombe several times as children," enthused Mrs. Crewes. "I actually loved our time there because I'm so very fond of sea bathing. There's a little trail down the cliff to the beach on your estate, is there not?"

"Yes. Daybreak Walk, we call it," said Ryan, smiling. "What a very good memory you have. It's a delight to see you again, Highness—after everything that's happened."

"Killian," said Mrs. Crewes, spinning to her husband, "Lady Marianne's father was a very dear friend of our papa's. Their home was but a short sail from the French port of St. Malo, which is a port on d'Orleans lands. Our families have a long history as neighbors. And our fathers arranged for Gabriel and Lady Marianne to marry when they came of age. It was to be an exchange of property, mingled fortunes, that sort of thing. In all that's happened, I'd forgotten about the betrothal."

"Oh yes, I can see how that might slip one's mind. And I should like to hear more, truly—but *on the topic* of abandoning this stoop . . ." Killian prodded. "Perhaps Lady Ryan's suggestion of tea in the garden would be the thing? Can we settle on that for the moment?"

Ryan glanced at Gabriel, hoping to covertly gauge his level of comfort with the notion of a garden tea.

"But have the two of you reunited?" asked Mrs. Crewes, looking back and forth between Gabriel and Ryan. "But of course you have. If not, how would Lady Ryan find us? Although—how did Lady Ryan find *Gabriel*? I don't understand." She laughed a little, clearly unsettled and confused and delighted all at once.

"I'm going to make a command decision," cut in Mr. Crewes. "We'll ask Wallace to have tea brought to the garden. In the meantime, I wonder if you, Lady Ryan, and my wife might discuss your unlikely journey from Guernsey to Wiltshire. Also, perhaps the two of you could oversee staff as they set things up in the garden? While you manage this, *I'll* avail myself of Prince Gabriel. His expertise with horses precedes him, and I have a mare about to foal. I'm deuced worried about her."

"A mare about to foal?" repeated Mrs. Crewes, spinning to him. "You can't mean to take him to the *stables*, Killian? *Now*? No. He's only just—"

"I should be happy to look in on the mare," Gabriel cut in, descending the first step of the stoop.

Ryan exhaled in relief. Mr. Crewes understood.

"I've given everyone quite a shock, I know," Ryan interjected, "turning up with no warning. I can try to explain. If Mrs. Crewes will—"

"Please call me Elise," Elise said, waving a hand. She wasn't looking at her; she stared only at her brother.

"The stables are in the back," Mr. Crewes said lightly, leading Gabriel down the steps.

Gabriel looked again to Ryan and she nodded. *Yes. Go. Look at the horse.*

And then they were gone, disappearing around the corner of the house.

Elise Crewes watched them go like she was watching an heirloom burn in a fire.

"Will he stay?" asked Elise Crewes softly.

Ryan, of course, had no idea if he would stay, or vanish, or become the king of France. She'd thought she'd never see him again, and now here he was.

"Probably?" Ryan guessed.

"But should I go with them?"

It wasn't Ryan's nature to stride into situations and tell people where *not* to go, but it *was* her nature to solve problems. The problem here seemed to want a very slow pace and room for everyone to come accustomed to everyone else.

"Perhaps a more pressing task," Ryan suggested, "might be to oversee the laying of the tea? The less formal, the better, I think? And with few distractions?"

"Yes, alright. I understand," Elise said. She gathered up her skirts and then stopped. "But how well *do* you know my brother, Lady Ryan?"

"I only met him yesterday. If you can believe it."

"Yesterday?"

"Well, when we were children—and then yesterday."

"*You* must stay on with us, I hope you know," she said, walking again. "As long as you are able. You will be our guest."

"Thank you. I find myself too desperate to refuse your offer."

"Desperate?" asked Elise.

"Yes, well, there's more to the story than simply

the old betrothal. I've come because of a conflict of interest with your cousin? A man called Maurice? But first . . ." and now she cleared her throat ". . . if I'm meant to stay, can I trouble you to admit my maid into your servants' quarters? I've left her cooling her heels in the carriage, and she becomes agitated in small spaces."

CHAPTER SEVENTEEN

THE STABLES AT Mayapple were thoughtfully designed and outfitted with every modernization. No expense had been spared. Gabriel had barely noticed, following his brother-in-law blindly around the paddock, grateful to be away from the house. But then he entered the barn, and he stopped short. A row of horses, their coats healthy and eyes alert, studied him from large stalls. On the opposite wall, tack and feed were organized like instruments in a surgeon's theater. The floor of the aisle had been raked and the straw lining each stall appeared fresh. Gabriel drifted to the horse in the first stall, a rose-gray gelding, and fingered his well-brushed mane.

"Look at you," he mumbled to the horse, running a hand over the light speckling on his coat.

"Elise has little interest in horses in general, but she's intrigued by exotic coloring. I've just bought a leopard stallion from America. The pregnant mare is champagne."

Gabriel walked by every animal, slowly perusing the stalls. When he'd seen and touched and whispered to each horse, Killian led him to the pregnant mare.

She ambled about a larger pen near the washing yard, belly heavy but eyes calm.

"My first attempt at breeding," Killian told him. "Both sire and dam belong to us here at Mayapple. Gratifying to be sure, but distressing if there's some complication. I'm sailing with no compass and the veterinarian in Marlborough is overwhelmed. He serves all of Middlesex and half of Wiltshire. There's no one in Pewsey. I've been reading up on foaling for months, and general opinion indicates no need for medical assistance. Even so, the larger she grows, the more nervous I become."

"May I?" asked Gabriel, eyeing the beautiful ivory horse. She seemed unbothered by Gabriel's scrutiny and did not spook when he climbed into the pen. She clomped over to sniff his pockets and nibble at his hat. It was a good sign; well-treated mares were curious and unafraid.

Touching her, whispering to her, felt like a brief respite from the overwhelming farewell to Ryan and the subsequent reunion with his sister. He ran his hands over her slick coat, tracing the muscled contours and listening to her contented whinnies and snorts. Gabriel moved around her, feeling her belly, examining a scratch on her hip. For a quarter hour, he asked questions and examined the stall where Killian intended for her to give birth. Next he followed Killian to the paddock outside to observe the sire. His brother-in-law gave him access to every corner of the stables and answered every question with no defensiveness. It occurred to Gabriel that he wouldn't mind calling on clients in their home stables if they were as open and agreeable as Killian Crewes. His guardian, Samuel, had had a strong preference for working alone, deep in the forest, with no input from owners; he'd believed house calls to private stables led to owners treating him like staff. There were also quarrels with other trainers and no distraction for the animals. Killian, in contrast, regarded Gabriel a little like an oracle. The deference was unnecessary but preferable to being treated like a stable boy.

In the end, Gabriel told his brother-in-law the mare appeared healthy and should foal in about a month. Killian swiped off his hat and hung his head in relief.

"I never fancied myself a horseman," Killian said. "I'm an amateur architect and builder. But one horse turned into two; two turned into three—and now here we are. They weren't necessarily on the agenda, but I refuse to neglect them."

The two men stood beside the paddock, elbows resting on the fence slat, watching grooms lead Killian's small herd out to graze.

"She's called Oyster—the mare," Killian said. "The girls named her. I'm aware that you rarely see horses outside of your camp and I should like to pay you for your time."

"You owe me nothing," Gabriel said. "You have delivered my sister. I am in debt to you."

"Your sister delivered herself. And me, for that matter."

"Even so."

"My gratitude then," Killian said. "I'm fortunate to have your opinion—your esteem in the horse world is legendary. In fact, it was Elise's search for you that started me on the path to building a stable. Every breeder seemed to know of the elusive healer called *Gabriel Rein*."

"I regret keeping myself so removed from Elise."

"Yes, well, I'll leave that for the two of you to discuss whenever she manages to pin you down about it. I am loathe to discuss my own complicated family, so you'll not find me hounding another poor sod."

Gabriel grunted, grateful for the reprieve. He hadn't lied, he realized, when he admitted regret for hiding from Elise. He'd kept away for too long. He'd thrown himself onto the stoop with no real plan. He meant only to stand between Ryan and the dogs. But he was glad his impulsiveness allowed him to see his sister. He wanted to meet his nieces and brother-in-law. Appointing words to this felt precipitous—like proclaiming the arrival of spring on the last day of February—but the regret was gone.

"What can you tell me about this earl's daughter?" Killian asked. *"Lady Ryan?"*

Gabriel rolled his shoulders. And now he felt the prickly discomfort of an obligation he couldn't fulfill.

"I'm not asking about your own circumstance, mind you," added Killian, "I'm an ally to you, just to be clear. But I'll be prevented from entering the house if I don't learn something about why the two of you have come."

Gabriel stared at the horses, considering how to answer. He would rather not reveal the stone-cold panic that Ryan represented to him; but God knew he needed advice.

"Lady Ryan," Gabriel said, "is being bullied into marrying the man who now holds my title. I'm presumed dead and he's the cousin who inherited. This man—Maurice is his name—is an avaricious, petty opportunist; and she has no wish to marry him. He's refused to take *no* for an answer and been rather forceful about it—violent, even. Lady Ryan and her sisters have little protection from him. Their father is alive but very ill. Their estate is large and ancient but depleted. In her desperation, she sought me out for help."

Killian made a low whistle—a sound that acknowledged the significance but also the relief that it wasn't *his* problem. For some reason, this response made Gabriel chuckle. Perhaps Gabriel didn't need advice so much as someone to curse the impossibility of it. Perhaps he needed a friend.

And so Gabriel told him; he rattled off the long, implausible story of Lady Ryan Daventry. He explained his boyhood letters to her; Maurice's designs on Winscombe and her younger sister; the dog attack; the ambush by Channing Meade and the screaming that led Gabriel to her—everything. (Everything except what had happened in the bedroom last night. Or the goodbye kiss.)

When Gabriel finished, Killian stretched back from the fence, holding himself at a slant. He shook his head. "I can't believe that a twenty-year-old betrothal would transfer from a presumed dead prince to the new prince. But God only knows. You'd not believe the convoluted arranged marriages I saw in my work at St. James's Palace. The ruling families of Europe are determined to protect the purity of royal blood above all things. It's an absolute miracle I managed to marry your princess of a sister."

"The tragedies in my life," said Gabriel, "have led me to view royal blood and purity as a soul-destroying plague to be avoided at all costs. That's dramatic, I know; but the story of my life and my sister's life reads like a gothic tragedy. I'll never exist in the realm of kings and queens, of palaces and courts, ever again. My father was executed because of it. Our family, torn apart. I've been hunted since boyhood because of my 'royal blood.' Now Lady Ryan is enduring more of the same. I stripped my life of all trace of *divine right* for a reason. I'll not be controlled by my heredity."

"Indeed," said Killian, studying him. He pulled himself upright and stared at the horses. "Well said, actually."

Gabriel grunted and kicked mud from his boot on the fence post.

"Considering this," ventured Killian, "what's to be done about Lady Ryan and your betrothal? It begs closer study, surely. I'm doubtful your cousin has a leg to stand on when it comes to modern laws, but it will take legal counsel to untangle. I've seen lesser aristocrats go ten rounds over who inherits a gamekeeper's cottage. A newly minted French prince? He will put up a fight over marriage to an earl's daughter and an estate in the Channel Islands. What do you intend?"

And here was the question of the decade. Saying the words, hearing his own name—his actual name and title—and explaining the threat forced Gabriel to acknowledge a new reality. This was *his* problem to solve. It would not be so easy as sending her to his brother-in-law and sister to sort out. Gabriel might be a recluse, but he was not without honor. He did not abandon women. He could seek out help, but ultimately, *he* should set this to rights. And perhaps he'd known this all along; perhaps that was why he'd followed Ryan every step from the outskirts of Pewsey to Mayapple. He hoped so. The evolution from ignoring her screams to standing in the stables of Mayapple had been lightning fast—but, he could now admit, it was not misplaced. This was his responsibility.

"She'll stay here as our guest, of course," said Killian, "and I urge you to remain at Mayapple until you've determined your next move. Our home is utter chaos—we cannot hide it, obviously—but take a room in these stables, if you prefer. The stablemaster and several grooms live in, but I'll instruct them to defer to you in all things—or I'll send them to the village for the length of your stay. The lodgings are modest, a room with a bed and stove for heat, a shared kitchen. But the stable will give you some relief from the mutiny of our daughters. And you can keep an eye on the mare. It would be unsporting not to mention this obvious benefit to me."

"I—thank you," said Gabriel. "It would never occur to me to remain, but it does seem ill-conceived to think I can be useful to Lady Ryan if I do not. However, I would be remiss if I did not mention that harboring me may be a threat to your young family. I've told Elise as much in my letters. I've had a price on my head since I left France. For as long as I can remember, mercenaries have hunted me. I cannot say it's safe for anyone with me on the property."

"I disagree, actually," said Killian. "The climate in France is not volatile toward remaining royalty—not at the moment; likely never again. The Revolution is long over and France is more concerned with fighting all of Europe than reseating a monarch. Make no mistake, I'd not invite you here if I thought it was unsafe."

Gabriel considered this. He didn't know Killian, but he was clearly a formidable man—not one with whom to trifle. He was no taker of careless risks. If Killian felt the threat had diminished, perhaps Gabriel was in less danger than he feared. Perhaps he could leave solitude long enough to see Ryan safe.

"There was a time when Elise felt threatened," Killian was saying, "but not since we've been married. These days, we go about our lives with no thought to it. You were right to take refuge in the forest for as long as you did. But trust me when I say that you're no longer a target. Look at this cousin of yours— Maurice. He's making no effort to conceal himself."

Gabriel thought of this. He read broadsheets from London and Paris every week. Even so, he'd not allowed himself to believe the threat had diminished. It seemed unbelievable, after all he'd suffered. And yet, Killian Crewes, a man who worked inside St. James's Palace for the king, believed there was no danger.

"I'll need to set things to rights at my camp before I commit," Gabriel finally said. "I've grooms in my employ who'll need instructions for my absence. Allow me to think on it. But I am grateful to you. Truly."

"Excellent," said Killian. "I'll tell my stablemaster. But let us face off with Elise together. She'll want you in the house. If you decide to stay with us, and if you prefer the stable, my advice to you is to stand your ground."

Gabriel nodded, thinking again of the potential of leaving Savernake Forest long enough to sort out Ryan's problem. He'd not envisioned one night out of the forest, let alone a week or a fortnight.

"I like what you've said of ruling families and royal

courts," Killian said. "I worked in St. James's for years and saw almost no value to their machinations. What a lot of vultures and vipers. And I feel terribly for this poor woman—Lady Ryan. But just to be clear, I would do anything for my wife. Her search for you has chewed a small hole through her heart, and—if possible—I would see it filled. There is no rush on this, but I cannot disguise the fact that her happiness is my top priority. In all things."

"I am grateful for your devotion to her. I will do what I can."

"As to Lady Ryan," continued Killian, "just a thought, but would you consider marrying the girl?"

Gabriel made a choking sound and covered it with a cough. "Ah—no. She'll not want to leave her sisters or her estate in Guernsey. And my life is in Savernake Forest. I've found some measure of peace that feels very precious, but it's specific to my camp."

Killian nodded thoughtfully. "Elise has told me what she suffered, fleeing France. She was fifteen at the time, but you were just a boy. I can only imagine what you've been through."

"It's not simply life in the forest. I'm unsuited to carry on as a gentleman in society. I've not been a prince since I was a child. If I'm being honest, it will be a struggle to survive your garden tea—how am I to go about as a prince? Not only am I unfit, making the effort feels destructive to my very soul. Lady Ryan is generous and versatile but she's also the daughter of an earl. She lives on a grand estate. No, I cannot marry her. Nor do I believe she wishes to marry me—or anyone. She and her sisters are settled and happy in Guernsey. She enjoys agency over her household and appears wholly self-reliant. Their family is respected by locals and their sheep earn a living. Except for this odd legal conundrum, she does not require a husband."

"Hmmm," said Killian, rubbing his jaw. "But you're fond of her?"

"Pardon?" asked Gabriel, the word came out on a choke.

"Lady Ryan—you enjoy her company? You're not ambivalent to her?"

"She is . . ." Gabriel began, searching for the correct word. ". . . I am not ambivalent. To her."

"Indeed," Killian mused. "Well, my first bit of advice—assuming you're open to my advice—is to keep your hands off. Of her. As you sort out all of this betrothal business."

Gabriel felt his cheeks burn red but he said nothing.

"Forgive my bluntness," said Killian, "I simply mean you've been very much thrown together, haven't you? An unresolved betrothal, but also new allies working against a common enemy. You've rescued her from highwaymen and have examined her various animal attacks and abrasions, et cetera, et cetera. And good for you; the world needs more knights gallant in my view. However, if you've no intention of *marrying* the girl, keep your distance, lest an already complicated situation become a total quagmire."

Gabriel cleared his throat. "I understand. There is no worry on this score. She is not at risk from me."

"Well, 'risk' may be overstating anyone's intentions—all I'm saying is, treat her like a chaste friend if you can. See if that doesn't make things easier for both of you?"

The memories of last night rose like a fog in Gabriel's mind.

"Thank you," he ground out, looking away, "for everything."

"Say nothing of it. Now, what of tea in the garden? Will my nephew eat everything before I've had so much as a crumb? Yes he will. Will his dogs be permitted on furniture and eat from the table? Also, yes. Can the London nanny my wife hired keep the children occupied before the tea goes cold? *Doubtful*."

SIX HOURS LATER, in the master bedchamber of Mayapple's family wing, Killian Crewes lay in bed beside his wife. He let out a tired sigh and drew her into the crook of his shoulder, absorbing the warm glow of her happiness. He'd spoken the truth when he'd named her as his chief priority. A side benefit of Elise's happiness was his own happiness; and a side benefit of their mutual happiness generally occurred right here in this bed.

"Is he anything like what you expected?" Killian asked, speaking into her hair. "After all this time?"

"My brother?" she clarified.

"Are there any other unaccounted 'hes' running about Mayapple at the moment?"

She chuckled. "Well, he looks like I thought he would; but he's far quieter, isn't he? *Stiller?* And he has such a humility about him. He looks like our father, but Papa was in no way humble. It's disorienting. I suppose I didn't know what to expect."

"He's not been jaded by the pretense of other men. He lives simply. I understand his unwillingness to invite vanity and covet and greed into his existence.

That's civilization for you; it's comfortable, but there is a pecking order."

"I love him, however he is," she said, snuggling more tightly into Killian. "Even if I must share him with your horses. Really, Killian, could the arrangements be more self-serving? I'd rather bring the pregnant horse into the house than relegate my brother to the stables."

"Trust me, Highness, I presented him with the only arrangement he would accept. In fact, I was a little shocked he said yes, even to the stables."

"He knows that our family should be reunited," she said. "Deep down, he knows."

"Well, there's that, but I also suspect him to be very fond of this *earl's daughter* he followed to our doorstep."

"Fond?" she asked, craning her head.

"Hmmm. To put it mildly. Think on it: We'd never clapped eyes on the man—despite scouring the countryside, despite years of correspondence, despite buying property on the edge of Savernake Forest for the sole purpose of drawing him out. And when do we finally encounter him in the flesh? On the heels of this young woman."

Elise sat up in bed. "But could you be right? Was this the impression he gave you about Lady Ryan? That is, do you think he—? But is it possible he has some romantic feelings for her?"

"The thought did cross my mind," Killian said idly. "I cannot say what went on between them in the forest, but I'd bet ten quid she did not complain about the bugs."

"Honestly," whispered Elise, folding herself back into his arm, "it occurred to me, too. That is—not about the bugs, but there is something between them. I saw it when we took tea. And she's very protective of him, isn't she? Oh Killian, if he formed some attachment to her, and she could see beyond his beard and his horses—if they would be open to the possibilities of a friendship . . ."

Killian made a snorting sound. "'Open?' 'Possibilities?' *'Friendship?'* Try marriage, Highness. That's where my brain has gone."

Elise sat up again. "What?"

Killian linked his hands behind his head and stared up. "He cannot remain in the forest forever. Or, if he does, he should have a companion. I'm hardly a matchmaker, as you know, but you should've seen the way he reacted when I asked him about her."

"How? How did he react?"

"He reacted like they got on very well—like they'd gotten on, and on, and he would consider himself the luckiest man in the world if they could get on again very soon."

"*No,*" Elise breathed dreamily, gazing into the distance.

"I've said it before, and I'll say it again. He'd evaded us for years; and the first sniff of Lady Ryan of Guernsey and he's suddenly knocking on our door? He fancies her. Mark my words. And she is good for him; she's unpretentious and unfussy and natural. She has a sort of evenness that suits him. And she's obviously infatuated."

"Is she?" asked Elise. "But how can you know? And how have I missed all of this?"

"Perhaps you're reeling from the shock of seeing him—and seeing him so transformed. Also, please don't forget that I formerly worked as King George's royal fixer. Before marrying you, I was constantly routing illicit lovers and or facilitating preferred matches in St. James's Palace. I can identify the spark of attraction at ten paces."

"Unless it's your own," she teased.

"Never say it. My own spark was painfully obvious."

"And yet you ignored it."

"Ignored? More like fled from it. Or endeavored to flee. My attraction to you, Highness, wasn't simply obvious, it was unthinkable. It was doomed."

She giggled. "And see how that turned out. I willed it into fruition."

"Thank God." He hitched his knee so their legs tangled beneath the covers.

"Absent your strong will," he went on, "or, perhaps working in conjunction with it, we can do our part to nudge them in the correct direction. When I worked as royal fixer, my job was to determine the most expedient solution to any given problem, with the fewest extenuating circumstances, the fewest players—or, I should say witnesses—and the most binding results. They didn't hire me for long, measured coercions that spanned years; I delivered results in a fortnight. This problem wants the same efficiency in my view. We've a tortured, exiled prince living like a lonely wild man in the forest and a spinster fiancée being stalked by an entitled coward. Their attraction is not only obvious, thus far it's proven to be very motivating. He's out of the forest. He's consented to stay on at Mayapple. We must strike while the iron is hot."

"How useful you are, Killian," Elise breathed, delving her fingers into the whirl of hair on his chest.

"And you thought my only function was sex." He closed his eyes, pressing his head into his linked hands. He could bask in her touch for eternity.

"Not your *only* function. Although I do seem to find myself *constantly* pregnant."

"You love being pregnant."

"I love *becoming* pregnant," she corrected, "and I love my girls, but I do not relish *being* pregnant. No woman does."

"I'll bet Lady Ryan will. She has that look about her."

"How could you possibly know this about her."

"I'm trying to be clever and failing. Let me just say, she desires a family."

"Fine. Has your fixer's brain determined how we might facilitate their attraction?"

"The shortest, simplest route is to keep them close in proximity and working toward a common goal. This is the real reason I offered him a room in the stables. If I hadn't, he would've returned to his camp and called once or twice more, monitoring Lady Ryan's problem from afar. He's been hunted and haunted and—understandably—he's very easily spooked. Think of how long you allowed the British royal family to, for all practical purposes, *hide you* away? He's still hiding; he's not yet had a motivating event to embolden him. He's getting very close, I'd say, but not yet."

"She is the motivating event?"

"He seems very motivated to me."

"And taking on our wretched cousin Maurice is their common goal?"

"Now you're thinking like a fixer," Killian said. "I have some additional ideas to encourage them; but

I need to make some inquiries in London. I'll send a messenger tomorrow. If you can summon your friend Sister Marie, she'll be needed before this is all said and done—if nothing else, to find a priest to marry them."

She looked up to him. "You're *that* certain? We're to the point of finding a priest?"

"Forgive me, I've yet to mention my secret weapon."

She rolled against him. "Do tell."

"Before I say it, I must secure a promise of gratitude from you. Because it's a very potent and effective secret weapon. It's practically guaranteed."

She chuckled and pulled herself on top of him, sliding onto his chest and hips with a delicious little murmur. "And what, specifically, am I to be grateful for?"

"I've advised him to keep his hands *off.* Off of her."

"You what?" She pushed up on his chest.

"Trust me on this, Highness. Time-honored method of pushing lovers together: telling them they must, must, must—above all else—*keep apart.* It's what I told myself when I fell in love with you. And see where that got me?"

But Elise was shaking her head. "I don't know, Killian. Gabriel seems very earnest and cautious. What if he restricts himself based on this terrible advice; advice that you don't even mean?"

"He won't restrict himself," breathed Killian. He unlinked his hands and slid them to her knees, tugging her legs on either side of him. "I've seen the way he looks at her. He'll not be able to resist. And if he abides by my suggestion—if he's perfectly able to keep his hands off of her—then we'll know I've misjudged their situation. And we'll leave it. An experienced solicitor can send your cousin packing with no harm done. Lady Ryan and your brother will go their separate ways. But I haven't misjudged; I'd put money on it. Be patient. Pretend you don't notice. Let's keep them close and working together.

"In the meantime," he rumbled, rising up to capture her mouth in a kiss, "about that gratitude . . ."

CHAPTER EIGHTEEN

ᏒYAN WAS TOLD at breakfast that Gabriel would
remain at Mayapple while they sorted out some solution to the imposter prince.

The announcement came from Mr. Crewes; an off-
hand comment as he'd salted his eggs. It was clear
to Ryan that Elise Crewes already knew, but she
launched into an odd battery of questions—"Did you
invite him to stay or did he ask to stay?" "How long
will he remain?" "Where is he now?" "Will he join
us for breakfast in future; will he come to any meal at
all?"—but her husband deflected them all.

"I've told you everything I know on the matter,"
Killian said. "He means to stay and get Lady Ryan
sorted."

Ryan stared into her plate, riding out the galloping
hooves that had replaced her heart. Gabriel would
leave the forest. Gabriel would be here, with her—or
at the very least, *near* her. Gabriel had arranged for
this with Mr. Crewes but not discussed it with Ryan.
She'd come all this way, she'd drummed him from
his seclusion, she'd caused him to admit his real
identity, she was his bloody fiancée—and she was
the last to know.

Even Gabriel's nieces seemed to know more about his intentions. The girls trundled through the breakfast room to pilfer scones and little Marie announced: "When Uncle Gabriel returns from checking on *his* horses in the forest, he will live with *Papa's* horses in the stable. And every day he will teach us something new about being horsewomen." She ticked off future skills on her fingers. "How to tie actual knots in actual ropes. How to braid the tails of the horses without danger from their powerful hind legs. How to examine their teeth."

"We mustn't overwhelm Uncle Gabriel, girls," said Mr. Crewes. "But will you eat your scone at the table? With a proper plate and napkin in your lap? Where is Nanny?"

"Nanny has eaten undercooked fish," reported Marie, walking out the door, a scone in each hand. Sofie hurried behind her.

"I worry Nanny has a weak constitution," tsked Elise, watching them go.

"That's the problem, is it?" drawled Killian from behind his newspaper.

Ryan smiled, in spite of herself. The Creweses were generous hosts, warm and accommodating; and their obvious affection and mutual respect made Elise feel safe and inexplicably hopeful. They talked openly about the work of running Mayapple and of raising their girls. If Ryan felt a trickle of homesickness for her sisters and her busy life at Winscombe, she reminded herself that she'd come to England to restore that busy life and protect those sisters. If she also felt a stab of longing for a family of her own, a husband and children, she pushed it away. Her life was so very full. She was under attack at the moment, but things were looking up. And Gabriel would (apparently) be nearby. Whether he'd simply *observe* Ryan from the safe distance of the stables or actually interact with her—she couldn't say. But she left breakfast feeling bolstered, and eager, and ever so slightly annoyed.

She made a silent vow to expect nothing from Gabriel Rein. She needed less disappointment and anxiety in her life, not more; and Gabriel was unpredictable and uncommunicative. And he would never leave Mayapple with her, he would not share any part of his life with her, regardless of what happened in their shared time on the estate. The fewer expectations meant less heartbreak in the end.

And then, just after breakfast, she saw him.

He stepped into a passageway in the servants' corridor and they came face-to-face. Agnes had been working her magic on Ryan's gown, a new-to-her frock given to her by Elise. The fit was good except for the sleeves, which needed lengthening, and the hem, which should be let out.

"Hello," Gabriel clipped, taking in the sight of her with a long, hard look. He stopped five feet from her.

Ryan wouldn't have been more surprised if the Prince Regent had appeared in the corridor. He wore buckskins and a jacket; both of which had seen considerable wear but were clean, unlike the rumpled, dusty clothes of the day before. He held his hat in his hand, exposing his hair, which was less uneven than she remembered. His beard had also been trimmed. He looked . . . if not, gentlemanly (or even civilized), then neat and respectable. He looked like a very large, very fit woodsman. Which she supposed he was. Was it wrong that she also found him devastatingly handsome? Ryan couldn't say; she knew only that the sight of Gabriel in tan buckskin and chocolate leather put her off of brocade waistcoats or linen cravats for life.

Beside her, Agnes gasped. Agnes hadn't liked the look of Gabriel when she'd seen him from the distance of the carriage the day before, and a closer view was unlikely to improve her opinion.

"That should do, Agnes," Ryan said, dismissing her. "I'll be mindful of the lace. You can sew it in earnest tonight."

The maid didn't waste time closing the door behind her and flipping the lock.

Ryan turned back to Gabriel. His initial appraisal of her had faded, and his regard for her now seemed detached. He was suspicious and remote, like he'd come upon a distrusted acquaintance. Only he could appear so very handsome and so very rude at the same time.

Ryan narrowed her eyes. She was accustomed to being overlooked by men, but she wasn't used to fickleness. *Expect nothing*, she reminded herself. Her new policy.

Finally, she replied to him. "Hello."

He said nothing. He loomed in the corridor, staring at her.

"How do you find the stables?" she continued.

Silence.

"What brings you belowstairs?" she asked.

"A stable boy led me to the kitchens," he said. "I'm due to meet Killian and Elise in a parlor."

"Ah. We're bound for the same destination then. I followed my maid to the sewing room to save her the trip."

"I hoped to keep away from the family and their guests until strictly necessary," he said.

"Well, your hopes have been dashed, because here I am."

"You're not put off by the servants quarters?"

She glanced over her shoulder. A clattery din of chopping and voices rose from the kitchens, but they were alone in the passage. "On the contrary, I trod every corner of Winscombe on a daily basis. This includes the dusty attic, the moldy cellar, and the servants quarters. In the absence of my mother, I am responsible for the house and the staff."

"What of your dress?" he asked.

Ryan furrowed her brow. *My dress?*

"This is your everyday wardrobe?" he asked.

Ryan looked at the smart white dress with tiny scarlet flowers. Elise had heaped a rainbow of beautiful dresses on her bed the night before, claiming three pregnancies in five years had left her with unwearable castoffs. Ryan had never been interested in fashion, but it would be impossible to miss the beauty of the dresses. Agnes had been ecstatic and suggested Ryan try the white and scarlet first. At Winscombe, Ryan would've reserved a dress of this quality for Easter or a wedding or— Honestly, at Winscombe, Ryan would've given any new dress to one of her sisters. But she was not at Winscombe, and her dress from the forest was ruined, and Agnes had been so eager to see her in something new.

"No, in fact," she said, eyeing him. "Elise has loaned

me a handful of dresses that she no longer wears. We've sent a messenger to my aunt in London, asking that my own clothes be delivered to Mayapple, but in the meantime . . ." She let the sentence trail off.

He stared at her, his face hard. With no warning, he turned away. "Do you know the way abovestairs?"

"I meant to take the back passage." She was speaking to his back. "Agnes and I came by this route. Staff can feel stalked when their domain is invaded, and so many are in the kitchens at this hour. You're going the best way. But we'll need light."

He swiped a candle from a sconce, and strode down the passageway.

"Is there an agenda for the parlor?" he called over his shoulder.

This was his invitation to join him, Ryan presumed. She started walking. "Mr. Crewes simply said he has ideas on how I might proceed."

The corridor came to a wall and turned sharply to the right. Gabriel made the turn. Ryan increased her speed to keep up.

"Please know, Lady Ryan, that I intend to find a solution for this," he said. And then he stopped so suddenly she almost collided with his back. He spun around. "I know my initial response was opposite of this. I was wrong, and I admit it. You took me by surprise. Obviously. You are my responsibility and I've no intention of sending you back to a greedy cousin who's bent on destroying everything you hold dear. I've limitations, but they are not greater than my responsibility to you."

After he'd said it, he turned and continued his march down the empty corridor.

"Just to be clear," Ryan called after him, "I am *not*, in fact, your responsibility. You're mistaken if you think I'm flinging myself into your care. My only request has been that you reveal yourself to your cousin."

"If I reveal myself to be the Prince d'Orleans, risen from the dead," he said, disappearing around the corner, "I'll have to carry on with the title until I can convince the royal court that I don't want it; that I disavow all of it, that I *abdicate*. It'll be an arduous process that could take months, if not years, and play out on the world stage. I will help you—I *want* to help you—but it must be done my way. We'll invalidate the betrothal by proving arranged marriages cannot be inherited. This should be obvious to everyone but here we are. I won't emerge from my seclusion, but Maurice can take the title and good riddance—so long as he leaves you alone."

She followed him to a dead end, with passageways forking to the right and left. "Where the devil does this lead?"

"It's to the left, I believe."

Gabriel turned left, ducking to keep from bumping his head.

"I never meant to direct how we do it," she told him. "Revealing yourself was just an idea. If we use lawyers instead, I can see it through by myself. I exonerate you from helping, Gabriel. Honestly, I expect nothing from you."

"How every man hopes to be perceived," he grumbled, "no expectations."

For some reason, this made her angry. Now she was responsible for how he was *perceived*?

"Gabriel, your request from the start has been 'expect nothing.' In hindsight, it was excellent advice."

They came to a thin stairwell with steep, narrow steps leading upward at a slight curve. There'd been no light for the last ten yards at least. Their only defense against the darkness was the candle in his hand.

"Is it here?" he asked, lifting the candle to push back the gloom.

"Yes."

"Up you go then. Forgive my terseness."

"Forgiveness is not necessary, Gabriel, but I would also venture that terseness is not necessary. I've been nothing but cordial to you. I've done everything you've asked."

"Yes, you have." A pause. "And what if I asked *you* something?"

"What? What do you mean? Ask me anything you like."

"Fine. What if . . ." another pause ". . . I asked you to marry me?"

"I beg your pardon," she chuckled. The acoustics of the stairwell had distorted his words. It sounded like he'd said, *What if I masked you and carried me?*

"*What if,*" he repeated, "we saw the betrothal through? What if you returned to Guernsey a married woman? My cousin could hardly marry you if you were *already* married."

Ryan stopped climbing. She could no longer blame the acoustics; she didn't understand because what he said made no sense. She turned back.

"You needn't answer right away," he said. "Think on it."

"*Forgive me,*" she began. She swallowed. Her chest

felt like the weight of the manor house was lodged on top of it.

"It was Killian who suggested it," he explained. "Yesterday. I dismissed the idea at first. But then, as I was riding to and from my camp, the notion began to take root."

She heard his words, but certain phrases hit her squarely on the head, like cold, fat raindrops that rolled down one's forehead and into the eyes; the prelude to a downpour.

. . . see the betrothal through . . . a married woman . . . dismissed the notion . . . take root . . . asked you to marry me . . .

". . . because clearly," he was saying, "you have a happy life in Guernsey with your family and—as you've said repeatedly, including just now—you don't mean to *fulfill* the betrothal. And I've my horses, and work, and my own home. We lead separate lives. But that doesn't mean a hasty marriage wouldn't protect you. While we carry on with these lives. Separately." He put a hand to the wall and cocked his head, looking at her.

"Gabriel, stop," she said. "I'll need a moment. The notion of marriage is . . . is . . ."

"Not to overstate the obvious," he said, "but don't think of it as marriage in a traditional sense. I believe it's called a union in name only? These sorts of arrangements are not widely seen, as far as I know, but certainly they are more common than for example the betrothal of infants as part of a loan."

"How well informed you are on marriage rituals."

"I take both London and Paris broadsheets and read voraciously. As anyone who has rifled through my possessions would know."

Ryan looked at the wall, flat and smooth and chipped from years of servants running up and down these stairs. She herself was beginning to feel a bit chipped and cracked.

"We needn't determine it now," he said. "I only raise it because we might explore this option when we speak with Elise and Killian. Unless you are entirely opposed to the notion."

"Alright," Ryan said simply. Her mind was a jumble of emotions and contingencies and hope and defeat.

"Alright, we'll not determine it now . . ." confirmed Gabriel ". . . or alright, you accept?"

Ryan wrinkled her brow and gaped at him, trying to understand him—to *really* understand him. It occurred to her that he was, in fact, very nervous to ask her this. The question had sort of popped out, and then he'd rambled. He was rambling still.

Certainly the suggestion of marriage—even a marriage where they lived separate lives—was a complete reversal. Earlier, he'd meant to lead her to the edge of the forest and deposit her on the side of the road. Now this?

His motivation was worth scrutiny. She would need more time; for now, she willed herself not to panic.

"I suppose I mean," she said finally, "'alright' I'll consider it?"

"Very good then," he said. "Thank you."

"You're welcome."

"No harm done?"

"No," she agreed, although there was a very great chance that she would never be the same after this conversation.

"Carry on?" he suggested, indicating the stairs.

"Indeed." She clipped out the word with confidence she did not feel, raised the candle, took up her skirts . . .

. . . and promptly missed a step.

The stumble caused her to tip sideways. She caught herself on the wall—or, she tried to catch herself—and fell back instead.

She let out a little yelp and *whooshed* backward. The candle fell from her hand, hitting the step with a thud; the flame sputtered but did not go out. The last thing she heard before Gabriel caught her was a muffled curse—then her shoulders collided with the immovable wall of his chest, his hand clasped to her waist. He closed his other arm around her and held her—her back to his front—in a long, tight, silent embrace.

For a full minute . . . two . . . three minutes (it felt like a blissful eternity), they remained very still, and very locked together. The only sound was their breathing. After a long moment, Gabriel ever so carefully, ever so gingerly, sank his face into her hair. She heard his slow, deep inhale as he breathed her in. His mouth touched her neck. She reveled in the stamp of his lips on her throat and tingled from his beard on her cheek.

"*Ryan*," he whispered.

She blinked, trying to orient herself in this backward lean, her toes teetering on the steps. It was a position she couldn't possibly sustain if he weren't holding her up—but he did hold her; and he called her name; and he *inhaled* her. The combination of touch and breath and beard set off a ricochet of flying stars inside her. The weight of the house was gone; now she felt buoyant and rising. Meanwhile, Gabriel fell against the wall, seemingly too overwhelmed to stand. He pulled her with him, balancing his shoulders against the plaster, clutching her back to his chest.

Ryan's thoughts matched the weightlessness inside her; all reason floating away. She retained enough sense to examine the situation—their hazy, breathless path from quarreling, to considering marriage, to now cleaving wordlessly against the wall. And then, for a reason not entirely clear, she started to giggle.

"What?" he breathed.

"I don't know." She bit her lip.

He made a growling noise and flipped her, spinning her in his arms until she faced him. Now they were nose to nose; he held her against him with an open palm to her bottom; his thigh between her legs.

"If we marry," he threatened, "there can be no more of this."

Now she laughed even harder. "Oh no, not this. Never this. Why not?"

"Because, it will confuse our resolve to live separate lives. Neither should have to choose between our established homes—the homes we love." He stared at her mouth.

"Oh please tell me more," she said, still laughing, "your offer gets better and better, the more you describe it."

"Go on then—laugh. How hilarious, this predicament. My freedom upended. Your life under attack. The only solution . . ." He trailed off, staring at her mouth. Ryan licked her lips.

"The only solution is a marriage in name only," she finished softly.

"If we can manage it—yes. *If* you'll not corner me

in dark passages." He squeezed her bottom, pressing her into his hardness. The contact levitated her, body and mind. She closed her eyes savoring the thrill of it.

"I've not cornered you," she told him. "I was minding my own business with my maid. *You* appeared from nowhere. *You* followed me down this dark stairwell. *You* have made this odd proposal."

He dropped his head forward, notching his face against her neck. He growled.

Ryan answered that growl with a little whimper. One of the first things he'd taught her in his dark bedroom was how very *good* his rough beard felt against her sensitive neck. From scalp to toes, Ryan's body buzzed to life. Every point of contact was suffused by heat; one place in particular burned with bright urgency. Ryan hiked up her knee, hitching her ankle over his hip, trying to satiate that burn.

Gabriel repeated the growling noise and tucked her foot behind his back, grinding her into his erection. Ryan let out a sigh of pleasure, the sound escaping through a smile. He was so . . . *dramatic*—and it thrilled her. Everything about this encounter was overblown and gothic and felt far more tragic than necessary. How had he survived the forest without the potential for forbidden stairwell embraces?

How had she survived her own life at Winscombe without the same? She'd always been measured and reasonable; the answer to everyone else's crises. She couldn't remember ever having experienced feelings so intense—hope, confusion, doubt, want—that stemmed from her own crisis.

With boldness she didn't know she possessed, Ryan

moved her head just enough to press her lips to his ear. "*Gabriel?*" she called on a low whisper.

For half a second, his body went very still, then he squeezed her more tightly, raised his head, and kissed her.

It started out gently—a nibble, a taste. Then, like a tinder catching flame, he slanted his head and dove in. His tongue plunged, his breath heaved, his body bowed off the wall to press into her. He propped up a knee, balanced her astride it, and used his free hand to roam her body. Hips, waist, ribs, the sides of her breasts—nothing was left unexplored. He tipped her backward over the steps, holding her secure at the waist, and palmed her breast. When that wasn't enough, he delved beneath the neckline of her pretty new dress, invaded her stays, scooping out her breast. Panting, he lowered his mouth to the burning tip.

He kissed her mouth and her neck and her breasts with the same frantic desire, his only way. He kissed so fiercely, traced her so thoroughly, Ryan stopped trying to keep up and simply fell slack in his arms. Oh, she tried to touch him. She had a vague notion of her fingers skating drunkenly to the neck of his shirt, searching downward, fumbling for warm skin. She liked touching him—she *wanted* to touch him—but oh, how she also loved surrendering to him and being kissed within an inch of her consciousness. She was invigorated—a taut, thrumming whip of sensation—but also limp with pleasure, all at once. She was malleable and fluid and responsive. She forgot about the meeting with the Creweses, and the servants in the kitchen, and the dim passage. She forgot everything but *him*.

After some time—what did time matter when it would never be enough?—after her mind had left her, after strumming, burning pleasure had become her sole existence, a *pungent smell* invaded her consciousness. An odor. It was heat, and leather, and—

Burning leather.

"Gabriel, the candle," she rasped, dropping her head back.

"What?"

"The candle," she panted, "I dropped it. Do you see it? Is it—"

Gabriel swore and slid to the right. "Bloody hell. It's singed a notch in the heel of my boot."

"But can you get it? We'll need it. We'll need . . ."

Gabriel swore again and bent sideways. He held Ryan around the waist with one hand and stooped for the candle with the other. When the candle was once again in hand, he rested his head against the wall, panting. He opened and closed his eyes. The candle sputtered and jumped but did not go out. Wax dripped to the floor.

For a long moment, they did not speak. They breathed in the stale air of the stairwell and the now familiar scent of each other. They dabbed lips and patted hair and allowed desire to, reluctantly, drain from their bodies. Ryan wiggled and Gabriel lowered his knee and slid her to the step.

"Can you manage?" he rasped. "How is the wound on your leg? Oh, God I've not upset it, have I?"

She clung to the wall, trying to put some distance between them. She forced her legs to work.

"I feel no pain, I assure you," she said. "But the

Creweses are waiting. We're being rude. We should press on."

"Yes," he panted, not lifting his head from the wall.

"We're almost to the door, actually." She took the candle from his hand. She held it out and the flame shook.

"It complicates our situation when I touch you, Ryan," he said. "Certainly, if we were to marry, it would be . . . We couldn't . . ."

"Yes, well, this cannot fall to me," she said, taking up her skirts. "I am many things but 'complicated' is not one of them, so please don't ascribe it. Also, don't pin me with the burden of 'not touching.' Marriage or no. It's not fair."

"It's unsporting, I know—"

"Unsporting? Gabriel, it's misplaced. I don't want to be the gatekeeper of whether we touch or don't touch. On top of everything else. And anyway, *you* kissed *me*."

"You whispered my name."

"I called you by name. Lock me up and toss out the key."

He snorted. "I know it's misplaced. But please. I'm begging you. Will you keep away?"

Absolutely not, she thought, but she said, "I will carry on as I always have."

One step at a time, she ascended the stairwell. Her body was gangly and uncoordinated; she jangled from their embrace. Was she being obtuse or unco-operative? Possibly. What did she know of kisses and men and complications? No man had ever been so overcome by her mere presence. Before Gabriel, no

man had so much as walked her home from church.
She was patently ignored by men. So how, in God's
name, was *she* to blame if Gabriel seemed stricken
by her? Improbably. *Miraculously.* She was plain and
functional, not alluring or diverting. This was not her
fault. Keeping away from him would be his problem,
not hers.

Ryan's problem—because she did have one—was
heartbreak. This would be the only result of their car-
ryings on. Her vast inexperience did not mean she
wasn't afraid of a broken heart. After some solution
could be found for the imposter prince, they would
part ways. Gabriel had been very clear about this.

And perhaps *this* was the "complications" he was
trying so hard to avoid—heartbreak. But a broken
heart, surely, would be worth moments like this.

Almost anything, Ryan thought, straightening her
bodice, taking a shaky step, would be worth moments
like this. Gabriel was worth the heartbreak.

CHAPTER NINETEEN

If GABRIEL EXPECTED to be overwhelmed by the grand hall and bright salons of his sister's estate, he was not.

If he worried he might fumble the delicate utensils used to stir tea and scoop sugar, he was also wrong.

The licking fires in large hearths did not cause him to sweat; nor did porcelain vases shatter when he turned corners or made gestures.

His sister was not as easy to overlook. The strange experience of great familiarity but also "long-lost-ness" was unavoidable. She stared at him almost unceasingly, eyes large, expression disbelieving. He didn't know if she hoped to catch him in some colossal social mistake or burst into tears.

If only she knew his biggest social mistake to date—committed literally within moments of entering the parlor—had been riding Lady Ryan astride his thigh in a dark stairwell. Kissing her breasts. He'd been half a second from taking her against the wall before his bloody boot caught fire.

What was slurping his soup compared to this? Oh the irony; he was not, by nature, randy, or rakish, or a despoiler of women. And it wasn't simply that he'd done it, it was that he *wanted to do it again*.

Meanwhile, Lady Ryan sat primly beside him in her fresh white dress—now fully tugged and smoothed back into place—hands folded in her lap, a look of grateful attention on her pretty face. She gave them all a brief review of Maurice's arrival at Winscombe, all that he threatened, and his imminent return. Gabriel contributed what he'd known of Maurice as a boy and what his father had told him about the betrothal. Elise—balancing Baby Noelle on her lap—told what she knew of cousins and the family line of succession. Standing near the windows, Killian Crewes listened to all of it, jotting notes in a diary.

When they'd all presented every known detail of the problem, Killian joined his wife on the sofa, leaned back and draped an arm behind her. Noelle crawled into his lap.

"Do I know of a solicitor who can, most likely, disprove and disavow this imposter cousin?" Killian asked, idly running his fingers through Noelle's ginger hair. "Yes, I can think of one man in particular. I hope you don't mind, I've sent a messenger to London this morning, seeking an appointment as soon as he is able."

"I'll cover his fees," Gabriel said. "Whatever the cost. He'll need to eventually travel to Winscombe to be the voice of legal authority on Lady Ryan's behalf. I'll pay for this, too. All of it."

"Could we not," asked Elise, "have this solicitor write to Maurice now? Warn the man off? Cut him off at the knees?"

"I would not advise any advanced warning," Ryan said. "In my experience, it's better not to give him time to prepare. If he discovers that legal sparring is on the horizon, he will seek out his own solicitors."

"Indeed," said Killian. "I'd also hate to leave something so important as Lady Ryan's future in the unreliable hands of the post. The back and forth of it. I prefer Gabriel's idea of sending the solicitor in person. His name is Mr. Finley Soames, by the way. As a favor to me, he should make himself available, as long as the schedule is set out in advance. It's lucky we know the date this cousin intends to return. That will be the week Soames should make the journey to Winscombe."

"And you believe Mr. Soames can put a stop to all this?" Elise asked. "Because Maurice would not be swanning about Guernsey, terrorizing Ryan and her family if he believed it was anything but valid. Will the word of your Mr. Soames be sufficient?"

"Yes," said Killian. "Well, probably." He thought about this. Finally, he said, "I assume. He'll show precedent—other arranged marriages that were dissolved; other heirs who did not inherit arranged brides-to-be; and—I don't know? Argue this before the local magistrate? I cannot say exactly, but I know Soames has untangled betrothals and inheritances far less obvious than this.

"That said," continued Killian, handing the baby to Elise, "if you want the very fastest, most direct way to send the cousin packing, Gabriel himself should turn up in person, prove he still draws breath, and challenge Maurice for the d'Orleans title."

Gabriel felt himself begin to sweat. The teacup in his hand rattled and he set it on the table. From the corner of his eye, he saw Ryan glance his way.

"Gabriel's claim to the title would need only the authentication of a courtier called a 'royal adjudicator,'" Killian went on. "This is the fellow who would vouch for Gabriel's legitimacy. He cannot simply pop up from the forest and say he is the prince, I don't care how much he resembles his late father. He'll need to dredge up any and all proof of his former life."

A queasy, clammy chill began to slowly rise inside Gabriel's chest. Courtiers and authentication and attaching himself to the Prince d'Orleans title—he'd sworn off all of this. Hearing them ticked off elicited a bone-deep exhaustion. His freedom, the control he held over his life, was put in deeper jeopardy with every new piece of this plan.

Lady Ryan reached out and settled a hand on his knee. Gabriel stared at the five fingers. The warmth of it sank to his skin—to his bone. He wanted to cover her small hand with his own. He wanted to encircle her wrist and tug her against him.

Lady Ryan cleared her throat. "Gabriel's 'return from the grave' is less of an option. Entering public life undermines Gabriel's home and work in the forest, and I've no wish to save myself only to lay waste to everything Gabriel holds dear."

She took a sip of tea; a calm, careful gesture that conveyed reason and patience. There was a finality to it. An authority. Across the room, Killian and Elise observed her hand on his knee and listened to her words. They watched her drink. Baby Noelle raised her hand and seconded her statement with an enthusiastic, "*Gah*."

"Well said, Noelle," observed Killian.

"She is fond of you, Lady Ryan," chuckled Elise, giving the baby a squeeze.

Gabriel looked back to Ryan. She was laughing at the baby, making a face, balancing the delicate tea-cup and saucer in one hand, holding to his knee with the other. An unnamed emotion, buoyant but also immense, seemed to squelch the cold dread in his chest. He turned back to Killian.

"Yesterday," Gabriel said, "you mentioned another option. You raised the potential of marriage. Could we discuss how this might work?"

And now his sister paused in lifting the baby above her. She shifted the child to search Gabriel's face. Killian cleared his throat and tossed his diary on the table, rattling the tea service.

"Now we're getting somewhere," said Killian. "Marriage. To each other."

"Well, not the sort of marriage where we live as man and wife. I mean, a sort of protective union that allows us to live separate lives."

Slowly, subtly, Ryan slipped her hand from Gabriel's knee and attached it to her teacup. Using both hands, she replaced it on the table. The hopeful portion of this conversation had ended. Now they would commence with tearing out her heart.

"It would be the sort of union," Gabriel explained, "where Lady Ryan returns to her family at Winscombe, and me to my horses and camp. She would have my name but also the freedom to resume her old life without the burden of me."

Ryan wanted to tell him that he was no burden.

She wanted to tell him that she would entertain some compromise where she left Winscombe for a time and lived a portion of every year in Savernake Forest.

She wanted to ask him if the only way for her to win was to embrace "her old life," exactly as it'd always been. She'd sought him out to protect her old life—she knew this. And there were three people and many sheep in Guernsey who relied on her, but so much had changed. Was there no room for compromise? Was it impossible for everyone to have what they wanted—including her?

And what Ryan wanted—what she wanted most of all—was to marry Gabriel but *not* live separate lives. To save her family and to also save Gabriel.

But Ryan was not accustomed to placing her wants ahead of what others wanted. And she didn't think Gabriel wanted to compromise. He'd just said what he wanted with no hesitation. If anyone in this room, anyone at all, sought some modified version that allowed for a real marriage, no one put voice to it. And Ryan could not be the only one to say the words. She was brave enough to want it—just barely—but she was not brave enough to say it. At least not yet.

"*Maman!* There you are," sang a voice from the doorway, interrupting the conversation.

Little Marie and Sofie peeked into the room, hopeful smiles on their faces. Baby Noelle cried joyfully at the sound of her sisters. Elise and Killian sighed and admonished the girls gently for interrupting. Ryan turned and waved at them, grateful for the reprieve.

"You've made your interruption, so now you must present yourselves and apologize to our guests," called

Elise. "Can you say 'excuse me' to Uncle Gabriel and Lady Ryan?"

The girls scurried into the room and dropped into shallow curtsies.

"I beg your pardon Maman, Papa, Uncle Gabriel, Lady Ryan," intoned Marie.

"I beg your pardon, Maman, Papa, Uncle Gabriel, Lady Ryan," parroted Sofie.

"Pray, where is Nanny?" asked Killian.

"Nanny has breathed rancid air deep into her lungs."

"Ah," said Killian. "Of course she has. And where did she encounter *rancid air*?"

"The cellar," reported Marie.

"What business have you in the cellar?" asked Elise.

"We are helping Bartholomew! We've only come out because we are in search of paint. But is there *paint* in the house, Maman?"

"For the two of you? No. For Bart? Also no. But I cannot attend to you at the moment. We need twenty more minutes to speak with Lady Ryan and Uncle Gabriel. What I need from the two of you is: *not* to return to the cellar. Instead, go to the *nursery* and practice your letters until I come for you. Papa will investigate what Bartholomew intends. Understood? No paint? *Or cellar*, for that matter."

"Off you go then," Killian told the girls. "And if you happen upon Nanny, will you tell her that we rely on her to be more robust."

"More bust, more bust!" repeated Sofie. "We will tell her, Papa."

And then they were off.

The room fell quiet. The baby whimpered, disappointed that the bright, loud, twitchy sisters had left her behind with the boring adults.

The adults in question regarded each other across the tea service. Talk of marriage had changed the mood of the room.

"Here is my view of the marriage option," Mr. Crewes finally said. "First, it's simple enough to arrange—so you have that in your favor. Some manner of wedding *can* happen, and it can be done quickly. Elise has remained very close with the nun who helped her escape France. Sister Marie could locate a cooperative priest. He may balk at marrying an Anglican to a French prince, but we can explain that you've been betrothed for years and also overpay him. It should be enough."

"Wait," said Gabriel. "I thought to marry her simply as Gabriel Rein, not invoke the betrothal."

"Right," drawled Killian. "And is Gabriel Rein a Roman Catholic like Prince Gabriel is?"

"Why not?" Gabriel shrugged.

"Very good. So Sister Marie will produce a cooperative priest, we will *not* mention your royal blood, pay him handsomely, and use your current identity. After that—"

"Forgive me," cut in Elise. She shifted the baby in her lap. "May I ask Lady Ryan: Are you willing to marry my brother 'in name only'? Is this what you want?"

Ryan tried to smile, but the expression was painful. She recovered her teacup and took a sip. She cleared her throat. "If I might speak for both of us, I don't think marriage is the preferred way. However, it is a tidy little means to an end, isn't it? It is a sacrifice for

Gabriel and—yes, for me—although I have the most to gain if it means the imposter is sent away. How can I complain if marrying Gabriel will restore my home and family?"

"But of course you can complain," insisted Elise, "quite easily. What of marrying someone else? What of children? If you enter into this *farce* with my brother, it will remove these opportunities. Marriage is forever, Lady Ryan."

With no warning, tears flooded Ryan's eyes. She looked into her cup, trying to blink them back. "Forgive me," she sniffed. "I am moved by your concern—truly. But, I have devoted my life to my sisters, and father, and Winscombe. Perhaps, once upon a time, I could have prioritized marriage, a *real* marriage, but not now. This is the only proposal of marriage I'm going to get, I would be foolish not to take it."

"But—"

"*Elise.* Please," cut in Mr. Crewes. He cleared his throat loudly and shot his wife an unreadable look. She frowned and some silent communication passed between them. In the end, Elise went quiet, although she glanced once more at Ryan. She sighed and turned her attention to the baby.

Ryan peered up, watching them through her tears. It was impossible not to feel a little jealous of the wordless shorthand between husband and wife. But Ryan hadn't lied when she'd said she'd devoted her life to Diana and Charlotte and her father. If she was meant to have silent exchanges, it would be with them.

"Just to be clear, Gabriel," Mr. Crewes said, "when you intend to carry on 'living separate lives,' does it mean you will not escort Lady Ryan to Winscombe when she goes? You intend to marry her and then send her home alone?"

Gabriel cleared his throat. "I meant to give her my name and protection and then allow her to return to the life she knew before. Everything as it was. *That* is my intention."

"But—" interjected Elise.

"In that case," cut in Mr. Crewes—and now he leaned and kissed his wife, right on the mouth. "*In that case*, Lady Ryan will require Mr. Soames to accompany her, because I'm doubtful your cousin will accept her word that she's now a married woman. You also come at this with a disadvantage because yours would be an unposted wedding."

"Unposted?" asked Gabriel.

"No banns read. *Rushed,*" he explained. "There is legal paperwork that will take care of a special license, which we can speed along; but my point is that hasty marriages are, by definition, suspect. You'll require either your own presence or Mr. Soames to argue the validity of the union to the cousin."

"Even if I'm marrying her as Gabriel Rein and not the Prince d'Orleans?"

"Even if you marry her as Robin of the Hood, Prince of Thieves. But I should warn you, Finley Soames will be disinclined to *lie for you*."

"Meaning?" asked Gabriel.

"Meaning he's very talented and devoted to his clients but meticulously honest—rare for a solicitor, I know. So, if you marry, and if he comes here to build an argument that thwarts the imposter prince, the two of you will need to *really convince him* of your affection for each other. Your loyalty. Your future together."

"We will?" asked Gabriel and Lady Ryan together. Elise seemed just as shocked. "They will?"

"Oh yes," said Killian, turning away to show the baby something outside the window. "Absolutely. Your playacting will be crucial. After Maurice is sent away, you may do what you will with your so-called separate lives; but when Mr. Soames interviews you, he'll need to believe the union is real. Remember, he must eventually prove that Ryan is *too married* to be married again. If Gabriel doesn't escort her to Guernsey, you'll need to convince Soames of some plan to reunite in the future. You must prove to him that you're devoted—a family. A real family."

Now Ryan felt another rush of hot tears. She couldn't look at Gabriel. She couldn't look at any of them. She stared at her hands in her lap.

"For how long?" asked Gabriel. "For how long will we need to pretend?"

"Oh, he shouldn't stay more than a few hours? The length of an afternoon at most. But it's not *those* hours that are crucial. It's all the days leading up to his consultation. You'll want to practice, and learn to behave like a proper couple, and cover up all evidence that you're . . . well—strangers. You'll want to get in the habit of appearing to be fond of each other—*deeply fond*, I should say. For the benefit of Mr. Soames. Between now and then. *That's* what I think."

"And after he's convinced?" asked Gabriel.

"After he's convinced, Lady Ryan will return to Winscombe and you will return to Savernake Forest. Mr. Soames will return to London and travel to Guernsey in October when the imposter is due. It's . . . it's what you've said you want, no?"

For a long moment, silence held the room.

It wasn't what Ryan wanted—not at all. She didn't want to pretend to have affection for Gabriel; she wanted to show her real affection. She didn't want to appear like a family; she wanted to be a family. And this said nothing of what Gabriel didn't want. He hadn't even wanted to leave his camp. Now he was living in the stables at Mayapple, pretending to be in love.

Ryan swiped her wet eyes with the back of her hand. She cleared her throat. "I think this is more than Gabriel was prepared to take on."

"Well," said Killian, "it's less than marrying in earnest *and* proving he's the Prince d'Orleans, which is what I would have done."

"Oh yes," scoffed Elise, "how eager you were to marry, darling. Spare me, please." She rolled her eyes.

Mr. Crewes grinned. "Leave nothing to chance, I always say."

"I'll do it," Gabriel said. "I'll do anything to save Lady Ryan if it means I don't have to cede control over my life to the d'Orleans princedom and to France."

Ryan stared out the window. The dog bite on her leg burned. The abrasion on her neck stung. She hated Maurice, and the d'Orleans princedom, and the French Revolution. She hated all of it, so very much. She wanted her old life back—not the life she would claim as Gabriel's not-really wife; but the life she'd known before she'd ever met him. Was that true? Was it better to have never known him than to meet him, and be touched by him, to pretend to love him, and not have him?

She didn't know. And it didn't matter, not really,

because this was happening. She could feel the momentum of the plan building in the room. Mr. Crewes spelled it out so very clearly. They were rescuing her—rescuing all of Winscombe. How could she be anything but grateful?

"Lady Ryan?" Gabriel asked gently. "What do you think? Can you pretend to be married to me for the length of an afternoon?"

"Yes," she said simply, turning to him. "I can pretend."

CHAPTER TWENTY

"*H*AS IT BEEN difficult," Ryan asked Gabriel later that week, "being away from the forest, engaging in manor house life?"

They were hunched over a stack of parchment, making notes about the fake story of their fake courtship they would tell the solicitor.

"It has not been difficult," he said.

"Not at all?" she wondered.

"Mayapple is pleasant," he clipped. "It's not as if I cannot navigate proper doorways or stair rails or Persian rugs. Until five years ago, I made trips to villages on market days. I met clients. I called to shops and forges and granaries. I don't live in the forest because I'm . . ." he exhaled "feral; I simply prefer the out-of-doors. My sister and Killian have made a happy life here." It was mostly true. He was, perhaps a little feral. Less than he'd once thought, but even so. He *was* sleeping in the stables.

"I suppose it's more unsettling that we are seeing the betrothal through."

"Well it's not a lasting transition, is it?" he said. "It solved a large problem without inviting sweeping changes in either of our lives."

He said this because he didn't know what else to say. He could hardly tell her that her dress, which was the color of whipped butter, set off the dark shine of her hair. He could hardly tell her that he'd wondered, all morning, what color she would wear, and that when she'd walked into the library, he'd thought she was the prettiest woman he'd ever seen. He could hardly tell her she smelled sweet and natural, like salt air with the slightest hint of a wildflower.

He knew only that the fewer compliments he paid, the less real their impending marriage would feel. Compliments were the result of paying attention. And it was *imprudent*, surely, for him to pay too much attention.

It was also imprudent to be left alone together in the library—or share one pen and a single sheet of parchment. Because honestly? The challenge of both Mayapple and their marriage was not feeling hemmed in, the challenge was *her*. He found himself categorically unable to *not want* her. He felt like a boulder rolling down a hill: hard, unstoppable, and wild. Being alone with her only made it worse—and it was uncanny, really, *how often* they found themselves alone. As hosts, Killian and Elise were gracious and warm; as chaperones, they were shite.

"Have you spoken to your sister?" she asked.

"My sister? Yes. She was just here five minutes ago." Gabriel frowned at the closed door. "Where she's gone, I cannot tell you."

"I didn't mean, have you uttered words. I *mean*, have the two of you had a proper reunion, have you spoken about your years in exile, or your flight from France, or finding your younger sister?"

"No."

She studied his profile. "Oh."

Gabriel wouldn't look at her. Not for the first time, he wondered why list making was a two-person job. She was creative and presumably, as a citizen of the larger world, knew far more about what constituted a believable courtship than him. Meanwhile, he could barely focus on the page. He found himself transfixed by the delicate bend of her wrist. The small bone, the tendons, the little freckle. Lady Ryan was an island girl, and her skin was tanner than that of a well-shaded London lady. He liked the freckles on her nose.

"Well," Ryan was saying, "you needn't sit knee-to-knee across from Elise and struggle through a formal conversation. You could walk with her or ride with her. Now that you've come to Mayapple, you can return whenever you like—you can pass Christmas with her family. You needn't stay away, after I'm gone. There is time to rebuild your relationship with Elise."

"I know almost nothing of 'relationships,'" he said. "And even less of rebuilding them."

For a long moment, she said nothing. She looked back to the parchment. This was her way, he'd learned. Unless she urgently required an answer, she did not press. She made inquiries and allowed them to hover, no expectations, like a moth in the air. Eventually Gabriel was compelled to swipe at it.

"We could say that I knew you when you attended the boys' school," Ryan said, pointing to their notes. "Perhaps I summered in Marlborough with a relative, and I sought you out because of our letters. We could say our correspondence continued from that point. We could tell Mr. Soames that we've been writing ever since."

"I regret," Gabriel blurted, "that I did not come to Mayapple sooner. It has been wrong of me to not seek out my sister."

Ryan paused. She turned to him. "I think your regret is misplaced. The reasons you did not leave the forest are valid. Savernake Forest was a necessary sanctuary and we all understand this. Certainly, I understand it."

"Really?" he said, rising from the desk, "well, that makes one of us. No—that's a lie, of course I understand. I may *regret* it, but I understand it. I felt safe there . . . and I wanted to learn horses . . . and other options did not immediately present themselves to an eleven-year-old prince on the run for his life." He exhaled.

Beside him, Ryan waited patiently, brushing the feather quill against her chin.

"Savernake Forest is a great source of fear to most people, did you know it? They're afraid of spirits and highwaymen and faeries and God knows what else."

"It is a dangerous place," she agreed, "at least in my experience."

"I've *no* fears in the forest. It is a haven. This is what Samuel Rein believed, and he passed the belief on to me. Before this belief, I was gripped by fear all the time—I was seized by it. Sometimes it felt overwhelming and incapacitating; other times, it was a tiny, painful pinch at my shoulder—but it was always there. Samuel and his forest delivered me from that. He never said, 'Your fear is not legitimate,' or 'You should conquer the fear.' It was simply, 'You'll be safe here.'"

"It's a powerful message, indeed," she said.

He shook his head and turned his back to the desk, propping his hips on the edge. Ryan stood beside him, facing the paperwork. His bicep touched her shoulder, and he felt a tingling at the point of contact. The smell of her enveloped him. He was touching her, and smelling her, and revealing life truths to her. How could he also resist her?

"In my experience," she ventured softly, "beloved parents—or surrogates, in your case—shape us in profound ways, and their views can become nearly impossible to dislodge. The world may present an alternate view, but, so what? We know only what we've been taught. Take for example my mother. She was the parent who shaped me. For better or for worse." An exhale.

Gabriel braced, uncertain if he could hear about Ryan's mother, and her shape, and her worldview. He worried he'd learned all he could about Ryan Daventry without becoming irreversibly attached. He liked every single thing that he'd discovered. Whatever she had to say about her girlhood would be, undoubtably, just as endearing. Of course he would hear it, because he was incapable of not listening. He hung on her every word.

"My mother was a remarkable woman," she began. "Clever, and confident, and proficient in so many things, but also compassionate and cheerful—an encourager. She was perhaps better suited for a grander life than our remote estate in Guernsey. Her choices were limited, obviously. As a woman, she could hardly run for parliament—although I've no doubt she would've been excellent in the Lords. For a variety of reasons, she married my father; and by the time

I came along, she was running our estate. My father was a true gentleman of leisure; she was called countess but she might as well have been the earl. I lost her when I was fourteen years old. For better or worse, the running of the household fell to me. I was young, but she'd taught me well and honestly there was no one else to do it. As I broached each new challenge, I always thought, 'What would Mama have done?' Her memory has informed my every decision. In hindsight, I'm not sure this has been the correct guiding force."

"What do you mean?"

"Well, we allowed my father's health to deteriorate without seeking better doctors, or second opinions, or forcing him to be mindful of how much he ate or drank. It would've meant coercing him, and Mama had always indulged him. She never commanded, she only suggested, and I did the same. Now he's so infirm, he cannot leave his bed.

"Also, my debutante year came and went, Diana's, too, and I did nothing about a Season in London, despite our aunt imploring us to take advantage of her sponsorship. I did this because my mother put little stock in the social whirl of London. The result is, Diana and I are unmarried and we have no reasonable guardian to stand in the way of your cousin. My mother was so very fearless, so capable. It's all I know. But I am not her, am I? And I've not been able to manage it as she would have done. I'm not as bold; not as direct. This makes me vulnerable in a way she was not." She chuckled sadly. "My experience is almost the opposite of yours, isn't it? Your guardian would have you so very protected; and my mother would have me take on the world—and perhaps neither was exactly right. And that says nothing of whatever values and priorities you learned from your early childhood, living in a palace, being influenced by royalty."

Gabriel made a scoffing noise. "They were not so much guides as aspirational figureheads. We were raised primarily by nannies and nursemaids and tutors. I only saw my parents when their late nights overlapped with my early mornings. Or at state affairs with extended family. I felt as if I belonged to them, but they were hardly invested in the raising of me. My parents did not know me—obviously, because they arranged for me to marry *you*."

The feather quill in her hand, previously flickering back and forth, stopped when he said this. Ryan sucked in an almost imperceptible little gasp. In his peripheral vision, he saw her head drop. Carefully, silently, she settled the pen into the inkwell.

"Ryan?" he asked.

She looked up and her eyes were bright. She was crying.

Panic, sharp and frigid, stabbed his chest. Something inside Gabriel collapsed, like a giant oak felled by a storm.

He looked closer, trying to remember what he'd just said.

"What?" he said. "What is it?"

RYAN WAS BEING foolish. She knew it. And she must stop—she knew this, too. There had been no promises or declarations.

My parents did not know me, he'd said. *Because they arranged for me to marry* you . . .

The offhanded comment hit her so very squarely and painfully in the heart, it took her breath away. Her eyes flooded with tears.

Any sane person would agree that childhood betrothals were relics of the past. They were self-serving to families and confusing to children and strange to everyone. The chances for a future happy marriage were next to none.

And yet.

And yet she'd come to believe that the two of them were somehow well served by the betrothal. Their childhood meetings had been happy and agreeable. Their letters had become keepsakes for both of them. And now, when she'd appealed to him for help, he'd tried to help her. He was *trying* to help her.

But help was not affirmation of the betrothal. And an affirmation did not mean he loved her.

Even so, must he say he resented it? Must he say he resented his parents for uniting them? Must he say it *to her*? Oh, God, how had she allowed herself to become so attached? To hope?

He did not mean it as a personal affront, she told herself. And she wasn't crying because of him. She was crying because she'd been overlooked for years—totally unnoticed by men—and now he'd piled on his indifference and she was universally rejected. His resentment was the straw that broke the camel's back.

When he said the *betrothal* was unacceptable, it was the same as saying *she* was unacceptable. As ever. Again. Always.

And that's why she was crying.

"My ramblings have offended you," he was saying, "and why am I not surprised? This is why I'm loathe to . . . to *expound*. My wretched life story should be discouraged at all costs, not goaded and prodded until I—"

He stopped. He looked over, and she could feel him studying her. They were shoulder to shoulder, leaning over the desk. She ducked her head, squeezing her eyes shut.

"Please, please don't cry," he whispered. "Oh God—Ryan. The very last thing I want to do is cause you distress."

She shook her head. And now he would be sympathetic? She would never compose herself in the face of his compassion.

"Is it all this talk of your mother?" he wondered. "But your memories are mostly happy, are they not? Forgive me, my parents were preoccupied on the best of days, strangers on the worst. It's a revelation to me each time I learn about the proficient ones."

"You seemed very adherent to your parents when your family visited Winscombe," she said, trying to change the subject. "Your letters mentioned your father in glowing terms."

"Yes, well, I'd been conditioned to sort of reflect his brilliance; it was part of my job as a prince. If you detected a glow, it was manufactured. This is what I've been trying to say about the poisonous legacy of royalty. If the indoctrination begins within, the control becomes second nature. I was told from the earliest age that I'd been chosen by God to be a member of this ruling family. My father had been likewise anointed— even more 'chosen,' as he was more closely related to the king. The result was, I should feel honor bound to revere him and imitate him. And not because of any fatherly effort on his part—simply because he was a prince. If the royal family itself does not believe it, how will the people?" He glanced at her. "Wait don't say it—woe is me, the neglected princeling. I know this isn't the reason you're crying."

She sniffed and wiped her eyes. "I suppose the people of France stopped believing in your divine right. In the end."

"That's putting it mildly," he said. "But before the riots forced us to exile, I was a prince in every way. You saw this in my letters, I'm sure. I believed that I was so very fortunate to be one of the Chosen Ones. That's the whole song and dance, don't you see. You're so very happy to be included, you don't realize the control exerted over your own life."

"Such as the time or attention your parents might give you . . ."

"Such as whether your parents notice you at all; where you live; what you learn from tutors; later, what you study at university. For a male, military service is mandatory, whether you wish it or not. You must align yourself with people who annoy you; and feign affection for people you despise. You cannot go to a pub, or browse in a shop, or walk down the street. You have every luxury but no freedom. Control of your life is ceded to the Crown."

"Including control over who you marry," she said, speaking on a sigh.

"Especially who you marry," he enthused, looking at her again.

Ryan closed her eyes, blinking back another wave of ridiculous tears.

"Hold on," he said, sliding a hand across her shoulders. He flattened his palm in the center of her back.

"Is this what's upset you? My spouting off about having the Crown choose my wife?"

"I'm not upset," she lied. "I'm . . . exhausted. I came here to locate the real Prince d'Orleans and instead I'm fabricating a fake courtship." She swiped up the parchment and waved it in the air.

"I don't believe you," he said lowly. He gave a little tug to her shoulders, trying to pull her to him but she didn't move.

"You know," he began gently, "I came to these conclusions about the royal family years later. When, after years of fear and anger, I could think of my father's execution—which, despite his detachment as a parent, was still very traumatic. And after I'd read editorials about the Revolution, and the history of France—the history of all of Europe. Only when I could reflect on these and also had the opportunity to live as a normal man did I understand the lack of basic freedoms afforded to those 'divinely chosen.' That is to say, I didn't begrudge any of it when I met you, nor when I wrote to you."

"Yes," she said, "when our betrothal was acceptable to you, you were still under the influence of the 'indoctrination,' of your family. And you were a child."

"Make no mistake, Ryan, my resentment is with the control exerted by my parents, not the girl they chose for me."

Ryan failed to suppress a bitter laugh. Faint praise, indeed.

Gabriel swore and shoved from the desk. He moved behind her and tugged gently at her shoulders until she pivoted. Now she faced him but she didn't look up.

Gabriel bent at the waist, like he was looking through the slats of a fence, trying to meet her eyes.

"I've offended you by suggesting that I did not want the betrothal," he said.

"I am not offended," she corrected. "And not wanting the betrothal makes perfect sense. Who wants their marriage decided in infancy? No one would choose this if they didn't have to. As I said, I'm—"

He cut her off by grabbing her around the waist, lifting her, and plopping her down on the desktop.

Ryan yelped and threw out her hands. "*Gabriel*," she gasped.

"I value control over my own life above all," he said, looking her in the eye, "but that doesn't mean I resent being pledged to you, Lady Ryan Daventry. Not ever. I enjoyed you from our very first meeting, I lived to receive your letters—obviously, they were the only thing I took when I fled France—and I have relished reuniting with you as a grown woman. My opposition to being a prince and my fondness for you are two entirely separate things."

"Stop," she rasped. The tears came rushing back. She hadn't meant to make him declare all of this— truths, lies, excuses, whatever it was. She'd wanted it too much, and he'd said it too perfectly. She didn't dare to believe.

"Stop crying, please," he cajoled, nudging closer, bumping into her knees. He'd loosened his hands on her waist but hadn't let her go.

She nodded, but the tears continued to come.

"Ryan?" he called softly. "Ryan? If you don't stop crying, I'll kiss you."

She let out a tearful snort.

"Don't test me," he threatened. "I'm capable of many things, feats of strength and skill, but managing a crying woman is not one of—"

She kissed him. Not only did it end the conversation, it was what she'd wanted to do all morning.

Gabriel froze when she did it, eyes open, hands reclasping her waist. But then he gave in—he always gave in . . . she bloody *loved it* when he gave in—and kissed her back.

And why shouldn't she kiss him? It was preferable to weeping when he claimed resentment and weeping again when he claimed fondness. And really what did he expect after he'd plopped her on the table and essentially issued a dare?

Don't think of it, she thought. *Relish it while you can.*

Relishing seemed to be the most effective thing to curtail the tears. He leaned over her, devouring her mouth. One hand cupped her hip, the other palmed the heavy, aching contour of her breast. Who could find dissent in this?

"Are you still crying?" he breathed, moving from her mouth to her throat. His beard scraped the skin of her neck. And wasn't this one of her favorite sensations in all the world? His beard created a full-body thrum that made her nipples tighten and her belly clench. She dropped her head back and arched, offering herself up.

"Probably," she moaned. "Don't stop. I feel a veritable waterworks coming on. Please, Gabriel . . ." she lifted a hand and clasped the back of his neck, pressing his head into her bodice "kiss it; make it better."

"This cannot be fair," he panted, "but I can't mud-

dle through the injustice. I *did* make you cry, but then
you . . . you . . ."

Ryan was rapidly losing the strength to hold herself up by an arm, and she wound both hands around
his neck. Now she hung from him, suspended above
the desk. He scooped her up and lowered her onto the
blotter.

"Mind the quill," she mumbled, hoping the ink was
dry on the list beneath her back. Gabriel's legs bumped
up against her knees and she tried to widen them, but
she was restricted by her skirts. She made a noise of
frustration and reached down, dragging the fabric to
her waist, giving her knees room to slide apart, hitching her ankles around his thighs to pull him in.

Gabriel made a groaning sound and toppled over
her, bracing himself with palms on the desktop. His
hard, dense weight felt heavenly; a warm solid answer to the call of her body. Every burning part of her
now had something to push against. Ryan constricted
her legs, cinching her ankles more tightly around his
thighs, sliding herself to the edge of the desk. Gabriel responded with a thrusting motion, aligning his
hardness with the fiery demand that burned between
her legs.

All the while, he ravaged her throat, her neck, her
décolletage. He freed her breasts from the bodice of
her gown, sucking, raking her with his beard, leaving
a trail of sensation. She cried out and he covered her
lips with a hard kiss, trying to swallow the sound.

She kissed him back, digging one hand into his
hair, clawing against his hip with the other; urging
him to thrust again. He kissed her hard and rocked
against her.

She was just about to ask what would happen next, after the kissing and the rocking; to ask how they might kiss more and rock without the frustrating barrier of their clothes, when voices floated through the library door.

"No, no I've *found* Nanny, Killian," came Elise's voice. "It was a fleck of paint from the windowsill. It flew in her face and she needs an eye wash. She'll have recovered by luncheon, surely."

Ryan dropped her head onto the desk with a *thunk*. Gabriel whipped up, staring at the door. He swore, rolled up, peeling Ryan from the desk as he went.

"Can you repair your bodice?" he whispered. "Tell them the dusty books gave you a sneezing fit."

"A sneezing fit?" she whispered. She was dizzy and burning and not entirely able to stand.

"You're very pink," he said, reaching to his breeches and adjusting the fall. "I'll examine their collection of Shakespeare."

Before Ryan could reply, he stalked between two bookshelves, disappearing into the back of the room.

Ryan drew in two deep breaths and blinked. She looked down. Her dress was hiked to her waist. Her bodice sagged. The exposed skin of her chest was whisker-burned and blotchy.

Ryan swore and began frantically shaking skirts and straightening darts and patting down flyaway hair.

"Sorry, I'm here, I'm here," Elise sang, rattling the door handle. "Fair warning: I'm accompanied by an infant. *Again*." She pushed open the door and bustled in with little Noelle on her hip.

Ryan cleared her throat. "Are the children alright?" she called, not turning around.

"Oh yes," said Elise. "Sorry to have vanished. Our nanny suffers from a myriad of challenges to her health. The girls roam the house with no supervision and Killian worries. But where is Gabriel?"

"He's searching for an, er, sonnet," said Ryan over her shoulder.

"A sonnet?"

"Yes. He has a fondness for poetry. His library in the forest is large but not so big as this."

"Take whatever you like," Elise called to her brother. "Killian's nephew will not stop until he owns every book in England."

Slowly, Ryan pivoted to face the desk. To her horror, their notetaking was bent and creased at strange angles, like a wild animal had nested on the desktop. Casually, calmly, she endeavored to smooth the crumpled parchment.

"Deuced dark in here, isn't it?" Elise was saying. She went to the window and yanked on the drapes, letting in the daylight. "That's better. Very good. Oh look at you, Ryan—but are you overwarm?"

"Just a touch," Ryan said. The truth.

"We can open the window as well as the drapes. But how is the progress on your faux courtship? Not too many unchaperoned hours spent alone in his camp, I hope. Should we scandalize the solicitor? I suppose it's better than claiming no passion at all."

"Passion would probably . . ." Ryan ventured, her voice high and squeaky ". . . not be remiss."

Somewhere in the back of the library, a book hit the floor with a *thunk*.

CHAPTER TWENTY-ONE

AFTER SIX DAYS, Gabriel began to take meals with the family. Not only did he have to eat, he'd discovered a latent but robust appetite for fine cuisine prepared by a talented chef. Some things, perhaps, were *not* better in the forest—foie gras, just to name one of them. Properly baked bread, for another. Beef Wellington, glazed potatoes, poached eggs with fried herbs, the list seemed endless.

On the first night in the dining room, he'd worried that Lady Ryan would somehow feel responsible for him. He could survive scraping his knife against the porcelain or drinking from the wrong goblet, but he would not allow himself to rely on her to smooth over gaffes.

He didn't want to catch her eye across the table, reassuring him; nor see her gesturing to a footman to bring him clean linen. This had been their dynamic on that first day at Mayapple. He'd burst onto the stoop and she'd managed the intrusion by requesting the outdoor tea and making pleasant chatter.

In the end, he'd worried for nothing. His first meal in Mayapple had come and gone without incident, and Lady Ryan had scarcely regarded him. She'd been seated next to his sister's old friend Marie, the nun who'd delivered Elise from France when she exiled. Marie was fierce and resourceful and was working to locate a priest who would agree to marry them within the fortnight. She was also the namesake of his eldest niece. Ryan and Sister Marie had been immersed in their own conversation while Gabriel was engaged with Killian's nephew, Bartholomew. The youth was eager and curious and almost completely without guile, and he'd launched himself at Gabriel with a litany of questions—French philosophy; Roman artifacts in the forest; the best spurs—and the meal had been a blur of delicious food and stimulating conversation.

On the whole, Gabriel's time at Mayapple was nothing like he'd expected. He was very raw and primitive—it was impossible to deny—but no one seemed to care, least of all Gabriel himself. When a dinner party was planned for a classmate of Bartholomew's and the classmate's family, no one cared that Gabriel elected not to attend.

He'd not yet reckoned with his sister; but not for fear of disappointing her. His regard for Elise was fueled by a deep mine of emotion that he wanted—at the moment—to keep tightly sealed. It felt reckless and unnecessary to open it, and he would not rush it.

Finally, everyone regarded the in-name-only marriage to Ryan as an excellent plan, and they all agreed to go along with it. No one seemed to blame them for getting married only to live apart. They spent their days rehearsing the testimony they would give the solicitor and crafting the story of their courtship so all of it sounded legitimate. Reckoning with Maurice

was a constant source of speculation and debate, but
they did not expect Gabriel to do more than what he'd
agreed to do. No one felt he owed Ryan a life debt.

He quickly found that family meals were the easiest
time to engage with her because there was no temptation to also touch her. Given half the chance—given a
secluded library or an empty passage—he *would* find
a way to put his hands on her, and then his mouth, and
he existed in a suspended sort of agony for what he
really wanted to do to her.

In fact, the more she avoided his gaze, and ignored
him at dinner, and occupied herself elsewhere around
the estate, the more he wanted her—which was remarkable, considering his preexisting level of want.
Gabriel went about his day with an underlying current
of desire that roiled and bubbled like a fever. He was
never *not* aware of her. He knew the rhythm of her
footfalls, the sound of her laughter, the smell of her.
He knew her favorite phrases, her Channel Islands ac-
cent, the way she tapped her knuckles against her lips
when she thought. He knew that, given the choice between the shade or the sun, she drifted toward the sun.
He wanted all of her, all the time.

The tears she'd shed in the library haunted him
still, but he knew there were many painful levels of
unfairness to holding her and kissing her only to send
her away in the end. The pain of playing both sides
was no mystery. Hell, the duality of it made him want
to cry, too.

The only solution he saw was to keep away. He did
not range far from the stables; instead, he watched
her from afar. He allowed her to write the story of
their faux courtship, and their first meeting, and the

reason he would not return to Guernsey with her. When they strategized about convincing the solicitor of their marriage, he made certain at least three others were present. On the rare occasions he encountered Ryan alone, he fled. It was cowardly and rude but better than the alternative. If they did not interact, he would not upset her. If he wasn't alone with her, he would not touch her.

By far, his favorite part of visiting Mayapple had been the burgeoning relationship he had with his nieces. If the reunion with Elise was gradual, and his avoidance of Ryan was a daily test, his interactions with Marie and Sofie and Baby Noelle came very easily and were a genuine delight. He'd developed a love and affection for the girls so suddenly and unexpectedly; and it brought him such joy, he allowed himself to embrace it without caution. They laughed, they said clever things, they adored him, and he simply basked in it. It didn't hurt that the two older girls were largely untended by their so-called nanny. Gabriel had only ever glimpsed the woman on one occasion, when she was being chased from the garden by a bee. As a result, the girls flitted in and out of the stables at will. They were omnipresent and he loved it.

A week after Gabriel had made Ryan cry in the library, the girls sought him out to play a game of hide-and-seek. As with all of their games, this one involved less playing and more arbitrary rule following. His eldest niece, Marie, managed playtime like a general at battle, telling everyone where to stand (or in this case, where to hide), and what to say, or how they should best enjoy themselves. As it turned out, hide-and-seek

was always played in pairs (for safety's sake), out of
doors (so as to not disrupt Nanny), and with no fully
closed hatches or doors (because of that time Sofie
had been locked in the hayloft).

Today, Marie was partnered with her cousin Bartholomew. Gabriel's partner was not named until the
moment he was instructed to crawl beneath a wagon
and hide beside her.

"And now you will hide *here*, Uncle Gabriel," lectured Marie, pulling open the door to the carriage
house and pointing to the hay beneath a parked wagon.
"Take care that your boots do not poke out the end of
the wagon because Sofie will see them immediately."

"And what of me finding my own hiding place,
Marie?" Gabriel inquired.

"Oh no, Uncle Gabriel, I must know where everyone
is, in case you are never found. Remember the hayloft."

"And who is my partner?" Gabriel asked, dropping to his knees, grabbing the slats of the wagon, and
swinging dutifully underneath.

"*Lady Ryan*, of course," exclaimed Marie, bending
over to supervise Gabriel's position beneath the carriage.

"*Wait . . .*" Gabriel rasped—but it was too late.
Ryan rolled from the shadows and blinked at him.
She was lying on her side beneath the wagon, head
propped on her fist.

Gabriel startled, nearly bumping his head. Ryan
cocked a brow, idly picking straw from her hair. Gabriel's heart began to thud. He tried to reverse, but—

"No, no, no, Uncle Gabriel," scolded Marie, swatting the sole of his boot with a stick. "You must keep
hidden. Sofie has already begun to count and she can
only count to ten."

"Best just to submit, mate," suggested Bartholomew sagely from beside the wagon.

"Now *we* shall hide beneath the steps to the house!" proclaimed Marie. Her stick landed on the ground with a *tap* and tiny shoes retreated. The carriage door creaked and the daylight dimmed to a narrow crack. Marie and Bartholomew were gone and Gabriel was alone beneath a parked wagon with his soon-to-be wife.

"Hello," Ryan said to him.

Gabriel frowned at her. His nieces were sunny little balms for the soul, but they were bossy. He needn't—

"I find," said Ryan, "that if you comply for the first five minutes, she'll soon be distracted by the next flight of fancy and you may go about your business."

He removed his hat and dropped it in the hay.

"Or perhaps you cannot abide the underside of the wagon for five minutes," she said. "With me."

"Did you tell her we should hide together?" he asked.

Ryan laughed. "Ah, *no*. If you believe Miss Marie Loretta Gloria Crewes is open to suggestions, you are not well acquainted with the child, clearly."

Gabriel considered this. He felt a piece of iron dig into his shoulder, and he reached into the hay and found a wheel bolt. He tossed it aside.

"Also," she continued, "I've made a point not to stalk you about the property. In case you haven't noticed. Your avoidance of me is very clear. Far be it for me to infringe."

"I'm not avoiding *you*," he said. "I'm avoiding being *alone* with you."

She'd been looking at him, but now rolled onto her back and stared at the underside of the wagon.

Gabriel swore and lowered himself beside her in the hay.

"Perhaps we needn't wait five minutes," she said. "Go now if you prefer."

Gabriel thought about this. "Is that what you want?"

"What I want," she said softly, "is to save myself from another encounter where I feel unwanted."

"*Ha*," he guffawed bitterly; the sound was out before he could stop it. "*Unwanted*. You feel *unwanted*. Oh the irony."

"What does that mean?"

It means that I've never wanted anyone or anything like I want you. The sentence took shape in his brain—the absolute truth—but he bit down, refusing to allow the words to leave his mouth. Declaring *this*—declaring *himself*—served no purpose but to hasten heartbreak.

Even so, he couldn't *not* respond. She was unhappy, and the very last thing he wanted to do was to make her unhappy. The point of keeping away was to leave her no worse than when he'd first encountered her.

He would answer her question with his own question. "You think I don't want you?"

"I think . . ." she sighed ". . . that you have been alone for many years, that you are—if you'll excuse my dramatic phrasing—'starved for a woman's touch.' I think you are, in a way, *primed* to seize upon any woman who happens along. I've been that woman, both conveniently available and enthusiastically willing. Also, we have this odd history between us. So. Do you want *me*, in particular; or would any woman do? Unclear, really, but I've learned not to hold my breath.

"Furthermore," she continued, "I think you're plunged into guilt by our encounters, and so you vow to yourself that you'll not indulge again, that you deserve better than passages and libraries—better than *me*, when it comes right down to it—and you won't allow yourself to succumb. *That's* what I think."

"I'm no virgin," he said.

"Noted," she replied.

A stalk of hay stuck from her hair and he wanted to pluck it away. The muted blue of her eyes was almost gray in this light, the color of a stone on the bottom of a stream. He'd known her as an adult for such a short time, he was still learning her face. Also, it was the most familiar face in the world.

"The one thing you gleaned from all I just said," she asked, "is that I need reminding that you're no *virgin*? When I said 'starved for a woman's touch,' I did not mean starved to the point of death. Just to be clear."

"I never claimed to be gracious or well-versed in the art of conversation."

"I know, Gabriel," she said tiredly, "your manners are not courtly—I know. Forgive me, I simply—"

"Allow me to tell you something about life in seclusion."

She sighed, the sound of someone bracing to be lectured on an obvious topic.

Gabriel pressed on. "I am deeply, painstakingly discerning about *when* I leave seclusion, and *why*, and with *whom*. Certainly almost no one *enters* my sanctuary."

"I remember," she said.

"*Not*," he corrected, "the *physical* sanctuary."

"Oh? I seem to recall being asked to shield my eyes when I was hauled into your camp."

"Fine," he ground out, "I'm also particular about the physical sanctuary. My point is, I also guard the sanctuary of my soul. But I allowed you in. I'm preparing to marry you, Ryan."

"Well, you're preparing to *pretend* to marry me. Let us not award anyone with medals for emotional courage just yet."

"I've revealed things to you. I've bared my soul."

"Right. And still, you *resist* our attraction because—"

"I *cannot resist you*," he bit out. "Don't you see? This is the point I'm trying to make."

"Alright—fine. Why? Why 'bare your soul,' engender this great intimacy between us, and then work tirelessly to keep away from me? Why avoid me and glower at me as if I'm a seductress, trying to lure you into wicked temptation beneath wagons? Actually, don't answer that. I've already said I've no wish to feel unwanted again."

Of its own accord, Gabriel's hand reached out. He dropped it onto her hip, fastened hold, and tugged. He rolled her to face him like he was spinning a log in the water. Ryan let out a small sound of distress, but she allowed it, turning until they faced each other. Their eyes met. Her expression was sad and cautious and something else. Wary? Reticent? She looked like she had grim news that she hoped someone else would deliver. But they were alone, and she must be the one to say it.

Outside the carriage house, rain began to fall. The drops fell suddenly and evenly, like someone tipped a watering can in the sky. Marie and Sofie could be heard shrieking and fleeing for the house.

"I've never thought of you as a temptress," he said.

"Obviously."

"Forgive my lack of eloquence," he ground out. "Everything I do is to protect you, Ryan—not heap on more offenses. You know that I will return to the forest and you will return to the English Channel and it will be easier if we've not . . ."

He stared at her mouth. He edged sideways, crowding her in. His knees bumped her shins. His boots tangled in her skirts. He was close enough to feel her breath on his cheek.

"Easier for who?" she asked softly. "Not for me. If I'm being honest. Gabriel, if the notion of 'sanctuary' means that you may never indulge in mutual desire, then I feel sorry for you. More sorrow than I've felt for your boyhood, and that is saying quite a lot, because we can all agree you've had a wretched go. Why survive all of that, reach adulthood, control your own destiny—only to choose . . . scarcity? Scarcity of affection, even for a fortnight. Even with me."

"You're not 'a mutual desire I want very much,' Ryan," he said. Of its own accord, his hand slid from her hip to the curve of her bottom. He palmed it and scooted her against him. "You will soon be my wife. We have a history together. And there are consequences to touching a woman we both agreed would live hundreds of miles away. It's reckless and cavalier and cruel of me. It's not the behavior of a prince, or a gentleman, or any man of honor and decency. Even I know this. You're not just *some woman*, Ryan."

"Ah, yes, back to the great many women who've made your virginity a faint memory, I see."

That did it.

He kissed her.

He lowered his mouth, silencing every forthcoming challenge or accusation or joke. He'd tried to explain and he'd failed. She was the most clever, most beautiful woman he'd ever encountered, and she could win any debate. Her body had an allure that drew him like the earth drew the tides. She was soft and responsive and smooth. She was also reasonable, and patient, and calm, and level. He wanted to devour all of it. He wanted to absorb every trait, every nuance, every compassionate leaning and glimmer of grace—including the multitude of subtle, unnamed qualities that followed her around like a cool, serene mist, so many that he couldn't count. He wanted them all.

But of course she was not consumable or absorbable, and there was probably something broken inside him that caused his desire to be so very all-encompassing. But he wouldn't think of his brokenness now. When he kissed her, he did not feel broken, he felt whole.

He used his right hand to scoop her bottom, pressing her into his hardness; with this left, he cupped her face. Canting her chin, he deepened the kiss. He kissed her like a man who'd come upon a beautiful woman under a wagon; playful and erotic. When their side-by-side positions became insufficient, he hiked a knee over her and rolled them, pressing her into the hay.

"Are you . . ." he panted, sliding on top of her ". . . are you—? How did you describe yourself? 'Enthusiastic and willing?' Still?"

Her hands were at the collar of his shirt, unfastening buttons. His boots were tangled in her skirts, his knees digging into the straw. She kicked a little, spreading her legs until he rested between her thighs.

"Ryan?" he prompted, kissing her hard.

She took the sides of his collar in two hands and yanked, popping buttons into the straw. When his throat was exposed, she nuzzled and smelled and tasted his skin.

"Ryan?" he rasped, rapidly losing the ability to ask permission. "Have you heard what I've said?"

"I've a problem," she admitted. "I *don't* listen to what you say so much as *interpret* the things that you *do*."

"Oh God no—don't do that." He buried his face in her hair. He found her ear and traced it with his lips. "Do as I say, not as I do."

The thing about almost making love to his not-really fiancée was it only felt like a mistake before he'd touched her and after they'd been together. During? During felt like the most natural, most correct thing he'd ever done. Previous women had felt totally necessary before and wholly forgettable afterward. In the middle, the encounters were anonymous and lonely. Holding Ryan was as different from other sexual encounters as a bed was from the ground. Ryan was soft and familiar and unforgettable.

"Will you remove your shirt?" she breathed. "That night in your bedchamber, you wore all of your clothes. I wasn't able to touch your skin. I want to feel you."

"You're killing me, Ryan," he said. But tugged his shirt over his head and tossed it into the hay.

She gazed up and made a little gasping noise. "Just look at you," she marveled. "You're perfectly formed." She walked her fingers over the muscles of his chest, feeling her way from his waist to his collarbone like a sculptor, putting the finishing touches on a masterpiece. Every point of contact was a worshipful caress.

He'd thought he couldn't get any harder, but he was wrong. He'd thought holding her and kissing her had been the most intense pleasure on earth, but he was wrong. There was more.

It was impossible not to answer the scintillating pleasure of her touch and he collapsed on top of her, recapturing her mouth in a desperate kiss.

"Do you think the girls will return?" she breathed against his jaw.

"It's still raining," he huffed. "And I don't regret it. I hope it rains for hours. Are you alright?"

"Oh yes," she breathed, "I am alright." He kissed her ear again and came up on his elbows. He eyed the bodice of her gown, wondering how he might free her breasts without taking the time to unfasten it or (what he really wanted) destroy the neckline.

"But Gabriel . . ." she said, massaging her hands over his shoulder ". . . the girls? Their nanny will keep them inside while it's raining—she wears a corrective shoe that must be kept dry—but if the rain stops . . ."

"I'll close the carriage-house door. I'll lock it," he breathed. Was it still raining? He didn't know. The world was on fire and he didn't care. He wanted the world to burn. He slid a hand beneath her neckline to fan across her nipple.

Ryan let out a moan and closed her eyes. He pumped his hips against her and the moan turned into a breathless cry.

"If we made some arrangement to meet," Ryan said, eyes closed, body arched, "after everyone has gone to bed perhaps, we could do whatever we wished. With no interruptions. We could have all night."

"And not in a bed of hay," he added, "not beneath the wagon."

Ryan's eyes flew open. "Yes," she said. She propped up on her elbows. "That's right. In a proper bed. Like in your camp."

Gabriel slid his gaze away. He'd not meant to agree to her suggestion. The words had just come out.

Of course she deserved a proper bed. She deserved privacy. He'd only agreed to the *theory* of these, not to a plan to make them happen. It was dangerous and reckless to arrange an actual rendezvous. Kissing was one thing, touching, his shirt off, her bodice disrupted; but to risk her virginity? As much as he hated to think of it, she might wish to share her life with another man in Guernsey. Perhaps they could later annul their marriage and she could marry again in earnest. He would not take this bit of it from her. He couldn't.

"Gabriel?" she prompted. He'd cradled her head in his hands and massaged his thumbs down her jaw. Slowly, he rocked back and forth against her, bumping his hardness into the apex of her thighs. Their clothes were a barrier, but not much. The erotic sensation was blinding.

"Don't tell me," she whispered, "we're back to noble resistance again? Avoiding complication?"

"You're mad if you think I'm bedding you and then sending you back to Guernsey." He kissed her. "Mad. I am a recluse and a rustic, not a blaggard."

Ryan broke away and turned her head to the side. "I'm leaving Gabriel."

"Leaving . . . the underside of this wagon?" Gabriel's heart stopped.

"Leaving *Mayapple*," she corrected. "Not today, but sooner than we thought. The solicitor is arriving from London next week."

"What?"

"Killian had a letter at breakfast," she said. "The post had been delayed and several days' worth of letters came at once. Including a note from Mr. Soames. He is expected to arrive Monday or Tuesday. Wednesday at the latest."

Gabriel frowned. The fire beneath his skin extinguished. He went cold all over.

"Killian didn't mention it to me," he said.

"Have you seen him since breakfast?"

"No."

"Well, when you do, he'll tell you. You can read the letter. It's happening. Next week, Mr. Soames will come and our time together will be over."

"Unless the man is detained," Gabriel offered, an unhelpful comment if ever there was one.

"I would not depend upon it," she said. "We must have Sister Marie bring the priest and perform the wedding right away—in the next day or so. Next week, we'll meet Mr. Soames as husband and wife and convince him of our great love story. When that's done, I'll have everything I need to return to Winscombe. And then I will return."

"Is it precipitous," he asked, "to believe a single meeting with this man will give us 'everything you need'? Should we not first speak to the man? He may interview us for days. He may require case files or clerks brought from London. We'll want him to—"

"He may do any number of things," she cut in quietly, "but he'll not require *me* for these. My story is unorthodox, but it can be explained in an hour or less. We'll have a marriage license; it will take very little to convince him of the fake story of our relationship. We can easily demonstrate affection. *I* needn't linger after next week. And in fact I can't justify lingering—no matter how much I've enjoyed my time here."

"You're so anxious to get back?" The question was out before Gabriel could stop it.

She chuckled and reached up. Gently, she flattened her palm on his chest above his heartbeat. She spread her fingers. A star-shaped imprint radiated from her handprint, burning away the chill. "My responsibilities have been abandoned for far too long. Diana and Charlotte cannot manage everything alone. And I miss them. I can't stay here forever. Neither can you. I know you miss your camp and your animals. You have commitments to clients.

"I do not mean to manipulate you with this news, Gabriel," she continued. "Truly. I've no misguided notions that you'll volunteer suddenly to commit to anything more than we've already— Well, to anything more. I know I'll never see you, ever again."

"I believe it's too early to say Mr. Soames won't interview you for days—for a week or more. If we knew what the solicitor required, we would not need to hire the man."

She shrugged and teased a hand through his hair. "I disagree, but we'll find out when he comes, won't we?"

Gabriel dropped his face to her shoulder, pressing his lips to the bare skin beside her sleeve. "When were you going to tell me?"

"When I saw you? After I played hide-and-seek with the girls? How can I tell you if I cannot find you? You can be difficult to locate, Gabriel."

"I'm sorry," he said—and it was true. He felt sorrow so very deep, all the way to his bones, to the soft center of his heart. She couldn't leave him yet. How could he let her go?

"I found you once, but I grow weary of seeking you out. Really I do. With the solicitor in place, I'll have what I came for. If, also, I found what I did *not* come for, I will leave that behind. That has been our arrangement from the start, hasn't it?"

He slid his arms beneath her and bundled her against him. He buried his head in her hair and squeezed with all of his might.

I've fallen in love with you, he thought, tears stinging his eyes.

"We have no arrangement," is what he whispered into her ear.

CHAPTER TWENTY-TWO

ᎶABRIEL SURPRISED THEM all by asking to hold the wedding at his camp in Savernake Forest. Sister Marie located a priest who was willing to marry them, but the man was disinclined to preside over the already unorthodox wedding in an Anglican chapel. If they must have the wedding outside, Gabriel said they might as well enjoy something different than their everyday experience in the well-trod garden of Mayapple. And if they convened in his camp, his grooms might stand witness.

With Mr. Soames expected at the beginning of the week and the priest only available for a day, their timing was limited. The chosen day happened to fall on the very same as the dinner party Elise planned for Bartholomew's school friend and his family. Elise offered to cancel the party but Ryan begged her to carry on. There was time enough for a morning ceremony in the forest and the evening dinner. The family would be away for the wedding and Mayapple staff could prepare for the party. The forest venue allowed for two events to occupy the same day.

It also allowed Gabriel to reveal his camp to Elise and her husband without an official unveiling. If the

wedding took center stage, Gabriel could share Savernake Forest without having to explain his life there in
quite so many words.

Ryan would not make more assumptions about
the logistics of the wedding than that. It was a gesture meant to heal a family, not a sign that their
marriage was anything more than—

Well, anything more than what it was. Which was
a means to an end that protected her. She could also
acknowledge that his camp was comfortable and familiar to him. He was being forced to marry her after
all; why not do this unwanted thing in the place he
wanted most of all?

If Ryan also found favor with the forest . . . if she
looked forward to returning to his cave-cottage, well . . .
they'd both gotten what they wanted. Or, half of what
they wanted. Ryan wanted the wedding—though it was
"in name only." She didn't want a marriage of convenience, but that was her destiny. At least she would do
the thing in a beautiful ancient wood, in the cool September air, with the leaves just beginning to turn, and
Gabriel's cabin as a backdrop.

"But were you really blindfolded the first time
my brother brought you to his camp, Ryan?" asked
Elise, nudging her horse closer. They rode through
Savernake Forest in a long, winding procession. Gabriel led the way with little Marie in his lap. Killian
Crewes rode with Sofie next. After that, Sister Marie
and the priest. Bartholomew, God love him, drove a
small wagon containing the maid Agnes, wide-eyed
and clutching the sides, and a trunk with Ryan's wedding dress. Elise and Ryan were last in line. Only
Baby Noelle had been left behind with Nanny. The

woman had suffered a severely burned tongue from hot chocolate but was convinced to mind the baby for the morning.

"No, not blindfolded," Ryan told her, "but he did ask me to close my eyes. It's a very great honor, I assure you, being invited to this camp. You should count yourself lucky."

"Well, the journey from not knowing him at all, to his sporadic letters, to being a wedding guest has been a long one, indeed. But the real champion today is you, Lady Ryan. It's no small thing to forsake all others and marry my brother, especially because he promises you so very little."

Ryan chuckled sadly. "I've had my own journey with him, haven't I? When I first met him, he told me Prince Gabriel d'Orleans was dead. He wouldn't even tell me his name. And now he's marrying me. So. He does things in his own time."

"That is a very gracious view for someone who is—I hope you don't mind me saying—obviously very fond of him. It has been clear to all of us that you share some affection."

Ryan smiled. "It's an open secret that we are not enemies, I suppose. Matters were not helped by these last weeks together at Mayapple. You are terrible chaperones, which I suspect was by design. It was sweet, your subtle encouragement."

"Not enemies, indeed," said Elise. "But he refuses to claim you as his actual wife in every way. This could be seen as short-sighted at best. At worst? Selfish. If I'm being honest."

"Our faux union is not a rejection of me, it is a safeguard of his own freedom."

"Yes but will that freedom keep him warm at night?" asked Elise.

Ryan cleared her throat but made no reply. The caravan of horses had turned eastward, bearing into the steadily rising sun. Dappled sunbeams illuminated the canopy overhead. All around them, autumn leaves twirled from the treetops. They dropped to the forest floor and created a patchwork of orange, and yellow, and brown. It was so beautiful, it made Ryan's heart ache. Or perhaps Ryan's heart ached because Elise was right. Gabriel had chosen his freedom over her. She did not begrudge him this, but there was sadness to sacrifice.

"Lady Ryan?" Elise asked, "if my brother asked you, would you leave your family and live in the forest with him and raise a family?"

Ryan closed her eyes, shutting out the beauty of the forest. This was a painful question. The answer—*yes*—floated into her mind like a falling leaf. But living in Savernake with Gabriel—which, it should be remembered, he'd not asked her to do—would steal her purpose as caregiver and steward to her own family. The real answer was more like, *maybe*. Someday. After her father's health improved or he passed on. After Diana and Charlotte were married and the estate was self-sufficient. When everyone could get on without her. If, after the great many years it might take to achieve these, he still wanted her—of course she would come. If he hadn't met someone more convenient or beautiful or bold. She hadn't lied when she'd said he was starved for a woman's touch. Another truth: Any woman would want him. He was beautiful, and passionate, and capable, and—even if he fought it—regal in his own, rustic way. Reuniting with his sister was only one of many returns to civilization that he would make. Next, Pewsey. After that, Marlborough. The women would come.

But Elise had asked her a question. After a long moment, Ryan said, "Maybe." The truth. Maybe if fifty things could be accomplished and the stars aligned and if he still wanted her. But she'd learned long ago not to pin her hopes and dreams on some man. She was invisible to most men and a sacrifice that Gabriel could not make. She had been remarkably *unchosen* for as long as she could remember. She could allow the reality of this to make her bitter and resentful or she could choose herself.

"I'll take your maybe," said Elise, "and I'll not let anyone in Wiltshire forget it. You have my word."

Ryan smiled. "You have been so very kind to me. Everyone in your family has been lovely. I will miss you terribly when I go."

"Well, let's not think of that yet. We have the wedding, we have the dinner party tonight, next comes Mr. Soames. I did not mean to dampen the festive mood of the wedding by pressing you on these serious topics. Forgive me."

"No forgiveness is necessary. Oh, but look, we're almost to the camp. I remember this bit. Here the trail will disappear and we'll weave through this copse of trees. Gabriel takes a different route every time to conceal the way. When we emerge on the other side, we'll round a hillside and then you'll see it. I was so very impressed the first time. I know we tried to describe it, but he lives in a sort of modified cave beneath a hill. He has an underground waterfall next to his bedroom."

Elise cleared her throat. "Does he?"

Ryan felt herself blush. "And the stables and horses are incredible. He's a kitchen garden, a cellar for grain and winter storage, a smokehouse, chickens, of course; and—oh, look . . ."

They cleared the grove of trees and rounded the hill and Gabriel's camp came into view—rough-hewn but tidy, just as she remembered it. Beside the cottage, in front of the kitchen garden, an arbor had been erected, the arch adorned with leaves of every shade of burgundy, and crimson, and aubergine, and pink. Coral-colored ribbon had been twined between the branches and streamed out, flapping in the breeze. Before the arch, a collection of chairs, mismatched except for their unsanded knobbiness, had been arranged in short rows. Stoneware vases containing bouquets of wildflowers—harebell, rockrose, wild parsnip, and others Ryan didn't know—had been positioned beside the innermost chairs, creating an aisle. It was like a beautiful little outdoor cathedral, with the grassy hill on one side, the garden behind, and the forest in gleaming autumn color all around.

Ryan blinked back tears, taking in the simple beauty and natural splendor of the scene.

"Someone's been busy," said Elise, kneeing her horse forward. "Can I assume the outdoor vignette is not a permanent installment."

Ryan, unable to speak, shook her head.

"Well, I knew he'd been gone from Mayapple for two days. What an effort he's made. Good for him. I dare say, this is rustic," she added, looking around. "I cannot believe my brother lives in a cave."

"Please don't remark upon it," Ryan said, recovering quickly. Elise looked at her, cocking an eyebrow.

"That is," Ryan added, "he believes that outsiders will not see it as he does. He is anxious for you, in particular, to accept it, I believe."

"Oh, I accept it," said Elise, reining around. "I'll accept anything to be a part of his life, even saying goodbye to you, which is the most difficult part of accepting him. But you did say you might consider returning. Perhaps what I mean is: How could you possibly live in a cave? If you did come back? Life in the forest is no small request."

"Yes, well, no one has made this request, have they?" said Ryan.

"No," mused Elise softly, "I don't suppose they have."

TWO HOURS LATER, Gabriel stood beneath the arbor he'd built, sweating in the only waistcoat he owned, waiting for Ryan Daventry to emerge from his front door and be escorted to him by his nieces.

His sister Elise and her husband smiled at him from the chairs he'd arranged in rows. His two grooms, Smith and Tucker, sat behind them, looking uncomfortable in their only waistcoats—and also a little confused. The nun Marie hovered on the periphery, checking the trees for anyone who might have followed them. Killian's nephew Bartholomew stood to the side, tuning up a mandolin. Gabriel had not asked for music, but Bart had insisted and Gabriel had thought, why not?

From the moment he lit upon the idea of marrying Ryan in his garden, his plan for the ceremony had mushroomed from an exchange of vows to a proper wedding. Instead of thinking about the meaning of getting married, he'd occupied himself with guessing how a proper wedding might look and what Ryan might enjoy. Gabriel had not attended a wedding since he was a child; and even then, he hadn't been a guest. He'd been a page boy who trailed behind his cousin when she walked the aisle at Notre Dame. After that, he'd been swept away by nannies so he did not fidget during the hours-long Mass. But he'd read about weddings in books and newspapers, and he knew the beauty of his own garden, and he knew that if he could extract Ryan from her existing life and install her in his own, he would seal the union just like this. They would marry in the beauty of the forest, with only his family and grooms, secluded from the world.

He could *not* extract Ryan from her life—he knew this—and she'd refused to commit to any preference for the wedding whatsoever, so he'd simply done what he wanted. One thing led to another and, in hindsight, maybe the little stage was a test for all of them. Would a rudimentary, outdoor ceremony be enough for Ryan when it came to something so important as a wedding? She'd been very comfortable at Mayapple and her own home was very grand indeed. If, in another life, at another time, she was able to leave Guernsey and consider life with him, would Christmases and May Days celebrated at outdoor parties be sufficient?

And what of Elise and Killian? His sister had never *not* been a princess. She'd exiled in St. James's Palace and now lived on a lavish estate. Her husband literally referred to her as "Highness." After the ceremony, she would leave this forest glen and host a dinner party for esteemed guests. Likewise, her husband's stables boasted every modernization. Killian managed Mayapple, his nephew's estate near Hampton, and various other properties throughout Britain. Compared to these, Gabriel's camp was so very modest. He didn't mean to test their acceptance so much as show them the reality of his life. They'd been asking to be let in for years. They'd opened their home to him, and now he would open his home to them. Could Elise reconcile her memories of him, also her future hopes for him, with the man he'd become?

So far, they'd been lovely. Killian had marveled at his horses and stables. Elise and the girls had seemed charmed by his cottage and waterfall. And Ryan had been—

Well, Ryan had not regarded him beyond quick glances and questions about where she might change clothes. It had been this way since they'd kissed beneath the wagon. She'd become single-mindedly focused on the logistics of returning home. Her only interest in the wedding had been the time and place and the procurement of the priest. Her only interest in their faux courtship had been how they would present themselves to the solicitor, and for how long, and how soon she could depart when it was over. Her attitude was, in every way, what they needed and also nothing like he wanted.

It was unfair and painful to confuse things. She would return to Winscombe—she was already there in her mind—and he would return to the anonymous life he wanted as Gabriel Rein. They'd said everything there was to say—each conversation ended in a small fight and a riot of nearly making love. They'd come so very close beneath the wagon. He would not dishonor her by taking her virginity and then sending her into the wide world alone.

Going forward, he would have a sister and nieces, but he would not have a wife. Ironically, that didn't mean he could not have a wedding. He would give this to her, if nothing else—a proper wedding that hopefully she could remember with fondness.

"Ah, here she is," said the priest, inching his pointed hat back on his head.

Gabriel looked at the man, confused, and realized he meant the bride had emerged. He would promise himself to her; he would rescue her and then desert her. In his gut, the pinch of a sharp thorn began to throb. Gabriel looked at the priest and looked at the sky. From somewhere to the side, Bartholomew began to strum the mandolin.

What am I doing? he thought.

Little girl laughter and snatches of conversation could be heard from the direction of the cottage.

"Come, come, Lady Ryan . . ."

"Bartholomew has begun the music . . ."

"No, Agnes, she wants her hair loose . . ."

Gabriel turned to the sound of the voices. Coming around the corner of the house, each hand pulled by one of his nieces, Ryan Daventry floated toward him. She wore a dress of deep magenta, the color of a stalk of foxglove. Her hair was long and flowing, with a crown of ivy and wildflowers ringing her head and streaming down her back. She looked to the girls, smiling and laughing, and Gabriel thought he'd never seen anything so beautiful in all his life. The pinch in his gut dug deeper.

She looked up and around, raising her eyebrows at Bartholomew and his instrument; she nodded to the grooms who'd staggered to stand, staring at her wide-eyed, clutching their hats to their chests. She smiled to Killian and Elise.

When, finally, she looked to him, she stumbled a little, pulled off balance by the girls—but locked onto him with a gaze so intense. It was her first time to look at him, to really look at him, since he'd held her beneath the wagon.

I'm sorry, he wanted to say.

I want you.

I did this for you.

I want you.

Stay.

These were the vows he wanted to make. This was what he wanted to tell her. When she reached his side and the little girls fluttered and spun to their parents, the priest began. Gabriel repeated the words after the priest, only changing one thing. His name.

"I, Gabriel Phillipe d'Orleans . . ." he said. *Not* Gabriel Rein.

It seemed less like a lie that way, and he did not want it to be a lie. He wanted it to be a wish. How long, he wondered, listening to her repeat her vows to him, had it been since he'd made some sort of wish? He'd stopped being afraid when he moved to the forest; started living on his own terms. But he'd also stopped hoping and dreaming and wishing. He *existed.*

Was this a foolish, unnecessary notion, he wondered. To wish?

CHAPTER TWENTY-THREE

"*B*UT YOU CANNOT leave so soon, Lady Ryan," said little Marie Crewes. "You've married Uncle Gabriel and he must stay with the horses. Oyster will have her baby soon."

Ryan stood over her open trunk, packing with Agnes. Although the wedding had been this morning and the Crewes's dinner party was tonight, Mr. Soames could come at any time. He could come tomorrow. She would depart as soon as she'd met with him, no stalling to pack. Marie and Sofie Crewes sat on the foot of her bed, fingering the lace and crystals on the three dresses splayed out for her perusal. After she packed, Ryan would choose a dress to wear to dinner.

"I am loathe to leave you all," Ryan said, smiling sadly at the little girl, "but I've sisters and a very sick father back at my home in Guernsey, and they need me. If your sisters and father needed you, you would go to them, wouldn't you?"

"Well, my mother and Nanny look after my sisters and our father," reported Marie thoughtfully.

Ryan smiled at this. She'd had a mother who looked after things once upon a time, too. In hindsight, it was reckless to put all the caregiving into the lap of one person; not only did it restrict that person, but what if she died? What then?

"What's happened to Nanny?" Ryan asked, trying to change the subject.

"She has leaned too close to the fire and singed her eyebrows," reported Marie.

"Ah yes. Well, there is no Nanny and no mother at Winscombe, so I must go, I'm afraid."

"But when will you come back?" Marie asked.

"I'm not leaving tonight, so never you fear," Ryan told the girls. "You're selecting my dress, remember? When I do go, I've suggested to your parents that you might visit me. I live on an island, as I've said. How would you like to travel across the English Channel to a little island, to swim in the sea or stand on a cliff and watch ships come and go? We can awaken while it's still dark and see the sun rise from the water like a creature emerging from the depths. What do you say to that?"

Ryan tried to make it sound as magical as possible, hoping to compel the Creweses to visit. She'd grown so very fond of this family; and now that the wedding had come and gone, she couldn't envision herself returning to Mayapple. Gabriel had broken her heart with the beauty of the ceremony, with vows and the heartfelt look on his face. Wiltshire was simply too close to him. Ryan wasn't certain she could survive her current broken heart; certainly she'd not survive having it broken again and again.

Her sole consolation was this: life as she knew it— her home, the independence, the lives of her sisters— was being restored. She'd achieved her goal in coming to mainland England. The only new piece would be her newly broken heart. It was better, she supposed, than *not* achieving her goal and *also* having a broken heart.

"But have your parents said you may meet Bartholomew's classmate?" Ryan asked. "This dinner for him and his family is meant to be quite the affair, I believe."

"We may not meet him," Marie recited. "We must remain with Nanny from supper until bedtime and there are no exceptions to this rule. Even if Nanny *dies*."

"Well, I should hope we aren't called to test this rule. But never you fear, I'll come and tell you goodnight so you may see my gown. Can I rely upon you to give me your honest opinion about which dress to wear? I wouldn't want Bartholomew's friends to think of me as a bumpkin."

"We will help you, Lady Ryan!" declared little Sofie. "You will not look like a pumpkin."

Ryan was less concerned about her appearance and more concerned about *keeping away* from the stables. Chatting over a formal dinner with strangers was hardly how she'd wanted to pass her wedding night, but it was as good an excuse as any. She would not, *could not*, see Gabriel—not an accidental encounter and certainly not (God forbid) a moment of weakness where she sought him out. Gabriel had rejected her for the last time. He'd married her in a beautiful show of natural splendor, and when Elise had suggested that the family return to Mayapple and Ryan remain in the forest for the night, he had refused. He'd gotten a strange look on his face, and said he didn't think that would be prudent. He said he would help dismantle the wedding arch and put away chairs and return to Mayapple after dark.

The answer had doused the warm and festive glow of the ceremony in colors of gray. What choice had she but to attend the dinner? With strangers? *On her wedding night?* When a few hours alone with her new husband was *imprudent*.

"Careful not to partake of anything too rich at the meal, my lady," Agnes warned her a half hour later. The maid was helping her with the dress chosen by the Crewes girls. "Or undercooked. Or that hasn't been properly *deboned*."

"Goodness, Agnes, you've begun to sound like the children's nanny." Ryan stood beside the maid as she mended the short sleeves on her borrowed gown. The silk was thick and difficult to sew, and Ryan held out her arm like a bird with a broken wing.

"I honestly don't care what I eat, Agnes." Ryan sighed. "I'd bow out of the dinner altogether if I could think of anything else to do."

Meanwhile, Gabriel could do . . . whatever it was he did in the stables, or in the forest, or—

What difference did it make? She would ride away from him—possibly as soon as tomorrow, depending on the solicitor—and this bizarre chapter of her life would end.

Perhaps, she thought, Gabriel had known what was best all along. Perhaps it *was* less complicated and easier to survive if there was no passionate wedding night or emotional final goodbyes. Her heart had already been broken, why lash it back together for one night only to have it painfully pulled apart another time?

"Your choice of the aquamarine came as a surprise, my lady," Agnes said, whisking her hands down the fabric, brushing away lint and smoothing the line of the skirt.

Elise Crewes had given Ryan *ten* of her former day dresses and evening gowns—an abundance of riches that Ryan couldn't wait to share with her sisters. Agnes had altered most of them, and she could work her magic again, adjusting them for Diana's curves or Charlotte's slightness.

"It was Marie and Sofie's choice you'll recall," Ryan said of the dress. "I'd never choose something so bold, but it will please them, I think."

"I believe the bright colors suit you, my lady," Agnes said. "How pretty you look."

"It will do," Ryan said simply, glancing in the mirror only long enough to see a blue-green blur, then hurrying to tell the Crewes children good-night.

An hour later, Ryan stood in the drawing room of Mayapple, nodding along to introductions of dinner party guests. Bartholomew's classmate was a chatty, bookish boy called Dennis Stanhope. His father was Sir James Stanhope of Marlborough; thankfully the family lived close enough to pack into their own carriage at the end of the night and ride for home. Ryan could barely manage a dinner party; overnight guests would be a stretch.

Sir James was accompanied by his wife, a woman Ryan suspected was already drunk when she arrived; and his aging mother, Lady Glennis. Mrs. Stanhope trembled and twinkled in feathers and gemstones and the grandmother was relegated to a dark corner and covered in wool blankets.

There were also two unexpected guests to the party: an older brother to Dennis Stanhope and that man's friend. Both young men were also on school holiday—but not from Eton, these gentlemen were in their final year at Oxford. The addition of these two men forced a slight delay as the kitchen plated more of the first course and the seating was rearranged.

The Oxford men were introduced as Mr. Nevil Stanhope and Mr. Charles Fielding, and they exuded the sort of slick and cynical arrogance that Ryan associated with London dandies. They took in the furnishings and fittings of Mayapple's entry hall and scrutinized Elise and Killian with thinly veiled judgment. It was appallingly rude, Ryan thought; not to mention misplaced for men so young. They were the most formally dressed of the night; upright and tight-necked in sculptural cravats, gleaming shoes, intricately woven waistcoats, and walking sticks.

As far as Ryan knew, Gabriel remained in the forest. Elise had not set a place for him. Together, Ryan and Elise had decided not to mention her marriage when she was introduced. None of them would ever meet again. It was simpler to identify her as an old family friend visiting from Guernsey and to use her former title of Lady Ryan. In truth, Ryan struggled to think of herself as Gabriel's wife. And here was another way he'd done her the favor of guarding her heart. The wedding had almost seemed like a game of make-believe; too dreamlike to become part of her identity. She was as she'd always been. Among allies but without a companion, together but alone, Lady Ryan Daventry.

In the mad scramble to accommodate last-minute guests, Ryan found herself seated directly beside the two Oxford men. An effort to separate couples put Mr.

Stanhope on her left; and her rank as the daughter of an earl saw the elderly Lady Glynnis on her right. Oh the irony; if she'd acknowledged her marriage to Gabriel, she would've been a princess and seated at the head of the table with Elise. If only.

When it was time to promenade to the dining room, Ryan told Mr. Stanhope, "Hello again," and reached for his arm. Their position as tablemates meant he would escort her.

The young man made no reply. He was stiff and twitchy and made a sort of snickering noise—a half mumble, half snort—and refused to look at her. He held her arm like someone had balanced dead vermin across his wrist.

Confused by this overt rudeness, Ryan began to second-guess herself. Had she inadvertently offended him in some way? She looked about her, checking the progress of Elise on the arm of Sir James; of old Lady Glennis on Killian's arm; of Bartholomew's friend Dennis escorting his mother. There was no lapse in manners; the group was simply making their way to the dining table. Bartholomew led the way and the second Oxford man walked behind Ryan and her escort, muttering what sounded like a joke under his breath. Ryan couldn't hear what he'd said, but he and her escort smothered a laugh, snorting to keep their merriment contained. Ryan glanced at the two young men, and that's when it occurred to her: they were making fun.

With no warning, tears shot to her eyes. These young men—boys, really, who'd only just made her introduction—would hardly acknowledge her. They recoiled at the thought of walking beside her for the length of ten yards, and now they made jokes at her expense? It wasn't worth her tears, she was a grown woman, for God's sake. And yet . . .

And yet the anticipation of leaving Mayapple, combined with Gabriel's refusal to be alone with her after their wedding, meant she must navigate this evening with sharp pieces of her heart jostling around inside her chest.

Why, she wondered, blinking rapidly, could they not simply *overlook her*? Why must they also poke fun? Ryan knew herself to be well beneath the interest of men. She'd made peace with this long ago. Even Gabriel, who'd both chosen her and not chosen her, would never *ridicule* her. Ryan was aware of her plainness and forgettability; but she'd not thought of herself as unseemly or unsightly or worthy of ridicule. Where was there humor in this? Save cruelty?

She didn't know. In fact, the only thing she knew for sure was that she'd been mistaken about attending this dinner. It wasn't a feasible distraction or a way to avoid her new husband. And she didn't want to touch this brittle, acrid-smelling young man. Or make conversation with him. She also didn't want to crawl alone into her bed at the end of the night, knowing Gabriel was alone in his bed but that he wouldn't come to her—not tonight and not ever.

And now her mind was running mad. And she didn't care. She blinked back tears. She'd fallen in love with Gabriel d'Orleans Rein. She'd actually managed to locate him in a deep, dark wood and then fallen in love with him. But he would not have her. He would leave her to these immature, hateful young men instead.

By the time they reached the dining room, Ryan's

eyes were, to her mortification, swimming in tears. Her escort took her to her chair and retracted his arm. If he spoke a civil word, she did not hear it. If he pulled out her chair, she didn't see it. A footman stepped up to cover the rudeness, and Ryan dropped into the seat, head bent over her bowl of steaming soup. She breathed in and out, trying to compose herself; willing the tears away, determined to see the meal through. She was being ridiculous. Nothing had been done to her—she was unharmed and, in fact, not even addressed. It was silly to cry. It was silly to have any reaction at all save boredom and endurance.

Thankfully, Killian Crewes stood to pronounce a toast, congratulating his nephew for making at least one friend at school. The distraction allowed Ryan to regain control. She glanced at her escort. He was seated beside her, oblivious to her descent into tears. Perhaps, she thought, she should give the young man the benefit of the doubt.

She cleared her throat. She smiled at his shoulder. In an effort to catch his eye, she leaned, and leaned, and *leaned* so far over, a lock of her hair nearly dropped into her soup. She strained to hear the conversation he was having with his friend. Finally, she simply interjected.

"Mr. Stanhope? Did you attend Eton like Lord Bartholomew and your brother?"

Nevil Stanhope paused in his eating, the gesture of someone stunned that he'd been addressed. He did not answer. He glanced at his friend who blew out a laugh.

"But have you ever traveled to any of the Channel Islands, Mr. Stanhope?" she tried again. "We're not so cosmopolitan as London or even Oxford, but the view of the sunset will take your breath away."

Again, he blinked straight ahead. He regarded her like a small dog who had escaped its owner and nipped and barked at his heels, as if he couldn't believe the affront.

And now, as the fragrant courses of dinner were served, one by one, Ryan's reaction became laughter, not tears. The audacity of these men to be inconvenienced by her simple bid for dinner conversation. She could, she realized, do this all night.

"Is there particular coursework at Oxford that interests you most?" she asked, speaking as if they were having a real conversation instead of a one-sided list of questions.

"But have you had the opportunity to attend the opera in London?" she wondered.

"There is a spice in these vegetables that I cannot name, but do you taste it?" she inquired.

"Is there some sentimental value attached to the jeweled pin on your lapel?" she ventured.

After the fourth course, Ryan gave up. The men were determined to ignore her, and Elise was staring down the table with real concern. Ryan had no wish to distress her. Soon, pudding had come and gone, and the ladies were invited to retire to the drawing room for sherry and hot chocolate. The gentlemen would linger around the table with the port. By the time they joined the women, Ryan would have made her excuses and gone.

Mayapple's formal drawing room was lined with windowed doors that opened to a stone terrace. The terrace was bordered by a wide railing that overlooked the garden. When the weather was fair, the doors were opened so ladies might enjoy the breeze or drift outside to view the night sky. Tonight, the servants had opened the doors to a gorgeous September moonrise. Ryan had never been so grateful to flee into the darkness. She'd passed her wedding night enduring the rudeness of arrogant dandies. She wanted nothing more than to pass ten minutes alone in the cool, cleansing air, then bid Elise and Killian Crewes good-night.

Unfortunately, her defection inspired a terrace migration. Soon the other ladies were spilling onto the flagstones. Lady Glynnis tottered to the railing, squinting into the dark garden. Elise Crewes led Mrs. Stanhope, now almost too drunk to walk, to the iron table and chairs. Five minutes later, the gentlemen meandered onto the terrace with glasses of port and pungent cheroots.

Ryan smothered a groan. She'd not expected the men to descend before she'd made her excuses and retreated to her bedroom. Moving quickly, she turned the corner where the terrace wrapped around the side of the house. Here the flagstones ended, but there was a door to the solarium or—even better—steps that led to a garden path that would take her to the kitchen entrance. It would be rude to slip away without saying good-night to Elise, but—

"Look at you, hovering in the shadows like a creature of the night."

Ryan spun around. Remarkably, unbelievably, Nevil Stanhope and his friend had come upon her in the secluded corner. They hovered, drinks in one hand, smoky cheroots in the other.

"I beg your pardon?" she said. The words came out

on a bitter little laugh. *Now* they deigned to address her? *Now?*

"*Lady Ryan*," drawled Mr. Fielding, as if he were testing the sound of it in his mouth.

Ryan recovered her composure and raised her chin. "You'll have to excuse me, gentlemen. I was bound for—"

"Come, come, *come now, my lady*," entreated Nevil Stanhope, his voice a slurred singsong. He pivoted to the right, effectively blocking her exit.

Ryan was so shocked at the aggressive move, she skittered two steps back. The chill of the night felt suddenly ten degrees colder.

"Don't tell me you're *leaving us*," he cajoled. "We haven't had the opportunity to answer your great many questions. We've finally had time to think of clever answers. You'd not want me to be a bore, would you, Lady Ryan? You'd not want me to venture answers to your questions before I'd given them proper thought?"

Ryan wanted to tell him that she doubted he was capable of proper thought. She wanted to tell him that there wasn't enough time in the world. She wanted to inform him that "quality" did not directly correlate to money or fashion or even an Oxford degree; decency and manners were what set people apart. More than any of these, however, she wanted to *go*; but they were hemming her in.

"Help me out here, Fielding," mused Nevil Stanhope, "what did she ask? *Did we* attend the same school as Dennis and Bartholomew? Well, *I* did. Charlie here was too much of a degenerate and was asked to leave after the first year. Luckless bastard finished at—where was it, Fielding?"

"Sod off, Stanhope," his friend said, laughing. "Degenerate, my arse. Takes one to know one, I always say."

"Answer me this, Lady Ryan," inquired Mr. Stanhope, turning back to her. It was too dark for her to clearly see his face, but his tone was mocking. Ryan pivoted, hoping to shove between them and flee.

"*Tut, tut, tut*," discouraged Mr. Stanhope, stepping closer. "Let's not retreat into shyness now. We're just getting to know each other. Why the rush?"

He stepped up in the same moment Ryan moved sideways, and she collided with his chest. He reached out with cold, clammy fingers, steadying her with a hand to her arm. His fingers felt like wet rope. She jerked back.

"Where's the enthusiasm we endured over dinner?" asked Mr. Fielding, boxing her in on the other side.

And now Ryan felt the first stirrings of real alarm. They endeavored to . . . to *what*? Ridicule her? Menace her? Trap her here and openly shame her while she gasped like a fish on dry land? She had too little experience with men to understand their motives, but she knew that drunkenness and boredom could rapidly lead to a situation that was unsafe.

Blocked from pressing forward, Ryan backed away. She bumped against the terrace railing and began to strategize how she might lower herself down the side and climb into the garden. Or perhaps she could try again to push past them. Would they actively restrain her? She could also cry out.

"Did you know," Mr. Stanhope was saying, "I actually *have* visited the Channel Islands. Jersey, I think it was. And you know what *I* found unforgettable? Not the ocean views, I assure you." His teeth flashed in the moonlight. "It was the *girls*. There's something about being confined to an island, I think, that makes Channel Islands girls so very accommodating—"

"Step away from the lady."

A new voice broke into the night. It was low, and calm, and lethal.

Gabriel.

Ryan spun toward his voice, eyes wildly searching the darkness.

"Who's there?" clipped Mr. Stanhope, head snapping around.

"Step away," Gabriel repeated.

Ryan saw him now—or she saw half of him. He came up the steps from the garden path in a slow, heavy ascent. With every step, more of his broad shoulders and muscled arms came into view. He wore no jacket or waistcoat, simply his shirt, the sleeves rolled up to reveal his thick arms. His hands were balled into fists.

"But is it the *gardener* coming to your aid, Lady Ryan?" scoffed Mr. Stanhope. To Gabriel he said, "Sod off. This doesn't concern you."

"I'll not ask you again," said Gabriel. He'd reached the top step and his full height towered four inches above the heads of the Oxford men. He wore buckskins and tall boots and looked to Ryan like a giant, bearded avenging angel.

"There's a true statement if ever I've heard one," mocked Stanhope. "Last I knew, servants don't make requests of gentlemen. Nor do they concern themselves with ladies. If you value your job, man, *piss off."*

Stanhope glanced at Ryan, looked away, and then looked back again. "Hold on," he drawled. "Perhaps I'm mistaken. Perhaps Lady Ryan *is* your concern. My lady—you little minx. Is it possible we've disrupted some *hidden arrangement* you have with this . . . this . . . What are you, mate? Gardener? Groom? Stable boy?"

Stanhope looked back and forth between Ryan and Gabriel.

His friend Mr. Fielding had begun to back away. "Leave it, Stanhope. It's not worth upsetting your father."

Stanhope held up a hand to his friend and leered at Ryan. "Please, my lady, I beg you, do the first interesting thing anyone has done all night: Tell me you've some understanding with the gardener?"

"He is no servant," Ryan whispered, her voice unheard over the pounding of her own heart. And here was another challenge of their sham marriage. She wanted to proclaim to everyone that he was her husband. She wanted to tell skinny-necked Nevil Stanhope that she was a married woman—in fact, she was a *princess*—that she belonged to someone, and he belonged to her, and he should not address her if he couldn't show the most base modicum of respect. But of course she'd asked the Creweses to keep introductions simple, to not complicate the night by explaining her absent husband. In this, Nevil Stanhope had been correct. She and Gabriel *did* have a "hidden arrangement."

She looked to Gabriel. He did not meet her gaze. He stared at Stanhope with a narrow-eyed expression of simmering fury.

"I beg your pardon?" Stanhope asked her. He

leaned and slid a hand to the small of her back. Ryan jumped. "You'll have to speak u—"

Gabriel moved so quickly, Ryan felt the rush of air before she registered his lunge. One moment he was standing on the top step, watching Stanhope with a glacial stare, the next he had the man pinned against the side of the house with a forearm across his throat.

"You will apologize to the lady," Gabriel said.

Stanhope made a gurgling noise. Mr. Fielding inched farther away, following the railing toward the larger terrace.

"Here is what will happen," Gabriel told Stanhope. "I'll release your neck, and you will apologize to *my wife*."

Gabriel levered his arm to a slant.

"Who?" choked Stanhope, coughing and wheezing.

"Wrong answer," said Gabriel. He removed his arm altogether, and Stanhope slid down the wall to the ground.

"Get up," Gabriel said. "Apologize."

"Your wife?" wheezed Stanhope, turning to the wall for support, climbing his way to standing.

With no warning, Stanhope shoved off the wall and threw himself at Gabriel. Ryan let out a little scream. Gabriel dodged left, easily avoiding the lunge. Half a second later, Gabriel swung, landing his right fist in Stanhope's gut. The man grunted, doubled over, and fell to his knees.

"Try again," Gabriel said, pivoting to make room for the sprawling Stanhope.

"Nevil?!" called a new voice.

Stanhope's brother Dennis and Bartholomew Crewes skidded to the corner, gaping at the row.

"You're joking, Nevil!" Dennis Stanhope exclaimed. "Not again. You ruin everything. I told Papa not to allow you to come."

"Don't make a fuss, Dennis, there's a good lad," cajoled Mr. Fielding, now halfway down the railing. "You didn't see it but we were attacked by a member of staff."

"This man? He's not a member of staff," said Bartholomew, "that is the brother of my aunt. He's a bloody French *prince*."

"Bart?" Ryan cut in, angling for control, "will you fetch Killian, please? Extract him *quietly* if you can. Don't disrupt the others."

"Yes, yes," said Bartholomew, "if you can assure me you're unharmed, Lady Ryan?"

"Oh yes. But about your uncle? Quickly, please Bart?"

Bartholomew nodded and darted away.

"I cannot enjoy one, solitary, decent friendship, Nevil!" Dennis railed at his brother. "Not one—without you mucking it up. Bartholomew's family are nice people; I waited a month for this invitation. And you attack his relative like a common footpad?"

"What the devil is going on?" Killian Crewes strode around the corner with Bartholomew. He took in Ryan's expression, Gabriel's balled fists, and Mr. Stanhope doubled over on the ground.

"Lady Ryan, are you well?" Killian asked.

"Perfectly well, Mr. Crewes. Please do not worry. There was just—"

"Say no more," breathed Killian.

For a moment, Ryan thought she'd made a mistake—that Killian would challenge or question

Gabriel. One glance at Gabriel and she realized her husband thought the same. This sort of public reckoning was a primary reason Gabriel dreaded leaving the forest.

But Killian wanted no reckoning. He glanced over his shoulder, tightened his gloves, and then smiled coolly at the group.

"Bart, can you and Dennis escort Mr. Stanhope to his feet and then off the terrace? His friend, too. Nope, not another step, Fielding. Off you go. Take the garden path to my carriage. Tell Tom to convey them to the fountain in Marlborough—but not a mile farther. There Tom will *deposit* them and return home. This will leave the family carriage here for Sir James and the others when they depart. I'll make excuses for Mr. Fielding and Mr. Stanhope so as to not upset Dennis's parents and grandmother."

"Right, Killian," said Bartholomew. He and his friend each took one of Mr. Stanhope's arms and began dragging him down the steps.

"Don't just stand there, Charlie," Dennis called to Mr. Fielding. "You're no stranger to evictions from civilized company."

"Let go, Denny," growled Mr. Stanhope, staggering to stand between Dennis and Bartholomew. Dennis hissed something at him and kneed him in the hip.

"You're certain you're unharmed, Lady Ryan?" asked Killian, turning back to her. "I've worried over your wellness all night. I apologize for imposing these men on your end of the table. I should've asked them to leave an hour ago. I'd no idea they'd descended upon you here in the shadows."

"Do not think of it again," Ryan assured him. "No

harm done. I'll shed no tears over their departure, but I'm grateful the party has not been ruined for the others. Dennis seems like a nice boy."

"Dennis and Bart are having the time of their lives, never you fear," Mr. Crewes said. The sound of punching could be heard in the direction of the carriages.

He glanced at Gabriel. "Can you manage from here?"

Ryan swung her gaze to Gabriel. She had no prediction for what he would do.

Slowly, Gabriel nodded to his brother-in-law.

"Very good," Mr. Crewes said. And then he yanked on his lapels, spun on his heel, and disappeared around the corner.

And now Ryan was alone on the dark terrace with her husband. Her breath was frozen in her chest. Gabriel was so handsome, and avenging, and *here*—when she'd really needed him, he'd been here. Her broken heart tried again to beat—all fifty pieces of it, scattered about her chest, thumping and lurching to life.

He locked eyes with her—that warm, hazel intensity focused entirely on her. Ryan's inside dissolved into shimmers. Ducking his head, he held out one, tentative hand.

Ryan leaped, throwing herself into his arms. He swept her to him, burying his face in her neck. She wrapped her legs around his hips and he swept a hand beneath her bottom. Without another word, he carried her down the steps into the night.

CHAPTER TWENTY-FOUR

GABRIEL WAS MINDLESS. Mindless with rage at the man who dared insult Ryan, who put his hand on her; mindless with need because she was in his arms again.

He'd spent the afternoon trying to keep away from her. He'd given directions to his grooms about dismantling the furnishings for the wedding. He'd thanked them and given them an extra bag of coins for the vast change to their responsibilities these last weeks. He'd ridden to Mayapple and taken out each of Killian's stallions, urged them to run full out and jump hedges and cantor sideways like dancers. His goal had been to pound out the doubts and desires warring inside his mind and exhaust his body to the point of collapse.

He'd succeeded only in the exhaustion—although in this moment, striding across the garden to the stables, Ryan in his arms, he felt exhilarated and boundless. He wasn't exhausted, he was on fire. He could carry her to his camp in the forest, or to Scotland, or the moon.

He strode the garden path instead, across the stable yard, to the door of the small room. He kicked it open without slowing. Ryan had burrowed into him, pressing her lips to the sensitive skin just below his ear.

She kissed, and licked, and savored; and Gabriel's consciousness shrank to the sensation in that one spot and the echoing throb of his erection.

Once inside, he slammed the door with his boot and spun. He pressed her against the door and let out a moan. He released her only long enough to turn the lock.

"*I'm sorry*," he breathed, speaking the words against her lips.

"Sorry for . . . ?" she asked sharply. Her voice was demanding and accusatory, but she didn't wait for an answer; she kissed him hard and then pulled back. "For what are you sorry, Gabriel?"

"Sorry that I wasn't there—not at dinner, like a reasonable . . ." He couldn't think of what reasonable role he would've filled at dinner, so he kissed her instead.

"A doting husband?" she suggested, speaking between kisses. "A faithful lover?"

He pulled back and stared at her, breathing hard. He deserved this, and he knew it—but his excuses were shite. There was nothing left to say.

"It couldn't be either of those," she mused. "You are not doting, and we are not lovers, are we?"

As if to make a point, she glanced downward. Their bodies were pressed tightly together. He'd pinned her to the door.

"You're cross," he breathed.

"We are not lovers," she repeated, "and you're not really my husband, despite the fact that we stood for the most beautiful wedding anyone has ever seen, and it's been documented and witnessed and will prevent me from marrying your cousin."

She kissed him hard and then popped her mouth from his and took his face in her hands. "What are you, Gabriel? If you could not come to dinner and I was left to my own devices with those terrible men? Are you my devoted *friend*? Is that what we are, Gabriel? Friends?" She kissed him again hard, arching off the doorway, pressing her soft heat against his aching need.

It occurred to Gabriel that "crossness" did not accurately describe how she felt in this moment. She was angry—and she had every right to be. He lifted her from the door and carried her to the bed.

He would've doubted her willingness to be kissed and carried and pressed against doors if she weren't so tightly wrapped around him. Her legs hugged his hips. Her arms were at his shoulders. While he stared, panting, at her beautiful face, she launched herself at his mouth, kissing him like a woman starved. She was cross *and* she wanted him. And she would have answers, apparently. God knew she deserved them.

"I am," he growled, striding to the bed, "the only one permitted to touch you. No one but me."

He lowered her onto the mattress and came down on top of her. He searched her face, praying this answer was enough. It was woefully insufficient but also the bloody truth.

"So touch me then," she dared. "If you are the only one, *touch me*, Gabriel—*please*."

The miracle of this answer was a pardon and an invitation at once. It was mindless, and he loved descending into a mist of irrational need and possession with her. There was no logic or reason or tomorrow or next week. He'd come for her in the most primal way, and she'd allowed him to take her.

"Take off the dress," he rasped, peeling himself off of her. First *this*, he thought. He'd wanted to see her, to see all of her, since that first night in the dark cave. He'd wanted her splayed before him; to look his fill and touch with no limits and bring pleasure. He wanted to simply *resonate* beside her nakedness, like a cymbal struck; to thrum and vibrate and hum for her.

He balanced on a knee and rolled her toward the wall, giving himself access to the fasteners.

"The girls chose the dress," she said.

"I don't care," he said. He brought his hands to the fasteners and began, roughly, to unflick each of them.

She gave a shocked little laugh. "You don't care that your nieces chose it or you don't care that I'm wearing it?"

"My only care for this dress is that it's off your body."

"Of course," she said, and he paused. He was losing her. He'd said the wrong thing. All of this was wrong, of course; and they could only forge ahead in the wrongness if they descended together.

He dropped his head over her shoulder and stared at her upside down. "What would you have me say about this dress? Before it's on the floor—what would you have me say?"

"Nothing," she said.

He sat up and stared, objectively, at the dress. "It's blue," he tried.

She laughed and dropped a hand over her face.

"It's shimmery," he guessed.

Her eyes were shielded, but he could see a small smile. He was on the correct path.

"I can see," he added, "why it would appeal to children."

She made a noise of surrender and tipped over, pressing her face into the mattress, offering him the row of tiny buttons.

He pulled her back, balancing her again on her side. He leaned over her. "Tell me what you would have me say. The dress is, in fact, green?"

Ryan sat up, and he dodged her just in time to avoid bumping heads. "Why," she asked, "would I—or any woman—care about the shade of the gown, Gabriel?"

He panicked. His only regard for the gown was that it remained on her body. Also, she was no longer prone. Also, they'd stopped kissing. Also, he wasn't touching her. She—

"Forget it. This is my error." She sighed. "I was fishing for compliments."

Gabriel thought of this, he thought of what he knew of women and dresses and compliments (almost nothing); and he thought of what he knew of Ryan's face, and body, and her presence in any room, or standing in his garden, or on a dark hillside in the rain.

She was shaking her head, staring into the distance. "Foolish," she said to herself. She dropped to the mattress again.

Gabriel caught her up, taking her by the arms and rolling her onto her back. Her eyes went wide, and she brought up her hands to clasp his shoulders.

"Ryan," he tried, "my mind does not interact with beauty like that of a man who is socialized and accustomed to the guiles of a pretty female."

"Please—" she cut in, squeezing her eyes shut. She turned her head to the side.

He dipped and kissed her neck. "Allow me to finish."

She let out a little moan, and Gabriel exhaled. The damage was not irreparable. He'd not lost her.

He rooted up her neck and spoke directly into her ear. "I have taken your beauty for granted, Ryan, I can see that now. And the reason is—I take all beauty for granted. It would not occur to me to compliment the sky after a summer storm, no matter how radiant; nor the wing of a dragonfly, no matter how intricately lined or iridescent. I do not tell the deep green cavern of the forest that it's breathtaking, nor the brook that it's smooth. My life is awash in natural beauty—and I cleave to it, and derive my sanity from it, but I also take it for granted . . . because *I can*. You've seen how disinclined I was to leave the forest—this is but one of many reasons why.

"When first I saw you—nay, every time I look upon you—I see beauty equal to the untouched, natural splendor that has been my daily abundance for years. I see radiance and smoothness in your face, I see serenity in your bearing, I see perfection in your small, gentle hands, and your soft earlobe and delicate ankles. My breath is taken away when I look upon you; I cannot resist you—as we've seen. And I cannot share you, as we've also seen.

"In my very great entitlement, I've allowed myself to touch you, and kiss you, and see as much of your softly curved body as I possibly can. But it has *not* occurred to me to *say* any of this to you. Your dress, be it blue, or green, or the color of a riverbed after a drought, would have almost no impact, because I don't care about dresses. I see the body and the face, both made perfect in heaven but existing within my own reach here on earth."

He pulled away from her ear and studied her face. "Do you see, Ryan?"

She blinked up at him, tears in her eyes, bottom lip bit between her teeth, and nodded. Her arms went around his neck and she tugged him to her. His mouth found hers and they devolved into another kiss. The mindlessness returned, and he kissed her like they were descending into a wonderful, hazy trance. Only when he felt himself begin to press against her, to thrust and nudge to stoke the burn between his legs, did he pry himself off, tip her sideways, and return to the fasteners at her spine. She went easily, her body pliant and languid, and he worked quickly, his hands shaking, his body as hard as iron.

"I would see you," he rasped. "If you doubt my incredible regard for your beauty, Ryan, look no further to how desperate I am now to *see* you."

By some miracle, the dress opened easily, and she scooted and lifted and allowed him to peel it from her body. Beneath the dress, she wore a thin bell of petticoats and stiff stays. The petticoats went the way of the dress, revealing stockings secured at her thighs with garters and loose cotton drawers.

Gabriel swallowed hard, gaping at the resplendent display of sensual woman sprawled on his bed. "Now this," he rasped, "I feel compelled to remark upon. You are gorgeous. I can barely touch you, you're so gorgeous."

With shaking hands, he unfastened the stays, releasing heavy breasts with dusky nipples. The sight of them poised Gabriel on the precipice of what felt like a small crisis. He'd never wanted so urgently to touch, to feel, to weigh, to tease; but he also wanted her entirely naked before him, he wanted to finish what he'd started. His mouth watered, his hands trembled, he stared with his breath caught. His erection felt like a marble club between his legs.

And then she arched up, peaking her breasts in his direction, and he let out an agonized moan.

Moving quickly, he slicked the stockings from her legs, dragging the garters with them. After the stockings, he tugged down her drawers; this afforded him the glorious sight of the triangle of dark curls at the juncture of her thighs. Gabriel swallowed hard and exhaled again.

When, at last, she was completely naked, he staggered to a stand and hovered on the side of the bed, looking down at her.

She tried very hard to be shy; eyes downcast, arm draped across her breasts, knees together, tipping slightly to the side. But she was grinning; and her half-lidded eyes lit with delight.

"You're remarkable," he whispered.

Her head snapped up. "And now compliments suddenly spring to mind?"

"I'm sorry, Ryan; there are skies after a storm, and then there are *skies after a storm*. Looking at you is like seeing the most glorious blue illuminated by a golden sun. You are *incredible*."

Her shyness dissolved after that, and she preened a little—she actually preened—and Gabriel, mindless again, stripped from his clothes and dove for her, scooping her up and pressing every glorious inch against his bare skin.

"What are we doing?" she whispered, trying to keep up with his mouth.

"We are mindless," he whispered.

"Oh, good," she said.

"In fact, I may never have a functioning mind, ever again."

CHAPTER TWENTY-FIVE

"*W*HAT DO YOU want?" Gabriel whispered into her ear.

"I beg your pardon?" Ryan breathed.

"Que veux-tu que je te fasse, Princesse?" *What do you want done to you, Princess?*

Ryan opened her eyes. He'd never referred to her as "princess." If he called her princess, he acknowledged not only his own title, but their union, as well.

"I don't know," she said. "I want what you did before. On the first night. In your cave."

He kissed her. "So you do know what you want."

"Well, is there more?"

He made a grumbling noise and dropped his lips to her neck. His beard tickled her cheek, and her jaw, and her throat. Oh, how she adored his beard.

"I would have your beard on me," she said. "Everywhere. And I would touch you."

"Is that all?" He'd draped himself against her, but now he stretched, aligning the long, muscled heft of him squarely on her body.

She moaned at the delicious pressure. "I don't know."

Try everything, she thought. And, *It's only for tonight.* And, *Remember it, cherish it.*

"Don't think," he whispered in her ear. "We'll not survive this if we think."

She nodded, reaching for mindlessness. Now she would only *feel*.

"When you were in my cave," he said, "which, allow me to reveal to you, felt at the time like the most unbelievable good fortune that could befall any man. In case you couldn't tell. A beautiful woman knocking about my cave half-dressed? Imploring me to lie with her, to touch her? I wanted every inch of you. From your smallest toe to the hair on top of your head. I wanted to memorize you."

"Perhaps I might do that to you?"

He chuckled against her neck. "My good fortune does not run to that. Surely."

"That's what I want, Gabriel," she said. "Will you lie back? Will you let me touch you? All of you? From your smallest toe to the top of your head?"

He let out a half laugh, have moan, squeezed her, but rolled to the side, flopping on the mattress next to the wall.

"Oh lovely," she said, pressing up from the bed. She scooted to her knees and shimmied backward, working her way to his feet. The room was dim, only one candle and a low fire in the stove, but she could see him and she looked her fill. He was a large, thick man but with no fat; each muscle defined. His arms were like ropes; his abdomen a cluster of taut plates.

And then she saw his erection. She blinked, unprepared for the size and rigidity of it. It rose from a nest of dark hair, straining toward her, lifting off his belly. Ryan sucked in a little breath; she felt a rush of heat flood to her face.

"If your goal is to kill me, Ryan," he grunted, "you're very close. Very close."

She glanced at him, licked her lips, and moved farther down his body. In the cave, he'd started at her feet, and so would she.

"Can you move to the center of the bed, so I have room?"

He nudged sideways and the movement caused his erection to bob. Ryan narrowed her eyes, studying him, determined to miss nothing. She would savor, and test, and remember all of it.

She rose on her knees, dragging both palms down his hard thighs to the tops of his feet. She explored the arch, the round bone of his ankle, the space between each toe. She glanced up. He'd tucked his hands behind his head, the posture of a man in repose. He gazed down at her with half-lidded eyes.

Reposed are you? she thought, biting her lip. *I accept that challenge.* Her hands reversed and felt upward, savoring the scrape of the hair on his legs, cupping the long muscle of his calf.

Gabriel let out a noise, half moan, half sigh. She smiled and dusted her hands to the tops of his legs to rest on his knees. His thighs were powerful, bulging with muscle; his calves tight and hard. His knees commanded all of these, and she could feel the strength there, the flexibility, the parts he used to ride a horse or climb a hill. It was breathtaking to roam freely over the broad expanses, now naked and relaxed, twitching under her touch.

After she'd tickled the area behind each knee and elicited another groan, she moved upward to massage the hard muscle of his massive thighs.

"But do you ride, Mr. Rein?" she asked idly, trying to be clever. But her voice came out broken and a little trembly; she sounded like a bird. Coincidentally, Ryan felt as if an entire flock flapped inside of her. Her heart had taken flight; swallows did loops in her belly, and a thousand wings fanned the burn between her legs.

Above his thighs strained the *obvious*—his jutting erection, and she remembered what he'd done to her that night in the dark cave. He hadn't explored her so much as covered her body with his hand and pressed. He'd made her warm and alive and burn with little more than the heel of his hand. Dare she endeavor this? She wanted to make him burn, but she wasn't certain that she was finished exploring him—really, thoroughly, exploring him.

Shyly, she glanced up. He watched her still, but his expression was less languid; darker, more heated. He'd pulled his arms from behind the pillow and rested his palms on either side of his hips. She raised her eyebrows and licked her lips, a question. He slowly hissed one word: *"Yes."*

"Yes?" She wanted to be sure.

"Ryan," he growled, and his hands closed on the bedsheets, squeezing them in balled fists.

Taking a deep breath, Ryan closed her eyes and slowly lowered her face against him. She felt the prickle of his body hair; she felt the hot, smooth steel of his erection, she felt his pulse pounding in his groin.

"Actually," he grunted, reaching for her shoulders, "I'll not last. Sorry, love, if we're meant to carry on longer than five seconds more, I'll not survive *that*."

She raised her head, and blinked at him.

"In fact," he rasped, "I may not survive the vision

of you, hovering over me, naked and innocent—Oh
God. Will you touch me? Please? A hand? Hell, a
wrist? A lock of hair?"

Ryan had never before seen him so agonized. His
eyes were now closed, he breathed in and out in heavy
puffs. Ryan licked her lips and carefully, delicately,
settled her hand on his erection. It felt soft to the touch,
but also solid. The skin was loose but the density was
hardness and thickness.

"Is this alright?" she whispered.

His only reply was a whimper.

Ryan was intrigued and excited and she couldn't
believe she'd devoted so much time to toes and knees
and ankles when there was *this*. She knelt over him,
bobbing her hand, testing the feel of him. She checked
his expression, watched it shift from agony to bliss
and back again. His moans and sighs fluttered across
her like a caress.

The burn and need in her own body were rising;
too demanding to ignore. Had he burned for her when
he'd touched her that night in the cave? Had he wanted
her as much as she wanted him now?

"Enough," he rasped, reaching for her wrist. "I can't
endure. Mercy, please, Ryan. Leave it. If you carry on
with this torture, I cannot torture you in return."

She liked the sound of this, so she released him.
She massaged her hands over his flat belly, nudging
fingertips into the seams of muscles, tracing the broad
planes of his chest. She kneed forward and straddled
his hips to properly reach farther up. When her body
settled on his erection, the folds of her sex grazed his
hot, smooth skin, and she let out a sigh.

This, she thought, *this* was the answer to the heat

currently burning her up. She allowed herself an experimental nudge and yes—exactly, perfectly *this*. She snapped her head up, checking for his reaction. He stared back, his hazel eyes blazing with intensity and lust. She pushed against him once more, reveling in the blast of sensation that sparkled from her core.

"Careful," he warned. His hands found her hips. "I'd hate for you to become too distracted to properly complete this long, slow killing. Of me. You're killing me, Ryan."

Ryan ignored him and returned her attention to the muscles of his chest. Every few minutes, she thrust again, riding another blast of pleasure. Between the feast of muscles beneath her hands, and the hard, insistent erection between her legs, Ryan was rapidly losing her ability to navigate. She was distracted; she wanted to play, and ride, and touch, and taste. She'd paused to explore the hair on his chest, running her fingers back and forth, flicking his nipples, shaping her hands over his pectorals.

"I'm going to touch you now," Gabriel whispered.

Ryan blinked and looked up.

"Forget I was here, did you?" he asked.

"You are all that is here," she whispered.

"Let me touch you?"

"Yes."

His hands slid from her hips and found her swaying breasts. When his calloused fingers brushed her nipples, Ryan's hands went still, her eyes dropped closed, and her mind went white.

"*That's right*," he hissed. "It's ever so fun when one of us explores, but it's the very best when we both . . ."

And now his words dropped off, because Ryan had

begun to thrust more steadily, harder; she was riding him. Maybe he finished the sentence and maybe he didn't, because she'd stopped hearing.

"Enough," he growled and he rolled to the side, tipping her to the mattress. She whimpered, hating the loss of contact, but then he pinned her down, straddling her, rubbing his hands across her belly and over her breasts, and cupping her face in his hands.

"Enough," he soothed, dropping his mouth to her neck, nuzzling her with his beard.

"Are you ready?" he asked.

"Ready?"

"Will you have all of me?" he growled.

"Yes," she breathed, "all."

"Are you certain?"

"Yes, I'm certain. Please. Before the end of our time together. Give me this."

"We will regr—"

"Don't say it," she begged. "Don't say it, don't say it—don't you dare ruin this by saying that." She clawed at his shoulders, pulling him down.

"I'll pull from your body before I spill my seed. We mustn't get you with child, above all else."

"I don't care," she cried. "I would bear your baby. I would raise it and love it. Do what you want—I know I cannot ask that of you, above all—but *I don't care.*"

After that, he ceased talking. He kissed her. He nudged her thighs apart with his knee, he took his erection in his hand and slowly, smoothly, slid into her.

"Oh," she cried, unprepared for the tightness, the fullness.

"Are you alright?" he gasped. His voice was choked, struggling.

"Yes."

He nodded, sniffed, and sank all the way on a long, slow moan. When their bellies touched, he leveled himself on top of her and lowered his head, breathing into her neck.

"Still alright?" he huffed.

"I think so," she said. The pleasure was gone, but the new sensation wasn't *terrible*. It was intimate and heavy and tight.

"Give me a moment," he huffed. "You've cast the most sensual experience like a spell, and I need a moment to recover my control."

"Are you hurt?" she asked.

He laughed. "Oh no—not hurt. The opposite. My God, you're tight."

"But what comes next?" she asked.

"We kiss," he breathed, moving to her mouth.

Ryan's eyes were open, but she saw only shapes and shadows. The whole of her consciousness was focused on the wedge of his body inside her. It was tight, and slippery, and full. In her periphery, she saw him draw closer to her lips; she felt him nibble at the corner of her mouth.

"Breathe, Ryan," he whispered as he kissed her. "Breathe."

Ryan drew in a shaky breath. Gabriel added his tongue to the kiss, licking her, teasing the seam of her lips. She laughed a little, licking him back, and her eyes fell shut. The kiss grew deeper, more sensual; and slowly, magically, the tightness between her legs gave way to a restless need to *not* keep still. She wanted to move. She felt the familiar burn that wanted satiation, that wanted to press, that wanted *him*.

"Oh," she gasped, kissing harder, giving her hips an upward, testing lift.

Gabriel groaned. The sound only heightened the burn and she lifted again.

"That's it," he hissed against her mouth. "Are you alright?"

"Yes." A breath. "Yes."

And then they were off. Ryan moved freely, rocking her hips against him. She had the sense that Gabriel held back, that he wanted her to set the rhythm. When she raised her knees on either side of his hips and dug her heels into the mattress, he finally, let go.

Devouring her mouth, crushing her against him, he matched the movement of her hips, thrusting, rocking, leading them in a dance that was both new to Ryan but also somehow known.

She clung to him, met him thrust for thrust, kissed him with all of the love in her heart. When the hot, wet, burning sensation began to build, when she felt the demanding sizzle to her very core—when her only thought was satiating it—she knew what was coming. She'd experienced this on their first night. *This* was the glorious bit, the undoing, the moment where he took her to the edge of the world and swung her round and round over open air.

She cried out when it hit her, repeating his name, again and again.

He held himself still, allowing her to explode around him, kissing her all the while. Eventually, her breathing slowed to a shallow pant; and she opened her eyes, blinking at the ceiling. Slowly but deeply, he began to move.

"Alright?" he grunted.

She nodded, grasping his shoulders, holding on.

"Alright?" he asked again, his body rocking faster, harder.

"Yes, Gabriel. I am alright."

And then he let out a guttural sort of *roar* and pulled from inside her. Ryan flinched, unprepared for the loss of contact. He fell on top of her, spilling his seed on the sheets.

"Gabriel," she said. Not a request, not a call, not a question. She simply said his name.

He lay across her, panting.

She settled one hand on his back. His skin was wet with perspiration. She dipped another into his hair. She hooked an ankle over his leg. He slid an arm beneath her back and scooped her tightly to him. He buried his face in her hair.

Ryan's mind floated in a shimmery pleasure haze; but questions, a million questions, crowded in. *Why had they waited so long? Why would he not want this for always? When could they do it again?*

She would ask this—she would ask all of this—but at the moment she was so very sleepy—exhausted, even. And he felt so good; damp and heavy and languid on top of her. She allowed her eyes to fall closed; sleep had just begun to drip down the corners of her brain, when they were startled by a knock on the door.

"Gabriel?" came an insistent voice, from outside. "Gabriel, it's Killian, are you there?"

Gabriel tightened his hold with one hand and took up the sheet with the other, draping it over her.

"We're in search of Lady Ryan," Killian continued, "and we cannot find her."

And now Elise's voice came through the door. "We've an urgent letter by messenger from her aunt in London. Her sisters at Winscombe have written that Maurice has returned to Guernsey. He did not wait until October; he is already there."

CHAPTER TWENTY-SIX

$\mathcal{K}$ILLIAN CREWES HAD known both of them would be inside Gabriel's room; likely in some manner of half dress. Elise had been less prepared. When Ryan stumbled from the bedroom, clutching her unfastened dress to her body, Elise reacted like a bird flew at their faces.

Gabriel, clad also in only a sheet, rushed behind her and rested two hands on his wife's shoulders.

"When did the letter arrive?" Ryan asked, reaching for the paper in Killian's hand.

"Just now, actually," Killian said. "We were seeing off the Stanhopes when a rider clattered up. It's expensive to dispatch a runner in the night, but your aunt was right to do it. Based on what you've said of Maurice—especially as it pertains to your youngest sister—there is no time to spare."

"No," Ryan agreed. "No, there's not. I must go. I must go *now*. Diana wrote this letter on Friday. That was six days ago. This means Maurice has been prowling around Winscombe for nearly a fortnight. Diana will protect Charlotte—but who will protect Diana? She is impatient and outspoken and prone to arguments. If he launched his dogs at me, what will her insubordination invite? I must leave here. I must go to them right away." She scanned the stables like a woman who intended to ride away in a bedsheet.

Finally, Gabriel spoke. "You cannot travel in the middle of the night, Ryan. Remember Channing Meade? You'll make the same progress if you pack tonight, sleep for a few hours, and leave at sunrise. You'll make London by Saturday and Portsmouth by the next day."

"I cannot spare the detour to London. My aunt will understand. I'll go to Portsmouth directly. This will save time, correct?" She looked around frantically, searching each person's face.

"A little," consented Killian. He dared not look at Gabriel. His brother-in-law must step up; he *must* do the correct thing. But the decision had to come from Gabriel. Neither Elise nor Killian could coerce him. If nothing else, Gabriel could ride with her as far as Portsmouth—they'd make better time on horseback. Killian was happy to put them in his carriage, but if she meant to sprint to the coast, she should leave her maid and her trunk and ride on fast horses.

"What of Mr. Soames?" Ryan asked suddenly, looking up from the letter. "We've not yet met with him."

Killian shook his head. "He's expected any day, but he's not here now. Obviously."

"Right," she said. "Well, I have our marriage license. It'll be Maurice's word against mine. If nothing else, my claim of being a married woman will slow things down. Perhaps this will give Mr. Soames time to travel to us."

"I'll go."

The words came from Gabriel.

Thank God. Killian steeled his face to have no reaction, but Elise was not so controlled. She slapped a hand over her mouth and gave a small, ecstatic bounce.

Lady Ryan swung about, gaping at her husband.

"I'll go," Gabriel repeated; his tone broached no argument. "You cannot go alone. I can help you. I am not without honor, Ryan; please don't insult me with the suggestion that I would send you to face him alone."

"But—" began Ryan.

"Please," Gabriel said, his voice as hard as rock.

"Fine," Ryan said. "What of your horses and your camp?"

"We'll leave at first light, just as Killian said," Gabriel told her. "If his driver will convey us to Pewsey, we'll hire horses there and change mounts every few hours. It's the fastest way."

"Thank you," she breathed.

"Elise, can I impose on you to assist her with her dress and see her safely and discreetly inside?" Gabriel asked. "I must ride to camp to set things to rights and fetch a few items."

"What can I do?" asked Killian.

Gabriel shook his head. "This is my responsibility."

"It's not," insisted Ryan firmly.

"Go," Gabriel ordered. "We ride at dawn."

CHAPTER TWENTY-SEVEN

𝒥T TOOK THEM two days and two nights to reach
Portsmouth. The first night was spent in an inn, but
the second night, they rode straight through—not Gabriel's preference, but Ryan knew there was only one
ship sailing to Guernsey every day, and it left at ten
o'clock in the morning. If they spent a second night in
an inn, they would miss the sailing and be stranded
on the mainland for a third day.

Gabriel did not argue with her. He threw himself
into the logistics—minding the horses, discovering
where they could change them out for fresh mounts,
studying the map. This left her to train her eyes on the
horizon, say very little, and *ride*.

She was an excellent horsewoman; he'd noticed
that she was comfortable on a horse when he'd escorted her out of Savernake Forest, but he'd not fully
appreciated her natural ability until they'd left Mayapple the first day. Killian and Elise, along with her
weeping maid, Agnes, had gathered in the drive at
sunup to wish them well and worry over provisions.
Ryan had apologized for her rudeness, spurred her
mare forward, and left them. Gabriel had shaken
Killian's hand—he'd shaken Elise's, too; they'd hadn't

yet worked up to an embrace—promised he'd write, and galloped after Ryan. He'd been galloping after her for two days since.

They'd shared the room at the coaching inn on the first night. Ryan had proclaimed herself too stricken by anxiety to sleep, but then she'd burrowed into his side and exhaustion had claimed her. He was glad. Her mindset was wrong for lovemaking—his, too, for that matter, considering the great *reckoning* into which he was flinging himself—and although he was never *not* aroused whenever she was near him, she needed sleep.

They'd traveled, largely, in silence. They spoke only of routes, and hours, and when they would eat, and whether the horses were fit and watered. Only when they were on the ferry to Guernsey, standing at the bow, staring across the churning waves of the English Channel, did they finally engaged in a real conversation.

"I'm hearing seven hours to cross," he said to her. "Has that been your experience?"

"At least," she said, blinking when the sea threw mist into her face.

"Will you sleep? There are berths. You can close your eyes; recover from riding through the night."

"I'm not sure I can."

"You said that the first night and you slept like a rock. It would be useful, I think, to be rested when your family sees you."

"I look so very wretched?"

You look beautiful to me, he thought. She was wind-whipped and sun-kissed, and her riding habit was black at the hem from days of hard travel. It was, he thought, precisely his idea of beauty. But he wasn't prepared to compliment her. He felt stalked by impending heartbreak if he couldn't cope with what came next. He was careful not to allow either of them to hope.

"No," he said. "Not wretched at all. Me, on the other hand? I will appear—well, there's no disguising my appearance, is there?" He ran a hand over his beard. "Your siege on the imposter will benefit from one of us looking civilized and not like a cave-dweller, surely."

She looked down at her dusty cloak and muddy boots; at her cracked and peeling gloves. Her hair fell from beneath her hat in sticky clumps. Idly, she patted it with her hand.

"Is that what you intend?" she asked, studying his face. "We'll besiege him together?"

"I—" Gabriel gripped the railing. "Probably? I'm sorry, Ryan. I've no idea what to expect—not from him, not from any of it. Mayapple was a revelation. A very sweet, very promising revelation. But taking on Winscombe is more than an indulgent sister and her besotted husband and daughters. If ever I intended to leave the forest—"

"—which you did not," she provided softly.

"—the very best place to do it was Mayapple. I can see that now. Winscombe sounds lovely—truly it does—and I will endeavor to stand with you. I'm not afraid of Maurice, but I'm unwilling to commit to becoming the Prince d'Orleans."

"Maurice is evicting three women and a sick old man because he is too weak and too lazy to take on anyone else. What could be more cowardly?" She tugged her mangled hat from her hair and rubbed her forehead. "Sorry. I know it's far more complicated than that. Let us simply reach the island, get the lay of the land, and take it as it comes, shall we?"

Gabriel snorted. "Devoted these last three days to building this intricate strategy, did you?" He was struck by such love for her in that moment. Even chasing across England, riddled with anxiety for her sisters, she was careful not to overcommit him. She was thoughtful and resourceful and loyal.

She turned back to the railing, dangling her hat over the water. "Here is my intricate strategy. We'll make landfall in St. Peter. We'll hire horses to ride to Winscombe; this will be a journey of another hour. The sun will be setting then, and Diana will be locking up for the night. You may ride the property or walk the grounds—whatever you wish. We've stables, just like the Creweses. Not quite so lavish; and it's teeming with bleating sheep, but there are horses, too. If it pleases you, you may . . ." she took a deep breath ". . . take refuge there while I locate my sisters, look in on my father, and discover the location of the imposter."

The boat deck rose and fell in a stomach-dropping swoop. Ryan lost her hat overboard—one minute she held it, the next it was snatched by the sea—and she cried out. She turned back to him with the most adorable look of consternation.

"Go below deck," he told her, speaking over the rough sea. "Wash, change, rest. I'll be down shortly to check on you. I'll bring you something to eat. I want to look at the sea."

Ryan studied him. "You've not been on a boat since you fled France, have you?"

"No," he said. "It's safe to say I am awash in all the things I've done since I fled France."

Two days earlier, back at Mayapple, Elise Crewes stood in the center of Bartholomew's bedchamber and whistled. Loudly. Her two daughters paused in their raucous marching and clapped their hands over their ears. Her old friend Sister Marie looked up from the map she was studying in the window seat. Bartholomew peeked from his open wardrobe, a stack of neckcloths in one hand and a pair of boots in the other. Various dogs ignored her, as did Baby Noelle, who sat in a sunny spot on the rug and gummed a cricket ball.

"Quiet, everyone," Elise called, "I must think. Bart, you've packed too much. How is one horse to bear the burden of a case so very large? Remember you and Sister Marie are *riding* to Portsmouth, not bouncing along in the carriage. Your goal is to be only a day behind them."

"Killian told me we're taking the carriage," complained Bartholomew. "The maid cannot ride on horseback for two days to Portsmouth. Besides, why am I going if not to bring the trunk of clothes to kit him out?"

"Oh that's right," said Elise with a sigh, resting a hand on her forehead. The plan had changed so many times. Even now, she wasn't certain they were doing the correct thing. In the correct order. With the correct friends and family as uninvited conspirators.

"Fine, the carriage," Elise amended, "but hurry, will you? The sooner you're packed the sooner you may leave."

"What if we hire a private boat to make the Channel crossing?" said Bartholomew. "Then we won't have to wait for the ferry."

"He's right," said Marie.

"Fine, good—yes. Do that. Just remember, Bartholomew, when you encounter Gabriel, your interference calls for a very light touch. Private boats and carriages are not my brother's style. You're there to offer Killian's suits—and only if Gabriel seems open to transforming his appearance. Chances are, he'll wish to remain exactly as he is. Which is fine. Don't make the offer if he seems annoyed you've followed him. The maid should stand ready to tailor everything— but again, only if he will allow it. Gabriel is larger than Killian, but Agnes is a genius with needle and thread. She's afraid of her own shadow, but she can be bribed with chocolate."

Killian strode into the room, carrying a traveling case and boot bag. He stepped over two dogs and tossed both items onto the bed. "I never thought marrying royalty would be such a drain on our wardrobes. How many dresses did you give Ryan? And now this."

"Ah, the magic weapon," Bartholomew called to the traveling case.

"*You* are the magic weapon, Bart," corrected Killian. "*You*. Not my suits. It's a delicate thing— playing valet to a long-lost prince, returned from the dead—but I wouldn't send you if I didn't think you could do it. You'll need to be observant and discreet and prepared for anything. Or nothing. Whatever Gabriel may need. Or doesn't need. We cannot send Elise, because she's too overbearing and like a mother hen. I would go myself except, *I don't want to go*."

"You would go yourself," corrected Elise, "except Gabriel must direct this on his own, as he sees fit. It's not our place. We've done enough—we've done *too* much. Me, overbearing? As if you've not manipulated them from the start." She shook her head at her husband.

"Perhaps I have done." Killian sighed. "Old habits die hard, I suppose. Which is why Bart is the perfect man to finish the job. He's never worked as a palace fixer. He's not too old, not too young; sweet and helpful and quick with chocolate."

"Sweet?" groused Bartholomew. "I am not sweet."

"You're very sweet," Elise said, sailing past him and plucking Sofie from his leg. "It's one of my favorite things about you."

"I've only agreed to this because it's a chance to see Guernsey. *And* it's so very close to the start of my school term. If I'm detained, I'll miss the first week of classes."

"You will *not* miss the start of the school term," lectured Killian. "You will deliver the maid Agnes, you will support Gabriel as needed, and vanish when you are not needed. We're sending you to be a non-intrusive, nonthreatening, friendly face—and to deliver a fresh set of clothes and the maid who can make them fit. Follow Marie's lead, she'll strike the correct balance."

"Follow my lead, Bartholomew!" called little Marie, climbing inside his traveling case.

"Not you, darling," said Elise, pulling her out. "*Sister Marie*, your namesake. You must stay here with Maman and Papa and your sisters and Nanny."

"But Nanny is—"

"Wait," said Killian, "don't tell me. Let me guess."

"Suffering from a toothache," suggested Bartholomew.

"Has a papercut," said Killian.

"A spider bite," said Bart.

The girls began to laugh. Elise crossed her arms over her chest and shook her head. "Stop."

"Has gotten her bun caught in the headboard," said Killian.

"Has seen a ghost," said Bart.

"Is plagued by a nosebleed," said Killian.

"I mean it," threatened Elise.

"One more," hooted Bartholomew. He narrowed his eyes, thinking. *"Has discovered she's really a French princess."*

"Careful," said Killian, "that one could actually happen."

"They could all actually happen," said Bart. "Poor Nanny."

"Ready?" asked Sister Marie, folding the map.

"If someone will fetch Agnes," Bart said, buckling his case.

"I'll get her," said Elise. "She's cowering in the servants' kitchens. She's confused and frightened, so be gentle with her. I think she would refuse to go along if she weren't so desperate to get home."

"We can go without her," said Bart. "You think I can't wrestle Gabriel into Killian's clothes? Let her come by mail coach at her own pace."

"No," said Elise. "He must look as fine and tailored and fitted as he possibly can. *If* he'll consent to a transformation. Being royal is ninety-five percent wardrobe."

"*Ninety-five percent*," said Bartholomew on a whistle. He glanced at his uncle.

Killian shrugged. "She's not wrong."

CHAPTER TWENTY-EIGHT

IF ABSENCE MAKES the heart go fonder, Ryan thought, cresting the hill that would put Winscombe into view, *what does vengeance do?*

And wasn't this a robbed moment? To see her beloved Winscombe for the first time in weeks and not feel heart-swelling love and joy . . . but instead to gird herself for battle. There hadn't been time to show Gabriel local landmarks or points of interest. He'd not been here since he was a boy and—tiniest hope in that relentless corner of her heart—she wanted him to love it as she loved it.

But Ryan had veritably sprinted from the boat, hired two horses, and pushed the animals up the road toward Winscombe at a punishing pace. She managed to tell him that the island was lovely in September, that the freesia were blooming, that the water was warm enough for bathing, but it was a rushed sort of overview, shouted over her shoulder. And her heart was not in it; she thought only of what crisis awaited her at home.

"There it is," she breathed, pointing to the estate, the pastureland, the cliff that overlooked the sea. "Do you remember it?"

"I think so," Gabriel said.

He'd been quiet since they'd disembarked in St. Peter. On the boat across the Channel, she'd done as he'd suggested and repaired to a belowdecks berth to wash and rest. An hour later, he knocked on her door, waking her from a half-sleep state. He'd said nothing, just stepped into the small space and closed the door behind him. Ryan had taken him in, wind-whipped, wet from the mist, his face grim. When he flipped the lock on the door, she'd launched herself at him.

He'd caught her up, embracing her for the first time since that night in the stables. They'd lain together in the coaching inn along the road to Portsmouth, but he'd not touched her like this. His hands were voracious, possessive, wild. Ryan answered with her own anxious, pent-up need. They didn't speak; he barely looked her in the eye. He walked her backward onto the small platform cot, kissing her hungrily, and reached a hand for her skirts. She raked them up, pushed her drawers to the side, and welcomed him. He released the ties on his buckskins with one hand and tilted her in position with the other.

He sank into her with no preamble, just a grunt and a sigh. Ryan had cried out at the pleasure of it, the possession, the consuming. They'd rocked together, using the sway of the boat to heighten their pleasure; a pulsing, throbbing tangle of knees, and hair, and breath.

"Please," she'd cried when the climax hit her; an invitation and a plea. She wanted him to find release inside her; she wanted him to *claim* her. But he repeated his withdrawal from the first time, pulling out just in time to spill his seed on the bench. Tears had swamped Ryan's eyes—the convergence of love, and want, and frustration, and fear.

Maurice, she'd vowed, *would not* ruin this. Gabriel *could* consider a life together that suited them both. This couldn't be the end.

After they were spent, they'd fallen asleep, burrowed in each other's arms. She woke to the sound of sailors, shouting their arrival. She'd sat up, listening for the familiar call of an osprey or island scrub jay; the salty, briny smell of home. Then they heard the anchor drop, and she hustled Gabriel out the door. An hour later, they'd been on horseback, pressing to Winscombe.

"I want you to have something," he said to her now, reining his horse to the side of the road.

"What is it?"

Her mare plodded to his gelding and Ryan reined her around, not wanting to lose sight of the house.

"You'll need a wedding ring," he said, pulling a velvet pouch from his coat. "Let us try this."

He turned the pouch upside down over his gloved palm, and a heavy gold ring, twinkling with stones and intricately carved with ebony recesses, dropped into his hand. He picked it up between his fingers and held it out.

Kneeing the mare forward, Ryan reached for it. "What is it?" she whispered. The gold was dense and heavy in her hand. It was a signet ring with jeweled crest.

"Will it fit?" he asked.

Ryan bit off her glove and tested it on the ring finger of her left hand. "It's a bit big, but—yes, it fits. What is it, Gabriel?"

"It was my father's signet ring. It's a pinky ring for men, but I hoped it would fit your ring finger."

Ryan looked closer, turning the mare so she could see the ring in the last rays of the setting sun. Tiny script spelled out some Latin motto. Another arc of text said, *d'Orleans.* She looked up.

"Gabriel?" she breathed.

"Wear it. We'll see what happens. If it's necessary for us to declare my true identity, it's another layer of truth. If it's not necessary, keep it as a token of my— well, as a token."

"Thank you," she said, sliding her glove over the ring. "Yes. We'll see what happens."

"We've made it before sunset," he said, urging his horse on. "Just as you planned."

"Yes. We were fortunate. The horses must have been expensive to hire. Thank you."

"You are an accomplished rider."

"Winscombe is vast," she said. "I've been riding the roads of this island since I was a child. You see that ridge there." She pointed to the west. "Our lands stretch from that ridge, which overlooks the sea, to the other side of that hill. It runs from the house *there* . . . into the wooded parkland that goes on as far as the horizon. Does none of this seem familiar? From when you visited as a boy?"

"Perhaps," he said, scanning the landscape. Ryan wanted to ask him if he thought it was beautiful, as she thought it was beautiful. She wanted to ask him if he could see himself living here, training horses here, abiding and existing here with a sense of well-being. But she would not press. She reminded herself that her most immediate goal was to catch Diana when she left the barn and before she entered the house.

They turned the last corner and the road descended a hill. The horses were forced to step carefully, and they slowed to a walk.

"But what are . . ." Ryan began, squinting at the long drive that led to the front gates of Winscombe. A chain of shiny vehicles lined the drive, their lacquer and gold trim shining in the setting sun.

"What is it?" Gabriel asked.

She exhaled. "Your cousin travels with an entourage and a retinue. These are his vehicles—all four of them, plus a wagon for his trunks and a curricle in which he zips about. He does not ride. I had forgotten the extent of his caravan."

Gabriel studied the row of vehicles. Ryan eyed him, her heart climbing into her throat. This was only the beginning. She squinted to the front gates, looking for a sign of her sister Diana. She saw only the liveried grooms and coachmen that operated and staffed the imposter's fleet of vehicles. They milled about the front gate in ridiculous powdered wigs and red velvet.

They had just passed the first coach when the grooms and drivers began to amble to the drive, looking out as Ryan and Gabriel rode by. Ryan glanced at them, neither smiling nor frowning, simply counting their number and wondering how the Winscombe kitchens were meant to feed so many servants. Again. She also tried to see them as Gabriel would see them. Each vehicle was lacquered black, painted with gold trim and a golden crest exactly like the crest on her

new ring. Velvet curtains hung from the windows and
silky pennants snapped at four corners.

She was just about to look back, to check Gabriel's
progress, when she saw two d'Orleans servants—
old men both; a groom and driver, from the look of
them—step from between carriages to the edge of
the drive. Ryan tightened her hold on the reins, worried they meant to rush up and grab her mare's bridle.
When she looked again, she realized their attention
wasn't on her. They were gaping at Gabriel with eyes
wide and mouths open.

Next she heard gasps and whispers; they called to
each other in French. When her horse passed the two
old men, she heard the whispered name of Gabriel's
late father, Prince Phillipe d'Orleans.

Ryan glanced at Gabriel, and then back to the
grooms. The two old servants—and oh, now a third—
had dropped to their knees in reverent bows. They
called to him in French.

"Your Serene Highness," they said.

"Prince Phillipe?"

"He has returned."

"He *lives*."

Up and down the line, servants in white wigs and
crimson livery emerged to observe Gabriel ride by.

Oh God, thought Ryan, a wave of dread rising in
her chest. How was this happening? Now? They'd not
even reached the house. Must this be the first thing
they encounter? His worst fears, coming to life?

Carefully, with as much nonchalance as she could
muster, she stole a look at Gabriel. He'd gone ghostly;
his tanned skin looked like the underside of a fish. He

kept his eyes fixed ahead. His chest rose and fell. She could hear his breath.

"Carry on," Ryan called in French to the bowing servants.

They did not move.

"On your feet," she tried. This time, she didn't look to see if they complied. She kneed the mare forward, rolling into a trot. Gabriel followed suit, and they sped through the front gates.

"I'm so sorry, Gabriel," she called to him.

"Where is the stable?" he called back.

"There." She pointed to the large, drooping structure surrounded by pens and paddocks. "It's there."

And then she saw her sister Diana. She was tromping from the stables to the manor house; skirts lifted to reveal muddy boots, hair tied in a knot at the nape of her neck.

"*Diana!*" Ryan called, her voice breathy and tearful.

"Go to her," Gabriel said. "I can find my way. Go."

Ryan glanced at him, her heart in her throat. She saw the set of his jaw, the rigidity of his shoulders. He wouldn't look at her but gave a dismissive wave. He reined the horse toward the stables and did not look back. He seemed to want to be left alone.

And Ryan wanted her sister.

"Diana!" she called again, kicking the horse into a sprint.

CHAPTER TWENTY-NINE

THERE WAS NO lantern in the stables. Also, no staff. There were, however, plenty of sheep. Gabriel tied the gelding to a post and drifted from stall to pen in the fading light. He found water for the horse and then feed. He stood at the edge of a pen and observed the sheep. They appeared rather thin at the moment. Ryan's sister must have ordered a second shearing. They'd been divided into various holding lots; with a larger group ambling about an outdoor paddock. They bleated and watched him with their strange, rectangle pupils. Gabriel was careful not to look at the line of carriages parked along the drive; with the golden crests as familiar to him as the flag of France.

He did, however, think about them. He'd learned in the last month that his mind could explore the possibility of something without putting his body at risk. He could survive remembering. He could survive speculation.

Remembering the strange and eerie sight of the servants, ruddy in their bloodred livery, *bowing* when he passed . . . calling out his father's name . . . was a trial, but it happened, and he could remember it, and the earth still spun. He was still standing. He was still free.

Unless he was mistaken, he recognized the older, fatter face of one of the bowing servants—he'd known this man, a coachman, and this man had known him. But how? It was a very far stretch to say Gabriel resembled *English* country gentry, let alone *French royalty*. It was almost as if the old men had wanted to see a prince.

And this sparked a different memory. He remembered the pervasive attitude of adoration, of reverence, of a sort of *love* (if he was being honest) that friends and strangers alike—certainly devoted servants—felt for his parents, and indeed, for him. This strange worshipfulness had been lost to his memory, likely because it'd been overshadowed by the strange hatred in the end. Before, his family had been loved to the point of bended knee; after, they'd been resented and hunted and executed.

The old servants had reflected that devotion and the sight had not panicked him, but he didn't like it. And certainly he didn't want it. He understood how quickly it could turn—he'd seen heads chopped from necks while crowds cheered—but also, he knew real adoration. And real, authentic adoration was the only sort of worshipfulness he wanted in his life. He'd adored Samuel Rein and his boys. Now he adored Ryan. He adored Elise and her family. What need had he for strangers to love him—and, potentially, to scream for his head—when Ryan might return his love in earnest?

The fealty of strangers was suffocating and conditional and misplaced. It was not love, it was control. The love and loyalty between husband and wife could be, he thought, liberating. And unconditional. He'd seen this in his sister's home. This was how Samuel Rein described the marriage between himself and his late wife. Maurice could take the royal esteem and rot. Gabriel's only interest was this more intimate, purer love. Authentic love.

When the moon was high and the dimming sunset had been replaced with a bright white glow, Gabriel walked from the stables to the hitching post and recovered Ryan's mare. With every step, he prayed that she was safe, and happily reunited with her sisters, and didn't resent him for sending her inside the house alone. Was it ridiculous, he thought, that he'd come all this way only to abandon her for the stables?

I'm not ready, he thought, leading the horse in.

I'm not ready.

If I face him—if I face any of this—before I'm in the correct state of mind, I'll bungle it. I'll behave like the maddened forest dweller I've been trying, for years, to become.

I'll be nothing like the prince she needs me to be.

Walking to the stables with the horse, Gabriel took in the looming mansion and verdant garden. The house was larger than Mayapple, but the roof drooped and vines sprouted between stone blocks. The garden was wild; tended only in pockets, scattered with fruit trees and a leaning sundial.

Maurice's grooms and coachmen kept, thankfully, to the vehicles; although Gabriel was certain he saw crimson shadows watching him from behind hedges and walls.

He'd just finished feeding and watering the mare and was brushing her coat when he heard footsteps crunching across the garden in his direction. Gabriel froze, a jolt of readiness coiling inside him, preparing him to pounce. He would fight, or he would shout, or he would—

"Gabriel?" called a familiar voice.

Ryan—thank God.

He laid his head against the curve of the horse's back and closed his eyes. *Let her be well. Let her be safe. Let her be alone.*

"*Here*," he called back and stepped around the horse.

She hurried to him, swinging a lantern before her to light the way. Two women followed behind, peering into the stables as if she was leading them to the cage of a trapped bear.

"Are you—?" she began but didn't finish.

"I'm alright," he said.

Her gait was neither slow nor fast, she simply walked, leading her sisters (the women could be no other than her sisters), her face tight with concern. She searched every corner of the stables, lifting the lantern high.

"I'm alone," he assured her. "Except for the sheep." He gave a small smile. "And the two horses. Have you no stable help?"

"We do," she said, "but they are tenants and they go home to their families at night.

"We brought you something to eat," she said.

The smaller, fairer sister—Charlotte, he guessed—clutched a basket with both hands. Her eyes were huge; she watched him as if he might rip it from her and bite directly into the straw.

"Thank you," he said.

"Diana, Charlotte," called Ryan, "I would like to introduce you to my husband, Gabriel d'Orleans, also known as Gabriel Rein. He has come to help us."

Diana and Charlotte stared at him like Ryan claimed to be married to one of the sheep.

"How do you do?" said Gabriel.

The two women said nothing. They looked from Gabriel, to Ryan, and back to Gabriel.

"Of course you would never be *rude* to the man I've dragged from his home and work to *save us*," Ryan bit out impatiently.

Eventually, the women bent heads and bobbed in greeting. Gabriel lowered his own head. *This*, he realized, was the reaction he'd expected from his sister Elise. He felt a wave of love for his sister; for her openness and lack of judgment. She'd not batted an eye when he'd bounded onto her stoop.

"And he will not come inside the house?" whispered Charlotte, eyeing him.

Ryan cleared her throat. "Until we understand what the imposter intends, we feel it's best for Gabriel to keep out of sight. As I've told you, he's a hand we'll play when the timing is most strategic—and not before."

"Was Maurice aggressive with you, Ryan?" Gabriel asked lowly. "Lady Charlotte, Lady Diana, you've not been threatened or harmed since he's returned?"

Slowly Charlotte shook her head.

Diana said, "He's playing cards with the men who travel in his caravan—his steward and his herald and his equerry and such."

"Travels with that many, does he?" asked Gabriel.

"He is very important," Diana said, rolling her eyes.

"The salon has the largest fireplace," said Ryan. "It's brightest and warmest, and that is where they play cards at night. As long as Utley, our footman, keeps them in drink, they should remain in the salon until they stagger to their beds."

"We are safe if we keep close to our father," provided Diana. "We take our meals in his room; we sleep on cots beside his bed. Papa has suffered a fall recently and cannot rise without the help of his valet, but he is awake. To do us harm in the presence of our father and his valet would require a boldness that Maurice does not possess. That said, we cannot remain locked in Papa's room forever."

"I told him," Ryan blurted out.

"What?" Gabriel asked.

"Maurice," explained Ryan. "He caught sight of me between his dinner and his game, and he demanded to know where I'd been. And so I told him. I said I'd been married—to a friendly correspondent I'd known for years. A man from the mainland. As such, I told him, 'I cannot marry you because I'm married to someone else instead.'"

"What was his response?"

"Honestly? He responded like I was a child who threatened to run away from home. He asked, 'What friendly correspondent?' He wanted to know what had become of this nameless man. He said he didn't believe me. He called me impertinent and told me I was disrespectful and a disgrace to both our families. He asked to see the ring, and I flashed my hand. But Gabriel? When he stepped closer to study it, I think he *knew*. I think he recognized some feature on it, because he turned a very strange shade of pink and his eyes bulged. He swiped for my hand, but I jerked away before he could touch me. And then I told him I expected him to take his leave tomorrow. I told him I had legal precedent on my side, that betrothals do not pass down like houses and land."

"God, Ryan, your courage is a marvel. I'm sorry you were forced to do this on your own."

She was shaking her head. "I wanted to be the first to tell him—and I wanted to be the one to do it. He has underestimated me in every way. Why stop now? He was unnerved by the ring, perhaps, but he's retired to the salon for his game. I heard him laughing as if he hasn't a care in the world."

"He simply accused you of lying and left it?" Gabriel asked.

"Well, he told me I was fatigued. That I should go to bed. That we would speak of this again in the morning. He said he didn't appreciate my fresh boldness and would not tolerate insubordination. He urged me to reflect on the ancient bond of our two families."

Beside her, Diana tapped her fingers and thumb together like a yapping mouth, the universal gesture of someone droning on. "He is insufferable," Diana said.

"Do you feel comfortable with him under the same roof?" Gabriel asked.

"Far more comfortable than we'd feel *in the stable*," said Diana. Her shyness, Gabriel realized, was waning.

"There's not even a cot in the stable, Ryan," Diana pointed out. "How is he meant to sleep? He could—"

Ryan raised her hand. She turned to Gabriel. "I think word of what happened on the drive—with the old servants bowing down—will have reached Maurice's entourage by morning. I've already noticed far more whispering and corner peeping than before. When Maurice looked at the ring, he wasn't shocked and confused, as one would expect. It was more like uneasy."

"Uneasy?" asked Gabriel.

"Suspicious," Ryan clarified.

"Perhaps word has spread," said Gabriel. "In my uncle's court, gossip was valuable currency. When you ask the world to believe you are divinely appointed, rumor can be a dangerous thing. Regardless, I don't like you under the same roof with him. You should not have to face him alone."

"Well, I hope you don't expect her to also sleep in the stables," said Diana.

"We are with our father," Ryan cut in, speaking over her sister. "I've sorely missed Papa and am delighted to find him so lucid. We've not seen this from him in more than a year. Maurice will not attack us at breakfast—in fact, the pattern of his last visit was to sleep very late and have a tray sent up midmorning. We will have until noon before we encounter him again, at least. We should all get some rest and I'll show him the marriage license tomorrow. Perhaps it will be enough."

"It won't." Gabriel sighed. "But I think you're correct. I should keep myself concealed until the most impactful moment. However we play it, whether you're married to Gabriel Rein or . . ." he exhaled ". . . Gabriel d'Orleans, the revelation of a living, breathing husband should be timed correctly."

The sister called Charlotte sucked in a little breath, presumably because of the ease with which his name and title rolled off his tongue in perfectly accented French.

"What can I bring to make you more comfortable?" Ryan asked. "Are you well?"

"Nothing. I'm alright. There'll be no howling at the moon or sacrificing your sheep, never you fear."

"Right," Ryan said. "Well, I'll leave the lantern. And the dinner . . ."

Charlotte crept forward and settled the basket in the center of the aisle and scurried to the safety of her sisters.

"Forgive me," Diana began, "but if *this* is the marital regard the two of you intend to demonstrate to the imposter, we're doomed. Are you certain you're *married*? To each other? You are newlyweds? You speak to each other like colleagues."

"Yes, Diana." Ryan said on a sigh. "I've told you we're married, and it's true. I've also told you our situation is complicated. Also we're both exhausted. And the fate of this family and a bloody princedom rests on Gabriel's shoulders. Please be gracious."

"Remind me never to marry a prince," Diana said.

"*Diana*," scolded Charlotte, eyeing Gabriel like this statement might be the final insult; like *now* he would lash out.

Ryan rolled her eyes.

"Not impressed," sang Diana, turning away. "*Not* impressed."

Charlotte hurried after Diana. Ryan stood a moment more, staring at him. *I'm sorry*, she mouthed.

"Go," he whispered tiredly. "Stay together and near your father. We'll talk again in the morning."

CHAPTER THIRTY

*W*HEN MORNING CAME, Ryan hurried to the stables to find that Gabriel and the horses they'd hired in St. Peter, were *gone*.

She stood in the center of the paddock, holding a tray of poached eggs with beans and a cup of black coffee. She stared at the milling sheep.

He'd gone.

She'd dragged him from his sanctuary, and he'd come along as far as he could tolerate, and now he was gone.

Their chance at a real marriage was over. She was alone again. Everything from here, she would manage on her own.

As ever.

The phrase "remarkably *un*chosen" echoed in her head.

Not everything revolves around you, she reminded herself, lowering the plate to a passing sheep. The ewe eagerly lapped up the steaming eggs.

He has his own demons, and they are significant.

With trembling hand, she took a sip of the coffee, and then poured out the rest. Swiping away a tear, she trudged back to the house.

CHAPTER THIRTY-ONE

"*I*F ONLY THEY'D had a white horse," said Bartholomew, trotting along beside Gabriel on the road to Winscombe. "Think of how princely you would look if you rode in on a *white* horse."

"There were no white horses," Gabriel said, shrugging his shoulders in the tight waistcoat beneath the even tighter jacket. Everything he wore was constricting and hot. His brother-in-law, Killian, was a tall man, but he wasn't as thick as Gabriel. Even Agnes could only do so much when there wasn't enough fabric.

"But shouldn't you have a crown or some other headpiece?" Bartholomew continued. "The hat looks *almost* better on you than it does on me—almost, but not quite—but if we're meant to send a message, and that message is 'The prince has come,' I think perhaps a crown might be more obvious. I could fashion you a sort of ancient Grecian halo out of olive leaves. Are there olives, do you think, on this island?"

"No thank you," said Gabriel. "Crowns are only used in ceremonial dress, Bartholomew. Nothing looks more fake than overplaying the part."

They were ten minutes from Winscombe—Gabriel,

Bartholomew, and Sister Marie—and they'd crested the hill that gave view to the English Channel and the ocean beyond. Bartholomew and the nun had turned up at the Winscombe stables seven hours ago—just after midnight. Gabriel had almost run them through with a pitchfork before he'd realized who they were.

"What are you doing here?" Gabriel had whispered, raising his lantern to their faces.

"We're here to return the maid of Lady Ryan," Bart had whispered back.

"Return who?"

"The *maid. Agnes.* Lady Ryan left her behind."

"Ryan left everything behind. She traveled only with a small satchel. What are *you* doing here?"

"Your sister sent us, Highness," the nun, Sister Marie, had told him, speaking in French.

He'd turned to stare, stunned by the use of his title. He'd blinked into the darkness allowing the words to hit him over the head, to see if they knocked him out.

Your sister sent us, Highness.

Elise, trying to reach him still. The title; popping up to startle him like a ghost.

But the nun hadn't sounded adoring or subjugated when she'd said it; she simply sounded practical. And a little impatient.

"Incidentally," Bartholomew had continued, "we've left the maid Agnes at the hotel in St. Peter."

Gabriel had looked back at him. "Why?" He'd been so confused.

"Because we've also brought a traveling case of Killian's clothes, and Agnes is going to"—and here Bartholomew had made the gesture of scissors—"sew you into them until you look like a proper prince.

Also, we left her behind because she's deuced annoying. Not an ideal travel companion in carriages nor boats. Riding horseback from the hotel to Winscombe was out of the question. I hope she's as proficient with a needle and thread as Elise claims, because she complains. A lot. Many tears. And repeated requests for the privy. But never you fear. We contained her in the hotel with hot chocolate. She's waiting. But we shouldn't tarry. She has the look of a bolter, honestly, and she's very close to home."

And then Gabriel—despite his fatigue, despite the lack of a solid plan, despite the fact that pretending to embody his real identity felt very similar to simply accepting that identity—had experienced an epiphany. He'd realized that a full life, richly lived, came with no guarantee of rest, or a plan, or control. There were compromises, and wild guesses, and degrees.

Perhaps humanity set up some men as princes and others as horsemen and perhaps he could—in the name of love—be both of them, come what may. For a time. In the name of love.

And so Bartholomew and Sister Marie had hauled him to St. Peter and set about kitting him out like a prince. He wore Killian's suit. He had a haircut and a shave. He'd squeezed into fine boots and a shiny hat and very tight kid gloves. When all of it was finished, Gabriel had looked in the mirror and barely recognized the man who stared back.

No, that hadn't been entirely true—he'd seen his father's face. The sight of this had caused him to step away from the others, to sit on the foot of the bed, to drop his head, and mourn. He'd mourned his father—a prince who'd given his life to starving, outraged people; people who'd loved him one summer and wanted him dead the next.

He'd mourned the loss of his mother, who sent her children away and never looked back.

He'd mourned his sister, who'd been lost to him for fifteen years—who'd suffered in her own way, and who'd started a new family when her own family was too dead, or too selfish, or too damaged to come for her.

Gabriel had also acknowledged that, despite the pain of exile, his parents had provided the boys' school in Marlborough as an escape route that might keep him safe. He had not been safe, but he had not been unhappy. And he'd also stayed alive.

Finally, he'd spared a moment for Samuel Rein—a man who wouldn't recognize him now, clean-shaven and wearing fine clothes. Samuel had taken an angry, terrified little prince from the forest floor and made him into a man.

When he'd thought of these things and smoothed them out like open letters inside his heart, Gabriel had told Bartholomew and Sister Marie that he was ready. They'd traded in the modest mount from yesterday for a stallion.

"Did you intend to reveal yourself as prince, even if we'd not come, Gabriel?" Bart asked now, riding beside him.

"Yes, I did intend to," Gabriel said. "But this is better. A very large part of being royal—"

"—is wardrobe!" provided Bartholomew. "Elise said the same thing."

"She knows. It's why I grew a beard and wore skins in the forest," Gabriel said. "It made me the opposite of a prince."

"I wasn't meant to force you to wear the clothes," admitted Bartholomew. "When we found you. They sent me to be a silent source of useful assistance. And only if you needed me. Also, to miss the first week of the new school term."

"You will not miss school, my lord," said Marie from behind them.

"It was Ryan's sister Diana who convinced me," Gabriel said. "Last night. Do you know what she said when she met me?"

"That you were large and hairy and frightening?"

Gabriel snorted. " 'Not impressed.' That's what she said. I'd spent years descending into this bearded, muscled, imposing man, but in the end, I made no impression at all. Not as a forest-dwelling woodsman, and certainly not as a prince. She saw me only as a lackluster husband for her sister. And, she wasn't mistaken."

"Do not deceive yourself," said Bartholomew, "my friend Denny and his brothers were terrified of you. You are worthy of a passing glance, I assure you."

"I don't care how I appear," Gabriel said. "Truly. But, I can be compelled to make the necessary impression, if only for a day. I can do this for Ryan."

"*Brilliant*," sang Bartholomew. "Will there be fighting?"

"No there will not be," said Sister Marie from behind them.

RYAN WAS SEATED at the breakfast table, her marriage license laid out before her, the d'Orleans signet ring on her finger. She'd dressed in clothes from her own wardrobe; a pale pink day dress that had been her mother's, the fabric turned, the darts removed, and the waist raised to be less old-fashioned. Her hair was tied back with a ribbon. Her mind was clear of Gabriel Rein. She would deal with his abandonment and her shattered heart later—after she'd saved her family and restored order to her home. There was something about a broken heart that helped put this business with the childhood betrothal into perspective. She was not afraid of Maurice, not anymore. After the chaos of emotions she'd experienced in the last month, fear had moved to the back of the line. She was resolved.

She heard Maurice's two dogs before she saw them; their claws tapping on the stone floor and ravenous sniffing. Ryan closed her eyes. The dogs preceded him to any room; he would be moments away. It was time. She would not, she vowed, indulge the pretense of small talk. There'd been too many shows of mannerly reserve when he'd first come. Manners made most things easier, even unlawful subjugation. But the takeover of a family should not be easy for Maurice. It should be very, very difficult. As someone who'd devoted her life to making things easier for everyone, Ryan was long overdue to be difficult.

She would say the words the moment he entered, no preamble—not even a hello. She would invite him to see for himself; to study the license. She would extend her hand and offer the ring for his scrutiny.

She would say, *This will not happen* again, and again, and again. If necessary, Diana waited in the next room with a musket.

"Ryan!" called a breathless voice from two rooms away. It was Charlotte, racing down the stairs. They'd tucked her safely away with Papa and bade her not to come down for any reason. And yet—

"Pardon me, er, Highness," Charlotte could be heard saying next, her voice surprised and excited. Ryan head footfalls on the marble in the great hall. Next came dogs barking and Maurice's snarl.

"Pardon me, pardon me, pardon me," sang Charlotte. "If you'll excuse me."

Ryan looked to the door that concealed Diana and her musket. Her sister poked her head out, confused and worried.

What? Diana mouthed.

Ryan shook her head.

"She *promised* to remain with Papa," Diana hissed.

"Ryan!" Charlotte called breathlessly—and then she was there, skidding to a stop in the dining room doorway with Maurice's hateful dogs on her heels. She clung to the doorjamb, panting.

"Look out the window, Ryan!" cried Charlotte. "Someone is coming! Look!"

"Either stop shouting or stand on a chair, Charlotte," Diana called to her. "He'll not call off his dogs and they become agitated when voices are raised."

"*The dogs*," came Maurice's voice from the corridor, "have done no wrong. They are perfectly well-mannered unless provoked. What is the fuss—"

"*Look!*" insisted Charlotte, pointing to the window as she climbed onto a chair. "Out the window. Ryan, you must look!"

Ryan glanced at Diana—and then, heart in her throat, she stepped to the window. Diana crowded in beside her, musket in hand. With shaking fingers,

Ryan pressed back the sheer drapery. The day was cloudless and bright; she blinked in the morning sun.

"*My God*," whispered Diana.

"What *is* it?" Maurice snapped from behind them. "Lady Charlotte, get down from there. You girls have the manners of rabble, I swear it."

Ryan ignored him. She ignored the sun in her eyes, and the dogs sticking their pointed noses into her skirts. She ignored the laughter bubbling from Diana beside her. She saw only the man riding slowly, proudly, mounted tall on a gray stallion, to the gates of Winscombe. Behind him, the grooms and coachmen of Maurice's caravan bowed on bended knee, faces to the earth.

"But is that *him*?" whispered Diana in disbelief.

"*Who?*" demanded Maurice, striding to the next window, yanking back the drapes.

Maurice drew breath to make some comment, but he fell silent at the scene outside the window. He gaped.

Finally, he asked, "And who is that meant to be?"

But he knew—Maurice *knew*. And Ryan knew. And anyone with eyes could see that an actual, honest-to-God *prince* had just cantered through the gates of Winscombe. His Serene Highness, a Prince of the Blood.

"I told you!" cheered Charlotte from atop her chair. "I saw him from Papa's window. Jenkins has hauled Papa from bed to see it. Papa believes him to be his old friend, Prince Phillipe. But I said—"

Ryan didn't answer, she snatched up the marriage license and fled the room, sprinted down the front hall, and threw open the front door. Maurice's dogs bolted beside her, running to the horses with a chorus of barks.

Gabriel looked up, working the reins to control his mount. He made his familiar clicking noise, settling both the stallion and the dogs. Then, he lifted his face to the house and looked at her.

The sun beamed down, warming her, reflecting a pink glow from her dress. The breeze died; the ocean over the distant cliff went still. Ryan was suspended in a blinding moment of deliverance.

He'd come. He'd come for her.

And oh, God, just look at him. He was every bit himself and also every bit a prince. For a nervous moment, Ryan lost heart. He looked so transformed with a clean-shaven face; in the hat of a proper gentleman; with gleaming boots and a riding crop and a wool jacket. He looked magnificent. The most refined, handsome, brilliantly turned-out man she'd ever seen. Tears of pride and love filled Ryan's eyes. She sucked in a breath. Charlotte and Diana crowded on the stoop beside her but came up short, gaping at the striking figure of a proud prince on a dancing horse.

"There is nothing to see!" Maurice was insisting from behind them. "The Daventrys have a caller—a neighbor or a peddler, no doubt . . ."

Ryan glanced back. Winscombe's curious staff and Maurice's twitchy entourage pushed behind him, straining to have a look.

"Come," whispered Ryan, taking her sister's hands. "Let everyone see. Make room."

She clipped down the steps, pulling Diana and

Charlotte with her. A scrum of mystified staff and courtiers spilled onto the stoop.

"Is this the *same person* from the barn?" marveled Diana, squinting at Gabriel.

"Everyone curtsy," whispered Ryan breathlessly, pulling them toward him. "When we reach him, we'll curtsy."

Ryan knew he'd seen her, but she had yet to catch his eye. He'd affected a detached sort of arrogance; he kept his gaze elevated and remote. He spoke in French to—

And now Ryan looked more closely . . .

—to *Sister Marie and Bartholomew*, who trailed behind him on their own mounts.

But how had they—?

But when had—?

"Good morning, Princess," Gabriel said in French, spinning his stallion.

Ryan locked eyes with him. His expression was formal and resolved.

Ryan stared at him—looked deep in his eyes—searching for some sign that he could manage it, that he *wanted* this, *really* wanted this. His horse spun again, and he whipped about, seeking her out. When their eyes met, he cocked an eyebrow and . . . winked.

Ryan let out a little gasp. Immediately she dipped into a curtsy. Beside her, Diana and Charlotte dropped into their own deep curtsies.

"Good morning, Highness," she said.

"What is the meaning?" demanded Maurice, pushing his way through the crowded stoop. "What, I ask you? Truly? You must be joking." He clipped down the steps. "Who the devil are you? What is this? Playacting?"

Ryan and her sisters turned to watch him. His voice was bold, but Ryan could see the careful study he made of Gabriel's face. All around him, Winscombe staff had followed Ryan's lead and dropped into bows and curtsies. Maurice's courtiers looked uneasy and confused.

"Get up," shouted Maurice. "Get up—all of you. *I* am the Prince d'Orleans. Where was this respect and supplication when I arrived? Pray?"

"*Hello, cousin*," Gabriel said in French, his voice bored and weary. He dismounted and Bartholomew leaped from his mount and took the reins.

"Careful how you address me, sir—you're no cousin of mine," Maurice said, answering in English. "I've never before seen you in my life. What is your business here?"

"Forgive my tardiness, I was detained yesterday in port. But I'm here now; come to join my wife, the Princess Marianne, and to see her family. We were married in a private ceremony in England."

Gabriel dusted his hands, slapping them together. He turned and tossed his whip to Bartholomew who caught it and smothered a youthful shout.

"I'll not stand for this charade," threatened Maurice, speaking now in fast, spitting French. "If you believe yourself to know me, sir; or to know this family, be prepared to prove your identity with more than a proud gallop and a shiny hat."

"And what did I say about a crown?" Bartholomew asked beneath his breath.

"Servants are easily fooled," Maurice declared, "and Lady Marianne and her sisters have ample motivation to play along. She was averse to me from the very beginning—and for no reason. Stupid chit—"

And now Gabriel lunged. It was, Ryan thought, one of her very favorite things to observe. She'd seen it first with Channing Meade and again with Nevil Stanhope. He'd also lunged at Ryan herself several times, although with a different purpose. He was ever so quick and light on his feet.

Now he took Maurice by the shoulders and backed him into the side of Winscombe's great stone facade. He pinned him there, lowered his face to Maurice's, and spoke rapidly in whispered French.

Maurice summoned his courtiers to pull him off, but no one moved. He made a general cry for help in English and in French. He shouted for his dogs. The assembled staffers, courtiers, sisters did nothing. Even the dogs kept back. All of them watched as Gabriel informed his cousin of who he was, and who Maurice was not, and what would happen next.

"Oh brilliant," Bartholomew was saying, "I'd hoped there would be fighting."

"My lord," warned Sister Marie.

Bartholomew ignored her and sidled his way to Ryan's sister Charlotte.

"Hello," the boy said to Charlotte. "In the spirit of revealing true identities, I'm actually *not* a royal page, but an earl, if you can believe it. Earl Dunlock. How do you do? But can you tell me: If *your* sister is married to the *brother* of *my* aunt—are you and I related, do you think?"

It was funny, and marginally concerning, and so very much in character for Bartholomew, but Ryan couldn't warrant it. She saw only Gabriel, clean-faced, poshly dressed, blindingly handsome, avenging and confident and walking toward *her. Choosing* her.

She let out a little whimper, watching him come.

"Princess Marianne," he said, walking to her.

"Yes?" she whispered.

"Where is my welcome?"

He was close enough then, and she threw herself into his arms.

"You came," she breathed. "Look at you. You came for me."

"Sorry for the delay," he whispered into her ear. "We wanted to head off any and all arguments, didn't we? We wanted it to stick. Bart and the nun arrived, and I recognized the opportunity to do it up properly."

"You're brilliant."

"I'm in love," he told her, kissing her neck. "I'm so very in love with you, Lady Ryan Daventry d'Orleans. If you'll have me, I want to have a go at a real marriage."

"Yes," she said, crying against him. "Yes. I want that too—so much. It's all I want. I love you, too, Gabriel. I love you so very much."

CHAPTER THIRTY-TWO

"*T*HE FINAL TEST." Ryan closed them inside the last door on Winscombe's family wing. She flicked the lock.

"*Can you*," she teased, "pass the night in a proper bed, in a proper bedroom, within a proper house? Will you survive the very great conventionality of it all?"

"Too soon to tell," he mused. "Will *you* be in said bed, in said bedroom, in said house?" He was leaning against the wall, watching her fold coverlets and fluff pillows. And this was the real test of his civility, standing patiently by while she walked *around* the bed, and *tended* to the bed, and *discussed* the bed, but he didn't toss her into it. Yet.

He elected not to tell her this; he was trying so very hard to be princely. He would wait.

That is, if the waiting amounted to five minutes or *fewer*, he would wait. After that, he could not be held responsible. He was, at heart, a cave dweller. And she'd already proclaimed that he was . . . how had she put it? Starved for a woman's touch.

"Yes," she said brightly. "We will broach this bed together. Although . . ." she said, looking around, and Gabriel thought, *Surely bloody not.* Employing brisk, jerky movements, he began to undress.

"This *is* my childhood bedroom," she was saying. "Now that you are here—now that you are the *owner* of Winscombe and I am your wife, perhaps we should consider one of the larger, more stately bedrooms?"

"I am not the owner of Winscombe," he said, dropping first one boot, then the other, to the floor.

"According to the marriage contract set forth by our fathers," she recited, "Winscombe fell to you whenever we married."

"I don't care," he said. "I don't want the responsibility of this estate—or any estate. Your sister Diana may operate the lands and you may run the household, just as you've always done. I will reside here like a sort of man-of-all-work, compensated in room, board, and sex."

"*Hired*," she said, watching as he pulled his shirt over his head. He'd skinned himself of Killian's restrictive clothing as soon as Maurice had gone. He'd never been so relieved to slide into his buckskins and work shirt. Except for now, when he was relieved to wear nothing at all, and to have his wife observe him with a look of hungry admiration.

"Speaking of work," he said, "I've walked around the estate, looking at tiles and railings and drains. Much of the needed work amounts to repairs I can manage myself. Especially if you've tenants who are willing to assist me."

"Yes," she said breathlessly. "Yes—my God, that is almost as wonderful as hearing you say 'Hello, cousin,' to the imposter."

"That was rather inspired, wasn't it?"

"The look on his face, Gabriel. He *knew*, he knew it was you. And to hear the great lies he was willing to perpetuate to cover up the obvious? What did he try to claim? That you were an actor? It shows just how determined he was to have all of it. If you'd wavered even an inch, he would've challenged you. He wanted this house. He wanted my sister Charlotte."

"Honestly," Gabriel said, "it was far easier after I saw him with my own eyes. He was always a petty, selfish boy, weak and grasping. I saw those same characteristics in the set of his jaw, his posture, his outrage. My sanctuary in the woods was never to hide from particular people—not Elise, and not my cousin. It was to be free of the control that royal blood exerts over the life of a chosen son. And to be safe from the mob rule that killed my father and sent trackers to hunt me like an animal when I was a boy. This was always my hesitation. Not a stray cousin who wanted to marry my wife. It was my pleasure to send him packing."

"Are we really married, Gabriel?" she asked, sitting on the bed. Finally, to his great relief, they were *embarking on the bed*.

"If the answer to this question restricts, in any way, whether I may, at long last, *finish* the act of lovemaking, tell me now. I will lie if I have to."

She laughed. "I am ready to bear your children, Gabriel. Beyond ready. And besides, the priest who performed our marriage seemed very thorough to me. If there is paperwork, we can sort it out. Although the license looks very official."

"God only knows," he said, stripping from his buckskins and padding to her. "We'll add it to our list of legal conundrums. I've told Maurice that I wish to abdicate my title to him, so long as he'll leave you and Winscombe—and me, for that matter—alone in peace. Forever. In fact, I made it a stipulation: take every last carriage and coach and crest and standard and vanish. Be gone."

"Except the ring," she said, staring at the signet on her finger.

"Except the ring," he repeated. "But only because you seem to enjoy it. Any missing family heirloom that bears the d'Orleans crest will make the abdication difficult for Maurice. Worst of all, my life outside the forest will make it difficult. Can he properly parade about as the Prince d'Orleans if the previous prince is alive and well on an estate in Guernsey? Another question for the lawyers. I want to make it official—all of it, the wedding, the abdication—and be done with it."

"But is a life outside the forest what you want, Gabriel?" she asked. "Life here at Winscombe? It's been a very complicated week for the two of us. There is a lot to say."

"I know." He kissed her. "And the question of where I will live—where *we* will live, is a serious one. The forest has been my salvation for so long. My animals are there; I've ignored my clients' horses for nearly a month. But I would be lying if I said I did not want to be where *you* are. I love Savernake Forest, but I love you more. And I can see great potential in Winscombe. It is remote and wild and unpretentious. There is woodland. There is a stable—rather ramshackle at the moment, but it could be perfectly serviceable; especially if your sister will allow me to combine its function to include horses."

"Yes—yes she will allow it."

"I'd not speak for her, if I were you," he commented. "There is a woman who knows her own mind."

"She doesn't scare me."

"She was armed with a musket when we arrived at Winscombe," he said, reaching for the hem of her night rail and skimming it off her body. "Coincidentally, Marie travels with a pistol. Little known fact. I thought, my God on top of everything else, let us not have a firefight."

"I cannot believe Marie and Bartholomew came all this way. Your sister loves you very much."

"Oh, God, my sister." He sighed, gathering her up. "I owe her . . . a letter—at the very least. And a conversation. Many conversations. I owe her a proper reunion. And then we will put our heads together and search for our baby sister, Danielle. Elise has held the tattered remains of this family together with sheer force of will. She will not relent until she finds us all. Unfortunately, Danielle was taken so young that she will not know us. But we may know her. If nothing else, we want some peace of mind that she's healthy . . . and loved . . . and looked after." He rested his lips on the crown of Ryan's head. "If she is somewhere hurting or alone . . . if she has *needed* us and we . . ."

"It is impossible to speculate," Ryan said, tipping her face up, kissing him. "You'll combine forces with your sister—this is progress. And perhaps I can help. I did find you, after all."

"Yes, you did," he said, pushing her back on the bed, sliding his hands up her body. "Thank God, you found me."

AUTHOR'S NOTE

As WITH ALL of my trilogies, the hook for Hidden Royals came before the plot. I knew the name of the series, but not the identity of the royals or why they were hiding. Aligning a book with actual history is one of my favorite parts of writing, and I devoted more than a month to researching this series. In the end, the real-life history behind Hidden Royals was only a jumping-off point; from there, my imagination sailed past uncooperative facts. This note, some of it repeated from the end of *Say Yes to the Princess*, seeks to explain what history is accurate in Hidden Royals and what has been manipulated.

Here is what's real in *The Prince's Bride*:

The French monarchy boasted several "cadet" branches—these were cousins and nephews to the king—who lived the royal life in palaces throughout France. They enjoyed lavish wealth and extreme privilege and were married to other royal offspring across Europe. When the people of France, starving and oppressed, revolted and executed the king and his family, these "lesser royals" were also targets. In the end, King Louis XVI and Queen Marie Antoinette, along with seventeen thousand other people, were beheaded in the

French Revolution. Royal relatives who weren't killed fled France and lived as exiles. They settled throughout Europe, including Britain, like Gabriel d'Orleans and his sister Elise.

One of the cadet branches of French royalty was (and is) the Orleans family. During the Revolution, the father, Prince Phillipe d'Orleans, was beheaded and his wife did flee France for Spain. Their children were secreted out of France and entered exile. Some siblings lived quietly with allies and retained their true identity (like Elise from *Say Yes to the Princess*). Others (like Gabriel, and the prince on which he was loosely based) kept hidden and created aliases.

Here is what is not true (or less true):

Instead of three children, there were five Orleans siblings. Four of these siblings were, unhelpfully, named either Louis or Louise. For this reason, and also because I'm particular about the names of my protagonists, I invoked the Orleans surname but renamed the siblings Elise, Gabriel, and Danielle—and reduced their number to make a tidy trilogy. The real-life eldest Orleans son and heir—known in my trilogy as Gabriel—really did pass much of his exile on the run for his life. My research shows him sleeping in haylofts and forests, never spending more than two days in one hiding place before moving on. He adopted a new identity and apprenticed with various trades and also worked as a teacher. For a time, he traveled to America and lived in New York and Philadelphia. In the end, after years of court intrigue, depositions, and deaths, the Prince d'Orleans returned to France and ascended to the throne as King of the French (as he styled himself).

The biggest historical discrepancy in this series

may be my upgrade of the Orleans branch in the order of succession to the French throne. In essence, I amalgamized the Orleans branch, who were *cousins* to King Louis, with the king's *brothers*. I did this for timeline reasons and because the bloodlust for a *nephew* to the king seemed more acute than the threat toward a mere royal cousin.

The notion of an arranged marriage between an English earl's daughter and a French prince is both convenient and interesting—but not really commonplace. The same goes for a newly inherited prince gaining his predecessor's fiancé along with his new estate. That said, the vulnerability of women with no power and few resources—in essence, *most* women in the nineteenth century—is no exaggeration.

Finally, the first act of the book, where Lady Ryan travels into the forest to haul her absent fiancé back to civilization to face his responsibilities, was inspired not by history but by Nala in *The Lion King*.

READ MORE BY CHARIS MICHAELS

AWAKENED BY A KISS SERIES

A DUCHESS BY MIDNIGHT   **WHEN YOU WISH UPON A DUKE**   **A DUCHESS A DAY**

THE BRIDES OF BELGRAVIA SERIES

YOU MAY KISS THE DUKE   **ALL DRESSED IN WHITE**   **ANY GROOM WILL DO**

THE BACHELOR LORDS OF LONDON SERIES

ONE FOR THE ROGUE   **THE VIRGIN AND THE VISCOUNT**   **THE EARL NEXT DOOR**

THE HIDDEN ROYALS SERIES

SAY YES TO THE PRINCESS